THE SNAKE STONE

Margaret James

PAN BOOKS

This edition published 1999 by Pan Books
an imprint of Macmillan Publishers Ltd
25 Eccleston Place, London SW1W 9NF
Basingstoke and Oxford
Associated companies throughout the world
www.macmillan.co.uk

This first world edition published in Great Britain 1993 by
SEVERN HOUSE PUBLISHERS LTD of
9-15 High Street, Sutton, Surrey SM1 1DF
First published in the USA 1994 by
SEVERN HOUSE PUBLISHERS INC of
475 Fifth Avenue, New York, NY 10017

British Library Cataloguing in Publication Data
James, Margaret
Snake Stone
I. Title
823.914 [F]

ISBN 0 330 39648 X

Typeset by Hewer Text Composition Services, Edinburgh
Printed and bound in Great Britain by
Mackays of Chatham plc, Chatham, Kent

1

Deborah Tanner

1830–1840

Chapter 1

I was sitting on the green rug in front of the living-room fire, playing with some shiny pieces of scrap copper. It must have been nearly dinner-time, for in the scullery I could hear the clatter of pans and the squabbling voices of the two girls who cooked for us. Now and again I caught the scent of something savoury wafting from the back kitchen.

Then one of the children who was boarded with me shuffled in. He sniffed and wiped his nose on his cuff. "Dere's a wubban in the frub roob," he said. His catarrh always made him hard to understand. "She's cub to see about you."

"Why's that, then?" At five or six years old I was far more interested in my pretty copper offcuts and my dinner than in any woman come to see about me. "Eh, Benny? What's she want?"

"Dunno. Cub an' listen."

So, taking my precious bits of metal with me, I sidled up to the door. By pushing it open a crack I could see into the front room of the house, which was also the place of business.

Mrs Haskell, my foster mother, was indeed talking to a woman. Or rather, she was grumbling to one. In a low voice she was muttering about the cost of bread and milk, and all the while she was sewing a seam in some length of black material which I suppose might have been a cloak.

"I know times are hard," Mrs Haskell was saying, as she stitched, "but I can't feed the child on fresh air. Not that there's much of that around here." She glanced up at her visitor. "She likes her food, does Deb. An' I suppose she'd not have me starve the poor little thing?"

"No, indeed." The visitor, a young woman in gaudy clothes whose skirt was way up past her ankles and whose bodice was cut lower than any I'd ever seen before, shrugged her shoulders. "Look, Mrs H," she wheedled, "it's only for a week or two. Couldn't you see your way clear to – "

"No, I couldn't. The cheek of her!" My foster mother snorted. "I'm not like some round here," she cried. "*I* don't take them in and starve or work them to death, then tell their mothers they died of the flux or whatever. *I* feed them well. I give them a bit of kindness, even. But I can't live on promises and neither can they. If you can't pay me now you'll just have take the girl with you."

"I can't take her."

"Can't you?" Stabbing viciously with her needle, Mrs Haskell sewed on. "Why's that?"

"She's not – well, she's just not in a position to have the child."

"She's lodging with some man, then?"

"In a manner of speaking."

"What's that supposed to mean?"

"It's a player this time." The visitor shrugged. "He's not with a regular company, though; he takes what he can get. Often he's away. But he's a terrible one for the drink, and this week he's too sick – "

"You break my heart." Mrs Haskell grimaced. "Why is she always taking up with these fellows?"

"She's never been a judge of men." The visitor sighed. "Her own health isn't good. She coughs and she coughs – "

"Yes, yes, I dare say she does." By now Mrs Haskell's patience was exhausted. "I'll go and fetch the child," she said.

"No!" The woman grabbed my foster mother's sleeve. "No, you can't do that!"

"And why not?"

"He – he's not fond of children. Even if he were sober, he'd not treat her well. But when he's on the drink, he's savage. You know how the players are."

"Oh yes, I know. I've seen them. Drunk in the streets with their women. Brawling and shouting."

"Then?"

"Then pay me what she owes me. And she can pay you." Mrs Haskell's beady black eyes narrowed. "There's twenty-three shillings and odd pence owing. You leave me a round twenty and I'll take the rest up with her. When I see her."

"I haven't a pound in cash," said the woman. "But there's this – "

"I'm not a pawnbroker," interrupted my foster mother. "I deal in cash only."

"Just look at this." From her pocket the woman drew a package. "She asked me to sell it for her. But you could take it as a pledge."

"What is it?"

"Open it and see."

So Mrs Haskell did. Fascinated, Benny and I craned our necks to look, but since our foster mother merely undid the twine and glanced inside the packet, we were to be disappointed.

"Well?" asked the woman.

"Well." Mrs Haskell was evidently tempted. "Oh, I suppose so," she muttered crossly. "Very well, I'll keep it for now. But you tell her, mind. The full account this day week, or the child goes on the parish. I can't keep her – "

"On fresh air." Saucily the woman grinned, and twitched her shawl over her bare shoulders. "Yes, I understand that. I'll tell her."

The woman went out of the front door. Mrs Haskell put the package in a drawer, which she locked. She tidied her sewing away then came into the living-room, where Benny and I were innocently playing. "Come, Deb," she said, sharply.

That very afternoon I was put to work in the button shop.

* * *

I tell you this, I'd never been so cold in all my life. As trials and tribulations go, a night spent bumping about in the grubby straw of a farmer's second-best cart may not sound such a terrible hardship, but the straw had been damp and the night freezing. Too chilled to sleep I'd sat slumped in a corner, counting the hard, white stars.

But the sun was up now and the day was going to be bright. The thaw was coming too, for although it was still very cold, patches of meltwater could be seen in the ice in the middle of the road, where the Birmingham coach had driven by. There, dirty slush had replaced the clean, crisp snow.

The farmer's man put us down at the crossroads. From there, he told us, we could easily walk into town. "Mile an' a half," he said, helping us jump from the tailboard. "Two at the most." He glanced down at our boots. "You ladies used to hoofing it, are you?"

"We can walk, if that's what you mean," replied my companion, rather too sharply.

"Thank you very much for the lift," I said quickly, seeing the man frown.

"My pleasure." He grinned at me. "You tell your friend, it don't cost nothin' to be cheerful."

We started walking.

The hem of Esther's skirt was very quickly soaked through and her stockings were soon disreputably muddy. As for me, my own dark blue dress looked like a rag. Creased and rumpled, the overstretched seams showed white, the cheap material was shiny, and now it was grubby as well.

The day grew clearer and the sky became blue. "Is my face clean?" I asked, as we stumped along. "Essie, look at me. Am I very dirty?"

"What?" Irritably, Esther glanced up. Although she was about the same age as me, she hadn't grown well and at fifteen or sixteen or thereabouts – her exact age was a deep secret – she was just over four feet tall. Gin and opium, Mrs Haskell had always said. Gin instead of mother's milk and opium in place of meat.

"Am I dirty?" I repeated, crossly now.

"I should say so." Esther grinned. "You've smuts all over your nose and a great big smudge on your forehead. You look like a sweep."

"Oh." Mortified, I rummaged up my sleeve, looking for a bit of rag. "Well," I muttered, "you don't look so elegant yourself. I'd guess *you* were a gipsy's child. One of those that goes begging from door to door with a basket of white heather and a mouthful of curses." I spat on my bit of rag. "So there."

Insults duly exchanged, we lapsed into sulky silence. We trudged on, getting colder and colder, and hungrier and hungrier. Coming to the outskirts of the town, we walked past several merchants' houses, bulky and fortress-like in the early morning light. Then, finally, Esther found what she was looking for. "Ah now," she said, "I reckon this must be the one."

I looked. "Here?" I whispered, my teeth chattering.

"Here," Esther replied.

A squat grey cube of a place, the house in front of us had great stone gateposts guarding the gravel sweep before it. A brass plaque was let into one of the posts and now Esther squinted at it. "The Orchard House," she read. "Yes. This is it."

She retied the strings of her bedraggled bonnet and pulled the bodice of her gown straight. It didn't much improve her appearance, for after a night of sleeping in them our clothes were of course hopelessly crumpled and awry. "Very well then, Deb," she rapped. "Step smartly now."

Frozen and miserable, I did my best.

Soon we stood on the stone steps leading up to the front door of the mansion. "You know," murmured Esther, as she rang the bell, "you really should learn to read and write. It's not difficult. I know you're slow and ignorant, but even you could – "

"Hush. Somebody's coming." I grabbed at Esther's arm, and shook her. "Remember," I hissed, "this was all your idea." We heard chains being rattled and bolts drawn. "Just don't forget, Essie, it was you who thought up this great scheme – "

"Oh, shut your mouth, you half-wit," she hissed back, as the door finally creaked open.

I was born in 1824, or so I had been informed and did believe. In those days, I might add, I believed everything I was told.

My mother was a woman of the streets, so they – that is, the neighbours – said, who'd left me at Mrs Haskell's to be reared, and until I was five or six years old she regularly sent money for my maintenance. I was in no position to doubt any of this. My mother might have been anything from a common labouring woman to a royal princess for all I knew to the contrary, for I never visited her and she never came to see me.

Esther Harris, these same neighbours said, was Mrs Haskell's niece, or cousin, or some sort of relation. This may well have been so, but all the same Esther never called my foster mother Aunt, or Cousin, or anything of that sort. It was always Old Haskell or the Old Bitch behind her back, and Mum – as in Madam – to her face.

Esther's father was commonly supposed to have been a wandering tinker, a kettle-mender who had happened upon her mother on the Wolverhampton road, and gone home to lodge with her for the winter. In spring he went on his merry way, leaving Mrs Harris with a baby in her belly but without having paid a single penny in rent. Mrs Harris wasn't too pleased about this, being a travelling pedlar herself who spent only the winter months in lodgings.

When the child was born, Mrs Harris had tried to drown it in a bucket. That was the story, anyway. The woman lodging in the house opposite had heard its screams, however, and rescued it.

"She was one of them as went about saving souls," said Mrs Haskell, telling the story. "She was with some travellin' band of real peculiarities, the Congregation of Modern Saints I think they called theirselves. Anyway, she fished young

Esther out, dried her off, then the whole congregation went rushing round to see what was what. They prayed so hard over Sarah Harris that she begged them to leave off. Then she promised to look after the child to the best of her ability." At this, Mrs Haskell had cackled. "The best of Sarah Harris's ability wasn't committing nobody to very much."

So Esther's mother brought up her little bastard in an off-hand sort of way, leaving it for long periods with Mrs Haskell, while she went off on the tramp. "Looking for that tinker," the neighbours said. She never found him.

While Esther's mother walked the highways and byways of England, then, Esther stayed in Birmingham. While she lodged with us, Mrs Haskell set her to work in the button shop. But then, when she was ten or eleven, Esther was sent to school for a year.

This was only the local ragged school. It was a dark room down a back alley, where thirty or forty scruffy labourers' children crouched over their slates while a nasty ginger ferret of a master thrashed some minimal learning into them. But all the same, it was school. Esther became a scholar while I stayed a little labouring hind, and I was as jealous as sin.

I have no idea who paid for this great education of hers. If I'd known, I'd have asked them to pay for mine, too. As it was, I never found out, and I grew up a dunce.

Esther and I lived all our childhoods in an artisans' court. It was condemned before I was born, but even today those old buildings are still standing, still close and insanitary, still high and dark, still shutting out what light does come out of a grey, smog-laden Birmingham sky.

There were hundreds of these courts, but Parker's Court was just about the rankest of the lot. It was near the canal, so it was always damp. Rotting, even. Mouldering redbrick buildings three storeys high surrounded a square brick yard, and down the middle of this ran the waste from the twenty or so homes and businesses of which Parker's consisted then.

On rainy days this muck and mess overflowed the central gutter and spilled into the houses. "It's not as if I mind my own dirt," complained my foster mother, as she and I worked frantically with yard brooms, brushing the stinking, filthy water back out of her front room, "but other people's rubbish I will not have. I run a tidy business. I keep a clean home!"

Home and business was usually the same place, for most people carried on their occupations on the ground floors of their houses and lived above their shops. A rabbit-skinner had his premises by the common gate, and to this day I associate the smell of curing skins with coming home. To the left of the skinner a japanner carried on his trade, and going on round there was a pin-maker's, a paper-box manufacturer, a small brass-founder and – oh, I've long forgotten the rest, but you have the idea.

The noise was constant. The air was always dancing with smuts.

Mrs Haskell's own trade was that of button-maker. Birmingham buttons these were, stamped from metal. In her work she was assisted by Joseph Taskman, a great, strong, half-witted boy who worked the stamper all day long, asking nothing in return but a bed under the work-bench and three meals a day. I think the incessant thud, thud, thud of the stamper had permanently addled his brain.

Certainly the factor thought so, the factor who in his greasy breeches and dirty coat was the middleman, who brought us the metal sheets which supplied the stamping machines, and who collected the finished products.

"Far gone, that boy," he would say, shaking his head. "But then, that's what it does to them. I see it all the time." Grinning at poor Joseph, he'd tap his own temples. "Nobody at home. Eh, lad? Candles lit and the table laid for company, but nobody at home."

"No, sir," Joseph would reply stupidly, just about understanding that his agreement was required.

Button making, then, was my trade from the age of five or six. As a little child, not strong enough to work the machines, I collected the buttons and rubbed the edges smooth with jeweller's wadding, rubbing my poor fingers raw in the process. Later on I learned soldering, fitting the shanks to the finished button discs. At other times I stood by Joseph to place the metal in the machine.

When I grew strong enough, I worked a stamping machine myself. Unlike Joseph, I hated it. I watched wearisome days drawing into dreary twilights, I heard the thud of the stamping machines in my sleep.

Mrs Haskell was supposed to pay me eight pence a day, and to feed me. When the factor came to collect the buttons I saw that gold and silver changed hands, but few silver coins ever came my way. I was paid in dull greenish coppers, in pence, halfpence and farthings. Sometimes I wasn't paid in money at all. In lieu of wages I occasionally had a second-hand gown, some stockings. Once I had a cloak. Just once.

By the time I was fifteen I was sick to misery of buttons, so when Esther suggested we might make our fortunes in service, said she had heard Old Haskell talking to a factor who knew of a nailmaster in Dudley wanting maidservants, I thought I'd found the solution to all my problems.

"Is Dudley countryside?" I asked Esther, as we discussed it. I loved the countryside. Mrs Haskell had taken me out of town on half a dozen occasions and I knew that heaven was green fields, huge branching trees and a great, clear blue sky. "Esther, is it a country place?"

"Country place? I dunno," Esther shrugged. "It's a smaller town than Brum, so it might be." She wasn't really bothered. "Look, are you coming or not?"

"Yes, I'll come."

"Good." Esther grinned and rubbed her hands. "I thought you would."

I was so green in those days that it didn't seem odd to me that Esther had eavesdropped so thoroughly on my foster mother's conversations, nor that she had, as if by magic, produced the name and address of the Dudley nailmaster. The thing is, I was just so tired of buttons. I needed, I was dying for novelty. I think that just then an offer of being apprenticed to a chimney sweep would have appealed to me. Anything to get away from that tyrant machine.

Looking back, I suppose I could have remained with my

mistress and tried another trade, for in addition to making buttons Mrs Haskell was a fence. In a small way, in a very small way, she received and sold stolen property. Of course, she never told me as much, but when times were particularly bad and the factor hadn't been by for a week or two and we were reduced to eating bread and onions for dinner, my foster mother would produce a ring, say, or a necklace. "Run along to Mr Reuben," she would tell me, naming the pawnbroker on the far side of the court next to Parker's. "Take this and ask him what he'll lend me."

So I'd take the thing and dash across to Mr Reuben, who'd screw in his eye piece and squint at the object in question. "Three shillings," he'd say. That was his invariable offer, whatever the nature of the pledge; old Reuben would have offered three shillings for the crown jewels themselves. "I'm robbing my family and starving my children," he'd add, as he handed over the coins.

Yes, there were opportunities in crime. I could have been a thieves' runner. But I was scared of the constables and I'd heard such tales of the Bridewell – where they tied women up half-naked to whip them – that I was afraid to be dishonest.

So it was that Esther and I stood on the steps of this grand house on the outskirts of Dudley, waiting for someone to answer the door to us. Rattle, rattle, rattle – somebody was having no end of trouble with the locks. Finally, however, the last bolt was thrown back, the door creaked open a couple of inches, and a peaky-looking maidservant said, "Yes?"

Esther was handy with her mouth, always had been. While I stood there like a natural, she launched into a prepared speech, addressing the grubby, weazen slavey as "Ma'am", and humbly requesting that we might be allowed to speak to the lady of the house, "For just two minutes, ma'am, or even less."

Her humility was rewarded. Blessed are the meek, I thought, as the mangy little housemaid grinned. "Go round t' the kitchen door," she said, revealing a mouthful of gums and stumps. "Go round the back, an' I'll meet you there."

We did as we were bidden. Entering the house, we were led briskly down a brick paved passage, then hustled into a small, bare parlour; where we were left to cool our heels for half an hour by the Dutch clock. Eventually, however, we were collared by another servant, marched up some wooden stairs on to a carpeted landing, and then shown into a large drawing-room, where we were brought into the presence of the mistress of the house.

"Say nothing," muttered Esther, as a lady turned from her writing desk to scrutinise us. "Let me talk. You just hold your tongue, d'you hear?"

I nodded, quite happy to do just that, for by now I was terrified half out of my wits. I looked about me. Such splendour! Such carpets, such wall hangings, such highly polished furniture, such a blazing fire – it was luxury I'd never imagined. As for the lady herself, she was dressed in purple silk, her sleeves were half lace, she wore jewels on her wrists and at her throat. She looked like a queen.

"What is it you want?" she demanded curtly, and Esther promptly explained that we had come to the town to find work. That we had heard of servants being required in this house.

"We understand washing, baking and cleaning," she lied. "We are honest, hard-working and quiet."

"Are you, indeed." The lady sniffed. "In my experience, girls of your age and class are untidy and dirty about their persons, noisy and rude in their behaviour and far from diligent in their work."

"Not us, ma'am." Esther glanced down at her dress. "We've been travelling," she said. "This accounts for the state of our clothes and boots, but otherwise, ma'am – "

Esther tailed off, as if embarrassed. She sniffed a bit, as if distressed. All in all, she was so humble and so meek that the lady eventually smiled at her and whispered to her servant, who left the room and returned five minutes later with a heavily whiskered man.

"References?" demanded the man, without preamble. "Have you references, girl?"

"Oh yes indeed, sir." Esther pushed her hand into her sleeve and drew out two grubby sheets of paper, which I'd never seen before in my life. "Here is Miss Tanner's," she said, "and here is my own."

My eyes were already as round as glass marbles. Now they began to bulge with astonishment, for Esther went on to describe a wholly fictitious past employment, ending her narrative with a strangled sob and a great dabbing of her face. "I'm sorry, sir," she choked, knuckling her eyes. "Mrs Haskell was such a good lady, such a dear lady, God rest her soul – "

I was sure now that Esther had gone too far, that such huge fibs would be seen through at once, and I was wondering about making a dash for it rather than be kicked down those hard wooden stairs. But, to my amazement, the mistress of the house seemed moved by Esther's counterfeit demeanour and sympathised with her distress. "We certainly need two under maids," she was saying now. "Two strong girls, to scrub, wash and clean. And you could do all that?"

"Indeed yes, ma'am. Indeed we can. Thank you, ma'am!" In her ecstasy, Esther bobbed a sort of curtsey; but since she was as graceful as a rheumatic sow, I don't know how I kept a straight face.

"Good." The mistress smiled. "So what are your Christian names?" she enquired.

"Mine is Esther," said my inventive friend. She elbowed me in the side.

"Mine is Deborah," I choked.

"Esther and Deborah." The mistress nodded approval. "Two excellent servants' names. Two excellent, *Christian* servants' names! Well – Susan will show you where to take your things. I shall speak to you in an hour's time. I will explain your duties then."

Susan took us to a room in the attic. It was full of ancient furniture; leaking chairs and broken tables were piled up anyhow and I thought it must be a lumber room, but Susan told us it would be our bedchamber. It was as cold as charity. "You do not have a fire," she replied, when I enquired. "If you wish to warm yourself, you come into the kitchen."

I looked at my bed. At Mrs Haskell's I'd slept on a mattress of soft flock with a pile of old quilts to cover me, and in winter time I'd always had a hot brick taken from the oven. The bed in this attic was a board covered with two thin blankets. "I shall freeze tonight," I thought.

If I had decided that a button-stamper's life was one of drudgery, it was partly because I'd had no other trade with which to compare it. Now I learned that housemaids were not necessarily blessed, and certainly in this house they had nothing to be grateful for.

The mistress managed the household herself. She kept the keys to every cupboard, storeroom and larder, and each day she doled out ungenerous portions of this and that as required. Nothing was ever left out and available. As a result we were permanently short of soap, soda, flour, tea, dried fruit – of practically everything. The mistress was so frugal that I'll swear the used tea leaves with which we cleaned the carpets were weighed and measured.

The rooms in which the family lived were light, plentifully furnished, warm and pleasant. But we servants – Esther, Susan the upper housemaid, Hannah the slavey, Mrs Matthews the cook, and me – lived in the basements and the attics, and these were cold and uncomfortable.

Our lives were grim. We were always half-frozen. We were always hungry. I have since known families where the cook kept as good a table for the servants in the kitchen as for the family in the dining-room above, but Mrs Matthews was old, her skills were limited, her employers never entertained and she had no chance to provide us with anything but plain fare. I suppose we had just about enough to eat, although Hannah's bones stuck out shockingly.

The mistress preferred Esther to me, of that there was no doubt at all. Perhaps Esther was the more skilful housemaid. But I have long since understood that mistresses do not like their female servants to be handsome, and if plainness was a recommendation, Esther had plenty of that.

For Esther was no beauty; far from it. She was short and squat, with bulging eyes and a nose and mouth much too big for her face. Her complexion was muddy, the result of catching the smallpox at thirteen. Her figure was lumpy. Her arms and legs were too short.

In fact, she resembled nothing so much as a toad, but whereas a toad's eyes are bright and dark, Esther's were a viscid, watery grey, which always reminded me of the smears of oily rainwater on the windows in Parker's Court. Once, angry with her for some reason and returning one of her own insults, I'd told her she looked like a toad.

"A toad?" she'd cried; surprisingly, she'd seemed hurt.

"Yes, an ugly, scabby, dirty toad." As a child, I'd never minced my words. "Esther Harris is a slimy, crawling, bulgy toad," I'd shrieked, to whoever cared to listen.

She'd blinked rapidly. But then she'd laughed and gone hopping round the courtyard, grinning and croaking in play.

If I was miserable at Orchard House, it was mainly because the mistress was never satisfied. On a diet of poor food and Adam's ale I worked as hard as I could, but somehow I never polished a table brightly enough, I never cleaned a grate to an acceptable standard, my washing was never sufficiently white and my ironing was a disgrace. Branded an idle simpleton, I hated Orchard House and everything in it.

Esther, though, seemed to be contented enough. She worked hard, much harder than I did. Her hands bore witness to this, becoming red raw from soda and labour, but she made no complaints. She went to bed apparently satisfied with her daily round of washing, scrubbing, carpet-beating, polishing and ironing, and she slept peacefully under her threadbare quilt.

As for me, I felt as if I'd jumped from one rat hole straight into another. I wondered if Mrs Haskell might have me back.

Chapter 2

Dudley makes nails. All along its mean little back streets there are squalid nailers' workshops, dirty little brick-built dens turning out thousands upon thousands of horse nails, hob nails, cricket spikes, pig rings, clinkers, bellows nails, dowels, rivets – the list goes on and on.

Mr Taylor, my employer, was a nailmaster; that is to say, a warehouse owner who bought iron rod from the local slitting mills, distributed it among the nailers, and received the finished nails back for payment. Payment, I should add, fixed by the master, not by the nailer himself.

The nailmasters were little gods, with powers of life and death. Together they controlled and regulated the nailers' wages, and since during the thirties there was an excess of labour available, a nailmaster could give out work or withhold it, could feed or starve a family at will.

"A hard, hard man – hard as his confounded nails themselves," was how I heard Mr Taylor described in the town, and I knew it was so. He and his kind were a set of villains who conspired together and manipulated their workforce as if the nailers themselves were so many puppets on strings.

Their methods of control were simple. For instance, if the nailmasters' warehouses became overstocked with, say, hob nails, they would use their own agents to foment a strike in those areas where hob nails were made. While the striking nailers argued among themselves and their wives and families quietly starved, the nailmasters smirked and sat on their fat behinds, comfortably aware that by the time the nailers went back to work the glut would have been disposed of and profits could remain as high as before.

And whereas the nailmasters could make out they were stout fellows, anxious to provide work for the lower orders and make the area prosperous, they could also pretend that the nailers were a seditious, ungrateful rabble, anxious to bring the government down and the country to its knees.

"We showed the devils, by God we showed them," growled my kind master one evening, as I served his wife's hot chocolate and wished I could have just a sip of it myself. "They won't tangle with Fearis and me again, by God they won't!"

Each time he said "by God" Mrs Taylor flinched. "Are they all back at work now, Mr Taylor?" she enquired. She always called her husband Mr Taylor.

"Some of them are, some aren't." Mr Taylor cradled his glass of whiskey in his fat red hands and stared into the fire. "Fearis sent his agent round the villages to find out who was speaking out against us. There were plenty of troublemakers, believe you me. Radicals, they call themselves. Radicals! Well, they can go and root around somewhere else, because they won't ever work in this area again."

"Will that be all for tonight, ma'am?" I asked. I thought they'd forgotten I was there.

"Ah – let me see. Well, you may clear away the tea things." Mrs Taylor always referred to her husband's whiskey bottles, flasks of seltzer water, dirty glasses and so on as the tea things. "And then you'd better go down to the kitchen. I was looking at the knives today, and some of them are distinctly spotted. Clean them all before you go to bed."

"Yes, ma'am." Together with the mistress's china, I loaded the old soak's dirty tumblers – six tonight, I noticed, the drunken sot – on to my tray, and stumped off down to the kitchen. I hated cleaning knives, for my fingers were scraped raw by the wadding. But the kitchen was warmer than the attic, and Mrs Taylor had, by some miracle, left half an inch of chocolate in the bottom of her jug. This residue was full of sediment, so I added more water and boiled it up. Then I filched a sprinkling of sugar and stirred it in.

I drank this soupy brew from a teaspoon, slowly, so

slowly, a sip at a time. They tasted of heaven, these dregs which, while I lived at Mrs Haskell's, I'd have emptied into the waste.

At first I'd wondered why Mrs Taylor had no local people in her employment, but by now I could well understand why Dudley girls preferred the drudgery of the nail shops to the stone-cold comfort of Orchard House. I came to envy the nailers' girls. At the end of each working day, the nailer's time is his own, but Esther and I had only one miserable afternoon a month to ourselves. Otherwise it was slave, slave, slave from five in the morning until past nine at night, seven days a week.

We were fed and clothed, it was true – indeed, for the first time in my life I had a new gown, albeit a coarse cotton thing too flimsy for winter time – but I felt we more than earned our rewards.

Why, then, did I not go? Why did I not give notice, and seek my fortune elsewhere? I suppose I was afraid. I would, after all, get no great reference from my mistress and I feared that if I left Orchard House I might end up a vagrant, like some we had seen on the road from Birmingham to Dudley, wretches in filthy tatters with feet bound up in bloodstained rags.

I've said we slaved seven days a week, but on Sunday mornings, we didn't work. We worshipped, which was harder still.

When I'd lived with Mrs Haskell I'd sometimes gone out on a Sunday to listen to and jeer at the itinerant preachers who came to the artisans' courts on purpose to convert the likes of us; so I had, as it were, heard miscellaneous snippets of the Good News. But now, sitting meekly amidst the chapel congregation of which the Taylors were members, I had the whole Message positively hammered into me.

Wide-eyed, scared as a mouse, I heard of hell-fire and damnation in wonderful detail, and I got it into my head that in the afterlife the worst sufferings were probably reserved for thieving servants who, without explicit permission, drank up the dregs of their employer's hot chocolate toddy.

We servants were required to wash before going to chapel,

so on Saturday nights we lugged jugs full of hot water up all those flights of stairs and tipped it into a large china bowl which sat on the floor, there being nowhere else to put it. We'd remove our clothes piecemeal, and wash quickly, since it was too cold up there to linger.

There was a small mirror in our attic, a square of glass in which we could see just our faces. As Esther and I combed our hair back from our foreheads we pushed and jostled each other to see our reflections in the glass. "Oh, move, can't you?" Esther would demand crossly, trying to see herself.

"When I've finished," I would reply.

"When you've finished. You think I'm going to stand here like a donkey while you take all day and all night?" And then, sometimes, Esther would elbow me in the ribs so sharply that I'd double up, which no doubt was her intention, for she could see her own ugly chops then.

I must admit that I liked looking at myself. When I studied my reflection I could see that my face was pale and doughy from lack of air; but my eyes were dark and well-shaped, my nose was small and straight and, better than that, my teeth were good. Every evening I did as Mrs Haskell had taught me, rubbing my teeth all over with soot from the kitchen chimney; then I swilled mouthfuls of water from the stoup round and round my mouth until the water ran clear. Esther never bothered, and her teeth were green, with black streaks on them. Horrible.

As for my hair, this was a very ordinary brown, but it was thick and naturally wavy, and I liked to put it up and take it down, trying different styles, which I anchored in place with a handful of hairpins filched from Mrs Taylor's stock of thousands.

"Really fancy your face, don't you?" demanded Esther one morning, as she shoved me to one side to see her own fair features in our mirror. She jammed pins in her cap so viciously that I thought she must be sticking them in herself. "Think the world of that mug of yours, you do."

"It's nothing out of the ordinary, but it'll do me," I replied.

I smiled at my reflection in the glass. "I'd rather have my mug than yours, anyway."

Esther scowled. "Pride," she said, "comes before a fall. Just remember that, Tanner. Just you remember that."

I just laughed at her. A mistake, that was. A bad, bad mistake.

We had been at Orchard House for several months now, but time dragged by so slowly that I was surprised when Mrs Matthews glanced at the almanac one morning and said, "Well, bless me, where's the year gone? It's the first of June."

"Washing this morning, then." Susan nodded to Hannah, Esther and me. "You three get started now. I'll see to the rest of the house."

We didn't argue. As far as I was concerned there was nothing to choose between blackleading grates and scrubbing dirty sheets. Both jobs ruined your hands.

It was a fine day, so we took the laundry into the back yard. Esther, Hannah and I pummelled away at linen pillow cases, cotton chemises and Mr Taylor's disgusting underclothes, then half an hour later Susan came out from the kitchen to tell us Mrs Taylor wished to see us in the parlour, immediately.

"Must be payday," muttered Esther, as we rolled down our sleeves and straightened our caps.

Our wages were supposed to be paid twice yearly, and I imagined she was right. So, with unusually light steps and silly smiles on our faces, we trooped upstairs to the parlour, which, as far as I was concerned, was no longer a splendid apartment fit for a queen but a hateful hole which I could never polish up to her ladyship's satisfaction.

But when we filed in, the mistress was not sitting at her desk. There were no little piles of coins on her blotter. Instead, Mrs Taylor was sitting slumped in her easy chair, looking thoroughly disconsolate. She was wearing a blob of a new cap which made her look as if a flock of pigeons had done their business on her head, and although I tried to control my face, a smirk *would* come. Mr Taylor was standing beside her, smoothing his beard with his sausagey fingers. Moses in trousers and a frock-coat. What a pair.

"Close the door, Susan," said Moses.

Susan did so.

"Now." Mr Taylor fixed us with his stare, the same stare with which, I suppose, he terrified striking nailers into submission. "Now, all of you, listen to me. There is a thief at large, perhaps even in this house."

We stared back at him. None of us dared move.

"A *thief*!" he repeated. He banged his fat fist on his wife's desk.

Hannah jumped.

"Now." Mr Taylor left his wife's side. He walked up to us and let his gaze rove to and fro.

"A silver inkstand," he growled, glaring at Susan, who looked steadfastly back.

"A set of napkin rings." He peered hard at Esther.

"A child's ivory teething ring," he barked, making Mrs Matthews flinch.

He stood in front of me. "Mrs Taylor's own silver needle case!" he shouted.

At that, his wife gave a little whimpering sob. Poor thing, I thought, that must have been upsetting. For in the lid of her needle case Mrs Taylor kept a tiny red glass bottle of laudanum, and we all knew perfectly well that she couldn't get through the day without recourse to her little comforter.

"I don't accuse any of you of stealing," said Mr Taylor graciously. "But you must all be vigilant. You must secure all doors and windows, at all times. If you see any suspicious persons loitering about my premises, you must tell Mrs Taylor or myself immediately. Is that understood?"

"Oh yes, sir," we chorused.

"Good." Mr Taylor pushed his hand into one trouser pocket and brought out a silver half crown. "That," he said impressively, "is for any information leading to the conviction of the thief."

"Sure you can spare it?" muttered Esther sarcastically, under her breath, making me choke on a stifled giggle.

Mr Taylor glared at me. "You find something amusing?" he demanded.

"Oh no, sir." I blushed scarlet. "I wanted to sneeze."

"Hm." The master sniffed. "Sneeze in your own quarters, not in my wife's parlour. You are all dismissed."

We trooped out.

"What about our money, then?" demanded Mrs Matthews, as we went down the wooden servants' stairs.

"I'll mention it to her later today. When he's gone out." Susan touched my arm. "Get off to the pharmacy in town and fetch her a bottle of her drops. She can't do without them."

"Shall I go now?" I asked. It was a nice day and I didn't mind the prospect of a walk at all.

"Wait until he's cleared off to the warehouse, then go." Susan sighed. "She ought to have some babies, give her something to occupy her time. But I don't reckon old man Taylor knows how to do it."

We heard no more about thieves and thefts for the rest of that week. Then, on Sunday evening, I was called from the kitchen into the parlour, where I found my master, mistress, a parish constable in all his rig – and Esther Harris.

"Ah, Deborah." Mrs Taylor's voice was slurred and she seemed drowsy, so I assumed she'd spent the afternoon on the sofa in the company of her bottle of drops. "Ah, Deborah. Um – "

"Let me deal with this." Mr Taylor glared at me. "Now, Esther," he growled. "Say again what you just told the constable and me."

"Well, sir." Esther's face was flushed. Her habitually dull eyes were bright. She was standing between the master and the mistress and she was grinning, exposing a great acreage of red gum. She looked so ridiculous that I felt a smirk twitching my own face.

That was my undoing. "Don't you dare grin at me, you little wretch!" Mr Taylor thumped his fist on the mantelshelf, and winced in pain and rage. "Esther," he howled, "speak!"

So Esther spoke. "I saw her," she said, pointing at me. "I saw her take that stuff. She hid the napkin rings in her sleeve.

She put the other things in a bag, and she handed it out of the window." Esther's gums glowed scarlet. "There, master. There's your thief."

Such bare-faced lies dumbfounded me. I stood there like an idiot, gaping at them all, and as I opened and closed my mouth like an ornamental goldfish, failing to make any sound, Esther began jabbering again.

"I saw her sneak down to the kitchen, master," she continued. "I followed her, and I saw what she did."

"And what was that?" demanded Mr Taylor.

"She opened the big press. She took the silver tops from the best cruet, and something else. It was too dark for me to make out what it was."

I couldn't believe what I was hearing. Or seeing, for that matter. The look of smug triumph on Esther's face, that grin of delight which played about her ugly mouth, was the stuff of nightmares. "She's hidden them in her room, I'll swear," said Esther. "Search her room, master. You'll see."

The master bade the constable remain in the parlour. Then, taking me by the elbow he practically hauled me upstairs. We were followed by his wife and Esther, who was still grinning.

It didn't take more than a moment for Mr Taylor to discover a silver salt cellar lid and a set of napkin rings, all underneath my mattress. They had not been there an hour ago when I'd taken up some clean underclothes, fresh from laundering, for Esther and myself. They made such lumps and bulges under the thin mattress I'd have had to have been blind not to notice them there.

"But I don't know how they got there!" I cried, finding my voice at last. "Master, believe me – "

"Why should we believe you?" Lunging forwards, Mrs Taylor scooped up her precious napkin rings and clutched them to her chest. "I saw you grinning at me on Tuesday last!" she screeched. "I saw you smirking, you bold-faced thing!"

I could hardly explain that I'd been laughing at her new cap, could I? "Mrs Taylor," I began, "I never grinned, or smirked – "

"Liar!"

"That's enough." Mr Taylor touched his wife's arm. "Listen to me, Miss," he barked at me. "I saw you on Tuesday afternoon. I saw you with my own eyes, walking in the town, when you should have been here at your work. You were going to meet your accomplice, weren't you?"

"No! I went to town to buy – "

"Silence!" The master started towards me and I thought he would hit me, so I shut my mouth. "Esther," he ordered, "fetch the constable. No, wait. We'll take her down ourselves." He grabbed me by the elbow and the whole wretched procession trooped downstairs again.

The constable had perhaps begun to wonder if he was missing some prime entertainment, for he was now standing on the first-floor landing craning his neck to see upstairs, his fingers hooked through his lapels. He looked tired. No doubt he wanted to get home and have his supper.

As we reached the landing I was handed over. "Keep her under lock and key tonight," said Mr Taylor, investing himself with an authority to which he had no right. But such was the nailmaster's standing in the area that the constable nodded.

"She'll be kept close," he promised. "I'll see that she – "

I heard no more. I squirmed out of the constable's grasp and almost fell down the stairs, then I was up and running. As I dashed through the entrance hall I grabbed a cloak – I thought it was mine – which happened to be on the rack there. By great good fortune the bolts and chains on the front door were not yet fastened for the night, or I'd have been caught there and then. But as it was, I flung back the great heavy door and dashed out into the darkness.

It was Esther's cloak I'd taken, I realised that almost at once. But, although much too short for me, it was serviceable, and it was black. It would hide me in the shadows.

Chapter 3

I ran until my throat hurt enough to bring tears to my eyes, and my heart threatened to burst. I was making for the town. Not, I am sure, with any cunning design of hiding in one of the many dirty side streets, alleys and passages with which the place was riddled, but merely because I'd turned that way after leaving Orchard House.

The day had been wet and overcast. It was June, but by seven in the evening it had become almost dark, for lowering black clouds had come scudding over during early afternoon and now heavy rain made visibility very bad. I was soaked through. My hair was plastered to my head and I felt water trickling down my back.

Although I'd broken into a violent sweat and my breathing sounded like an old man's, I dared not stop. I darted into a side street. Pitch dark, it was as narrow as a needle and the warehouses on either side were so tall that they blocked out what light did filter out of the late evening sky.

I hurtled down this murky channel, then across a wider street, and then into a rubbish-filled alleyway. I felt my feet sinking into slime and refuse and mire, and I shuddered as my damp stockings became even wetter with God knows what filthy, stinking stuff. But still I ploughed on, and on – until I slipped on a heap of wet ash, and fell over.

I hit my head on a brick wall. It took all my powers of self-command not to cry out in pain, and I remember I bit my lower lip until it bled. I still have a tiny scar to show for it.

The constable chasing me was old, and encumbered with a heavy, old-fashioned lantern (which I was relieved to see had blown out) and a wooden club. I seem to remember that he even carried some sort of bill-hook. But to my dismay he'd kept up well with me, and now I could hear him huffing and puffing as he hammered on the door of the house against the wall of which I lay cowering, wrapped in my black cloak.

Soon he brought the occupants to the windows, and an anxious voice cried, "Who's that? The Watch? Is there a fire?"

"No fire. I'm hunting up a criminal." The constable gasped, catching his breath. "It's a young woman," he panted. "But vicious. Very vicious." He drew breath again, harshly. "Has a knife. Knows how to use it."

"I've seen no young woman. Haven't heard one, neither." The man who had opened a window slammed his shutter closed, and the rest of the occupants followed suit.

The constable stumped off across the wet cobbles then, but rousing the house opposite produced the same negative effect. "Clear off," shouted a shrill female voice. A lower casement opened a crack, then a man growled a few ripe curses, and a request to let a decent working chap get his sleep.

The constable stood puffing and blowing and swearing for a moment or two, but then decided he'd had enough. He went off, rattling his lantern and damning me to all the torments of eternity.

For an hour or more, or so it seemed to me, I sat motionless on the ash heap. The summer night was clearing now. The rain had eased off, the clouds were blowing away and on the outskirts of the town the sky was full of stars. Gradually I began to make out shapes.

I was leaning against a small, two-storeyed house, next to which was a brick-built shed. Unglazed windows in this allowed me to peer in and see an anvil, a pair of bellows and a central hearth, glowing very feebly.

A nailshop.

I touched my face and felt the stickiness of blood on my temples. I realised I was wet through. I'd caught one of my heels in my hem and ripped my skirt right up one seam, I had smears of dirt all over myself, and I'd lost the buckle of one shoe. But, in spite of the fact that I knew I must look like a hoyden, and although I knew full well that the inhabitants of the house might call back the Watch, I dared to knock upon the door.

This time, it was not the man who answered. Instead, a female voice cried, "Who's that now? What d'you want with us?"

"I want – I'd like – " My voice cracked and I started to sob. "Please, mistress, I need – "

"Just a moment. Stay there and I'll come out."

As she opened the door to me, I could tell the woman was even more frightened than I was. Glancing up and down the dark alley, she clutched her shawl nervously to her throat, and I saw she was trembling. She peered closely at me. "Well, what is it?" she rapped. "Explain yourself."

"I'm – I'm – "

"You're what? Speak up, girl!"

"I'm a traveller," I said, at last. "I'm looking for lodgings. Some place to stay – "

"A traveller, eh?" The woman's eyes were now fixed on the bloody graze on my forehead. "You have money?" she demanded.

I had a shilling and odd pence in my apron pocket. "Yes, I have a little," I replied.

"I'll have to ask my master." The woman shut the door in my face, and left me all alone in the dark misery of the alley.

While she conferred with her master – her husband, in fact, for all the nailmakers' wives referred to their men as "my master" – I wondered what story I should tell. Although I knew perfectly well that the nailmakers had no love for the masters, it seemed a foolish idea to declare myself a suspected thief; so I decided to say I was a tramper on the road, looking for work in the metal trades.

As I made this decision the door opened again and the woman held it wide for me to enter. Seated at a mean, scrubbed table just inside the tiny room was a gaunt, thin-haired man. The master? Yes, so it appeared, for now he rubbed his eyes and glared at me. "A traveller, is it?" he rasped. "Does that mean you're an honest working woman, or a thieving gipsy?"

"I'm a working woman," I replied. "I've lately been employed in a button shop, in Birmingham." Then seeing an opportunity, I added, "I dare say I could quite easily learn your trade."

"There's very little work at present," said the man. He knuckled his red-rimmed eyes. "You'd not make sixpence a day."

"I could cook, then. I could clean." Earnestly I gazed at him. "If you were to let me lodge here for a while, I'd pay you in ready money, and labour, too."

He looked at me as if I were a fool. I suppose I was. But at least he said I could stay, and so I spent the rest of that night on a wooden bench against the cold, empty grate, aching all over and failing to sleep.

I was set to work the very next day making shoe bills, which are the headless spikes used for studding the soles of workmen's boots. As I laboured over the fire, my wet clothes dried on me, and the aches in my legs eased off. Amid the noise and dirt and smell of hot iron and scorching leather aprons I could close my eyes and fancy myself back at Mrs Haskell's. I realised I could slip into my old ways again very quickly, and didn't know whether to be depressed or relieved.

There was, however, one big problem. My hands were rough from housework but the sinews had grown soft, and I was well aware that it would take a while to build up my strength and grip again. As I struggled with the hammer on my second day in the nailshop I saw Mr Correy, the master, looking at me suspiciously. I forced an apologetic grin. "I sprained my wrist a week or two back," I explained. "It's taking a while to mend."

"I'll get the missus to look at it," he said. He turned back to the fire. "Try using your left hand, if you can. Deborah?"

"Yes, master?"

"I heard tell in the town that old skinflint Taylor's house was robbed a few days back."

"Old skinflint who?" I faltered, blushing.

"Taylor. He's a nailmaster, a big man in these parts. You must have heard of him?"

"No, I don't think so."

"Ah." Mr Correy shrugged. "They're looking for some runaway maidservant, so I heard. She's suspected of passin' stuff out to the thief."

"Oh." My face was hotter than the fire. "Oh. I see."

"There's a reward out for her capture." The nailmaker plunged an iron basketful of hot nails into water, filling the nailshop with steam and noise. "Five whole shillin', so they say. A tidy sum to folks hereabouts."

"Yes, I suppose it must be." So I was to be betrayed. I looked down at my feet, and sighed. I had no strength to run away again.

But then, glancing up, I saw Mr Correy was grinning. "I think old Taylor'll keep his five bob," he said. "I mean t' say, I reckon that maidservant's miles away by now. Don't you?"

I looked at him, met his faded blue eyes, and understood. "I suppose she must be," I replied.

To my great relief and gratitude, Mr Correy never mentioned the Taylors again.

The nailmaker's wife was my instructress in my new trade. A nailmaker herself, she was apparently tireless, working all day to turn out hob nails, pig rings or whatever by the hundred, as methodically as a machine; and all the while she kept one eye on her children as they did their work in the shop.

Wiping her hands on her stained leather apron, she explained to me that she was lucky in that her rented house was right next door to the shop where she worked, because while they were babies she'd been able to keep watch on her children and prevent their coming to harm. Other mothers were obliged to leave small children at home and out of earshot, to get up to all sorts of wickedness.

Babies were no problem; they were usually swaddled and

hung up on hooks, to cry themselves to sleep. But unless they were doped into insensibility with Atkinson's or Gregory's, the older, mobile children got up to all kinds of mischief.

As Mr Correy had told me, there wasn't all that much work to be had. "Here in Dudley," he explained, "there's just too many o' we nailers, turnin' out far too many nails. Market's satterated." He sniffed and scratched his beard. "Soon, I reckon, Master'll stop giving out iron rod. Then we'll be in bad trouble."

I asked him why.

"Why?" He stared at me. "Well, Lord bless the girl for a fool! Because *then* we'll have to go to the fogger. That's why!" He glanced derisively at the small heap of hob nails, which was all I'd managed to turn out that morning. "Get on with your work, girl," he growled, "and don't ask so many questions."

I later learned that when the nailmaster's stocks of nails reached a certain level, he would stop supplying iron, and then the nailers had two options – to go to the fogger or starve. The fogger, a middleman who was usually the keeper of a public house, would negotiate directly with the slitting mills and supply the nailmakers with iron on credit; but he bought the nails back at well below the market price. Or insisted that the nailers took their wages in beer.

"Correy's a good man," said Mrs Correy, as she explained the fogging system. "He's a kind husband, he doesn't hit the children or beat me; but he does like his beer." She sighed heavily. "When he's working for the foggers there's many a Friday night he'll go off and drink his wages while the babies and I sit starving at home."

The babies were Mrs Correy's three surviving children – Michael and Ellen, ten-year-old twins, and Dick, who was six. In spite of his youth and size Dick stood at the fire with the others and could already turn out a hundred bore tips an hour. I myself could manage about twenty, so you can see I was a liability rather than an asset to the trade. I must stop daydreaming, I thought, and looking out into the yard.

In the yard next to the nailshop were the ash heaps, and adjacent to them stood great piles of rotting rubbish, made up of human, animal and vegetable waste. Rooting pigs, pecking fowls and children too young to work in the nailshops spent their days rummaging in these noisome heaps, the children arguing over finds, and hitting the pigs on the snouts to make them squeal and give up whatever delicacies they'd uncovered in the course of their own excavations.

This was where I went to take a breath of air. After the acrid smoke and choking dirt of the nailshop, this atmosphere scented with decay was sweet to me, and in the evenings I sat on the steps of the Correys' house and breathed it in as if it had been Arabian perfume. I told myself I must improve, or the Correys would throw me out.

I did improve, but slowly. "Bit better today," said Mr Correy, about a month after my arrival, as he looked at my output for the day. "Pity there's no market for the buggers."

Improving or not, every night I went to bed totally exhausted. My sleeping quarters were a corner of the family's bare, cheerless living-room, my bed a wooden bench next to the grate. Across from me, at right angles to my bed, was the kitchen, and this was the family's bedroom. Here they had a sort of bed made of boxes and padded with rags, on which the parents and the two eldest children slept, covered with motheaten blankets. Dick had a straw-filled mattress on the floor. He couldn't come in with the rest of them, explained Mrs Correy, because he kicked like a donkey in his sleep.

My own bedlinen was my black cloak. A threadbare, tattered thing going green at the edges, it had once been Mrs Haskell's. In fact it still was hers, for she had not given it to Esther, and I could imagine how angry she'd have been when she'd discovered Esther had pinched it. Each night I wrapped myself in it, and, my legs sticking out and my feet hanging over the end of the bench, I would go to sleep.

One night I rolled over and hit my hip on something hard. Cursing Dick for having left a pebble or clay marble on the bench, I shifted. But still the thing bit into my legs and so, with a sigh, I sat up and rummaged around to find it.

There was nothing on the bench, and in my drowsy state

it took me some time to understand that the thing bothering me was inside the cloak itself. Since there were no pockets, it had to be in one of the seams, or the hem. I felt all round the hem and eventually came upon a lump like a knobbly stone. I got up, crossed the room to the shelf on which Mrs Correy kept her tea caddy, a china dog and a pair of rusty scissors, and borrowed the scissors. Unpicking the material, I drew out something made of metal. A chain. And hanging from the chain, winking at me in the feeble light from a dip left burning on the table, was a pendant of green glass.

My first reaction was one of horror. Was this something else belonging to the Taylors, which Esther had planted? But then I realised, of course it wasn't. If she'd wanted me to be accused of its theft she would have stitched it up in one of my garments, not one of hers.

Wondering if it were very valuable, I weighed the pendant in my palm. It was heavy for its size. I peered at it closely; and now I saw that it was rubbish. The chain was gilt, but much of the gilding was rubbed away, showing plenty of grey base metal through the gold finish. The pendant itself was oval, its metal rim in the form of a coiled snake, which was nicely worked, I thought. But the stone was just dark-green glass, and although it was faceted like a jewel it was badly chipped in several places. A cheap thing, the sort of stuff pedlars sold. All the same, it was pretty in its way.

I decided that I rather liked it. I also decided that Esther owed me this. I tucked it back into the hem of the cloak and pushed it tight against the side seam. In the morning I would ask Mrs Correy for a needle, and sew the hem up again.

I lay down again to sleep. From the kitchen came Mr Correy's grunts and snores, Michael's adenoidal whimpers and the noise of Ellen's bubbling gulping as she tried to suck air up through her permanently blocked nose.

Alone in the near darkness, I held out my hands. Even in that bad light I could see they were ruined, the nails all blackened, broken and split, the skin on the knuckles red and bleeding and raw. None of my previous labours had been half so cruel to my hands as the nailer's trade.

I considered my clothes. The cuffs and lower sleeves of my cotton dress were frayed and ragged beyond repair. I rubbed my eyes and sighed. At the rate I worked, I barely earned enough to feed myself, and I'd never manage to scrape together the cash to clothe myself for the winter.

I must leave, I told myself. I must go, there's nothing for me here. But then the spectre of myself as a roadside scarecrow, a tramp on the highway begging my food and set upon by dogs as I passed through the towns, made me realise the foolishness of just packing up and going. For the rest of that night I wept in despair.

When they could get any, the Correys took lodgers. I don't mean vagrants like me, whom they had taken in out of charity, but proper, paying lodgers. People with business in the town, journeymen passing through; that sort of person. It must have been about the middle of August when a company of travelling actors came to the town, and one of them rented the room Mrs Correy kept to let.

At first I hadn't realised the Correys rented the whole house. I'd imagined the big bedroom upstairs, with its sloping ceiling close under the roof tiles, was let to somebody who was away at present. But no. Mrs Correy now explained that without this occasional addition to her income the family would certainly have starved, and she was pleased when a certain Mr Rayner took the room, for a fortnight to begin with, or perhaps longer, depending on the run.

Mr Rayner was a thin, round-shouldered, elderly gentleman with a face like a gargoyle and a roar like a mad bull. He talked all the time, frequently to himself, and he drank brandy by the bottleful, so that by the time he'd lived there for three days the whole house reeked of spirits.

He'd got it into his head that in addition to being a nailer's girl I was some kind of errand-running slavey, so when he wanted a bottle he'd come stumping into the nailshop and bellow above the din, "God, I need a drink! Deborah! Go and fetch me a bottle! Best French!"

This would usually happen in the middle of the afternoon,

for Mr Rayner liked to be nicely tight before he went to the theatre.

"Go on, Deb. Oblige the gentleman." Mrs Correy didn't mind my running errands for Mr Rayner, for he was polite (in a roaring sort of way), he was conversational, and he was extremely generous, often sloshing out a great mugful of spirits for his landlord and lady, which he brought into the nailshop and offered to them while they worked.

Mrs Correy would sip gratefully. As for Mr Correy, his drink was beer, but he didn't seem averse to acquiring a taste for brandy, for he downed it in mouthfuls. And as for me, I always received a shilling for my trouble, so running errands was well worth my while.

By the end of August I had become handier with the hammers and could almost keep up with little Dickon, as Mr Rayner called him, but times were growing very hard. The nailmasters had closed their warehouses and even the foggers were supplying only the smallest amounts of iron to increasingly desperate nailers.

It was clear to me that Mr and Mrs Correy wanted me away. Toiling from dawn to dusk, they still lived on the edge of starvation, and under the dreary servitude which the masters and foggers forced upon them, their health and strength gradually ebbed away. Mrs Correy was thirty, but she looked fifty-five. As for Mr Correy, I didn't think he had ever been a child.

I suppose Mrs Correy must have said something about me to Mr Rayner, for late one afternoon he came stumping into the nailshop to roar out his request that Deborah should step across to Lyle's beer shop for a bottle of best French. Permission was given. But then, as I walked off down the alley, Mr Rayner himself came scuttling up behind me, and asked if he might walk along with me. I was mystified, but replied that I had no objection.

"No objection, eh? Good girl." Mr Rayner cleared his throat. "Been a nailer's girl for a long time, have you, Deborah?" he demanded. "Been turning out pig rings since you were a little squealer yourself, I suppose?"

"No." I shrugged. "I was born in Birmingham. I made buttons there. In fact, I spent all my childhood in a button shop."

"A button shop, eh? Making Brummagem buttons, out of tin and copper and brass and other metals beside."

"Tin and copper, mostly," I agreed.

"Quite so, quite so." Mr Rayner grinned. "But then you said to yourself, 'Ah me, this life is a precious, wondrous thing, but Birmingham's a sad place to lead it in,' and your thoughts turned to the open road. You longed to travel to distant lands, to meet outlandish peoples, to sample other climes. Am I right?"

"I suppose so," I replied, although I wasn't at all sure what he meant.

"I wonder what you expected to find." Peering at me from under his bushy eyebrows, Mr Rayner rubbed his red-veined nose. "The average nailer's life doesn't seem to have very much merriment in it," he observed.

"No," I agreed.

"In fact, I'd say it was a downright miserable sort of existence. A ceaseless round of thankless drudgery, near starvation and anxious care."

"Maybe," I said. "There's not much work to be had just now, certainly."

"It's the same everywhere, my dear. A universal malaise." He got out a pocket handkerchief and blew his nose loudly. "But all the same, I reckon this Dudley's the meanest little hole I've ever had the misfortune to be in. Just look at that."

"What?"

"That!" Glaring across the main street, down which we now walked, he snorted in derision at a group of fat, ugly women nattering round a fish barrow. "Woman, lovely woman," he muttered, sarcastically. Then he sighed. "They've been bad audiences," he said. "The house has never been more than half full, and I'd guess that a good third of the buggers there didn't understand a single word we said to them. We're leaving on Wednesday."

And with that he turned on his heel and stumped off down the main street, leaving me to go on alone to the public house.

After his last performance, Mr Rayner treated his landlord and family to a supper of ham, bread and pickles, then he addressed the problem of me. "I'll take her with us, if she likes," he offered. He winked at me, and as he did so I saw his left eye catch the light, and realised it was glass. "We're moving on first thing tomorrow morning," he continued, "packing up at first light in fact. Well, Deborah? Would you fancy another stab at life on the open road?"

A life on the road. It was the very thing I dreaded. But with the actors, would it be different? Less hazardous?

"Can you sew, child?" Mr Rayner was asking now.

"Yes," I lied. "Yes, I can sew."

"Wash?"

"Oh, yes, sir." That at least was true. I could blue and scrub and clear starch with the best of them.

"And I suppose you could be taught to pack up properties and generally help the ladies?"

By ladies I supposed he meant the actresses – a bunch of whores, if Mrs Haskell was to be believed. "Oh, certainly," I replied.

"There it is, then." Mr Rayner poured himself another glassful of spirits, then poured one each for his landlords. Before he began to drink, however, he had to attend to an itch on his nose. He rubbed and rubbed, and snorted and sniffed, he screwed up his face and – yes, out popped his false eye, which he began to massage vigorously on a corner of his neckerchief. Dick stared open-mouthed with horrified delight.

"You won't get wages," said Mr Rayner, busily polishing, "but you won't starve either." He glanced in distaste at my horrible dress. "When it's my benefit night I'll buy you a new gown. Velvet, if you like."

"Thank you, sir!" I was amazed, and thrilled.

"Don't thank me. You'll earn it, never fear." He popped his eye back in again and turned to Mrs Correy. "There it is then, ma'am," he said. "We'll take her. She'll be an asset to us, I'm sure."

I hoped he was right. At any rate, I was anxious not to be proved a liability and cast adrift again.

Chapter 4

Mrs Correy cried when we left, although I suspect she regretted losing her lodger rather than her least skilled pair of hands.

I walked into town with Mr Rayner. We passed the grimy Town Hall, turned right into Stone Street, walked on past the glass works, turned left into Priory Street, and eventually we reached the theatre, a small redbrick building very like a chapel down on its luck. Peeling paint flaked off its rotten woodwork, grime and soot stained its bricks, and its façade of mouldering plaster looked like dirty sugar icing. Two crumbling columns supported a canopy over the door, which was scratched and notched and defaced beyond repair.

We went inside and found ourselves in a narrow vestibule. I sniffed the air. "What's the smell?" I asked, for I'd never snuffed up anything like it before.

"What?" Mr Rayner sniffed too. "Oh, that," he said carelessly. "That, my dear, is the smell of the theatre."

"Oh." I looked blank.

"It's the most magical mixture in the world," he continued. He threw out his arms in a gesture of universal embrace. "It stirs the blood and quickens the heart. It stiffens up the sinews and – "

"But what *is* it?" I persisted.

"It's – well, I suppose it's oranges. And dust. And face paint. And lamp oil. And sawdust. And musty, fusty costumes." He grinned at me. "But most of all, my dear Deborah, it's the smell of the Drama. Of the perturbed spirits of a thousand Thespians past."

"I see." I wasn't any the wiser, but I tried to look as

if I'd been enlightened. And now, taking me by the arm, Mr Rayner led me through another door, so we were inside the theatre itself.

I'd never been into a theatre before. In those days, I need hardly admit it, I only dimly understood what a theatre was for. Dumbly I gaped all around this tawdry little provincial playhouse, with its rows of rough wooden benches in the pit, its half-dozen boxes, three on either side of the stage, and its abject apology for a dress circle, consisting of half a dozen rows of faded red plush armchairs fenced off by a brass rail; which I thought could have done with a good spit and polish.

"Stay there," said Mr Rayner, pointing to a dusty chair in a sort of cubby-hole in the wall. "I'm going to look for Henry Collis."

"Who?"

"Old Henry. Mr Collis to you, mind. He's the boss." Briskly Mr Rayner strode off, sweeping past all the benches, then jumping with surprising agility on to the stage in front of us. He disappeared.

From my gloomy cubby-hole I looked past the rows of seats to the stage. At the back of this, I could just make out a couple of men packing wicker hampers with what I later learned were properties – a strangely assorted selection of candlesticks, weapons, crowns, orbs, sceptres, and pots and pans – and clothes. Presently a woman joined them. Then a large, dark-haired man staggered on, half buried under a pile of costumes. These he dumped in the middle of the stage. Additional hampers were dragged on, and these too were filled with costumes, weapons and cooking things.

Amidst all this chaos Mr Rayner now reappeared, together with, I supposed, Mr Collis. A man of thirty or thereabouts, he was a fair-haired, stocky fellow in grubby white shirt-sleeves, a dark red waistcoat and threadbare black trousers. He jumped nimbly from the stage, walked down between the rows of seats, then stopped within a few feet of me.

"A nailmaker's girl," muttered Mr Collis, frowning. "I tell you, Charlie, you take far too much brandy, it's addling your brain. A nailmaker's wench! A dirty, verminous, illiterate slut. What use can she be to us?"

He must have thought I was stone deaf as well as dirty, illiterate and so on. Or hadn't he noticed me sitting there?

"Take a look at her, Henry. Just eye her over." Mr Rayner's habitually loud voice was low and coaxing today. "She's a handsome lass, a rustic Venus; a meadow flower who's languished grievously in this sooty soil."

"You mean she's a grubby little hoyden."

"She's rather grimy, yes, but washable I'm sure. She can cook, and sew. She could walk on as a page. She could – "

"No," said Mr Collis. "Absolutely, definitely no."

"Ah." Mr Rayner frowned, then tried another tack. "Henry," he wheedled, "you're a Christian?"

"I hope so." Taking a stump of pencil from his waistcoat pocket, Mr Collis scribbled something on the newspaper he was holding. "I very much hope I am."

"Then it's your Christian duty to aid this poor child." Mr Rayner's hand was now on Mr Collis's arm, stopping him from writing. "Henry, for the twentieth time, we need a general help. Someone who can pack and unpack, mend costumes, assist the ladies with their changes. Fetch food and drink from the chop house as and when required, wash stockings, get – "

"And your little trollop could do all this, could she? What a paragon." Mr Collis grimaced. "She's been wasted in a nailshop."

"I don't say she could do all of it, but she's a good and willing lass." Mr Rayner's voice was pleading now. "She's quick and clever, she'd find it easy to learn."

"Oh, very well, very well." Worn down, Mr Collis sighed. "Let me see this creature."

"Now?"

"Now." Mr Collis sucked his teeth. "I assume she's lurking hereabouts?"

"She's over there, by the box office." Looking towards me and grinning, Mr Rayner beckoned me over. Diffidently, I came.

"God, she's dirty." Mr Collis wrinkled his nose in distaste. "Couldn't you have stuck her under the pump before you brought her here?"

"She'll wash." Mr Rayner rubbed his hands together. "Look at her, Henry, just look at her. Did you ever see such a face? And that hair, those eyes – "

"Are very ordinary and may be seen on forty thousand other girls throughout the length and breadth of the kingdom." Effectively silencing Mr Rayner, the manager looked balefully at me. "You're a nailer's girl, is that right?"

"I've recently been in the nailing trade, sir, but before that I was in service and before *that* – "

"I don't need to know your life history, child." Mr Collis was eyeing me up and down now, making me feel like a cow in a market. "You can wash, and sew, and cook?"

"Oh yes, sir."

"Right." Mr Collis looked directly into my eyes. "Well then. Let's see your legs."

"M-my legs?" I stammered, astonished.

"Yes." Mr Collis glared at me. "I wish to look at your legs. Surely you understand me?"

"Yes sir, but – "

"You wish to work for me?"

"Yes," I replied.

"Well then, do as I ask you."

I lifted my skirt to my ankles.

"Higher," said Mr Collis.

I raised it to my knees.

"*Right* up!" snapped the manager. "God in heaven, these girls think I have all day."

I bared my legs completely. My face on fire, my eyes filling with tears, I stood there, humiliated. My stockings were in tatters. My shoes were so down-at-heel and filthy and cracked that they were fit only for the bonfire.

Mr Collis walked round me, assessing.

I wanted to die.

"She might do." Mr Collis was back in front of me now. Chin in his left hand while his right hand held his elbow, he examined my face, had a good stare at my chest and then seemed to measure my waist. He turned to Mr Rayner. "She might do," he repeated. "She could take the court pages and the serving boys."

"She wouldn't need plumpers," said Mr Rayner.

"No." Mr Collis glanced at my legs again. "No, she wouldn't. Well, now."

And the two of them strolled off together, leaving me standing like an idiot in the pit of that dusty theatre, glaring after the pair of them. I let my skirts fall to my ankles. What was a plumper, I wondered. And was I to be taken on or not?

I didn't stand there for long. It seemed Mr Rayner had won his point, for now the woman on the stage called to me and told me to come and help her pack some costumes into a wicker basket.

As I clambered on to the stage, she grinned at me. "Judith Glass," she said, holding out her hand to take my grubby paw. "Now then, if you could fold those black jerkins? Don't touch the white stuff, you're too dirty."

Mortified, I blushed. "Could I wash, then?" I asked.

"Er – yes. Perhaps you ought. There should be a pitcher here somewhere." She gazed around her, as if expecting one to come floating out of thin air. "Oh yes, over there, on the table in the wings," she declared, pointing to a bowl and ewer.

I went and washed my hands then went back and packed, white clothes and all.

We were joined very shortly by another woman, as little and round as Judith Glass was thin and tall. Dora Parry, I learned later, played children, while Miss Glass, lanky and lantern-jawed, played comic servants of either sex. Miss Glass and Miss Parry were great friends. They ate together, slept together, and if one grinned the other also bared her teeth. To upset or annoy one was to offend both.

I don't think they had any great opinion of me. For the next hour they talked over my head, ignoring me almost completely. They broke off their chatter with each other only to tell me to be careful with this or to mind how I folded that.

"Oh, her. Only Mr Rayner's latest piece of nonsense," said Miss Glass later that morning, as she and Miss Parry walked off to take their mid-morning break. She smirked at the gentleman who'd apparently asked who I was. "I doubt if she'll last long."

I rammed down the last cloak and fastened the basket, nodding to a man who'd been bearing them off that this last one was ready to go. As I did so Mr Collis came on to the stage, accompanied by a fat, florid, blonde woman and a slimmer, dark-haired one. Miss Gaynes and Miss Tolland, Mr Rayner told me later, the stars of the company. No, they didn't pack baskets. They had their baskets packed for *them*.

Gradually, as if Mr Collis's presence were a magnet, other people drifted on to the stage. The manager surveyed them all, as if counting. "Very well," he said at last, satisfied that everyone was there. "Time to be on our way."

So the company of seven men, four women and me set out in a lurching, jolting collection of vehicles, leaving Dudley, I most sincerely hoped, for ever. I was told to travel with Mr Rayner, Mr Denby (the man who had asked who I might be, and who was evidently not impressed when he found out) and a friendly black mongrel named Toss, who, I was told, walked on as Launce's dog and did some very clever business in the burlesques. I was none the wiser.

"Pretty well, Deb?" demanded Mr Rayner, as we left the smokey air of Dudley behind and rolled out into the green Worcestershire countryside.

"Oh yes, sir, fine." In fact I was feeling very ill. The jolting of the wagon, which lurched into ruts and bumped out of them with a great creaking of axles and shaking of all the passengers, was making me feel quite sick. Toss was crushing me against the side of the car, licking my face, and a bag which seemed to be filled with pots and pans was sticking into my back. "Yes, sir," I repeated, wanting to believe it, "I'm fine."

While the rest of the company made do with wagons, carts or old-fashioned gigs drawn by mules, donkeys or broken-down nags, Mr Collis, I noticed, went on a pretty piebald horse. He was a good rider, sitting easily in the saddle and holding the reins loosely while the horse fidgeted and bucked a bit, evidently irritated to be crawling along at this pace and longing for a canter. The manager drew close to our cart and looked in. "You're a bit green, Deborah," he observed. "Feeling queasy?"

"No, sir." I was struggling to keep down the bread and cheese I'd eaten prior to departure, and could not comfortably say more. "No sir, not at all," I mumbled, as Mr Collis continued to look at me.

He shrugged, then laughed. "A stoical lass," he observed, and moved on. Later that morning he left us, taking his horse for a gallop across the countryside, meeting us at an inn later that evening.

I was glad when he'd gone. I didn't like the way he looked at me.

At six the following evening we arrived in Worcester; a cathedral city, so I was now told, on the banks of a river called the Severn. As we rolled into the suburbs I stared about me, wondering, for I had never realised a town could be so clean. Where was the smoke, the soot, the dust? Where were the manufactories? Why was it so *silent*? There were plenty of people about, taking the pleasant evening air, but apart from the muted murmur of their conversation and the rumble of the occasional coach or cart, there was no noise whatsoever.

"It's so quiet," I observed to Mr Denby, as I hung, gawping, half in and half out of the wagon. "Somebody must have died."

We rolled down cobbled streets towards the city centre, which unlike those of Birmingham or Dudley was almost completely innocent of litter or any other sort of filth. "It's so clean," I added, overawed. "It doesn't smell." At that moment a brewer's dray drew alongside us and the handsome young driver grinned at me. I grinned back, delighted.

Mr Denby also grinned at the good-looking drayman, but for some reason he received only a grimace in reply. Unconcerned, he shrugged. He turned to Mr Rayner. "Charlie," he said, "I hope you haven't taken those lodgings by the tannery again. *They* stink enough to offend even the blocked-up nose of Miss here."

It hadn't occurred to me to wonder where we might stay tonight – but now the question of lodgings was eagerly discussed. Miss Parry and Miss Glass, who had travelled together in a sort of dog cart which I later saw double as Boadicea's chariot and Caesar's triumphal coach, took rooms at an inn halfway down the Shambles. Mr Denby and his particular friend Mr Wright went off to visit an old acquaintance, who'd promised to put them up. The rest of us took private lodgings.

Mr Rayner took me to a mean little house in a narrow street off the Droitwich Road. Here we were joined by Barty and Tim, the musicians, who would share a couple of rooms with Mr Rayner. As for me, I was to sleep in the kitchen with the slavey, who, as soon as the mistress of the house saw me, was told to heat water for me to have a bath.

I had my bath. While I was taking it, in the kitchen surrounded by a forest of towels draped over half a dozen clothes horses, my clothes disappeared. As I stared about in a panic, wondering what I should put on, the slavey brought me in a new set, a cotton gown and some underclothes. "Who sent these?" I asked, as she helped me into them.

"One of the actresses," replied the servant. "They come in a parcel just now, with a message to put your others on the fire."

Mr Rayner grinned when he saw me. "That's better," he said. "Thank Lucinda nicely when you see her."

"Lucinda?"

"Miss Tolland," he said, naming one of the stars. "She said it hurt her eyes to look at you in your beggarmaid attire."

I went to bed that night clean, warm and comfortable, lying next to the slavey on a mattress stuffed with straw. I woke the next morning feeling reborn.

That morning saw us all gathered at the theatre, to be given instructions and harangued by Mr Collis. Miss Parry, Miss Glass and I, chaperoned by a yawning Mr Denby, were sent off round the town to drum up interest in our enterprise. We posted bills, we went into shops where Dora Parry smiled winningly at the men behind the counters and persuaded them to put our notices in their windows, and we handed playbills to passers-by.

Our group took the north of the city. Mr Hammer and Mr Wright, two middle-aged fellows with lots of whiskers who affected a very flashy style of dress, went with Miss Tolland and Miss Gaynes to overawe the more genteel south. I suppose Mr Collis was organising everything at the theatre. I know Mr Rayner was comfortably getting drunk.

The first theatrical performance I ever saw was something I shall never forget. I had helped the ladies into their first set of costumes and Mr Rayner then told me that when I wasn't wanted by the ladies I could stay in the wings, if I cared to, and watch the evening's entertainment.

I could hear the audience, murmuring and rustling like a hive of giant bees. All around me actors were clearing their throats, muttering to each other, making feints with stage weapons, snatching a last look at a script.

Then the bells rang. The curtain came up, the lights flared, the music played. And the magic began.

I stood entranced. Here was Mr Rayner, paint plastered so thick that it hid his wrinkles completely, pretending – and pretending convincingly – to be a lovesick youth. Here was Miss Tolland, but she was now a princess in cloth of gold, with stars in her hair. In the course of that evening I saw Mr Collis become a Roman soldier, a ghost, a Scottish nobleman – and then become himself again. I made sandwiches for phantoms and fairies and giants, I brought in pots of ale and porter for earls and Moors and Indian savages. I passed that evening in a mad, frantic dream.

In those days, a night at the theatre was a lengthy business. In addition to a couple of plays (or more usually excerpts from plays, for provincial audiences had not the patience to follow a whole five-act piece) there were songs, tableaux, interludes, a burlesque – there had to be an opportunity, in fact, for everyone to do his or her party piece.

Everyone had their own little niche in the company, a niche which was theirs and theirs alone. Miss Glass always did comic servants. Miss Parry always played children. Mr Rayner had his own motley selection of specialities. Mr Hammer and Mr Collis played various heroes, as agreed between them. No one poached on anyone else's territory – there'd have been bloodshed if anyone had dared.

I earned my board and lodging. I was at the theatre from early morning until late at night, answering cries of, "Deb, where's my sword?" and, "Deb, run over to Mason's and fetch me a pot of rouge," and, "Deb, please to wash out these stockings and dry them carefully, mind you, away from the fire," and so on and so on until I was fit to drop.

One evening about a week after our arrival in Worcester, I was standing in the wings, gawping as usual, when Mr Collis came up behind me. "Now," he said, snatching off his wig and fanning himself with it, "I shall want you to go on later tonight."

"Go on?" I stared at him.

"Yes, go on." Mr Collis spoke slowly, as if to an idiot. "Judith is rather unwell. Too many ripe peaches, I suspect. You must take her part in the burlesque."

"But I, but I – " Like a fool I gaped at him. "But I can't," I mumbled. "I don't know how."

"Oh, it's nothing." Realising that his entrance was fast approaching, Mr Collis jammed his wig back on his head. "Look, Charlie will show you what to do, where to stand and all that. Miss Gaynes will take you on and you simply follow her out. Simple."

"But the words!" I could feel my knees turning to jelly. "Mr Collis, I don't know the words!"

"They're very easy. Six lines at most. Mr Wright will prompt you." He grabbed a sheaf of paper from a table in the wings and riffled through it. "Here you are," he said, "see for yourself. Four separate speeches, very short – nothing to it."

"I'm sorry, sir." I bowed my head in shame. "I can't read."

"You cannot read." Mr Collis slapped his forehead. "Of course you can't. What was I thinking of?" But then he glared at me. "You have a memory, though!" he barked.

"Yes, but – "

"Go and see Charlie, now. He'll get this into your head. Dora can get you dressed." His eyes bored into mine for a few seconds more – but then he smiled. "Don't be scared," he said gently. "The others will carry you."

"But sir – "

"Tonight's your début," he said. "Better go and get made up."

I took the script he'd thrust into my hands and stared at it. Going off to find Mr Rayner I stumbled straight into Barty, who was sitting on a hamper, cleaning his flute – he wasn't wanted during the dramatic interlude.

"You'll be right as ninepence," he said kindly. "Just watch me. I know that sketch backwards, an' I'll give you the cues."

"Thank you," I said, still disconsolate.

"Chin up." He grinned at me. "Tonight's the night, eh, lass?"

It wasn't so awful. As I stepped out into the glare of gaslight, I caught Barty's eye and he gave me a great big wink. He fed my few lines to me, hissing them so audibly that the audience must have heard, but since the character I was trying to play was a fool anyway, perhaps it didn't matter. After five minutes or so I found I was almost enjoying myself. I dared to glance at the audience. They were laughing! I'd said something funny, and they were laughing! I felt my power.

The burlesque was over in ten minutes, and as I scampered off the audience clapped. They weren't clapping me, you understand, they were applauding Mr Rayner and Miss Gaynes. But as I heard them cheer and clap, I was caught in that invisible silken web, caught sure and fast. I knew that I wanted to go on the stage again. I wanted to have people looking at me, and admiring *me*.

Chapter 5

We stayed in Worcester for three weeks, and we did very nicely, playing to almost full houses. So how did we entertain the citizens of Worcester? Well, our nightly performance usually consisted of a couple of complete one-act plays, a series of comedy sketches, two or three burlesques (very popular, especially if they made fun of the government) and various songs, dances and tableaux. There were excerpts from a serious drama in the middle of the evening, during which half the audience nodded off to sleep, waking up in time to throw nutshells at the cast as they took their bows.

I had made my début – my "first appearance on any stage" as the handbills would have put it, had there been time to print any, which there wasn't of course – and there was no going back. I was wanted every night now, walking on as a servant, standing at the back as a minor god or goddess, or just helping to make up a crowd. As a reward for good behaviour I kept my little part in the burlesque, and once a night I was tripped up, knocked about, fell over my own feet and was laughed at for my pains. I loved it, I loved it more than anything else in the world.

"From Tuesday he wants something light, to follow his bit of *Othello*." He was the manager, and the person required to produce something light was Charlie Rayner. He coached Dora Parry and me in a short sketch about a clever girl and an idiot boy.

Got up in a ragged smock and tattered pair of trousers, with a vile felt hat on my head and a straw in my mouth, I played the boy. The first time we did the piece the audience laughed, howled, and roared for more, and I was elated. Egged on by Dora, I fell over more often than I needed to, tripping and knocking and bumping myself merely in order to get even more reaction from the pit. The laughter was like strong drink, going straight to my head. I never noticed my bruises until I came off.

"A natural clown. A female Grimaldi," observed Mr Rayner happily, as Dora and I ran off the stage one night to stamps and yells of approval. "Listen to them!" he cried. "Got them in the palm of your hand, you have. Get back on and do that last bit again."

"*What* did you say?" Waiting in the wings, got up in a bedsheet as the Spirit of Victory, Miss Gaynes glared at him. She caught me by the collar. "You will *not* go on again," she hissed. Giving Charlie Rayner a look which, so he told me later, damned near froze his balls off, she swept on to do her solo recitation. The highlight of the evening. Her party piece.

"Take no notice of her," said Dora, as we watched Miss Gaynes declaiming magnificently. "She's only jealous."

"Jealous of what?" I asked, astonished.

"Our reception." Dora smirked. "You wait and see. They'll give her a decent hand, all right, but they won't call out for more."

I hung about in the wings to find out if Dora was right. She was; they didn't want an encore. And when Miss Gaynes swept off, she poked me with her spear as she passed.

After Dora and I had made the audience laugh, and Miss Gaynes had roused their patriotic fervour, Mr Collis made them cry. He gave them a dramatic monologue on the death of Nelson, and before he'd done most of the ladies in the boxes were sobbing their hearts out. Even the rowdies in the pit were quiet.

It couldn't have been that these weeping women were in love with Mr Collis, for he was old, and very plain. Not ugly, you understand, not hideous and repulsive like Charlie Rayner, but plain. Dull. He had the sort of face which could be seen on forty thousand men throughout the length and breadth of England.

So what did he look like? Well, his eyes were a nondescript grey blue. His face was round, sunburned and freckled like a labouring man's. His nose was too snub and his mouth was too big. Straw-coloured hair, cut very close so that he could get his wigs on easily, made him look even more of a bullet-headed rustic, and no hero of romance ever had a figure like his, all navvy's muscle in the chest and shoulders but much thinner and sinewy in the legs. If I'd had to guess, I'd have supposed he was a tenant farmer. A cousin of one of those brown-faced men who walked round the town on Wednesday afternoons and trod manure into the shops.

But being on stage gives height to the shortest figure, paint on the face can transform the plainest features, so when Mr Collis was made up and in a black wig, the shape of his legs improved by calf-plumpers and fleece-lined stockings, he looked almost handsome. He often played somebody called Hamlet, and, if I could, I watched from the wings as he performed. I don't know how it was, but as I watched him I found that somewhere deep inside me a chord was struck. And although I knew it was only Henry Collis under all that powder, paint and jet-black finery, and it was only blowsy Miss Gaynes sighing and dying as Ophelia, I was, in spite of myself, very moved.

But then, of course, the bubble would burst. Tonight it burst with a vengeance. "Oh God, these stays will be the death of me! Deb! Where the devil is the girl?" As she came off stage that evening I could see Miss Gaynes's make-up was running even more than usual, that her wig was awry, and that she was sweating rivers from exertion. Collaring me, she leaned over the props table. "Cut them if you must," she cried, tugging at the laces which bound her. "Oh God, oh great God in heaven, I'm going to expire!"

As I bent to unlace her, Mr Collis sat down on a hamper, pulled off his wig and fanned his hot face. "Hurry up, Deb," he rapped. "And when you've finished seeing to Pen, get over to the public house with a jug. I've such a thirst tonight."

"Yes, sir. Just one minute, sir." Struggling with the knots and trying to calm a squirming Miss Gaynes, I glanced at him. He was red in the face. His black-spangled cloak showed rusty spots and there were little rents all over the fabric. His jerkin was splitting at the seams, and the neck band was fastened by a couple of hat-pins skewered into the button holes.

So the illusion vanished in earnest, and Hamlet and Ophelia were just two provincial actors again, getting on in years.

If Miss Gaynes was well past her prime, her friend Miss Tolland was just about at the height of her grace and beauty. A pretty, dark-haired woman who wore her thirty-odd years well, she played Viola in *Twelfth Night*, Beatrice in *Much Ado* and Boadicea in the current tableau. She had already put me in her debt by giving me clothes, but then one morning she sent a message that I should go to her lodgings in Foregate Street.

There she washed and curled my hair for me. "Not bad. Not bad at all," she said when she'd finished, and opened the window to let out the smell of singed curl papers, hot tongs and baked hair. "Well, what do you think?" she asked Fred Hammer, who lounged in just then – without knocking, I noticed. "Look at her, Fred. Isn't she a beauty?"

Mr Hammer dropped into an armchair and gave me the full benefit of his appraisal. "She'll do," he said eventually, a grin splitting his dark, lank-jawed face. "What's the idea, Luce? What are you plotting now?"

"Plotting? Me?" Miss Tolland giggled. "Really, Fred, whatever gives you these ridiculous ideas?"

"There," said Mr Rayner, when I saw him later that morning. "Told Henry you were a nice-looking lass."

"Most girls are nice-looking, Charlie," retorted Miss Tolland, miffed.

"Hm?" Mr Rayner walked around me, a brandy-soaked grin on his rubbery face. "Well then," he said. "I think we have a *beauty* here, Lucinda, do we not?"

"Exactly." Putting her head on one side, Lucinda Tolland examined me. "A good profile, Charlie," she murmured.

"Very good," he agreed.

"And a nice figure. A little too slender maybe, but sweet. Just made for a white gauze gown."

"Naughty." Mr Rayner wagged his finger at her. He sucked his teeth. "A Juliet?" he suggested, archly.

"Maybe." Miss Tolland smirked. "Or perhaps a Cordelia?"

"Or even an Ophelia," put in Fred. "Oh, I see it all now. You'll be for it!"

"Well, we have a Spirit of Empire, anyway." Mr Rayner grinned broadly. "We'll get her up in the white and gold tussore, for a tableau at the end."

"The white and gold tussore belongs to Pen Gaynes." Derisively, Fred snorted. "If you honestly think she'll lend it to little Miss Nobody here, you must be – "

"Henry will deal with our dear Penelope." Mr Rayner tweaked one of my new curls. "Yes," he said, "a beauty. A rare, natural beauty."

I blushed.

"We're going to have to do something about her poor little hands now," said Lucinda, lifting up one of my red, roughened paws. "Lemon juice and almond oil, I think. Fifteen minutes in oil each morning, and a rub over with half a lemon before bed each night – that should do it. Then she'll be perfect."

"Perfect," agreed Mr Rayner.

"You just watch your step," muttered Mr Hammer, to no one in particular.

All this flattery delighted me, for I had never thought of myself as a beauty before. Oh, I knew I wasn't ugly. Esther Harris was ugly, and I didn't resemble her at all. But although I knew I had nice brown hair, was averagely well grown and had a reasonably good complexion, I had never, as Esther thought, fancied my face. To hear Mr Rayner call me a beauty made me redden, and I later decided that they were all teasing me for some private reason of their own.

The Spirit of Empire tableau was very silly, but as a finale to the evening's entertainment it was a great success.

Unaccountably, the white tussore gown which I should have worn vanished just before the first performance, so I made my entrance as Empire wound in a white bedsheet with spangles hastily sewn around the waist and throat. I stood in Miss Parry's and Miss Glass's old cart (now, by means of a bit of crêpe and scarlet ribbon, transformed into a Triumphal Car) and held a fixed smile, while at my feet a British Child (Dora Parry in a short white dress and lace-trimmed under-trousers) offered me a wreath. Other members of the company were variously Justice, Truth, Valour and Beauty (Miss Gaynes, in a white-powdered wig, a lot of face paint and far too much rouge).

Then one night, as I came off the stage, Charlie Rayner took my hand. "I've done it," he whispered excitedly. "I've done it at last!"

"Done what?" I asked dozily, yawning hugely, for it was past midnight and I'd been up since five.

"I've worn him down." He nodded over to where Mr Collis stood leaning against a flat, talking with Miss Gaynes. "He's agreed to let me coach you for Juliet."

"Juliet?" I repeated, blankly.

"Yes!" Now Mr Rayner was practically hopping up and down with glee. "Oh, you poor child," he cried, "you don't know what it means, do you? But you'll see. You'll see!"

Early the following morning Mr Rayner called me up to his room, and while Barty cleaned his flute and Tim shaved, he told me the story of Romeo and Juliet. Evidently, this particular drama had not been performed by the company for some time now, for among the female players there was no one really suited to act Juliet.

"But it's a slayer, you see," said Mr Rayner, "a proper slayer. The ladies adore it. So do most of the gents. If you have a young, pretty Miss Capulet, you can't go wrong. Packs them in, it does. Positively packs them in."

Reflectively, he rubbed his stubbly jowls. "People will fall over themselves to see a beautiful young girl stick a horrid great knife in her chest."

"Ugh," I said.

"There's more to it than that, of course." Mr Rayner grinned. "Well, Deb? Are you game?"

"Well." I shrugged. "Not a real knife, is it?"

"No, no, of course not. Property dagger, blade goes up into the handle, you must have seen some in the box. So will you give it a go?"

"I suppose so," I replied.

"Excellent. We'll have a drink on that." And so Mr Rayner, Barty and Tim drank a toast to my success as Juliet, and I wondered what I'd let myself in for. I hadn't long to wonder. Tossing off his tumblerful of brandy, Mr Rayner reached for a bulky playscript. "Very well, then," he announced. "We'll begin. I'm your nurse. So."

"It was all my idea, you know," said Mr Rayner, later on that morning. "*I* told him. I said, 'Henry, just look at her! She'd make a capital Juliet.'

"And do you know what he replied? He sniffs at me and says – cool as you like, mind – 'She's not doing it, Charlie. For one thing, she's too dull to learn the lines.'

"So I said nothing more. I just thought to myself, oh ye of little faith, I'll show you. And then I said, 'Let me give her some instruction, then. I'll use R and J as my text.'

"And so he sniffs and snorts and turns around, but then he says, 'Oh, very well. Try if you must. I'll get no peace until I say yes.' "

Mr Rayner grinned, and poured himself more brandy. "When I have a bit of spare time," he promised, "I'll teach you to read. And when you've learned Juliet, we'll get you up on stage with Fred Hammer. He'll pull you along."

To my great surprise, I found I had a good memory for lines and I learned the part of Juliet – or rather excerpts from it, for of course we didn't intend to perform the whole play – in a couple of days.

We'd moved on from the city by then, and were touring the countryside; we did a performance here, a concert there, we played in public houses, in private homes, in village squares – anywhere there was an audience, in fact. And so it was that I played my first Juliet in a barn in Worcestershire, with

"That's pretty," said Mr Collis, as I stood in the wings one evening, watching Dora and Judith acting out a short pantomime of Jack and Jill.

"Let's see." Got up as Old Capulet, Mr Rayner appeared at my side. He took the pendant in his hand. "I used to be a jeweller," he said, eyeing it.

"Among other things," said Mr Collis, grinning.

"I was a jeweller of repute, I'll have you know. Lords and ladies came to me." Mr Rayner turned the pendant to catch the light from the stage, tapped the stone and squinted at it.

"Glass," he said, pulling a long face. "Glass, set in some cheap alloy. Copy of a French piece, I'd say; but crudely done. Very crudely done."

"Typical Brummagem ware, eh?" put in Mr Collis, laughing at us both.

"That's about it. Pity." Mr Rayner let the pendant lie against my chest again. "Nice bit of costume, though," he added kindly. "Where d'you get it?"

But as my cue came just then, I had to run on to the stage, and could not reply.

2

Henry Collis

1840–1841

Chapter 6

So the nailer's girl played Juliet, the grandee's daughter. Well, I suppose this was no more inappropriate than a bankrupt drunkard like Charlie Rayner going on as the noblest Roman of them all, nor even than myself treading the boards as Lear, the widowed family man given so much aggravation by his daughters. I'm a childless bachelor myself, you see, and intend to remain so.

After Worcester we embarked on our autumn tour. In addition to theatres, we played in barns, town halls and public houses. I can't say I cared for public houses. There, the spectators spat streams of warm ale at us if they became bored.

We acted for polite audiences of the affluent middle classes, who clapped and smiled when we pleased them. We also played to crowds of ill-behaved yokels, who flicked nutshells on to the stage, hurled mouldy cider apples at the actors and picked fights with each other in the pit.

Most of our audiences that autumn were of the yokel variety, but the company as a whole could deal with barracking, hectoring and general abuse. One gets used to it, and invariably we coped, answering back or playing along, despising the hecklers for the peasants they were. But then, one night in Redditch, I almost had an uprising in the ranks.

This particular audience had been rowdy from the start, and as the evening progressed, they'd got worse. They howled, screamed and drowned us out, they threw apples, nuts and rotten oranges and they spurted jets of ginger beer right on to the boards, roaring with laughter as they did so. Pissing on the actors, they called it. Most amusing, you'll agree.

Halfway through the evening, when we were all due on together for a tableau, Lucinda put her foot down and refused to go on again. "That's it, Henry," she announced, folding her arms. "I'm not going out there. They're not bloody listening; they're having a free-for-all in the aisles. And I don't want to get my eye blacked by a rotten apple with a stone in it."

Pen was glaring at me as if it was all my fault. As for poor little Deb Tanner, she was as pale as her gown, and obviously wondering if this hour was to be her last. I glanced round the men in my cast. Charlie Rayner looked game, but as usual he was half-cut. Tom Denby and Harkess Wright were clutching each other in fear. "Fred?" I hazarded.

"What?" Fred wasn't keen to face that mob, either.

"We can't let the ladies go on just yet." I took his arm and led him aside, to talk man to man. "You come on with me," I said. "We'll get them singing or something. Eh?"

"You're mad, Henry. Quite mad!" Now that the safety of her precious Fred Hammer was involved, Lucinda positively spat nails at me. "Just let them carry on, why don't you? They obviously don't need *us* to complete the evening's entertainment. I think we should all pack up and go home."

"Fred?" I repeated.

"Oh – all right. But a singsong's a bloody ridiculous idea." Fred picked up a broadsword. "Let's go and do the duel from *Macbeth*. Might take the buggers' minds off their own boring little fight. Bring the blood."

So, with quaking hearts – for actors have been dragged off stage and as good as murdered before now – Fred and I went on. Amid a hail of missiles we lunged, and thrust and parried. Grunting and sweating, we fought each other all over the stage, as much to dodge what was being thrown at us as anything else.

Eventually, however, the combatants in the pit stopped hitting one another, and began to watch us. They shouted advice and put bets on who would win, Fred or I. It seemed we were fighting the longest duel scene in the history of the theatre.

But it worked. By the time Fred had run me through

the heart and I'd spewed fake blood all over the stage, the spectators were all more or less in their places again and the evening continued, albeit with sporadic outbursts of cat-calling and apple-hurling. Deb, Fred and Charlie even silenced them for five minutes, but after Deb had died on stage all hell broke loose again.

"Get up!" I hissed to her. "Up! Sing a song, or dance the polka! Now!"

She was a game little thing. She rose from her bier, and, shaking in her little velvet slippers, she stepped to the front of the stage and sang a sea shanty. Still dressed as Old Capulet, Charlie did a hornpipe all around her. When they came off, I went up to congratulate her, but the poor child burst into tears. Glaring poisonously at me, Lucinda led her away.

Not for the first time, I wondered why I did this for a living. Working as a miner or a chimney sweep would have been so much more uplifting, not to say safer in the long run.

Naturally, we tried to suit our performances to our spectators' tastes, but the basic formula for our standard entertainment hardly ever varied. We travelling vagabonds put on a show to please everyone, or at any rate we tried to. But actors can get heartily sick of constantly rehashing the trial scene from the *Merchant*, of trailing through the sleepwalking scene from *Macbeth* tomorrow and tomorrow and tomorrow, and there were one or two members of the company who'd privately combed through the Swan of Avon and hit upon just the part to show off his or her special talents.

These parts were always some bit of Bardery left deservedly unrevived since the seventeenth century. "No, Charlie, not *Timon of Athens*," I had to insist again and again, for poor old half-blind Charlie desperately fancied himself in a Grecian get-up and was anxious lest the state of his legs should disqualify him for a tunic not so many years from now.

His anxiety was not without foundation. Legs are always the last thing to go, but still, Charlie's were definitely on their way out. All the same. "Who's even heard of *Timon* in Hereford?" I had to ask him. "We'll give them the blasted heath from *Lear* and Portia's mercy speech."

"If you're using Pen for Portia and she wears that boned silk bodice she's so fond of, the quality of mercy won't be the only thing that's strained," muttered Charlie sourly, thwarted yet again. "Are you doing Lear tonight, or am I?"

"You take it this time. I'll do the Fool myself." I clapped him on the shoulder. "Charlie, Charlie, some men are born to play kings, and you're one of them. Timon? He's not worthy of you. Macready himself couldn't better your death scene in *Lear*."

He was mollified a little.

That autumn – through the rest of September, October and the first half of November – our engagements took us down the Wye Valley, that most beautiful part of England. There, the lovely melancholy of autumn stirred my soul. The golden leaves on great oaks and elms, sheep pouring like milk over the green fields, and the heavenly smell of ploughed earth, made me wish I were a poet. Well, dammit all, I *dream* of being a poet, always have done; but these are the twilight fancies of a poet doomed at last to wake a hack actor manager.

Oh, and a poacher, too. That golden countryside of Herefordshire teemed with rabbits, hares and pheasants. We vagabonds ate well that autumn.

Deb Tanner was useful. I have to admit this. Charlie Rayner was an old soak, a sentimental fool where a pair of pretty eyes were concerned, and he'd landed us with useless floozies time and time again. But this time he'd been right. In addition to being very handy with the packing and unpacking, and generally helping out with the thousand things with which a touring company has to cope, Deb could *act*.

She was indeed that rarest of unicorns, a born player. The dramatic pause, the expressive gesture worth a dozen words, the catch in the voice at a moment of pathos; all came naturally to her. "My only love sprung from my only hate," she would falter, that last word caught in an agony of despair, and as she spoke it I could see, I could actually *feel* the audience responding with a great wave of sympathy for poor doomed Juliet.

For my part, I had to teach her the mechanics of playing. She had to learn to exaggerate her movements, to start, to stare, to express her feelings in a larger, more powerful fashion – in short, to be dramatic. Charlie took it upon himself to improve her talents still further, tutoring her in the sort of stagecraft he'd learned as a young man and which still went down very well with the sort of oiks to whom we usually played.

"Now do fear," he was telling her, as I walked into their lodgings one morning. "Come along, child. Fear!"

"Yes." Deb opened her eyes wide. She let her jaw drop, she drew down her eyebrows, and she gaped in exaggerated horror.

"Hands!" Charlie shouted. "Don't forget your hands."

So then Deb raised her hands, palms outwards to fend off the object of her imagined terror. Her eyes opened still wider, her jaw dropped almost to her chest, and so on.

"Good! Excellent!" Charlie grinned. "That's the stuff to give the buggers. Now die."

Obligingly Deb clutched at her chest, rolled her eyes to heaven, groaned, staggered and finally collapsed on the floor in a tumbled heap. She must have been black and blue that night, for in spite of instruction from Charlie and myself she still had no idea how to fall.

"Let your knees buckle gradually," I told her, startling her now, since she'd been too wrapped up in her lesson to notice me come in. "Take some weight on your hands, and for God's sake don't jar your spine like that again. Try once more."

She did. I suppose it didn't look quite so painful that second time, but I made a mental note to give her some intensive lessons on movement, before she actually broke some bones.

So, eventually, Deb learned to *play* as well as any of us, mastering a stylised series of facial expressions indicating horror, pain, misery, joy or whatever, learning the stage embrace and the stage kiss for all occasions – in short, communicating what was going on even to the deaf old ladies in the back row. But at the back of my mind a voice insisted that she'd have been better as she was, and I longed for audiences which would have appreciated her soft sincerity.

Perhaps one day, I thought, we'd find them. In the meantime we wandering vagabonds stamped and roared and postured for the men of the Marches.

Charlie Rayner, a master of the ranting, honking, gargling, grunting, two-minute-long expiry, twisting and writhing like a dyspeptic serpent, was easily the most popular player in the whole company, eclipsing even the ladies. He came on to howls of approval and cries of, "Show 'em how to do it, Charlie! Show 'em how it's done!" And later he was implored to, "Give it us again, Charlie, give it us again!"

So frequently Lear or Macbeth got up and expired once more, just to please his fans.

In due course we reached Chepstow and put on our last performance at a little hell-hole of a theatre with rising damp and a rotting stage, through which I was daily praying Charlie would not put his foot. The trapdoor was broken and the resident carpenter was too drunk or stupid to mend it, so we could not do *Macbeth*. There was rainwater inches deep in the dressing-rooms. Everyone's lodgings seemed to be verminous and vile, and as we settled in at the theatre, Lucinda and Fred were carrying on some acrimonious private argument, choice morsels of which echoed all around the building. "Stupid bitch," yelled Fred as Lucinda flounced into her dressing-room and slammed the door. "Pox-faced, fat-arsed sow!"

"Disgusting, ignorant, *vulgar* oaf!" screeched Lucinda in reply. "Born in a ditch, son of a tinker and his half-witted, syphilitic *donkey*!"

This went on all day, increasing in rancour as it went. I imagine we all learned some foul epithets we hadn't known before. But somehow, as it always does, the performance came together and things picked up. Charlie surpassed himself, roaring like a wounded lion and making the ladies in the boxes shrink back in delighted horror. Even the pit went quiet.

"They're loving him tonight," whispered Pen Gaynes as she and Harkess Wright, got up in togas for the final tableau vivant in which the audience was invited to yell out the choruses, watched Charlie gasp and choke and howl his life away at the end of our excerpt from *Lear*, Dora Parry's prostrate form lying stiffly across his gouty knee. "Good old Charlie, now they'll be nicely warmed up for Britannia."

"Warmed up, my arse." Still smarting from Lucinda's reflections on his paternity, Fred picked at his dirty fingernails and scowled. "Bet you a sovereign to a bent ha'penny the buggers in this town don't know the words to a single song. God, I don't know why we bother. Oh Christ, here comes the Witch of Endor herself. Good evening, Lucinda. Got something stuck up your bum, my love? Or are you deliberately walking like that?"

"Shut up, Fred. Leave Lucinda alone."

"With pleasure. Oh God, if only I'd listened to my mother's advice and gone for a soldier – "

"I'm sure we all wish you had." Pen adjusted her helmet. "Listen to me, Fred. Tonight, you come on when you're expected, not five minutes after. And you don't crowd me. Ah," she added, seeing Deb approach, "here comes Justice, late as usual. Charlie won't be requiring your services tonight, dear. He looks quite done up."

Deb looked blank, and shrugged. It was obvious that she had no idea what Pen meant.

"Well then, ladies and gentlemen," I said, into the resulting silence. "Shall we go and give them our best?"

In spite of the fact that Deb was quite obviously Charlie's latest adopted daughter, their relationship was a subject for some crude backstage speculation, at least among the baser spirits.

"Beauty and the Old Soak," said Tom Denby, watching this unlikely pair walking out of the theatre after the performance that night. "Going home to bathe the old devil's bunions?" he shouted after them, as they went off to their lodgings.

"As good a notion as any," murmured Harkess Wright, Tom's particular friend. "Start at the foot and carry on up, that's what I always say." His blue pop eyes glistened and he patted Tom's hand.

"Nice little bottom on her." Shaking off Harkess's paw, Tom pursed his lips. "A Rosalind if ever I saw one."

"A Viola." Giggling, Harkess turned to me. "Eh, Henry?"

"Lucinda Tolland will have your liver if she hears you even *thinking* that." Tom linked his arm with his friend's. "Well, come on, dear. Time to go up the wooden hill. Say goodnight to Henry, now."

I bade them goodnight. I locked up the theatre and went off to my own lodgings, thinking.

Viola and Rosalind. These roles had been written for Deb, were crying out for her. But they were also Lucinda's private property, and I understood absolutely that if Deb was to keep her cheeks unscarred and her pretty nose unbroken, she must not aspire to either of them.

An actor manager must run a tight ship. And no, I didn't want a mutiny on my hands.

Chapter 7

Rosalind. Helena from *All's Well*. Viola. Deb had been born to play these roles, she had just the right air of innocence and naïve charm. Perhaps one day, I told myself. One day. In the meantime, I would coach her for Cordelia. Dora Parry wouldn't mind that at all; she'd only agreed to play Lear's silly little daughter because she was fond of Charlie Rayner, and there was no one else remotely suited to the part.

"Cordelia today," I told Deb and Charlie, as I walked into their fusty lodgings one sunny morning and found him in a cap and dressing-gown and her mixing his cordial, for all the world like the fond father and his most dutiful child. "Come along, Charlie, drink that down. Then we can begin."

"Begin what?" Charlie muttered. He turned his back on me and sat down by the window. "Thank you, Deborah. What would I do without you?"

"Good morning, Mr Collis." Politely Deb smiled at me, and my heart lifted. "Would you like some tea? It's just this moment made."

"He doesn't drink tea," growled Charlie, from his corner. "I can run through Cordelia with her myself," he added sourly. "Get along, Henry. Go and annoy the carpenters. I'll coach Deborah."

"No, you won't," I said. "Charlie, we're going to have some moderation this time. *Controlled* passion, eh? I don't want Deb tossed about like a rabbit in a terrier's jaws. Well then – shall we make a start?"

Charlie grumbled some more, but eventually he gave in. During the course of the morning he learned to let

Cordelia speak her lines uninterrupted, and he left off roaring.

He was fond of Deb. He wanted her to do well.

I'm not exactly sure how it came about, but soon after she'd played her first halting, hesitant Juliet, I found the nailer's girl was constantly on my mind. I blessed the happy accident which had landed her among us, and shuddered when I thought that but for Charlie Rayner and his little whim, her talents might have lain dormant and unrecognised for a lifetime.

But then, so many of us came into the theatre almost by accident; I myself was certainly never intended to be the manager of a company of beggarly strollers. *I* was destined for holy orders, and would have become a discontented vicar quietly mouldering away in some country parish, had not a crowd of third-rate actors playing at a provincial theatre so fired my imagination that I knew I had to act, or die. I was bitten so hard by the scorpion of ambition that it was either take up with a company of vagabonds or be confined in an asylum for the insane. There's not so very much to differentiate a stage from a madhouse, you might say. You'd probably be right.

My father was rector of Hafren Wood, in the county of Warwickshire. A respectable, learned, kindly man, he was well liked by his flock and beloved by the poor for his regular remission of their tithes. But he had one weakness, and that was for narcotic drugs. He needed his pipe of opium as a baby needs its coral comforter, and he went nowhere without his phials of laudanum, his drowsy syrup, as he called it, which he at first used only to pacify his nagging headaches, but to which he later became hopelessly addicted.

My mother had always rationed his allowance of the drug, but after she died there was no such check on him. He died when I was seventeen, demented, hounded by imaginary demons and persecuted by howling nightmares. He'd been poisoned by the stuff which he'd first taken to relieve a persistent little pain behind the eyes.

He left me nothing but debts. I took one look at the lawyers' letters and left, meeting up with a company of strolling players in Northampton. For eight shillings a week I walked on as a noble, a soldier or a page, and off stage I was general dogsbody. I graduated from pages to curates, to prosy fathers and villains' accomplices. In due course I came to play Macbeth, dying bloodily on stage almost every night for the next five years.

I fell in love with the leading actress, a married lady fourteen years older than me. Her husband was the prompter, a pleasant fellow who occasionally did comic servants and who wrote the burlesques. He loved gambling and drinking, but neglected his duties in the marital bed. The rest you can guess.

Actors came and went, retired or died, and my mistress became ambitious for me. "You should be the manager," she murmured, as we lay tangled in bedsheets at my lodgings or hers. "*You* should be in charge of the company. Not that old fool."

The manager was not a fool, but a once competent classical player who was growing old. He had been ill on and off for years, but steadfastly refused to consult any doctors, preferring to dose himself with laudanum. When he finally did seek medical advice, he wished he hadn't, for he was told he needed an immediate operation to remove a growth in his side. Rather than face the knife, one cold January morning he walked into the river; and it was up to Harkess Wright to take over. Or to me.

Harkess very kindly let me. I took on the debts, the irritations, all the difficulties of keeping a company of volatile temperaments below simmering point. I became an actor manager and went grey before my time.

Charlie Rayner thought he'd talked me into it, but the truth was, when Deb Tanner joined us, I was actively seeking a young actress capable of playing Juliet, Cordelia, Bianca and so on.

I'd wondered about poaching someone from another company, I'd suggested to Dora that she leave off playing brats and start taking adult roles, I'd even advertised now and then; but the girls who had come forward had been such donkeys that I hadn't been at all tempted to take on any of them, and had sent them and their mothers on their way complaining.

Lucinda Tolland, our born comedienne, who took all the breeches parts, had consented to lumber through Juliet once in a while, but she hated doing tragedy, so I knew she'd be relieved to give it up. And she was.

As it happened, Lucinda took to Deb immediately. Dora Parry and Judith Glass at first tolerated but then became quite fond of her. I knew all the men in the company rather fancied our little nailer's girl, and if Charlie Rayner had not guarded her like an old dragon breathing brandy fumes fit to poison the atmosphere, one of them would have corrupted her long before now.

But Pen Gaynes hated her. With Pen I had nothing but trouble from the first. Dear Pen. Poor, fat Pen. One of the best Miss Capulets of her generation, she was too old for Juliet now, for at thirty-five her bosom had sagged, her hips had spread alarmingly, and her teeth were almost gone. Perfect for Lady Macbeth, ideal for Portia, and, at a push, just about acceptable for Desdemona, it had nevertheless been a great wrench for her to relinquish her favourite role.

As long as I let her keep Desdemona, however, she was just about controllable. If she could be throttled twice a week by Fred Hammer, preferably as Lucinda looked on sourly from the wings, she was reasonably happy. Being half strangled in public always excited her, and when that evening's performance was over she'd come tripping along to my room or wherever I happened to be, cheeks aglow, eyes glittering, streaks of black paint still on her neck and her gown stuck to her with sweat.

"Was I wonderful tonight?" she'd demand, tossing back her tangled blonde hair and widening her eyes.

"Wonderful, my dear," I'd reply. If I was in the mood, that is. "Quite superb."

And then I would find her in my bed that night.

I admit it, I was fond of Pen. She made a comfortable cushion and although I haven't ever married, my needs are the same as those of other men of my age. As I lay on her I let her grumbles about the other actors' lack of style, lack of taste, lack of any acting ability whatsoever, wash over me. In a way, her low, murmuring complaining was quite soothing.

But then, one evening when she'd been at Charlie Rayner's brandy, she began to annoy me, for she started to complain about Deb. We were lying comfortably tumbled in a mess of sheets, blankets and quilts when she sat up and glared at me. "She can't act," she announced. "She can't dance, she can't sing. And her eyes are too small."

"Are they?" I said. "I hadn't noticed."

"They're tiny. Piggy." Pen blinked owlishly at me. "Think about it, Henry, and you'll agree. She looks like a mole."

Now, Deb's eyes were indeed smaller than Pen's, whose enormous, bloodshot gig lamps could fix the front row of the pit like a snake charmer mesmerising a basketful of cobras. But Deb's brown eyes, fringed with long, silky lashes, were of well-above-average size and perfectly beautiful. With her sweet little freckled nose and full red lips she looked like a pretty pixie. "There's nothing wrong with Deb's eyes," I said carefully, not wanting to be kicked in the groin. "Although, of course, they're not as large as yours. Nobody's are."

Apparently satisfied, Pen smirked. "Her chest is quite flat," she went on, taking my hands and laying them on her own pectorals, for which "billowy" is the word which always comes to mind. "She looks like a boy."

Indeed she did. In doublet and hose and a velvet hat, the nailer's girl looked quite ravishing, a Viola come to glorious life. "She's pretty. She's sweet. She's very biddable." I wasn't going to be bullied by Pen. "She has a long way to go before she could compare with you, but she's willing to work and learn. I have great hopes of her."

"Pretty! Sweet! Biddable! She's conceited, scheming and sly!" Pen's lower lip began to wobble, and her gig lamps filled with tears. "She's trying to take you away from me!"

"Oh, come now." I stroked Pen's plump, white shoulder. "She's a child," I said, laughing. "Not jealous of a little girl, are you, my sweet?"

"Do I need to be?" Sulkily, Pen glowered. "Henry, do I need to be?"

"I've never in my life fancied boys. And, as you yourself point out, Deborah has the figure of a lad."

"Ah." Pen dabbed at her eyes. She sniffed, and a ghost of a smile hovered round her lips. Then, like a great white dolphin, she flopped backwards on to my bed. "Come here," she whispered.

I did as I was bidden.

In spite of my assurances that she would always be the leading lady in my company and in my heart, Pen never referred to our new Juliet as anything but "the nailer's brat". She snarled and glowered at poor Deb Tanner, and it was pathetic to see such jealously so openly displayed. But then again, provided Pen could declaim the mercy speech at regular intervals and get into my bed for a grumble, she was just about bearable.

Who wants a mistress who is just about bearable?

I don't know what planted that first seed of affection, but from that time on, as I ploughed Pen's well-furrowed field, my thoughts would be of Deb. As I kissed Pen's rouged lips I imagined opening Deb's soft mouth with mine. As I tried to contain Pen's wobbling flesh in my embrace, I thought how pleasant it would be to have Deb's slim young body in my arms.

But old men should not run after young girls. Also, I was fond of Pen Gaynes.

As I have said, Deb was a natural player. She spoke long-dead writers' lines as if she'd just thought of them herself, and sentences first set down two hundred years ago tumbled from her lips as fresh as flowers in May. She was anxious to improve her stagecraft. Whereas the others bellyached incessantly about rehearsals – "Unnecessary, my dear fellow, I know the part backwards, and we always keep the business the same" – Deb was at the theatre early each morning, declaiming to the pit and breaking her heart to the gallery. Practising, practising, learning to be player.

Sometimes, unobserved, I watched her. She *was* Juliet. She *was* Cordelia. I wondered about her ancestry. Who was her father? David Garrick had had no known issue, but in my more sentimental moments I liked to fancy that this child was the result of some illicit union and that she might be a descendant of the great actor himself.

She certainly had what I thought of as an actor's face, mobile, expressive, displaying the widest range of emotions with apparent ease. When she looked sad, she reminded me of someone I'd once known, but I could not place her. I meet so many people, after all.

As well as acting, she sang, in a pretty but thin soprano which Charlie and I decided to fatten up. "Breathe now!" Charlie would cry, as I coaxed an accompaniment out of some rickety old piano in the wings. "Now. And now. Good girl. And again." Obediently Deb would go through the air or anthem or whatever again and again, until Charlie and I agreed she'd got it right.

She was in the theatre again one cold morning in November. Singing her heart out to nobody, she did not hear me slip in, so I sat down to listen to her. She finished her song, then came to the front of the stage and began to recite the mercy speech from the *Merchant* – Pen's lawful property.

She did it very well. When she spoke those lines:

"Though justice be thy plea, consider this,
That in the course of justice none of us
Should see salvation – "

she made them such an earnest, such a heartfelt appeal that I would have sworn the little simpleton knew what they meant. I waited until she'd finished, then I coughed. She peered into the gloom and saw me.

"Oh, Mr Collis." She was Deb Tanner again now, the nailer's girl. She plucked at her gown and blushed.

“Come and sit down.” I smiled at her encouragingly, and patted the bench beside me.

She came.

I saw that today she was wearing a new gown, a present from Charlie, I assumed, with a pattern of little blue flowers and demure blue piping at the wrists and neck. It made her look like a governess. Lucinda had charge of her hair now, and had looped it prettily round her ears. Such sweet little ears, I caught myself thinking, such kissable little ears.

I coughed again, to correct myself. “I heard you just now,” I said, in what I intended to be a reassuring way. “You know, you have an excellent ear for verse.”

“Oh.” Her blush became deeper. “I – I was only t-trying it out,” she stammered. “M-miss Gaynes is so clever at it, I wanted – ”

“Yes. Quite.” God, she was a thousand times better than Pen Gaynes, and it was on the tip of my tongue to tell her as much, so you can see the sort of state I was in. “I was impressed,” I said.

No reply.

“I do feel you have a future on the stage,” I continued. I smiled in what I hoped was a fatherly fashion, but I might just as well have given her a hideous, goatish leer, for she stared back at me quite alarmed. “Deb,” I ploughed on, “do you intend to stay with us?”

“I’d loike to.” Her normal speaking tones had a strong Birmingham overlay which was quite absent from her acting voice. “Yis, I’d loike to, virry much.”

“Then I’m sure we’d be delighted to have you.”

“Thank you, Mr Collis.” She smiled shyly. “You’re very kind.”

That smile enslaved me. Without warning, my heart turned over. Worse, far worse than that, my member stood up and took notice, so I was obliged to cover it with my hat. “Mr Rayner’s teaching me my letters,” she went on. “I hope soon to be able to read.”

“That will be splendid.” I must have sounded like an usher at a public school, commending a favourite pupil whose father might endow the foundation. I wanted to cross my legs but I couldn't, I'd have injured myself.

Deb stood up. "I promised Miss Gaynes I'd fetch some things for her from town," she said. "I ought to go now."

"Yes. Fine." My smile was a rictus of agony. "Well then, I'll see you later."

I watched her walk out of the theatre. With Charlie as Lear, she would play Cordelia. I'd coach her for Ophelia myself. She could do it. She'd break hearts.

Chapter 8

Our autumn season ended in mid-November. Our winter engagements that year took us to the south of England, to a circuit of theatres in the Staines–Twickenham–Egham area. Those theatres were dreadful places. Cold, damp, riddled with dry and wet rot, inside there was dirty, faded scenery, scarred and broken seating, ancient curtains fast dissolving into motheaten rags and rusting, decaying stage machinery which didn't work. The scene shifters were unpunctual and surly and the carpenters habitually drunk.

Surprisingly, though, the audiences were good, and we played to near-capacity houses. Charlie said this was because his own splendid reputation had gone like a flaming sword before him, making it a matter of absolute necessity to the people of Middlesex that they should see the great Mr Rayner before he retired.

"Charlie," I said, "you'll never retire. Out of all the actors I've ever known, you're the one most certain to die in harness. You couldn't forsake the stage any more than you could give up your bottle."

"On the contrary," he replied, "I yearn for a thatched cottage and a trout stream." He dabbed his good eye, as if he longed for the rural tranquillity he might never enjoy. Unless I gave him more benefit nights.

Charlie might have been a crowd puller, but the others also had their fans. Lady players always attract followers, and Lucinda had a regular beau, an elderly gentleman with watery eyes and a wet moustache who'd trailed the company all over the Midlands, along the Welsh borders and across the green heart of England into the Home Counties. He sent her wilting flowers and cheap champagne. Pen and Dora also had their admirers, so after each night's performance there were usually six or seven gentlemen (of sorts) lounging about outside the theatre, ogling the females and hoping for a glimpse of bare leg.

Good houses and hard work lent Time wings, and before we knew it we were racing towards the next year. As Deb had no knowledge of her exact date of birth, aware only that she'd come into the world about 1824 and that her guardian had once told her she'd been born in winter time, we decided to celebrate her birthday on the first day of the new year. So on the first of January 1841 we held what we decided would be her seventeenth birthday party.

"A birthday party?" she'd demanded, when Charlie told her what had been decided. "What's a birthday party?"

"A birthday party, my dear, is a group of people well met together to be joyful," Charlie replied.

Poor ignorant child, she was still none the wiser. Afterwards she understood that a birthday party was just like any other other occasion when off-duty actors get together; an excuse for the whole company to crowd into Lucinda Tolland's lodgings to eat peeled prawns and rabbit pies, and for everyone except Deb herself to get rolling drunk.

It wasn't that she disdained the bottle, you understand. After half a glass of porter she fell asleep, so the party continued around her unconscious form. At two in the morning, Charlie hoisted her on to his back and declared his intention to carry her home.

"I'll come with you," I offered, afraid he might drop her in the gutter. "If you meet any constables, it won't look very good – "

"I'm not drunk!" Charlie drew himself up to his full height, and hiccuped. "I tell you, Henry Collis, I'm as sober as the next man. So there!"

All the same, I helped him take Deb home. We laid her on her bed and covered her with a quilt. "Sleeping Beauty," murmured Charlie mawkishly, looking down on her.

"Yes," I agreed. "Shall I just – "

"Hands off!" As I leaned over to draw the quilt up round Deb's shoulders, Charlie shoved me aside. "I'll do that," he muttered. "You get off home to your trollop. She'll be wondering where you are."

Our first performance of the new year brought in an exceptionally good audience. Families with children always help to keep the rowdies in check, and that particular evening there were several large family parties, with whiskered papas and frizzed-up mamas shepherding gaggles of idiot grandparents and over-excited children into the boxes and the best seats in the circle.

In the pit, of course, the lads were cuffing one another, chewing nuts, sucking oranges, swigging ginger beer and belching – oh yes, a noble and discerning crowd indeed – but they seemed a good-humoured rabble, and I felt fairly confident that tonight Fred and I would not suddenly have to leave off being Hamlet and the Ghost to go and break up a fight among the apprentices.

And in fact the evening went very well, the only untoward event being that Britannia got her helmet knocked off. An orange came spinning through the smoky air, and an ill-bred voice shouted, "You should've left that old bucket at home with the coal in it."

The yell of laughter from the pit set even the families in the boxes tittering, a fist fight broke out in one of the aisles, and Fred clenched his fists. "Time to go and break a few heads," he muttered. "Come on, Henry. Nip it in the bud now, before everything gets out of hand."

I grabbed his arm. "Give her a chance," I said. "Look – she's doing very well on her own now."

Indeed she was. Pen Gaynes is a trouper of the first order, and, unperturbed by the sudden disappearance of her headgear, she raked the audience with such a fierce blue glare that the laughter died. The pugilists stopped breaking one anothers' front teeth and went back to sit on their benches. Shaking her copious blonde locks free, Pen began to sing, and by the end of the song she had the entire audience roaring out the chorus, totally with her.

"She's wonderful," breathed Deb, who was standing with Charlie in the wings. "Absolutely wonderful. And so brave! I'd have run off and cried."

"You wouldn't have done anything of the sort. Not now." Charlie grinned at her. "You'd have carried on regardless and thought, be damned to the lot of them. Eh?"

"I don't think so," said Deb.

"You'd have coped." Leaning towards her, Charlie breathed brandy into her face. "You're worth a dozen fair Penelopes. Don't tell Henry I said that."

As if I needed to be told what I could see for myself.

As I have said, the actresses all had their particular admirers. These gentlemen come and go, and don't usually give us any trouble. One young fellow had been following the circuit since Staines, joining the club led by Lucinda's elderly Lancelot, and now he became one of our most persistent patrons. Each evening he could be seen in a box, gazing fixedly at Deb. Sometimes alone, sometimes he had company in the shape of two or three other young men; but he didn't indulge in the usual horseplay or foolery. He merely watched our little Juliet.

When Deb was off stage, his attention wandered. His companions cat-called and carried on as young oafs do, smoking and eating and drinking and hanging over the edge of the box, flicking cigar ash over the balustrade and threatening to be sick over the patrons in the pit. But the constant admirer took no part in this. He simply waited patiently until Deb came on again.

He looked like a well-set-up young man. Expensively dressed, neatly shaven, obviously he had a bit of spare cash in his pockets. He could have been a bank clerk. Or a trainee lawyer. But I tell you, all sorts follow actresses. Butchers' sons, sweeps' sons, dukes' sons, kings' sons even – Mrs Jordan was an actress long before she became a royal whore and set about presenting King William with I think it was ten bastards.

"Noticed that fellow in the left-hand box?" demanded Fred one evening, as we stood in the wings waiting to join Dora and Deb on stage.

"The one in the blue coat? Oh, yes. He's become quite a regular." Affecting a nonchalance I certainly did not feel, I lounged back against a hamper. I flicked a bit of lint off the sleeve of my robe. "Seems to be rather taken with our infant prodigy," I added, offhandedly as you please. "Look at him now. Eyes starting out of his head."

"Yes." Fred grinned. "Lucinda's jealous as hell."

Night after night Deb's admirer sat there, staring. But then, towards the middle of February, he disappeared. Perhaps he was sick, I thought, or had done away with himself for love. At any rate, a different young man was in his box that evening, so as he left the theatre I accosted him, just as he himself was joined by two other lads.

I suggested a jar or two, to which proposal all three readily agreed, so I treated them at a pot house near the theatre. As I'd assumed, they were indeed friends of the constant admirer, and during the course of the evening I established who this lovelorn fellow was.

"Father was a bookseller," said one lad, draining his tankard and holding it out for more. "Thank you, Molly my love, the same again. Yes, had a shop in the City, I believe."

"Large private fortune too," chipped in another boy, winking. "Pockets very well lined. Overflowing at times." He wiped his mouth on his sleeve. "Yes, has a few bob, has young Minot."

"Minot?" I asked.

"Thassis name." The third lad grinned. "Thassis name, see. Channing Minot."

"Ah." As I ordered more drinks, I felt a sort of angry pleasure that this independent, handsome, rich young man at least had a stupid name. But overall, it was little consolation. In every other way, he was a better man than I.

Channing Minot's illness was, most unfortunately, neither life-threatening nor of long duration. The end of the month saw him back in his accustomed seat, gawping at Deb and leading the sympathetic moan of pity when Juliet stabbed herself in the chest.

I have to admit that in addition to acting the part with total conviction, Deb looked heart-meltingly lovely as poor, doomed Miss Capulet. For the role Lucinda had got her up in a flowing white muslin gown, tight about the bosom and then tumbling in Grecian folds to her ankles. Her hair was loosely knotted and curled charmingly round her ears, and about her neck she wore her green glass pendant.

Thus attired, she was such a picture of youth, innocence and purity that even the ladies in the audience loved her, weeping extravagantly when she died. The men sniffed a bit, too. As she took her bow that evening, her admirer led the universal applause. I saw that she looked directly at him, and blushed with delight.

I am not, as a rule, in the business of prophecy, but I felt from the beginning that this Channing Minot would make trouble for Deb. Perhaps you will say it was just an old man's jealousy which made me feel this. Perhaps you are right. But still, I felt it.

Deb came off stage in such a glow of happiness that I could have sworn the very air around her was charged with electricity. "Oh, Mr Collis," she cried as she saw me, "oh, Mr Collis, what an audience. What a night. They did like me, didn't they?"

"Indeed they did." I pretended to be amending the prompt script. "Go on and take another call. Pen's not quite ready yet."

She dashed back on to the stage. The audience stamped, clapped and whistled. Deb herself blushed even pinker, and I saw that she glanced shyly towards the box where her lover was on his feet, still leading the applause.

For a minute or more they clapped her, and were still cheering when she tripped back off again. In her toga and coalscuttle Pen Gaynes stumped past her, treading on her little black-slippered feet and shoving her so hard against a flat that she grazed her elbow quite badly; but even this could not wipe the smile off Deb's sweet young face.

I felt I was expected to say something, so I did. But at that moment, extravagant, heartfelt praise was beyond me. "Well done, my dear," I muttered. I was fastening my jerkin for my next entrance, so could not look directly at her. "Very well done indeed."

I wished she'd go back to her dressing-room, but she didn't. She stood there, panting, watching Pen. I wanted to take her in my arms. To tell her that I loved her and would always love her, far better than any callow lad of twenty-odd, who probably loved himself much more than he could love anyone else. But if I'd done so, what then? She'd have stared at me in astonishment. She'd have slapped my face, perhaps. Or laughed. I couldn't have borne that. I realised I was trembling.

Pen Gaynes came off, followed by respectful applause. I could see from the way she clutched her trident that she was still livid. I didn't care. Jamming my wig on my head, I became Richard the Third and went on stage, still shaking.

I almost murdered Fred Hammer that night. He had to fight me off in earnest, hissing angrily that I ought to lay off the drink, that *I* was supposed to be the one who was bloody dying.

3

Deborah Tanner

1841–1843

Chapter 9

I could hardly have missed the good-looking young man in the nearside box who gazed so fixedly at me. It's not vanity speaking now – he did stare at me, and only at me.

Over those few weeks I watched him. When I was off stage I peered round the flats and studied him unobserved, and I saw that he paid no attention whatsoever to Miss Tolland and Mr Hammer, Beatrice and Benedicking away like mad, that he had no interest in Mr Rayner's noisy expiries, nor in Mr Collis's elegant soliloquies. While *they* were playing, he tore up little bits of paper and talked on and off to his friends. But when the tableau was set up and I came on as Justice, he stopped tearing and talking and his eyes became firmly fixed on the stage.

On me.

Was I imagining it, I wondered. That was, after all, a distinct possibility. But when we had done that tableau vivant three nights in succession and the young man still watched it as if he were memorising the songs and the very script itself, I was almost certain he admired me.

Then, one Thursday night, as Miss Tolland stepped out of her place in the picture to sing the first air, Miss Gaynes confirmed it. "The nailer's brat's made a conquest at last," she muttered to Mr Wright. "That scrubbery-looking fellow in the box. He's gawking at her now. See?"

"Eh?" Mr Wright glanced at Miss Gaynes, then his eyes flicked to the box and back. "Oh, him," he murmured, out of the side of his mouth. "Seen him there before. Not my sort of fancy. Cruel eyes. Don't you think so?"

"Perhaps." Miss Gaynes smirked as much as her inch-thick

paint would allow. "But, Harkess, cruel eyes are just what you like best, so – "

But then a sharp stare from Mr Collis's own cruel eyes buttoned her lips, so I was denied any further enlightenment.

Now my heart soared. Proudly I held up my cardboard sword and rusty scales and gazed benignly at the audience, glad indeed that Mr Collis had decided Justice need not be blindfolded as she'd probably trip over something, and the hicks in the audience wouldn't know she was supposed to be blind anyway.

I looked at my newest friend. His eyes, cruel or not, were light. Blue, I assumed, or palest grey. His figure, or what I could see of it, seemed good. He was young. Older than me, I guessed, but still only in his early twenties. I felt my heart turn over.

By the end of that week, I found that whenever I was due to go on and play, I came out in a great perspiration. For each time I appeared on stage there he'd be, in a side box, looking fixedly at me.

Then one evening our eyes actually met. As I stared out over the auditorium, he caught my gaze. He smiled. I felt myself grow weak, and how I got through the rest of that evening I shall never know.

A further week went by before my kind friend in the audience saw fit to declare himself. He'd been absent for two days, throwing me into a panic, but then he returned. Better than that, halfway through the evening –

"There's a note for Miss Tanner," said Mr Denby sourly, evidently provoked to be used as a messenger. "A boy brought it to the stage door. Had to give him threepence." He handed me a piece of thick, creamy paper, folded over.

Could it be from him? I snatched it eagerly. Feverishly, I opened it – and could not decipher a word. I'd never seen such a scrawl. Mr Rayner was teaching me to read; I had mastered print and was coming to terms with handwritten script, but this stumped me. This letter wasn't *written* at all. Instead, it looked as if a party of lively beetles with inky feet had danced a quadrille on it.

So, pretending even more agitation than I felt, I passed it to Miss Tolland. "Would you be so kind as to read this?" I faltered. "I'm too nervous – "

"Of course, dear child, of course." Kindly, Miss Tolland smiled. Taking the paper she scanned it as if it were a part. Then, heroically, she read aloud.

"'Dear Miss Tanner,' she declaimed, 'I should very much like the favour of a word with you and will wait outside the theatre this evening, in the hope of your kindness. In the meantime I remain your devoted admirer – ' "

Miss Tolland screwed up her eyes. "What's this?" she muttered. "Charing? Or maybe Channing? Well. Channing Minot – I think."

"Channing Minot. Channing Minot." I said the name over to myself, savouring it on my tongue. I wasn't sure if I liked it or not . . .

It was agony, perfect agony, waiting for that performance to be over and the audience to disperse, but finally they did so. They clattered out, the gaslights were extinguished, and straight away the bright, magical theatre became a darkened, empty shell.

For me, of course, the evening was only just beginning; but instead of dashing out to meet my friend, I stood like an idiot in a corridor, waiting for I don't quite know what. But then Miss Tolland found me moping and took charge. "Come along then, child." She snatched up my cloak and tossed it round my shoulders. "Whatever are you waiting for? Can't disappoint our admirers!"

"*Your* admirers, Luce?" demanded Mr Denby spitefully, as he pushed past us to leave.

"The child needs a chaperone." With a wide gesture which nearly knocked Mr Denby's hat off, Lucinda Tolland swept her own black velvet cloak about her shoulders. "Come, child," she repeated urgently. "Doesn't do to keep one's public waiting."

Miss Tolland was a born flirt. In spite of her understanding with Mr Hammer, who glowered at all her admirers and occasionally hit one on the nose, she smirked and widened her eyes at any man who looked at her, and tonight she beamed more than obligingly at the group of loungers lurking outside the stage door. After several fulsome "good evenings" however, my chaperone pushed through this little crowd, dragging me with her. Her bright eyes darting, she looked up and down the street while the stage-doorers eyed us in their usual desultory fashion. But then someone touched my arm and I turned to see Channing Minot standing there.

My stomach twisted. "It *is* Miss Tanner, isn't it?" he asked, smiling, for the light was behind me.

"Yes." Foolishly, I gaped at him. "Yes, that's right."

"I so much enjoyed the performance this evening. And some parts of it, of course, were particularly fine." He fidgeted a little now, aware that all the stage-door loafers were gawping at us. "I – um – "

But then neither of us spoke any more. *I* was completely tongue-tied. Never having had an admirer before, I didn't know what I was supposed to say. So I just looked at him.

Channing Minot was beautiful. His hair fell in black-blue curls around his face. His blue eyes were as clear as aquamarines. His features were neat and regular. In fact, he was the handsomest man I'd ever seen, and I was flattered to the point of imbecility that such a man should even glance at me.

Finally he muttered some offhand remarks which I did not properly hear. I replied, hardly knowing what I said. All we needed to do, it seemed, was gaze at each other.

Then he took his leave. He said he had to be back in London by midnight, and that he was late already. He disappeared into the blackness, and I stared after him, bewitched.

"He's positively in love with you, child!" cried Lucinda, whose very existence I had forgotten. Stepping out of the shadows, she took my arm and led me back into the theatre. "He's head over heels! Besotted! Lucky girl."

Back in the warmth of her dressing-room, where Fred Hammer stood waiting with the blackest of scowls on his ugly face, she sat me down and beamed at me. "Well?" she demanded. "Do you like him?"

"*Like*?" I stared at her blankly. A single meeting had done it all. A single light touch on my arm had kindled such an ache, such a longing, that I knew myself to be violently and eternally in love.

I agree, it seems ridiculous now. But before you condemn me for a fool, you must remember that I was playing Juliet almost nightly. I was just turned seventeen. I knew nothing of the world. All in all, I could hardly have been better prepared for a sudden infatuation which I was determined to believe was everlasting love.

Before slipping away, Mr Minot had apparently asked Miss Tolland if by any chance she and I took a walk in the High Street in the afternoons. Lucinda had replied that we often did exactly that, so the following day Channing Minot and I met again and dawdled past the shops together, with Lucinda and Fred Hammer trailing us at a discreet distance.

Channing Minot talked. I listened. I had no choice in this, for my tongue had somehow changed into a lump of metal which was soldered to the roof of my mouth, my throat had almost completely closed up, and the effort of articulating more than three words together made me feel quite faint.

"My father had shops," Channing was saying, as we stared absently into a hat-shop window. "He was a bookseller. He had businesses in the Strand, St Martin's Lane and the Tottenham Court Road."

"Ah." Having no idea where these places might be, I didn't know whether to say "How splendid" or "Oh dear, don't fret about that."

"Do you have the shops now?" I enquired.

"Me? Oh no. They're sold. My godfather managed that for me." Channing smiled at me. "I was christened after my godfather," he told me now. "He was Alexander Channing, a paper merchant. He had a very extensive business – perhaps you've heard of him?"

"No." I wondered even then why I should have heard of a paper merchant, but there again I was so ignorant I'd barely heard of anybody. I thought perhaps this Mr Channing was a great and famous man. I'd have to ask Lucinda. She read the newspapers, after all.

"I have rooms in a house in Holborn," Channing went on now. "I own the house, as it happens. I live on the first floor and let the ground floor to business gentlemen."

A man of property! A landlord! I really was impressed now, and my eyes grew round.

We were walking past a shop with a display of shawls in the window, and beside it Channing stopped. "Miss Tanner," he said gravely, "that blue and green cashmere, with the tasselled fringe – it would so become you. Do you think – "

So he bought me the shawl. He presented it to me with a kind of mock ceremony which I found delightful and then, seeing Lucinda and Fred approaching, he took his leave. But not without asking permission to walk with me again the following afternoon.

"My dear!" cried Lucinda, as Channing walked away. "My dear child, what a conquest. A three-guinea shawl! What a prize. What a man! Eh, Fred?"

"Fellow looks like a regular blackguard to me," replied Fred Hammer morosely, spoiling things a little. "That red waistcoat. Those horrible yellow boots. All those revolting kiss curls round his face. What's he mean by it, eh?"

Channing told me that his ancestors were originally French Huguenots – in other words, Protestant refugees, although for all I knew then, a Huguenot might have been a species of bear – from La Rochelle. His parents had, it appeared, both been the sole offspring of their own parents' unions, and Channing, I assumed, was also an only child.

His grandparents, he said, were buried before he was born, and so when Mr Minot died and his wife followed him shortly afterwards, Channing found himself solitary in the world, the sole survivor of his line.

I expressed my sympathy for his bereavements, enquired further about his family – but he declined to elaborate, so I spared him further pain.

"You know," I said, "you're just like me."

"How's that?" he asked.

"You're alone in the world, without family." Shyly, I looked up at him. "Mr Minot, how do you live?"

"I have a comfortable enough income." He smiled at me now. "My father invested wisely in the stock market and as I told you, I have property. I live in sufficient comfort."

"I see."

"But it's a cold, lonely, bachelor existence." He sighed. "I could wish – I could well wish it were otherwise."

Then he said he had an appointment and must take his leave; but he would, if I pleased, walk with me the following Monday. It was Wednesday afternoon then. Seeing my obvious alarm at such a long separation, he touched my hand, to comfort me. "I have urgent business in Town," he explained. "I shall not be able to get away until Sunday evening. But all the time I shall be thinking of you."

Channing Minot stayed away for rather more than a week, but each morning a bunch of fresh flowers was delivered to the theatre. These perfumed presents did little to relieve my feverish state of mind, however, and by the eighth day of his absence from his customary seat I felt I was dying of despair. When I stabbed myself that evening I half wished Fred's old property dagger had been real and that I could have put myself out of my misery.

After that performance, however, Fred appeared in the ladies' dressing-room, picking his great yellow teeth and lounging against the doorpost, a very sour scowl on his ugly face. "Person to see Miss Tanner," he growled. "Waiting by the box office he is. Won't go away."

Of course it was Channing. Of course he was full of apologies and distress at not having seen me for a whole week. He took my hands in his and almost mashed them; I heard the bones grind together. "I must speak to you," he said, his eyes glittering. "Will you walk out with me for ten minutes?"

"Yes. Yes, of course." I had half my make-up on, I was dressed for the stage, not the street, but I did not hesitate. Heedless of reputation or propriety, I stepped out on to the cold pavement and went with him.

We walked in the main street at first, but the pertinent stares of passers-by upset Channing and we turned down a side road. "I'm sorry I missed your performance tonight," he said.

"There'll be others," I replied. I smiled at him. "Mr Minot, was there something in particular – "

"No. Well, yes." Channing stopped walking. He laid one hand on my arm. "Would you – could you ever consider giving up the stage?" he asked.

"Maybe one day." I shrugged. "I might decide to try something else. Or if I were to marry, it might be difficult to – "

"Would you marry me?" His grip on my arm tightened. "You must know that I admire you very much. I feel positively bereaved when I'm away from you. Miss Tanner, I ask you again most urgently, will you marry me?"

Marry Channing Minot? Marry this gentleman, this landlord, this picture of manly beauty and charm? How could I refuse? I threw my arms about his neck. "Yes," I cried. "Yes, dear Channing, of course I'll marry you!"

"A gentleman of substantial private means," announced Lucinda proudly, as if the whole business had been managed and successfully concluded by herself. "Well, Pen – what d'you think of that?"

"He's a gentleman of substantial private debts, more like," retorted Pen. She sucked her gums and glanced sneeringly at me. "So, Miss, when's the great event to take place?"

"Friday fortnight." Happy beyond sense and reason, I beamed like an idiot. "There's no family to inform or invite, you see, so there's no reason for delay."

"It's a rum business. A very rum business indeed." Fred Hammer heaved a deep sigh and looked pityingly at me. "Is he all there?" he enquired.

"I'm sorry?" I asked, puzzled.

"Is anyone at home?" Fred tapped his forehead. "I mean to say: fellow like him, girl like you. Holy matrimony's not the usual arrangement, is it? Had it sewn up, have you? He gets the scissors on your wedding day?"

"Be quiet, Fred." Sharply, Lucinda dug him in the side. "He's so vulgar," she sniffed, glaring at him. "But what can you expect? Mother was a common stroller, you see. Tramped the country, scraping a living where she could. Carried him with her."

"She did, too." At the recollection, Fred sighed. "Up hill and down dale, through blizzard and tempest. A fine woman, my mother."

"Fine!" Lucinda tossed her head. "She had no more finesse than a donkey."

"Don't you malign my mother!" roared Fred.

"Well, she was a harlot." Lucinda wasn't at all abashed. "She gave you a harlot's example and a harlot's morals and you assume everyone brings up their children as she did. Well, they don't."

"Better a harlot than a hypocrite!" howled Fred. "I'd sooner be a harlot's child than a hypocrite's daughter!"

"And what, precisely, do you mean by that? My father – "

"*Your* father!" Fred snorted. "An excellent man, and no mistake. Honest shopkeeper, pillar of the community, a pious fellow if ever there was one. Cast you off without a penny when you took up with me. Oh yes. Kicked his precious daughter into the street to starve. Left you without so much as a shift to cover your arse. Told you to piss off and – "

"Are any of us invited to the feast?" piped up Dora and Judith in unison just then, as things began to look rather nasty.

"Oh yes!" I cried. "Yes, all of you; Mr Minot would like everyone to be there. I thought," I added humbly, "that I might ask Mr Collis to give me away. Miss Tolland, do you think he would?"

"I'm sure he'd be delighted," replied Lucinda, with a wobble in her voice. She dabbed her eyes and sniffed. "Yes, he'd be thrilled."

"Oh, thrilled indeed," echoed Fred, his voice heavy with sarcasm. "Well then – where's the merrymaking to take place?"

"At St Michael Archangel, in Chancery Lane. Then, for the wedding breakfast, we're going to a hotel."

I went to look for Henry Collis and found him and Charlie Rayner in a sort of dirty cubby-hole at the back of the theatre, drinking coffee and busy with the accounts. Brown envelopes were piled on the table, coins and banknotes were heaped all about, and the manager's fingers were black with ink. As I entered this makeshift office, he looked up and smiled. "Ah, Deborah," he said, kindly. "What may I do for you?"

Charlie Rayner also grinned, but as I told Mr Collis what I wanted, his grin was replaced by a frown. He took out his false eye and began to polish it vigorously with his pocket handkerchief, spitting on the glass to bring up the shine, harrumping all the time as he did so.

Wishing he'd go away, I looked at the manager anxiously. Surely he'd do this one small thing for me? After all, he'd never actually wanted me in the company, and now here was a golden opportunity to get rid of me, so surely a short walk up an aisle wasn't too great a favour to ask?

As I repeated my request – for he didn't appear to have heard it the first time – I saw Mr Collis was pale. I attributed this to surprise. Or perhaps a more likely cause was Charlie's uncouth behaviour, and again I wished him away. "Mr Collis," I began, for the third time, "do you think – "

"I'd be delighted, my dear. Honoured, I should say." The manager smiled again, a weary, patient smile. "I'm flattered that you thought to ask me, and I'd be glad to be of service to you."

It was my turn to be surprised. Mr Collis looked at me so gently. His voice was so kind. I wondered now how I'd ever been nervous of him, this tired-looking, middle-aged player who suddenly seemed to have the weight of the world on his shoulders.

"So we'll lose you," he said now, leaning back in his chair to look at me.

"Yes." I shrugged. "I'll be sorry to leave you all, but you see – "

"Yes, it's a great thing for you. I do see that. Deb?"

"Yes, Mr Collis?"

"Remember us," he said. "Remember your time with the company, and bear in mind that if you ever need us, we'll be your friends."

"I know that," I said. "And I thank you."

My side of the gloomy old city church, with its withered little pew opener and its dirty stained glass windows throwing dark blobs of colour on to the stone-flagged floors, was noisy and colourful; but Channing's was quiet and sombre. In fact it was almost empty, for his only guests were a very pale young man in a dull purple waistcoat and an older fellow in grubby navy-blue fustian, who looked badly hung over.

Both these elegant specimens sat slumped in their places, dozing quietly, throughout the whole service. Purple Waistcoat had to be nudged quite sharply before he'd hand over the ring.

My brand new husband and I came out into bright spring sunshine. Looking up at Channing, so handsome, so tall, I felt as if I would burst with happiness.

Behind me I heard the company talking. "I had the arranging of her hair," said Lucinda, agreeing with Charlie that I looked a picture. "And Dora did her dress and veil."

"Looks familiar, that veil. From the properties box, is it?" asked Charlie, in a booming stage whisper.

"No, we had it from a little shop in Byfleet Alley, just behind the theatre. Two shillings and three pence – wasn't that cheap?"

"Don't know why he wanted to *marry* her," I heard Fred Hammer mutter, labouring his old theme. Lucinda told him to shut up.

We went to the hotel by cab. There, we had a splendid breakfast and speeches from all the male members of the company, except Mr Collis. He said he couldn't think of anything to say. As we left, everyone but the manager kissed me heartily. I thought that rather ill-natured of him, but was far too happy to worry about it.

The only person I wanted to kiss that day was my husband.

Chapter 10

Until Fred Hammer brought the subject up, it had never entered my head to wonder why Channing Minot wanted to marry me. As opposed to make me his mistress, that is. Aren't all actresses supposed to be of easy virtue, you ask? Well, I imagine some are, but I'd given no one any reason to suspect *I* would be a complaisant whore. Until I heard what Fred had to say on the subject, I'd thought it was the most natural thing in the world that, having fallen in love with me, Channing Minot would want to marry me.

I was young, I was pretty, I was a virgin. I had no dowry, but Channing was rich. Naïvely I imagined there was nothing unusual about our union. Nothing at all. So on that fine spring day I looked forward to beginning another new life, as a married lady. I went into marriage with my head and hopes high.

Was I dreading my wedding night? No. In spite of being a virgin myself, I knew all about coupling. In the dark courts of Birmingham I'd frequently stumbled over or into pairs of bodies locked in that most intimate of embraces, I'd heard the grunts of the men and the moans of the women, and by about the age of twelve Esther Harris had supplied me with all the necessary technical information about the act of human congress. Esther's own sex education had been received at the keyhole of her mother's bedchamber, where Mrs Harris entertained many a gentleman lodger in order to eke out her rent.

As for the finer feelings, the things of the spirit rather than of the coarse, wayward flesh – well, playing Juliet night after night had made me hopelessly romantic, and I saw no reason why Channing and I should not love as wisely and well, if not as tragically, as *Signor* and *Signora* Montague. And naturally, for Romeo and Juliet, their first and last union had been perfect.

After seeing the last of our guests away, Channing took me back to his home, a dark, narrow, terraced house on three floors, on Holborn Hill. We took off our outdoor things and went into the sitting-room, a large, airy chamber on the first floor. Old furniture, thick carpets and heavy curtains gave this an air of solidity and comfort. We looked about us, a little embarrassed now, but then Channing reached out and touched my face. "Deb?" he whispered, his fingers stroking my cheek.

"Yes?"

"I think – I want – "

I understood. We went upstairs to bed.

"You're not afraid of me, are you?" he demanded, as he unfastened his shirt buttons and drew the garment over his head.

"No." I looked at him as he stood there half-naked, and am ashamed to say that the emotion uppermost in my mind was simple greed. As I gazed at his broad shoulders, tapering down to a slim waist, as I admired his smooth white skin, I wanted him as much as, when a child, I'd wanted sugar almonds or cinder toffee. If he'd been a plateful of cakes I'd have gobbled him all up. "No," I repeated, "I'm not afraid at all."

To prove this, I went to him and, raising my face to his, I kissed him. He tasted of aniseed water, warm and sweet. He took me in his arms. "Oh, Deb," he whispered, holding me close, "help me!"

I assumed he meant that he was as inexperienced in love as I was, so I kissed him again and ran my hands over his back and shoulders, warming him. He relaxed then, and kissed me back. He felt for the fastenings on my gown, and began to undo them. And instinct took over.

Channing had no notion of how to please a woman, but he knew how to please himself. For my part, I was so young and so wildly in love with him that even his few perfunctory kisses, haphazardly bestowed before he got down to the real business of the afternoon, more than delighted me. I was flattered to be the object of his desire and the instrument of his satisfaction.

"Are you hurt?" he asked, afterwards. "A woman's supposed to bleed, I know – but have I hurt you?"

"No, not at all." Indeed, he hadn't. All that travelling and leaping about on stage had made me so supple and elastic that my body had easily accommodated him, and a tiny trickle of dark-red blood was all I had to show for my loss of viginity. "I love you," I said, kissing him again, meaning it.

"Yes, well, I love you," he replied, but so offhandedly that a more perceptive woman would have been seriously concerned.

I played at house, shopping for delicate little dinners for the pair of us which were cooked by Kitty, the middle-aged housemaid who had been old Mrs Minot's servant. My husband was generous with pocket money, so I equipped myself with a whole new wardrobe, a task which took up six or seven weeks of my time. Leaving the narrow house on Holborn Hill, I sallied forth to the fashionable shops of Oxford Street and Regent Street to buy or order shawls, bonnets, gowns and underclothes.

I had six new dresses run up by a lady in St Martin's Lane, and as these arrived I put them on and paraded before my husband in my new clothes. These parades became a ritual which led to the same conclusion each time.

"Would you like to see my new gown?" I would enquire, thinking of the parcel upstairs, waiting to be unwrapped.

"Very much indeed." Channing would lay aside his newspaper and stretch. "Will you put it on for me?"

"With pleasure."

"Very pretty," he would say, as I appeared before him with five guineas' worth of silk and lace on my back. Then he would get up and come over to see how it was all held together. Turning me round, tickling me and hugging me and making me giggle, he would unfasten all the buttons, pull the laces undone, and take me off to bed. Leaving the expensive new dress lying on the floor.

So soon I was used to being married, and was harmlessly busy all day long. I was visited by old Mrs Minot's acquaintances and I even made friends with some other married ladies in the area, telling them, when they enquired, that I had lived in Birmingham where my family was engaged in the metal trades, and that I had met Mr Minot through a mutual acquaintance.

Soon I had my round of morning calls to receive and afternoon visits to make, and at the end of most days I wondered where the time had gone. I had no time to fret for my old friends. I meant to visit the London theatres, but there was never time.

Channing never brought his own friends back to the narrow, three-storeyed house in Holborn. He met *them*, he said, at his club, where women were not allowed. He enjoyed a game of cards and sometimes in the evening he went to a gentleman's house to play.

I didn't mind at all. I liked being at home, in the first real home I'd ever had. Kitty was chatty and companionable, and when Channing was out I went down to the kitchen and sat by the fire with her, listening to her talk about London, a great, sprawling, dirty but magnificent city, which was still a place of wonder and mystery to me.

Married to a handsome young man of independent means, living in a smart London house, how could I not be happy?

I think Kitty regarded me with mild amusement. Certainly she felt no malice towards me; but then, I was no threat. I had little idea how to run a household and never interfered with the system she followed. "Would you like to see the household accounts, Mrs Minot?" she had enquired, on the Saturday following my arrival. "They're all here, right up to date. And here are the rent records for the lodgers downstairs, if you'd care to look." She offered me a cloth-covered ledger and a leather-bound book.

I waved them away. "I'm sure everything's in order, Kitty,"

I said airily. I didn't understand columns of sums, but in those days I was too young and too vain even to admit my ignorance, let alone express a desire to learn. "Leave the books there," I said. "I'll look over the figures when I have time."

Of course, I never had time, and Kitty rapidly understood that she had *carte blanche* to cheat and rob me blind. It is to her everlasting credit that she did nothing of the sort.

Anyone coming to the house might well have mistaken Kitty for the mistress, for she wore a black gown with lace insets in the sleeves, and she put on an apron only for baking day. Tilda, a skinny, twelve-year-old girl who came in daily, did all the heavy, dirty work. She reminded me so uncomfortably of myself, at the Taylors' house, that I avoided her.

Time flew by. As I looked at the almanac one morning, I realised I had been married for almost a year.

"I have to go and see a gentleman today." Channing had come down to breakfast early that spring morning, and now he was wolfing toast as if he never expected to see food again. "A gentleman who mustn't be kept waiting," he added, through a mouthful of bacon. "Will you get my black coat, and have Kitty brush it well?"

I fetched Channing's coat and brushed it myself. "Who is this gentleman?" I enquired.

"A Mr Ezra, in Oxford Street." Channing pulled a long face. "It's business," he added. "Not pleasure."

"I'll come with you," I said. I had not been out for three days and I fancied a jaunt. "I'll walk over with you, shall I?"

"No," said Channing. He shrugged on his coat. "No, you can't do that."

"Why not?"

"Well – "

"Look, I'm up, I'm dressed, I can come now." I smiled at him. "Don't you want my company?"

"It's not that." Channing looked at me. He sighed. "Oh, very well," he said, wearily. "Come if you must. Don't complain if you don't like what you see."

Mr Ezra's house turned out to be situated at the bottom of a steep flight of steps which led, through a rusty iron gate, to a court more malodorous than any in Dudley or Birmingham. Rubbish-strewn, running with rats and sewage, smelling far worse than Parker's Court ever had on even a hot summer's day, this place was surrounded on three sides by blank, high walls. In the fourth wall there were merely three tiny windows, all stoutly barred.

"There are some shops further up the street," said Channing, seeing me twitch my gown away from a heap of what looked like mouldering offal just dumped on the flagstones. "Go and look at bonnets, if you'd prefer."

"I'll come and see this gentleman with you, then we'll go to the shops together." Brightly, I smiled at him. "I wish to buy a silk shawl. You must help me choose it."

"We'll see." Channing held out his hand to help me down some further steps, which were squeezed into one of the corners of the court and which I had not noticed before. In permanent shadow, they were coated thickly with black slime, and consequently were very slippery. They led to a very narrow passage, at the end of which was a door. "Well, here we are," said Channing. He jangled a bell fixed to the wall. We waited.

We waited a long time, during which I had ample leisure to observe that the door was very solid. And shabby. Ancient blue paint lay on it in flakes and its knocker was a crusted, evil-looking green; obviously this was never used. I began to wonder if the door itself was ever opened, for drifts of rubbish had blown against it and the keyhole was clogged with grime.

But as I wondered and fidgeted, Channing stood patiently, and eventually his patience was rewarded. A sound of bolts being drawn back was followed by the door opening a crack and a suspicious voice demanding, "Well? What is it?"

"I wish to speak with Mr Ezra," said Channing.

"Name?" demanded the voice.

"Mr Minot."

"Wait."

The door closed again. We waited. Then, three or four minutes later, it was opened properly and we were admitted. "Say nothing," whispered Channing. "Take your lead from me."

We stood in a spacious, gloomy vestibule while the person who'd let us in, a short, dark, elderly man, blinked at us with red, sore eyes. Mr Ezra, I wondered? Clad from head to foot in tight, rusty black, this fellow was hump-backed, splay-footed, and he resembled nothing so much as a dingy clerical gnome, or troll.

He coughed, and gouts of yellow mucus appeared at the corners of his eyes. He wiped these away with a very dirty handkerchief. "So," he said at last, "so you wish to see Mr Ezra."

"Please." Channing's voice was quiet, neutral, as if he feared to break a spell.

"Many people wish to see Mr Ezra," said the troll. He pointed to a thin man sitting silently in the shadows. "*He* does."

"Yes, but – "

"So does she." He nodded in the direction of a heap of rags, which I now realised was a woman crouched in the corner. "She was here before you."

"Yes indeed," agreed Channing, "but Mr Ezra – "

"Is very busy today. Very busy indeed." The troll eyed us up and down. "What for should he talk to you?"

"Tell Mr Ezra," said Channing, more sharply now, "that Mr Minot would like just five minutes of his valuable time. Tell him I've brought the papers. Come back and tell me what he says."

"Very well." The troll shuffled off through a second door, which he locked behind him. Ten minutes later he returned and we were taken through it, into a passage which led to a dark, fusty room.

At a huge desk, on which reclined two slim black cats, sat a very handsome, hook-nosed, middle-aged man. Before the desk were a couple of hard, upright chairs, on which Channing and I were invited to sit down. The cats blinked their yellow eyes. The clock on the wall ticked steadily.

"So," said Mr Ezra, "you need five minutes of my time."

"Yes," said Channning. "And I need some more of your money, too."

"You wish to increase your debt? Tsk." The money lender shook his head. "I read your proposal," he murmured, glancing at a letter on his desk. "You want we should bring all your affairs together, yes? Advance you a further sum, just to see you through this difficult patch?"

"Yes, that's right."

"And then we could calculate what you owe altogether, and work out a fair rate of interest for the whole."

"Whatever you wish." Channing was getting irritable now. "Look, a round five hundred will see me through."

"Five hundred." Mr Ezra considered. "You have for me the deeds of your house?" he asked.

"Yes." From his pocket Channing took some papers, which he passed across the table.

And what about me, what did I think of this? Well, ignorant fool that I was, I didn't understand what was going on. I knew nothing about collateral security and I had no inkling whatsoever that my husband had just made the money lender a present of my home. Or as good as. I just sat there smiling nicely, as if I were a duchess being entertained to tea.

Mr Ezra studied the papers, found them satisfactory and then reached for a pen. As he signed the necessary bills and documents, he glanced up at me. "You used to be on the stage, Mrs Minot?" he enquired, politely.

"Yes," I replied.

"You acted, of course. You sang?"

"Yes." Remembering past pleasures, I nodded and smiled more brightly. "Yes, I often sang during tableaux, sketches and such."

Mr Ezra returned my smile. "My daughter sings," he said. "Perhaps you'd like to hear her?"

"I'd be delighted." I ignored Channing's ungracious scowl. "Yes, it would be a pleasure."

So Mr Ezra summoned the troll, and two minutes later

in came a little girl of about ten, dark-eyed, dark-haired, pale-faced – a child obviously bred in close confinement, never allowed to run out of doors.

She went to her father and leaned against his shoulder, murmuring to him in some foreign language, in which he also replied. Then she stood up straight, folded her hands demurely before her, and opened her mouth.

The song she began sent shivers racing through me as they'd never done before. The hairs on my neck rose and my skin tingled. The music swooped and curved in a graceful arabesque of sounds, dipping and soaring, and it ended eventually in ecstasy, on a high-pitched note of such wistful hope – but not before all the misery and despair of a whole nation had been set down in song. I took out a pocket handkerchief and dabbed my eyes.

"Now something more cheerful," said Mr Ezra, who had been watching me the whole time, thoughtfully stroking one of the cats. "Something to send Mrs Minot away with gladness in her heart."

The child considered for a moment, then she whispered in her father's ear. "Yes. Perfect," he replied. "David?" he called.

"Yes, Master?" answered the troll, scuttling in.

"We need your help here."

So the troll beat time with his foot while the child sang, as her dark eyes sparkled and she clapped her hands to accompany herself in a charming, fast tempo song which also ended on a high note, but this time one of triumph.

"A wedding song," explained Mr Ezra. "You're recently married, Mrs Minot? So: this song wishes for you good luck, long life and seven handsome sons."

"Thank you." I smiled from father to daughter. "Thank you both, very much."

"It's nothing." Mr Ezra leaned back in his chair. "Mrs Minot, in your professional opinion, do you think my daughter would be well received on the stage?"

"She has a lovely voice." I smiled encouragingly at the child, who blushed prettily and then hid her face on her father's shoulder. "She's young yet, and very shy. But certainly in time – "

"A great career might be possible, eh?"

"Most definitely."

"You hear that, *kindeleh*?" Mr Ezra shook his head. "What a great shame it will never be."

"Oh but, Mr Ezra," I cried, "in a few years from now, when she's grown up and become more confident, your daughter could be the talk of London. The public would be enchanted to discover a fresh, new talent."

"Well, Becca! Mrs Minot thinks ladies and gentlemen would be flocking to hear you." Mr Ezra smiled sadly. "My daughter sings only for her family," he said. "And for God."

"But, Mr Ezra – "

"Mrs Minot, I thank you for your good opinion of my daughter's talents, and am flattered that she pleased you so much." He took the child's hand and pressed it affectionately. "Go now," he murmured. "Your mother needs you."

Obediently the child slipped away. And two minutes later Channing and I were climbing the dirty steps out of that gloomy court.

"What a nice man," I remarked, as we reached street level and sunlight.

"You little idiot." Channing glared at me so angrily that I shrank back a step. "God, what a simpleton. What a half-wit. What a judge of character. She thinks a disgusting villain like Joseph Ezra is a *nice* man!"

"Well, he was." I rallied, and glared back at him. "Channing, so he was!"

"He was mocking you." Channing ground his teeth in fury. "He was sneering at you, the dirty, thieving Israelite, and you hadn't the wit to see it."

"But, surely you don't think – "

"Even a Hebrew money lender thinks he's better than a player." Channing scowled at me. "Ezra would sooner see his daughter crucified than let her become an actress, and a whore."

Chapter 11

As we walked along Oxford Street the sun came out and this seemed to lighten Channing's mood. He stopped scowling and linked his arm through mine. "What shall we do for the rest of the day?" he asked. "You say. Choose anything you please."

"Anything?" I thought for a moment, then, glancing down at my new mauve silk gown, I decided I'd like an opportunity to show it off. "I'd like to take a drive in the park," I replied.

"Which park?"

"Any." I smiled at him. "You decide."

We spent a delightful afternoon in Hyde Park, skirting the Serpentine, feeding the birds and watching companies of Guards at their exercises. I thought how splendid Channing would look in a red coat, with gold braid and epaulettes; but when I said as much, he laughed. "Go for a soldier?" he demanded. "You see me as a man of war, do you?"

Perhaps not. Channing was a gentle person, and I could not imagine him firing a musket or trampling an enemy. "No, not at all," I replied.

As the sun was setting we hailed a cab and went back to the narrow house in Holborn, where we ate a good dinner and then went early to bed. And so, a perfect afternoon and evening more than made up for an unpleasant start to the day. I lay peacefully in my bed that night, watching the shadows dancing on the ceiling. I listened to Channing breathing sweetly and softly beside me, and thought I was truly content, that life could offer no greater happiness than this.

Fool that I was. From that day forward, neither my

bed nor even the sheets and blankets which covered me were mine.

One evening a couple of months later, two men called to ask if Channing were at home. I heard Kitty bring them up the stairs and, after rapping on the door of our sitting-room, she ushered them in. I was not introduced to them. Instead, Channing stood up and said, "My dear, these gentlemen and I have business to discuss. I think perhaps you had better go to bed."

Without arguing, I went. As it happened I had been on the point of going up, for a stomach-ache and griping cramps, the results of my monthly indisposition, were making me feel sick and wretched. I went down to the kitchen, took a heated brick from the range and wrapped it in a square of blanket. Hugging it to my sore stomach, I was fast asleep long before Channing came to bed.

The following night the two men came again. This time they were introduced to me as Mr Maclean and Mr Rogers, "Two business associates, my dear." Channing seemed rather ill at ease tonight; but the men, on the other hand, made themselves comfortable in the best chairs, patting the upholstery and looking about them with a satisfied air.

I did not wish to sit and listen to a discussion about money, so I excused myself and went to bed. Meeting Kitty on the landing, I wished her a good night. "Those friends of Mr Minot," I added carelessly, as she walked on past me, "have you seen them often before?"

"Never before last night, Mrs Minot." Kitty shrugged. "Mr Minot seems very anxious to have their good opinion, but I can't think why. They don't seem like gentlemen to me."

"No," I agreed. I felt Kitty was right. My acquaintance with gentlemen was limited, but I'd thought Mr Rogers and his friend looked decidedly rough, a pair of natural brawlers of the kind who were regularly ejected from theatre pits. And surely, if they'd been business associates, Channing would have offered them refreshments? Wine, or coffee, and maybe cakes? Instead, he'd made no move to offer them anything at all.

Kitty went off to bed, but tonight I was not sleepy, and curiosity led me back along the landing. Creeping noiselessly, I reached the door of our sitting-room. I placed my ear next to the keyhole, and listened.

I heard someone stir up the fire – we always had a small fire, even in summer, for the house was inclined to be damp – with a poker. There was a cough, a muttered comment from Channing, a reply from one of the men. I pressed my ear closer to the keyhole. That was better, I could hear perfectly now.

"Come now, Mr Minot," said one of the men, "we've heard all this sort of flummery before, and it won't do. Debts of honour, these are. Must be paid."

"Debts of honour, indeed." My husband sniffed. "Wheeler's a trickster. He cheats."

"Well, Mr Minot. *That's* a foolish thing to say. If your words were carried to Mr Wheeler – "

"Oh, it was just a joke." Channing sounded petulant now. "I'll pay you," he promised. "By Thursday week, I'll have the ready cash."

"Thursday's far too late." That sounded like Mr Maclean. "He wants the cash tomorrow. All of it."

"I can't get it all by tomorrow!" cried Channing. "Where do you expect – "

"Go to the Jews." That was Mr Rogers. "Go to the Hebrews, they'll help you out."

"I'd rather not borrow any more from them." Channing heaved a deep sigh. "Look, I know another person who might advance me something. I'll be seeing her tomorrow, so – "

"Her?" Mr Maclean laughed. "A lady, is it?"

"So what if it is?"

"Nothing." Mr Maclean was still chortling. "Well, all I can say is, if any lady's fool enough to lend you money, it's her look out. I'll tell him to expect you about noon then, shall I?"

"I suppose so."

I heard the scraping of chairs, so I hurried back along the passage and was in my bed by the time I heard the men leave.

Then I heard the street door bang shut again and assumed that Channing himself had gone out.

I dozed off for an hour or two, then woke, then dozed again. It was well past two in the morning when my husband finally came home.

He came to bed the worse for drink. Smelling like a tavern, he leered and slobbered all over me, grinning like an idiot and pawing at my nightgown with hands that shook like an old man's. Although I explained that I was bleeding, he insisted on taking what he said was his by right, pushing his knee between my legs, grabbing at me and eventually levering himself above me.

He tried to kiss me, but dribbled all over my chin instead. Half undressed, he could not undo the rest of his buttons and began to swear and curse like a drunken sailor; I'd never heard such language, not even from Fred Hammer.

"Go away, Channing." I pushed his face away from mine. "Go and put your head under the pump."

"Later." He grabbed at the neckband of my night-gown, and tore it. "Later, when I've – when we've – "

"Go away!" I struggled and squirmed, and since in his drunken state he was uncoordinated and clumsy, I managed to shove him off me, and right out of bed.

He fell on the floor, cursing. "Nasty little bitch!" he cried, mumbling and sobbing now. "Don't know your duty, do you? Well, I'm going to teach you who's master tonight!"

I stared at him. At the back of my mind, I wondered if this was indeed my duty; that since I had promised to obey my husband, was I obliged to let him use me as and when he felt so inclined? But then anger and disgust got the upper hand, and I decided that no, he was not entitled to take what I was unwilling to give. As he scrambled back into bed I gave him a great push which sent him tumbling out again. I snatched up the blankets and took myself off to the kitchen.

There I stayed for the rest of the night, to the astonishment of Kitty, who came down at six to find her mistress bundled up in her bedclothes, rocking herself to and fro in the fireside chair.

Channing came in a few minutes later. "Coffee," he demanded. "Kitty – coffee! Lots of it, hot and black."

"Make your coffee yourself," I snapped. "Kitty's busy."

"Oh?" Channing sat down at the kitchen table and nursed his aching head. "And I suppose you're busy, too?"

"Not especially." I glared at him. "But you know where the coffee things are, don't you?" I asked.

"Yes, indeed. But I'd always thought, that if a man keeps a bitch, he should have no need to bark himself." Channing grinned at me. "A good wife," he observed sarcastically. "A good, obedient wife, who jumps to do her husband's bidding, as a good wife should. A treasure. A pearl beyond price. That's you."

"Well, you're a great brute of a husband," I retorted. "A nasty, selfish hog."

"Oh? Then why did you marry me?" he demanded.

"I don't know," I muttered. "Why did you want *me*?"

"God knows." As a spasm of pain crossed his face, Channing winced. "God alone knows, for I certainly don't."

We glared at each other. His eyes were bloodshot, his hair awry, his complexion blotched and unhealthy. He did not look at all handsome today. While we had been bickering, Kitty had made coffee and now she placed a scalding bowlful in front of him, which he drank down straight off. "I have to go out," he said, wiping his mouth on his hand.

"Why?" I asked.

"None of your damned business." Channing scowled at me. "I'm going to meet someone. A lady, as it happens."

"Really? I do hope she'll be pleased to see you arrive. I'll certainly be pleased to see you go." I drew my bedclothes round me and shrunk into them. Channing got up and a few minutes later I heard the front door slam.

I looked at Kitty and she looked at me. Then she shrugged. "I'd like to get to market early today, Mrs Minot," she said. "So if it's all right with you?"

"Yes, Kitty," I agreed. "You go off now."

So I was left alone with my thoughts, which were not pleasant that morning. Letting my mind wander, I realised how much I missed the players, and I wondered where they were now. As I dipped my bread in my coffee and sucked at the soggy crust, I recalled the many pleasant breakfasts I'd had with Lucinda and Fred, with Charlie Rayner, with Judith Glass and Dora Parry, convivial meals of whatever we could get, taken at mid-morning in someone's lodgings, or seated round the properties table in the wings of some stage.

It occurred to me then that the theatre was where I belonged, and that in marrying Channing Minot I'd made a great mistake.

Chapter 12

During our tours of the provinces, the company had sometimes included in the evening's entertainment a series of tableaux entitled *Scenes from Modern Marriage*. One scene had been *Their First Quarrel*, closely followed of course by *Their Reconciliation*, in which the wife served up her husband's favourite dinner, which was invariably a grinning boar's head made of crumbling plaster, complete with ferocious papier mâché tusks and an apple in its mouth.

For this kind of burlesque we'd naturally exaggerated our gestures and facial expressions, and the whole series had been good for plenty of hooting and laughter from the pit. Not to mention a few genteel sniggers from the boxes above, as wives tittered prettily and husbands blew their noses hard.

But now I found my own life mimicking art. When he came in that evening Channing was in a deep sulk. He would not speak to me, he would not eat his dinner, he would not come to bed; instead, he went and lay on the rag rug before the cold kitchen range, curled up and shivering, like a beaten dog. This went on for nearly a week, and in the end I found it so trying that I resolved to make things up.

One morning Channing went out early, so I went back upstairs, put on my best dress, and coiled my hair the way he liked it. I sent Kitty and Tilda off to one of the local lying-in hospitals for poor women, with a basket of Kitty's excellent baking for distribution there. Then I made up the sitting-room fire and sat down to wait.

When Channing eventually came in, I met him at the door. I smiled. I put my arms around his neck and kissed him.

"Let's be friends again," I suggested. "Quarrelling is so tiring, after all."

He looked at me as if I'd struck him. I'd thought he'd smile back, shrug and say that of course we could be friends once more. But instead he covered his face with his hands. He sat down on the floor, and burst into tears.

"What did I say?" I sank to my knees beside him. "Channing? What is it? What's wrong?"

"N-nothing. Nothing's wrong." With an effort he controlled his sobs. And then, like a little child, he wrapped his arms around my neck and held me. "I don't want to lose you," he cried, his tears soaking my hair. "I don't want you to hate me – not you, not you! Oh Deb, help me!"

"Help you? How?" I found my pocket handkerchief and dabbed at his face. "Dear Channing, what do you want me to do?"

"Just stay with me. You will, won't you?" He looked at me so anxiously, so desperately, that I was afraid. "Promise me you'll stay?"

"Channing, I – "

"Promise me! Promise!"

"I'm your wife. I'll always be with you." I smoothed his damp hair back from his forehead. "Darling, we had a silly quarrel, that's all. We're friends again now."

"Are we? You mean that?"

"Of course I do." I smiled at him, a mother consoling a worried child. "Come and see what I've made for our dinner. Roast pork, potato dumplings, new greens, a cinnamon tart. All your favourite things."

Channing did not go out at all for the next few days, and whenever I suggested a walk he told me to go with Kitty, or a friend.

"But I'd like to go out with you," I said, one sunny afternoon, as he sat in his chair and refused to budge. "Channing, do come, just for an hour. The sun's shining, the air will do you good. It's not healthy to stay in here, all cooped up like a sick hen."

Eventually he agreed to come. He insisted, however, that we stuck to wide, public thoroughfares and he refused point blank to enter any shops. His eyes darted about all the time, as if looking out for someone. I wondered if perhaps he were starting a fever, and decided to take him home.

Then it began to rain. Great drops fell out of what had, only minutes ago, been a bright blue sky. "Come along," I said, taking his hand. "We'll get back now." If he was ill, there was no sense in getting him soaked to the skin as well.

He let me lead him. The rain was coming down very heavily now and I decided to take a short cut, through a rubbish-strewn alley near Covent Garden Market. We picked our way through a smelly mess of mouldy cabbage leaves, slimy, rotting fruit and broken boxes, and I was beginning to wonder if coming this way was such a good idea after all when I heard Channing give a cry of alarm.

And then the man walked out of the shadows.

At first I took him for one of the market porters, for he was dressed in ordinary workman's clothes and he wore a labouring man's greasy scarf around his neck. Then, to my surprise, I realised that Channing must know him.

Grinning, the man came up to us. He took Channing's lapel and rubbed the cloth between his forefinger and thumb. "Decent bit of stuff, Mr Minot," he said, by way of a greeting. "Your execution coat, is it? Mean to be hanged and buried in this?"

"Get out of my way." Pale as death now, Channing took my arm. "Come, Deb," he muttered. "Let's go home."

"Don't be in such a hurry." Still the man grinned at us. "I only want to talk to you," he said, pleasantly enough. "I've been wanting to talk to you all week, but it seems you've been busy. Too busy to spare even a minute for me."

"I've nothing to say to you," said Channing. "And so I'll wish you a good day."

"You know it's a hanging matter." Suddenly the man's grin disappeared, and now he looked very grave. "You're in deep, you know that. You can't go back."

"And if I try?" demanded Channing. "If I try to swim away?"

"I'll drag you back. Or see to it that you drown." Letting go of Channing's lapel, the man looked at me. Running his eyes up and down my body in a manner which I found – and which I was sure he intended to be – extremely offensive, he leaned back against the wall and began to pick his teeth. "That's a pretty little wife you have there," he observed. "Where did you pick her up?"

"None of your business," snapped Channing.

"I heard she was on the stage once." The man looked into my face. "An actress, I'm sure they said she was an actress. And we all know what actresses are." He leered at me. "Easy with her favours, is she?"

"You leave her alone!" Becoming angry now, Channing glared. "I tell you, Tripman, if you so much as touch her, if you harm a hair of her head, I'll make you sorry! I'll – "

"Brave words, my little hero, brave words." The man whom Channing had called Tripman grinned again. "So she's your private property, is she? Safe and inviolable, all yours? Well, Mr Minot, understand this. Not even the clothes you stand up in are your own. So I reckon that woman's mortgaged along with everything else. And I tell you this for nothing, there's those as are sick of you defaulting on your debts."

"I've told you before, I'll pay you when I can!" Still Channing glared. "You can't get blood from a stone, and you can't have anything from me."

"Oh, but I think I can."

As the man spoke, I became aware of two other men standing in the shadows, and now they joined the group. They stood silent, evidently waiting for orders. "So now," said the man called Tripman. "Are you going to pay up?"

"I've told you, I can't – "

"Then we'll have to have some other kind of satisfaction, won't we?"

"What do you mean?"

"You'll see." Tripman snapped his fingers. "Well, now.

Are you going to take your medicine? Or do you want that pretty little wife of yours to swallow it for you?"

One of the silent couple smiled at me, but it was an ugly, leering smile. Then the other pushed his hand in his pocket and produced a leather tawse, which he smacked against the palm of his hand. "Well?" demanded Tripman. "Choose."

"Take her." Loud and sharp with terror, Channing's voice rang and echoed in that narrow street. "Take her, do what you want!"

I could hardly believe what I heard. But hear it I did, so I braced myself, determined that whoever touched me first would regret it. One of the men, the leering one, came towards me now, his dirty fingers toying with the buttons on his trousers. I slid off my gloves, intending to use my fingernails to good effect. But even as I shrank back in terror, the man went past me. Then there was nothing but a mass of bodies, with one voice crying out for mercy.

I could have run away, but now anger made me reckless. I fell on the nearest man, kicking and hitting and scratching him, trying to pull him off my husband, whose moans were piteous. But I was slim and light, the men were all heavyweights, and I had no more effect on them than a mouse attacking a pack of wolves.

I don't know how long the men hit and punched my husband, but it seemed like an eternity. Eventually, however, one by one, they stood up. They stretched, scratched and yawned. Tripman gave Channing a final kick. "Get up," he said. "Get up, and be grateful for a fine, spirited woman *you* certainly don't deserve."

He nodded to me. "Mrs Minot, it's been a great pleasure to meet you, and I wish you a good day."

I stared at him, speechless. Then I glanced down at Channing, a dishevelled, bleeding heap on the wet, grimy cobblestones. "You evil-looking wretch!" I cried. "You and your friends, you're nothing but bullies and cowards, and I wish you all in the pit of hell!"

"As I said, a fine, spirited woman." Tripman grinned at me and replaced his hat on his head. "Get him to the road," he said, nodding towards Channing. "I'll stop a cab for him there."

"We don't need any help from you." I glared at him in fury. "You can all go to the devil!"

So the men slouched off.

The rain continued to pour down. Gradually Channing's moans eased off and I managed to convince him that he could tackle the few paces to the road ahead. I had great difficulty finding a cab, but eventually, by paying a driver in advance and promising him a big tip, I cajoled him into taking myself and my husband home.

"Don't you let him bleed on my cushions," said the man, as he saw the state Channing was in. "Robbed, was you?"

"No. He had an accident." I gave the driver a florin. "Please hurry."

Paid well over the limit and anxious for his upholstery, the driver made haste. As we cantered along the muddy streets, I went over and over what had happened. I had imagined some of it, of course. When I'd heard Channing offer me for the men's use, I'd been dreaming. No husband would have offered his wife to ruffians like that, not even to escape a beating. No decent man would have so much as contemplated such a filthy bargain.

We went and sat in the kitchen. Kitty and Tilda were still out doing good works, so I made tea and then I attended to Channing's hurts. I eased off his shirt. When I'd sponged away the blood and grit and gravel I saw that most of his cuts were superficial, that his bruises were not severe – he'd heal in a few days. Apart from a swelling under his left eye, his beauty was not impaired at all.

As I bathed his face I tried to talk to him, but it was difficult, for he didn't want to talk to me. I was, however, determined to get a few things straight. "Channing," I said gently, as I smoothed soothing ointment on his grazed forehead, "when you married me, you told me you had a private fortune."

"Did I?" he muttered.

"Yes, you did."

"Oh." He studied his bruised and broken fingernails. "Perhaps you misunderstood me."

"Perhaps." I wrung out lint in water. "But you did tell me that you had a comfortable private income, and that you didn't need to work for a living."

"I may have said something like that," he agreed. He shrugged. "Just recently," he admitted, "I've lost a little at cards. I've made some unwise investments, and I've been obliged to borrow money from men who won't scruple to use violence to recover what is theirs."

"Really? But Mr Ezra didn't look like that sort of man – "

"He's not my only creditor." As I touched a bruise, Channing winced. "I've debts all over the place at present."

"Have you? Well then – "

"Well then what?"

"I shall go back on the stage." This was the obvious solution, after all. I'd heard the company talk of summer seasons in Brighton, where even a walk-on could make three pounds a week. With the optimism of youth I imagined that I needed only to present myself to a manager to be taken on. "There's no need to worry," I said gaily, "I'll mend our fortunes, you'll see."

"You'd never earn enough to clear my debts," said Channing gloomily. "Never."

"Oh come. They can't be all that great." Encouragingly, I smiled at him. "We live modestly enough here. We have few day-to-day expenses. The lodgers give us a little income, and you have investments, which must bring in some return."

"You don't understand what you're talking about, so be quiet." Irritably, Channing pushed me away. "You're not going on the stage," he said. "That's the last thing I want, attention drawn to me."

"Why's that?" I asked.

"You've never heard of blackmail, I suppose." He grimaced. "I'm being blackmailed, Deb. There. Now you know. And those sorts of debts can never be repaid."

"But what did you do?" I asked. "Whatever did you do, that people can extort money from you like this?"

“I can’t tell you,” he replied.

“Was it so terrible?”

“I didn’t think so. Not at the time. I reckoned I was doing the world a service.”

“What do you mean?”

There was a long, long silence. “I had to do it,” he said. “I had to, I’d have gone mad if I hadn’t. Deb, Deb, don’t pry. I don’t want you to know anything about it. What’s done is done, finished.” He sighed. “Accidents can happen to the best of men.”

It was four days before Channing would venture out again, and when he did at last go out it was alone. He refused my company, saying he needed to think. He returned that night looking pale and sick, and lay on our bed moaning, curled up like a small child who’s been whipped. I left him there for an hour, two hours. When I went up to bed myself he looked at me piteously. “Pass me my coat?” he asked meekly, as if he were afraid that this modest request might be refused.

I handed it to him. He rummaged in the large side pockets until he found it. This was the first time I’d seen him open an envelope of whitey-brown paper and shake out some powder inside.

“It’s for my toothache,” he said, as he dabbled it in the palm of his hand. “You don’t object, do you, if I try to ease at least some of my pain?”

“Of course I don’t.” I sat down on the bed beside him. “Shall I get you something to help it down?”

“No, thank you.” He rolled the sticky powder into a ball and put it into the side of his mouth. “Deb, I’ve something to tell you,” he said.

“What?”

“Can’t you guess?”

Actually, I could. “There’s no money, is there?” I asked.

“Not much.” He shrugged. “Will the tradesmen give us credit?”

“No. The greengrocer and the coalman won’t deliver any more, and I had words with the baker today.”

"Miserable beasts." Channing looked close to tears. "What are we supposed to do now then, starve?"

"We owe them money, so they've a right to expect it. They need to live, too." I shrugged. "It's a pity you were bred to no profession," I added.

"Yes indeed, such a pity." Sarcastically, Channing grinned at me. "I was bred, my dear, to be a gentleman of independent means."

"Which you're not," I retorted.

"Which I *am*!" Channing glared at me. "I labour under a few temporary difficulties, which a good wife would help me bear."

"I want to help you!" I cried. "I've offered to go back to the theatre. I could earn maybe five pounds a week, more if I get good parts."

"You're not going back on the stage. Do you understand me? You're not to go anywhere near a theatre. I'll be seriously displeased if you cross me in this."

"But why?" I asked. He'd once been a keen theatregoer himself, after all, trailing all the way out to Middlesex to watch me. "Channing, why?"

"Actresses are whores," he replied. "I'll not have my friends say my wife is a whore."

What friends, I wondered. Those fellows who'd dragged him out to the sticks in the first place, who'd been the cause of his getting ideas about me? I hadn't set eyes on them since we married. These days Channing never went to his club, and the only visitors he had were creditors.

"I have a scheme," he announced, as he sucked on his opium pill. "A new scheme, it can't fail."

"No?"

"No." He patted my hand. "You're a good girl, Deb," he said. "You be my good angel, eh? God knows I need one. The devil and I have been far too familiar of late."

I was beginning to wonder if he was a species of devil himself. But I had something else to think about these days. I had seen a playbill telling me that my friends were in town.

Chapter 13

The playbills were, as usual, plastered over doors, fences, gateposts and especially those tempting flat surfaces like the blank walls of houses, on which there were stern notices stating "no bills to be posted here".

I read that, by popular demand, the Royalty Theatre in Lisle Street was putting on a short season of unparalleled entertainment, beginning on the twenty-second of that month. Today it was the twenty-sixth. Since the company had arrived in town I'd been anxious to see my friends; but I'd not wanted to antagonise my husband. This morning, however, Channing had gone out early, presumably to try to raise more credit, so I put on my new cashmere shawl and went out too.

In spite of waiting on Holborn Hill for a full ten minutes, I couldn't see a single cab for hire. The urchin whom I'd told to go and find one had taken my penny and disappeared, and now every hackney carriage which clattered past was occupied. Moon-faced passengers peered from each steamed-up window, and every driver ignored my waving hand. So I started to walk.

It had been a bad summer and this was the wettest and coldest of a whole month of damp, chilly August days. Rain stung my face, my soft leather shoes sank in the mire, and, caught by a gust of wind, my expensive new bonnet blew off and landed in a stinking midden. Disgusted, I left it there, so now my carefully arranged hair was knotted and tangled by the wind. But I hadn't far to go now, and I thought that since I was wet I might as well get a little wetter. I took the quickest way possible and within ten minutes I was at the Royalty Theatre.

A grimy little place badly in need of redecoration, with a fish-fryer's stall at the entrance and a couple of costermongers' wagons blocking the stage door, it was nevertheless a theatre, and from the moment I stepped inside I felt I was home.

In the foyer I could hear the rumble of voices and the chirruping of Barty's flute as he practised a new variation. Then I heard Dora Parry's giggle. Breathing in the smell of the place, greedily inhaling those mingled scents of oranges, musty costumes, stale tobacco and the dust of years, I hesitated for a moment – then walked in through the double doors and surprised them all.

At the sound of the doors banging shut, they all broke off from their rehearsal to stare. Henry Collis looked at me as if he'd seen an apparition. I suppose he had, for I must have looked just like Mad Margaret the Maid of Madrid, turned out into the storm by her evil stepmother. My hair was plastered to my head, my clothes were wet through, and I was shivering with cold.

"It's Deborah!" The first to recover, Lucinda Tolland jumped nimbly from the stage and lunged towards me. Enfolding me in a bear hug she kissed me on both cheeks, laughing and crying with delighted pleasure. "Oh darling," she cried, "darling, darling Deb, whatever are you doing here? Where've you come from? You're soaked!" She drew me towards a brazier at a corner of the stage, rubbing me with her own shawl and clucking like an old hen with one chick.

"How are you?" "Why are you here?" "Have you come back to the company?" These and a dozen other questions came tumbling all around me, and as I tried to answer them I became breathless and tearful both at once.

"Let the poor little bugger breathe," said Fred Hammer, picking Dora up bodily and pushing Judith away. "Luce, get Deb a cordial. She looks as if she needs it."

So Lucinda brought me a hot drink and, warmed and

welcomed, I sat by the fire and sipped it while I caught up with the news.

"Charlie's gone," said Judith, as she saw me looking round for him. "Retired."

"It was the tights and curly wig that did it," added Harkess Wright. "Them and the slashed doublet, of course."

"Did what?" I asked.

"Bewitched a widow. Landlady of a lodging house in Brighton." Judith sniggered. "So old Charlie's been made an honest man of, and now he's idling away his days on the promenade or in the warm brine bath."

"Does his rheumatism a world of good, that brine bath," put in Dora. "And the widow keeps a splendid table."

"She does indeed." Tom Denby grinned. "We were all there for a week in June. Came away with bloats."

I smiled to think of Charlie being fattened up. "Has Miss Gaynes retired too?" I asked, for I could not see her there.

"Pen? Retired? *She'll* go on for ever." Mr Denby began to pick his teeth. "No, she's temporarily absent, that's all."

"Giving concert parties in the frozen north," put in Mr Wright. "Touring all summer. Liverpool, Leeds, Manchester, Halifax. And so on."

"She'll be back on Saturday," said Judith.

"Throwing her weight around," said Dora.

"And there's even more of it these days," muttered Fred, with a grin. He glanced at Henry Collis. "Yes well, Henry, we all know how tenderly attached you are to dear Pen; but even you must admit that her embonpoint is becoming just a little bit – how shall I say – "

"You've said quite enough," said Henry Collis, speaking for the first time. "Ladies and gentlemen, I have some paperwork to attend to, so if you'll excuse me?" And he walked away, without even having acknowledged my existence.

"Temper," said Lucinda, as he disappeared through the flats. "He didn't want to come here."

"Why?" I asked.

"Oh, we needed to fill in a fortnight and he was promised

the Lancaster in St Martin's Lane, but then the management decided not to reopen until September, and all he could find at short notice was this hole." Lucinda looked around her. "But it's not so terrible. The houses are good. And as for the place itself, I've played in far worse rat traps than this."

"Only an inch of rain water in the dressing-room," said Dora.

"Scene shifters no more than averagely stupid," added Judith.

"Floorboards no more than usually rotten," put in Fred. "If Harkess stamps about a *little* less enthusiastically, they might just hold for the run."

"Ropes on the trapdoors've been there since Adam was a boy," muttered Mr Denby. "But we've got no more than the usual complement of vermin, and the curtains are held together nicely with mould and dirt."

"And we're off to America next month," said Lucinda, cheerfully. "Off to seek our fortunes! Well, some of us are."

"And some of us are booked for the Lane," added Mr Wright, beaming.

"So things are looking up." Lucinda smiled at me. "And you, my dear Deb," she said, "does being a married lady suit you?"

"Yes," I said. I forced a smile. "Yes, I'm very happy."

"Excellent." Lucinda looked around for Fred. "Well, since the slave driver has gone off to sulk in his den, let's go and have something to eat."

So we all trooped across the road to a chop house and ate hot rib of beef from grubby plates jostling on a gravy-stained tablecloth, and we drank porter from dented tankards, and I felt warmed and wanted and happy.

"Will you come with me to see my lodgings?" asked Lucinda. "They're above a chemist's shop, nice airy rooms, well fitted up, quite the best I've had in a long time."

"Don't go, Deb," advised Fred. "She only wants to bore you half to death with her bloody scrapbook."

"He's just jealous because my notices are so much better than his." But Lucinda laughed good-naturedly, and extracted from me a promise that I'd call on her the day after next.

I wanted to stay with them. You've no idea how much I wanted to stay! But now I invented an appointment and excused myself, leaving them to their chat and banter and laughter.

The rain had stopped, so I decided to go home a roundabout way. I'd call at my dressmaker at the bottom of St Martin's Lane, then walk back to Long Acre, where I hoped to find a baker who'd give us credit. Then I'd cut across to Bow Street to visit a poor woman in dismal lodgings there. This was someone who had been befriended by Kitty as she lay in hospital giving birth to her first child, and whose husband had disappeared while she was away.

I walked along slowly, chewing my lower lip and bemoaning my stupidity. If only I'd asked advice! If only I'd been less hasty! For I saw now that I belonged with the company. I wanted, I *needed* to act. It wasn't enough to be just me. As an opium addict needs his daily draught, I needed to stand outside myself and be someone else, to be Juliet, Ophelia or whoever, to love and suffer and die for them. And only then, as the curtain fell, would I be content to be myself again.

For the last year or more I'd been playing a part. That of a docile married woman. But now I was heartily sick of it and wanted to be a married woman no more. Especially one saddled with a difficult husband whom I'd once loved, but now didn't even like.

I walked on. And then, on the corner of Long Acre and St Martin's Lane, I saw them.

At first I noticed only the dumpy figure of a woman, shrouded in a merino cape topped by the most evil-looking lump of bonnet ever to sit on a female head. But then, as I came closer, I heard something familiar. I head Channing's laugh. My husband was talking to the creature in the bonnet, and what she was saying amused him a great deal.

Of course, I was fascinated. But since I'd been on a visit to the theatre, where I'd been more or less forbidden to go, I also felt rather guilty. I didn't want to speak to Channing in case my crime showed in my face, so I ducked into a doorway, muffled myself in my shawl, and watched him.

He and the woman went on talking, and eventually I saw my husband lay one hand on her arm. I bridled rather at that. Who could she be, that he treated her with such familiarity? I was soon to find out, for just then she turned towards him, her face came into profile, and I had a most unpleasant surprise. Indeed, I only just stopped myself from crying out.

The woman was Esther Harris.

At first, I thought I must be imagining things. Esther, of all people in the world – how could she be in London, how could she know Channing, and how could they be talking so familiarly together, how had they come to know each other so well? I closed my eyes. When I opened them, the dream would have melted away. But it was no dream. When I looked again, Esther and Channing were still deep in conversation, and now she was laughing too and playfully tapping his shoulder.

I felt sick. I stood in that doorway and great waves of nausea washed over and over me. I had thought I no longer loved Channing Minot, but it seemed I was mistaken, for I was now quite ill with jealousy. Why else would I feel so angry, so sick, so murderous, and all at once?

As I watched I felt my heart hammering painfully against my ribs, I almost *heard* my pulse race, and I knew I was soaking with perspiration. I was on the point of going up to them when suddenly Esther turned towards the road, hailed a cab – and before I could move she was inside it, disappearing, leaving my husband standing on the pavement, waving her off.

I don't know how far I walked that afternoon, but it was dark when I arrived home. Channing had evidently been unconcerned by my absence, for he'd apparently told Kitty that I'd been to visit friends, who had promised to bring me home.

"Did you have a pleasant day, Mrs Minot?" Kitty asked, as she helped me off with my shawl, and tut-tutted when I explained I had accidentally left my bonnet behind in the cab; for only loose women are seen in public bare-headed.

"I had a mixed sort of day," I told her. I kicked off my dirty shoes and muttered something about having stepped out of the carriage into a puddle. "One of those days that are a mixture of pleasure and pain."

Well, that was true enough. After a delightful morning and midday, I'd had a horrible afternoon. Walking by the river, watching the greasy black water slapping the dirty shore, I'd been wondering how I could kill Esther Harris without being found out and hanged myself.

I took a candle and went upstairs to bed. I meant to wake Channing and ask him why he'd invented stories about me. In fact, there were all sorts of things I wanted to ask him. But then again, I reflected, there might be questions he'd want to ask *me*. So I undressed and slipped into bed.

I left the candle burning for a moment, and I looked at my husband. He was not drunk or drugged. He lay on his side, breathing softly, his hair tousled, his left hand curled by his cheek, like a child.

He stirred and murmured something. "It's just me," I said. I snuffed the candle.

"Deb." Half asleep, he turned towards me. His body recognised mine, and now he embraced me. "Dear Deb," he whispered, kissing me.

Sober, he smelled and tasted so sweet. Tired, he was gentle and kind. I'll remember this night, I thought, as I lay beside him afterwards, warm and contented in his arms. Whatever happens in the future, I'll remember that he loved me tonight.

Chapter 14

"My dear, you *must* come to my benefit!" Lucinda pouted at me. "You, and your handsome husband – indeed, I was hoping you'd bring a large party of friends."

"I'll see what I can do," I promised, miserably. I could hardly suggest it to Channing, who had expressly forbidden me to go near any theatre. And somehow I doubted that Messrs Maclean, Rogers or Tripman were avid playgoers.

A week had gone by since I had seen Channing with Esther, and I had still not found a way to ask him how he knew her. We had been happy that week and I was reluctant to disturb his good humour. He was so cheerful and optimistic, in fact, that he'd suggested we leave the dusty city for a few days and take a jaunt to the coast, though with what he meant to pay for this excursion I did not know.

"Oh, we're in funds again," he replied airily, when I asked. "I told you I had a new scheme. All our worries are over now."

"What have you done?" I asked. "Channing, you haven't stolen, or done anything – "

"Of course not. Stop fretting." He grinned. "An investment has paid off, that's all. You can pay the coalman and tell him we'll be trading with his rivals from now on."

"So you've borrowed more money," I said. "Channing, how are you going to pay it back?"

"I haven't borrowed. I've made an investment. Something quite different." He laughed at me. "Poor little ignorance, don't fret about what you can't understand."

I suppose I was convinced. Well, there's no supposing about it, of course I was relieved that our money worries seemed to be over. But all the same, I was still anxious. Still concerned.

"So we'll go to Brighton next week?" demanded Channing now.

"Yes, I suppose so." I shrugged. "Yes, Channing, that might be a very good idea."

Late one afternoon, I returned from visiting Lucinda to find the house on Holborn Hill in darkness and apparently deserted. This was as I expected, for it was Kitty's monthly day off, and she had taken Tilda to visit some of her relations in Southwark. I imagined Channing was out somewhere about his own business, sitting in some coffee house in the City perhaps, deep in conversation, maybe, with his fellow investors.

I did not ring the bell. Instead I let myself in with my own key.

At first I assumed that the merriment I heard was coming from the ground-floor front, where two noisy young medical students, whose habits were somewhat irregular – now and again they even brought in women of the street – had rented rooms. But then, as I climbed the stairs, I realised the laughter was coming from my own bedroom.

"Channing?" I called. "Channing, is that you?"

No reply.

"Channing!" I was a little afraid now. "Channing, what are you doing up there?"

Still no answer.

Reaching the landing, I hesitated. Now I was aware of an unpleasant, smoky smell, familiar but at the same time strange.

I listened again.

Silence.

But then there was some indistinct grunting, the floor shook, and now Channing's laugh, loud and uninhibited, rang out again.

I flung open the door.

I had the shock of my life, for she was *in my bed*.

Rearing up naked, Esther Harris was the most horrible sight I ever saw. She was almost totally bald. Her chins obscured her short, fat neck completely. Her body, bloated and swollen, with skin so encrusted and scabbed that it seemed to be growing mould, wobbled and shook like some disgusting living jelly. She looked straight at me, but I'm sure she did not see me, for her eyes were glassy, blind and stupid; not questing and darting as I'd always seen them before.

She was astride Channing, facing away from him. Lying on his back beneath her, his hands on her ham-like hips, he pushed and bucked, groaned, then pushed again. Plainly they were at the climax of an act of love. But he held her in such a way that, ignorant and innocent as I was, I knew that with her he was slaking some perverted lust that he'd never tried to satisfy with me.

And then he began to laugh again, a foul, grunting, evil laugh. I knew now he was hurting her, for she winced and grimaced. She ground her rotten teeth, and tears rolled down her scabby cheeks like rain.

But then, through her tears, she laughed. Throwing back her ugly head, she screamed with laughter. "Go on!" she gasped. "Go on, go on, go *on*!"

I wondered about killing the pair of them. The kitchen knives were always kept sharp and I knew exactly where they were, I could have one in my hand in an instant. I could spill Esther's black blood all over Channing's white body and then I could stab him, too.

But suddenly I could bear it no longer. The warm vomit rose in my throat and I fled to the scullery, where I retched and heaved up my heart for a full ten minutes. Even down here I could smell that strangely perfumed smoke, and it made my head spin. I was sick until I could be sick no more. Then I jerked open the kitchen door and ran of the house, down Holborn Hill, into Farringdon Street, not stopping until I reached the river. Gasping for breath now I walked on to Blackfriars Bridge. Burying my face in my hands I leaned on the parapet. I began to cry, sobbing like a little child.

Five minutes later the first flush of tears abated and I stared down into the dirty Thames, wondering how it would feel to have the cold grey water close over my head and bubble into my lungs. That way I'd benefit a fellow human being, for I knew there were men who made a good living fishing suicides out of the river, dragging the bodies to the shore on hooks, in order to empty their pockets and steal their rings before giving them up to the river police.

And even as I stared down on to the flood, a man in a rowing boat came under the arches and looked up at me, as if to say, "Do it now, why don't you, do it while I'm here, nice and convenient, an impartial witness; save me the bother of rowing back against the tide to find you before another chap does."

But he grinned at me then, and asked when I came off duty, since if it was soon he'd like to take me out for a drink. "Or if you've had a good night's trade," he added, "p'raps you could take me out instead?"

I stared back at him coldly. I wished I had a brick to drop on his stupid skull.

I walked on the bridge for hours, trying to decide what to do. The moon came up and shone on the water, and I was still undecided. As eleven o'clock chimed, two blowsy women bustled up to me and, very roughly, ordered me off their patch.

I walked along Fleet Street, then made my way slowly up the Strand. Then, as the bells were all striking midnight, I made a decision. I'd leave him. I'd just go, I'd disappear, and if he looked for me I would not be found. That would be better than killing him. That way, I would not depart my own miserable life on a public gallows, with a rope around my neck.

I touched my throat and felt the cold metal of a chain, for I happened to be wearing my green glass pendant, the chipped, cheap ornament which Charlie Rayner had despised but which I thought had always brought me luck. Luck! Just now I wanted to tear it off and throw it in the gutter, but the chain was too strong to break and my hands were too cold and stiff to unfasten the clasp, so I left it where it was.

For the second time in my life I was alone and penniless, with nowhere to go. It was very late now, and all respectable people would be in bed. A night watchman eyed me suspiciously, then grinned and asked if I had time for a quick one. I drew my shawl tight about me and walked on.

There was nothing for it but to go to the theatre. I walked to Lisle Street, but when I arrived at the Royalty even that was closed and dark; so I went to Lucinda's lodging. Almost in tears again, I rang the bell. I rang and rang, but no one answered, and I was on the point of leaving when at last I heard footsteps in the passage, bare feet slapping on flagstones, coming towards me.

The door was opened by Fred Hammer. His great hairy feet were unshod, and his shambling body was wrapped in a woman's flannel robe. He glowered into the darkness, demanding who the hell was knocking people up at this time of night. He had evidently risen from Lucinda's bed, for I could smell her perfume on him and one of her hair ribbons had been tied, ludicrously, round his neck.

I tried to speak, but my voice failed me. Fred peered into the gloom – and saw it was me.

"Good God," he muttered. "The child bride." He reached out one hairy paw and took my wrist. "Come in, Deborah," he growled, "come in, do. You look half dead. What's happened, eh?"

"I – I went – " I tried to explain, but words wouldn't come. "Mr Hammer, I'm sorry, but I – "

"Oh, stow it. Tell Luce. Come on." He wasn't angry. He wasn't even put out. He held on to me and ushered me up the narrow stairs, shaking his untidy head, and mumbling to himself. He opened the door of Lucinda's bedroom and pushed me in. "Look what I found on the doorstep," he said. "Must've been washed up by the tide."

Indeed I was the most miserable, dishevelled, tear-stained wretch that could be imagined.

They sat me down on the eiderdown and although the smells and atmosphere of recent sex made me feel sick all over again, Lucinda and Fred were so kind and concerned that I wept with gratitude. I tried again to speak. "I w-went home," I stammered, "I s-saw them, and I – "

"We are in a bad way," murmured Fred, rubbing my cold hands. "So – hocked the family silver, did you, and the horse broke its leg?"

"Don't tease the poor child," said Lucinda. Spilling right out of her old satin dressing-gown, her make-up smudged and in places half licked off, and her hair like a stork's nest, Lucinda was the essence of motherliness all the same. "Let her get her breath, at least."

"Sorry," muttered Fred.

"I should think so, too." Kindly, Lucinda touched my hand. "Is it your husband?" she asked.

"Yes," I replied. "He – "

"Always thought that fellow looked a blackguard," ruminated Fred.

"Did you?" Sharply, Lucinda glanced at him, her dark eyes like gimlets. "We would like some tea," she said. She pointed to her little felt slippers, which Fred obediently slid on to his huge, gnarled feet. His heels hanging over the backs, he slapped off down the passage, then downstairs to the lodging-house kitchen.

Lucinda took me in her arms and held me against her soft maternal bosom. "Now, my dear, there's no need to tell me anything," she said. "But if it helps – "

I laid my head on her shoulder and told her the whole story of my life.

4

Henry Collis

1843–1845

Chapter 15

For the past eighteen months or so the company had been doing very well. So well, in fact, that it was breaking up, as its members were offered various separate engagements here, there and everywhere. Pen Gaynes wasn't the only one who'd earned celebrity, for Judith and Dora were booked for a season at the Haymarket, Harkess and Tom Denby had gone to Drury Lane – as mere walking gentlemen, it's true, but they hoped for better things as the season went on – and Lucinda, Fred and I had been offered something we could not even contemplate refusing. We were booked for a winter season of engagements in North America, to play with various native companies in Philadelphia, Baltimore, Washington and, of course, New York.

Lucinda's scheme was that we should also take Deb. She cornered me in the coffee house in which I usually took my breakfast to tell me so. "To have a fourth member in our party would be so *very* useful," she urged. "If we took Deborah, we could extend our range *enormously*. For instance, we could consider doing – "

"Do you think, Lucinda," I interrupted, "that I might trouble you to refill my cup?"

"Certainly." Obligingly, she poured. "More sugar?"

"Thank you."

"Not at all. Now as I was saying. She'd do Juliet, of course. She'd relieve me of Cordelia and Ophelia – and I tell you now, Henry, I really wasn't looking forward to doing either of them. And indeed why should I, since Deb can play them so well? And as for those three new plays you've just bought, Deb would be perfect for the dutiful daughter, and the jilted bride, not to say the broken-hearted young widow."

"I decide who plays whom, Lucinda. Not you."

"Of course you do, darling, and very well you arrange things, too." Brightly, Lucinda twinkled at me. "So if you agree, I could tell her – "

"Not before I've had my breakfast, Luce." I buttered a hot roll and looked around for the preserves. "Look, you know I don't make decisions this early in the morning."

"Then let me make this one for you." She smiled her most persuasive smile. "This is what we'll do. We'll take Deb. And then, with all our abilities, so wide and different, we'll be able to extend our range considerably, we'll not need to rely so much on native talent."

"If there is any," growled Fred, slurping chocolate.

"Exactly. I may as well tell you, Henry," said Lucinda, shuddering artistically, "that I fancy I shall find any colonial Cordelia or Yankee Juliet totally unbearable. Quite beyond the pale."

"Although she don't mind a Brummagem one at all," ruminated Fred. "Ain't that odd?"

"Fred Hammer, be quiet." Now Lucinda leaned against me and rubbed her soft bosom against my sleeve, a most agreeable sensation I must admit. "And in a new country," she went on, "poor Deb could forget that nasty fellow and begin her life anew."

"Well, I suppose she might." I shrugged the distracting bosom away. "Is Deb living with you at present?" I asked.

"Moved in lock, stock and barrel," replied Fred. "We've got bloody stockings draped everywhere. Curl papers all over the floors, female unmentionables on every flat surface."

"Resolved to leave her husband, is she?"

"Most certainly." Lucinda narrowed her eyes. "Henry, if you knew one quarter of what the filthy beast had done to her, you'd weep. Even your flinty heart would melt at that poor creature's plight. And you'd – "

"I'd take pity on the said poor creature and offer her our unconditional protection, I suppose." Heavily, I sighed.

"Lucinda, if we did take Deb with us, have you considered what – "

"Dear, dear Henry! I knew you'd agree." Head on one side like a pretty parrot, Lucinda beamed at me. "I'll tell her it's all settled, shall I?"

"You'll do no such thing!" I cried. The liberties the woman took! "Who's the manager of this company, Lucinda?" I demanded. "You or I?"

"Oh, you are, Henry." Lucinda smirked, and again the bosom rubbed against my arm. "And what a brilliant, wonderful manager you are. Quite the best. Look what you've done for the company this twelvemonth past. How we've prospered under your tutelage, how our careers have blossomed. And all because of you."

"Thank you," I said. "But Lucinda, flattery – "

"It's not flattery, darling. I speak the simple truth."

"Very well." Again I pushed Lucinda's chest aside. "Ask Mrs Minot to come and see me at eleven tomorrow. And now you must excuse me. I have some letters to write."

Mrs Minot, indeed. To me, she'd always be little Deb Tanner. As I walked along the Strand on the way back to my lodgings, the very thought of her lightened my heart; but the idea of being in her company again made me feel as nervous as a fifteen-year-old lad. Which, you will agree, is an absurd state for man nearing his thirty-sixth birthday to be in.

I spent that day writing letters, but to whom I wrote them I cannot now recall. I don't think I slept at all that night. When I got up the next morning I was bleary-eyed, my hair stood on end, and I wore a silly smile on my face which made me look like the village simpleton.

No matter.

Her marriage had failed.

She was coming to see me.

She did not come alone, of course. Lucinda and Fred were at my lodgings in Catherine Street at eleven o'clock sharp, bringing with them a pale, wan creature bearing very little resemblance to the lively, pretty child whom I'd thought the most promising Juliet of the age. "Mrs Minot?" I held out my hand in welcome. "I hope I see you well?"

"Of course you don't, Henry. She's not well at all." Elbowing me aside, Lucinda plumped herself down in the best armchair. "Very well, then. Shall we get on with it?"

So we sat round my table, toying with coffee cups and breaking biscuits into little pieces. I busied myself with papers, Lucinda fidgeted and sighed, Fred clicked his badly fitting china teeth, and poor Deborah looked down at her hands, ill at ease and quite possibly wishing herself anywhere but here.

I put my papers together and clasped my hands before me. "Has Miss Tolland told you what we propose?" I asked Deb gently, well aware that Lucinda would have done exactly that. With plenty of embroidery thrown in.

"Yes, Mr Collis, she has." Deb looked up and met my eyes. "It's very kind of you to think of me, and I'm very grateful for your kindness. But I'm sure there must be many other ladies, most anxious to – "

"No doubt there are. But it's you we need." The black circles under her eyes, the waxy pallor of her skin, together with her expression of utter dejection and misery, nearly broke my heart. "We would very much like you to come with us," I urged. "Or someone like you," added my evil inclination, to save my own face.

"Like me?" she asked.

"Another young lady." I coughed, to clear my throat. "A lady capable of taking the parts you could play."

"You might take Miss Gaynes," she suggested.

Pen. I grimaced. Things had gone rather sour between myself and dear Penelope. "I don't think so," I said firmly. "Mrs Minot, I should explain to you that we are already booked to appear in at least half a dozen different towns. On our arrival I hope to arrange further engagements. Since America is such a huge country, we will be covering very great distances."

"Through virgin forests full of naked savages, down swollen rivers turbid with raging cataracts, across sweltering deserts and disease-infested swamps," interrupted Lucinda, beaming happily. "Oh, Fred, you will take care of me, won't you?"

"Miss Tolland, if you please?" I glared at her, and she smirked in reply. "We'll be travelling hundreds of miles on river boats, we'll be cooped up in railway trains for days on end, and we'll be taking long coach journeys on what I am led to believe are atrocious roads. I do feel that at Pen's time of life – "

"She's pushing forty-five if she's a day," muttered Fred.

"– she would not want to undertake all that."

"She'd moan all the bloody time, is what he means," grinned Fred. "And *we* wouldn't want to undertake all *that*."

"In any case, she wouldn't come with us if we did ask her," said Lucinda. "She's got herself engaged to a greengrocer. Heard last Tuesday, didn't you, Henry?" Sympathetically, she patted my hand. "Never mind, darling. Better to have loved and lost – "

"Lucinda, do be quiet." I found I was blushing furiously, either with anger or embarrassment, or more probably both. Irritably I began to riffle through my papers, looking for our initial itinerary. "So anyway, Mrs Minot, if you – "

"He first saw her in *Coriolanus*," Lucinda told Deb, as if I wasn't there. "One evening, she was playing Volumnia with such style and panache, that – um – that her dress became disordered – "

"That her left tit fell out of her toga, is what she means," put in Fred. "Come on, Luce, get on with it."

"And a greengrocer in one of the nearside boxes was stricken with love." Lucinda giggled. "He began courting her that very night."

"Inundated her with edibles."

"Wooed her with cucumbers, cabbages and carrots."

"Until finally she succumbed."

"And that was that. The wedding will be in October." Expressively Lucinda shrugged. "So you see, my dear. Pen can't come."

"How long will you be away?" asked Deb, looking at

me with what I chose to assume was sympathy for my jilted state.

"Initially for six months," I replied. "Longer if we can arrange the work."

"It sounds perfectly wonderful." There was a wistful note in Deb's voice which cut me to the marrow. "But no, I can't come."

"Why's that?" demanded Lucinda.

"I'm married," Deb replied. "If I leave my husband, I lay myself open to all kinds of accusations."

"If you stay with the wretch, you lay yourself open to humiliation, penury, and worse." Lucinda took Deb's right hand and held it in hers. "Dear Deb, we need you. What do you owe that beastly man you call your husband, eh?"

"Better ask old Henry that one," said Fred. "His father was the vicar." He grinned at Deb. "Henry was born a gentleman, see; although he's come down in the world and certainly ain't one now. Being a vagabond and player, I mean.

"So come on, Collis. What's the official line on this one? Is Deb bound to love, honour and obey the fellow, or does his nasty behaviour release her from her obligations? And leave her free to come with us?"

"Oh, I think Deb should decide that for herself." Behind my back I crossed my fingers. "I'd never counsel a woman to leave her husband unless – "

"It was in your own interests," grinned Fred.

"Unless she were in grave physical or moral danger, was what I was about to say." I glared at Fred. "And in any instance, the final decision would always be hers."

Deb looked at Fred, at Lucinda, then at me. She sighed. She got up to leave and had bidden me good day before I could say anything more.

She went home with Fred and Lucinda, no doubt to be harrassed and bullied half the night.

In the morning she sent me a short note agreeing to go to America with us.

Chapter 16

We soon completed our short season at the Royalty. During this time Deb stayed with Lucinda and Fred. I don't know if she saw her husband. I didn't wish to know. On September the sixteenth we went up to Liverpool, to set sail for the new republic.

Our ship turned out to be a three-masted wooden barque of considerable antiquity, on which passages were considerably cheaper than those on a modern ironclad steamer. The barque's cargo was cheap Birmingham metalware, and its ballast, or so it appeared to me, the most wretched of Irish emigrants. Seeing this poor half-human detritus dragging itself on board and disappearing into the bowels of the ship was like watching so many ghosts and spectres of the damned being consigned to the pit of hell.

"God dammit all, Henry," muttered Fred, staring bleakly from where we sat on the quayside, as yet another ragged woman chivvied half a dozen wraithlike infants on to the ship, "dammit all to blazes, they must be crammed in like pickled herrings down there."

"I was just thinking that myself," I agreed. "I've counted two hundred and seventeen so far."

"Poor devils. Poor miserable buggers one and all." Fred sniffed. "I tell you this; if we do well over the bloody water, I'm coming back to Blighty under steam. Hey, you there!"

"Me, sir?" A scarecrow of a woman with a weazen little baby in her arms jumped in terror. "Please, sir, sure an' I'm sorry, sir, but I didn't know – "

"No, I dare say you didn't, you poor bitch." As the Irishwoman stood hesitating on the gangplank, Fred pushed his hands into his trouser pockets. "You got any provisions for the voyage?" he demanded.

"No sir." The woman hung her head. "I was hoping – "

"To scrounge off the other skeletons in the hold. God." Holding out his hand, he gave her a couple of half crowns. "Here," he growled. "Go and get yourself some dried stuff. Peas and beans and that. Or you'll be food for the fishes before we're halfway there, and that's a fact." He turned to me. "Henry, where're those bloody women?"

"Gone to buy something." I shrugged. As we stood on the quay, Lucinda had suddenly remembered she needed a pot of some particular rouge which was sure not to be available in America, and she'd dragged Deb off with her in search of it. "They'll be back in half an hour," I reassured him. "Or so Lucinda said."

"Don't trust that bitch." Morosely Fred kicked at a capstan. "Gone to buy something, my arse. I reckon she's swanning down Lime Street. Eyeing up some bugger just back from the Indies, with the cash coming out of his ears." He scowled down at his feet. "I can see her now. She'll be pushing her tits in sailors' faces, wagging her bum at any well-heeled – "

"For God's sake, man!" I stood up and glared at him. "She's gone to buy a jar of Mason's Best Carmine, that's all!"

"That's what she *said*, but can we believe the cow?"

"Oh, stop it. Let's go and have some coffee, shall we?" Although I must admit that what with watching Irish emigrants, and listening to Fred's lugubrious speculations on Lucinda's movements and motives, coffee wasn't really what I wanted just then. A stiff brandy wouldn't have come amiss.

The voyage was expected to last a calendar month at least. The captain, a mere lad of twenty-six, promised us a smooth passage, and at first the sea was indeed calm; in fact, there was hardly enough wind to belly out the sails. But the gentle rolling motion of the ship was enough to make at least some of us ill, and I for one began to wonder if it had been such a good idea to leave the safety of dry land.

Then, three days out, we hit a storm.

From the moment we left Liverpool, Lucinda had proved herself to be natural sailor, but the rest of us were not so lucky. At first, Fred and I thought it beneath our manhoods to admit to feeling a little seasick and to begin with we did our modest heaving in private. But as the storm worsened and the days of being churned like buttermilk became nights of being thrown from side to side like peas in a colander, we became less bothered about our reputations and were ill in public, like everyone else.

"Roast beef and bottled beer," muttered Fred, as he and I dolefully munched dried biscuits in the dining saloon one midday. "Prime rib and best ale, that's what the fellow in the red waistcoat suggests. Man's a fool."

"On the contrary, maybe he's quite right," said Lucinda, who was tucking in to a dangerously slopping dishful of thick mutton and vegetable soup. "Give your stomach something to bite on. That's the idea, you see."

"God." Fred pushed another biscuit into his face. "What's that bloody mess you're eating?"

"Mutton chowder, darling. An authentic American delight." She offered Fred a quivering spoonful of fat mutton, yellow peas and greasy stock. "Try to take a little nourishment," she suggested. "It'll do you good."

"Oh Christ," replied Fred, as his face turned greener than it was already. He dashed from the room, banging his head on the door frame as he staggered out.

As she heard him being sick in the passageway, Lucinda laughed cruelly. "That'll teach him to accuse me of making cow eyes at sailors," she observed. Complacently, she smiled at me. "What about you, Henry darling?" she enquired, offering me a spoonful of pearl barley swimming in yellowish gravy. "You really ought to try this, you know. It's extremely good."

I hated Lucinda Tolland that day.

And as for our other companion in adversity, what of her? Well, Deb – poor Deb – was prostrate. She lay in the cabin she shared with Lucinda and a certain Mrs Bradlaw, a widow from Manchester going out to seek her fortune in Cincinnati, and whimpered in misery and terror.

"Tell her to take some roast beef and bottled beer," suggested Fred sarcastically, as we loitered in the passengers' forward saloon the following horrible and heaving morning. The area around Fred's right eye was now swollen and black and his forehead sported a wide expanse of sticking plaster. "Tell her it'll do her good."

"Don't be so silly. The poor girl's very ill." From the steward, Lucinda had collected a plate of dry biscuits and a bottle of seltzer water, and now she was about to lurch off to visit the invalid. "Go away, do," she went on crossly, as the two of us staggered along the passage beside her. "Go and play cribbage or something. It'll take your minds off your heaving guts."

"I'll visit Deborah if I please." Now Fred grabbed my right shoulder, making me fall heavily against the rail. "I 'spect she'd like to see me. And good old Henry here."

"She'd sooner entertain a pair of ship's rats." Lucinda glowered at us both. "I told you before; she isn't at all well. And the sight of you two, with your faces of Lincoln green, would just about finish her off."

"Horse shit, woman. The girl dotes on me. Always has done." Just then Fred retched, but manfully he swallowed again. "Whassa matter with her, anyway?"

"She's indisposed."

"What's that supposed to mean? Got the pox, has she? Grown blue warts on her nose?"

"Go *away*!" Elbowed savagely in the ribs, Fred lurched against the wall, banging his elbow. He glared at Lucinda, who gave him a saucy grin in reply.

"Very well, Luce," he muttered. "You win. We'll take our guts elsewhere." And so, dragging me with him, he lurched off to the smoking saloon, swearing under his breath and cursing the equinoctial gales to all eternity.

In the smoking-room we ran into the first mate, so I left Fred haranguing the unfortunate man and walked, or rather staggered, back along the passage to Deb's cabin. I knocked twice, three times, and eventually Lucinda condescended to open the door. "We don't want any gentleman callers, Henry," she said. She went back in and slammed the door behind her.

Four or five days into the storm, the wind veered to the south and the sea grew marginally less rough. Better than that, Fred and I finally found our sea legs, and from then on we did as the gentleman in the red waistcoat had suggested, taking a daily breakfast of fried beefsteak and strong ale.

This set us up for a series of dangerous morning promenades about the ship, clinging to each other like a pair of elderly inebriates as we were buffeted about the deck and soaked with stinging spray. We watched in awe and admiration as the sailors on the rigging went about their dangerous tasks apparently unconcerned, while we staggered hither and thither and, I must admit it, occasionally retched over the side.

As the weather improved and I began to feel better, I managed to spare some pity for the poor Irish emigrants, packed like black slaves in the filthy pit of the steerage. Having nothing better to do, Fred and I daily took charge of half a dozen bony children and went staggering about the ship with these skinny brats, giving them some fresh air and exercise and seeing the wind whip some colour into their white faces. On calmer days we managed to set up some games of hopscotch or tag.

These calmer days became more frequent until the tempest ceased all together. One bright, starry evening I took some children back to their foetid hole and from its murky depths I heard a woman's voice raised in blessing, as she thanked Our Lady Star of the Sea for her gracious intercession, for the quelling of the storm.

I thanked her, too. And I wondered if I might trouble her further, and ask her to do something for Deb.

For although the storm had blown itself out, Deb still lay ill in her narrow bed. The sun sparkled on the sea, the wind was light and refreshing, and even the wizened Irish women struggled up on deck to take some air; but Deb lay prone and wretched. Fred and I, who refused to believe that she could still be seasick, were finally taken in to see her. She was fast asleep, but so pale and bloodless that it was obvious she was ill.

"Poor little cow," whispered Fred, his husky voice hoarser than ever with pity. "Galloping consumption. That's what it is. Seen it before." He fetched a deep sigh. "I give her three weeks."

"Perhaps she should see the ship's surgeon," I suggested.

"That little drunkard. Face as red as a flannel petticoat and accent as thick as a Yorkshire blanket, I can't understand a single solitary word he says. And have you seen how his hands shake?" Lucinda pursed her lips. "I wouldn't ask him to doctor a pig."

"Lucinda?" Woken by her nurse's tirade, Deb opened her eyes. Seeing us standing there like Faith, Hope and Charity, she merely blinked. Evidently she was too feeble even to show surprise.

"Could you fancy a bite to eat, my love?" asked Fred gently, his raw-boned features softened by sympathy. "A lamb chop, maybe? A small cutlet and a little mashed potato?"

"No, thank you." Deb shuddered. "No, I don't want anything."

"What about a little fresh air?" I suggested lamely.

"Yes. Perhaps you should try to get up." Encouragingly, Lucinda smiled. "The air's so sweet now, it'll do you so much good. Please will you come up on deck?"

"I can't," replied Deb. "I don't think I can walk."

"Stuff and nonsense." Cheerfully, Lucinda helped her sit up, then began to rummage around for her clothes. "Come along," she said briskly. "I'll help you dress. Shoo," she added, to Fred and me. "I'll bring her on deck directly."

On deck, it was obvious that Deb felt even worse. The sight of the glassy green waves on the glittering sea did nothing to lift her spirits, and the sharp, clean breeze on her face did nothing for her wan complexion. As she faltered past the mizzen mast we came upon a family of Irish emigrants cooking up some nasty mess in a smelly charcoal brazier, and this was too much for her. She rushed to the rail and was violently sick.

Having had no breakfast to speak of, it was merely thin, acid bile which spoiled her dress; but this public disgrace made her cry and Lucinda, glaring at me as if it were all my fault, took her back to her cabin.

"That young lady in your party, sir?" asked a young ship's officer, who was strolling by with a trio of very pretty female passengers.

"Yes," I replied. "But I'm afraid she's not at all well."

"Some can take it, sir. Some can't." The officer grinned at me. "Offer the lady some smelling salts," he advised, "then get her up here again. Let her sit in a sheltered spot with the sun on her face – it'll do her the world of good."

"Maybe it would," I agreed.

"Certain to." The officer shrugged. "When they've been brought up delicate, sir, they often can't take it," he said.

One of the three women he was squiring about smiled at me. "It's my first time up today," she volunteered, in the accents of one who had almost certainly been brought up extremely delicate. "Mr Robbins is quite right – an hour in the sunshine will do the lady a great deal of good."

And then, nodding politely to me, the officer and his belles moved on their way, as easily and casually as if they'd been strolling down Mayfair.

As for me, the knot of fear in my stomach was growing more twisted and tangled by the minute.

Chapter 17

"Deb would like to see you, Henry," said Lucinda, the following morning. "You'd better come now," she added bossily, "while the widow's busy sunning herself and ogling the second officer on deck."

I went without delay and found Deb half sitting, half lying on her berth. Wrapped in a thick flannel dressing-gown which I assumed was the widow's, her hair was loose and she was as pale as porcelain. Suddenly I had a premonition of death, which of course I instantly dismissed – but it was hard not to feel anxious, when she looked so like a living corpse.

"What is it, Deb?" I asked. I sat down on the widow's bed and tried to look businesslike but concerned, which was very difficult as I actually felt nothing but blind panic and stomach-churning fear. "Look, my dear," I began briskly, "if you feel able to get up, I'm sure an hour or so on deck would set you – "

"Mr Collis, I'm going to have a child." Deb's tone was one of such dejection and despair that it was as if she had announced she was going to be burned at the stake the very next morning. "I'm very sorry, Mr Collis, but I'm going to have a baby."

Relief washed over me. I could see the tears in her eyes, but my own relief was so great that to this day I don't know how I prevented myself from taking her in my arms and kissing her in gratitude.

"A baby, eh?" I said cheerily, beaming all over my face. "Well, that's not a tragedy, is it? Come now," I went on, in my hearty, favourite uncle voice, "don't cry. It's perfectly natural, after all. And I'm sure there are plenty of midwives in America."

"It's not that." Her tears spilled over and coursed down her cheeks. "It's Channing's child," she wept. "I'm carrying that man's *baby*! Oh God, I hate it so much! The very idea of it makes me sick with hatred!"

Now her sobs choked her, and she hid her face in Lucinda's bosom, crying as if her heart would break.

I waited for the sobs to subside a little, then I patted her hand. "When's the baby due?" I asked. Such a practical man.

"March. April, at the latest. I don't really know – or care." She raised her tear-stained face to mine. "I'm so sorry," she whimpered.

"Sorry for what?" I smiled encouragingly, or tried to. "My dear Deborah, you're going to have a baby. That's nothing to fret about, is it? We'll look after you, of course," I added, in case she thought she might be cast adrift in the New World, pregnant and destitute.

"Thank you. You're very kind." Deb sniffed. "You're always kind."

"And when you're on dry land again," I went on jovially, "you'll be so much better. Probably you'll feel like working."

"Well, of course I hope to be able to work. Mr Collis, I shall do my best."

"I know you will." She was becoming agitated again, so I held her hand and rubbed it in what I hoped was a consoling fashion. "Don't worry, my dear," I went on. "Most actresses – or those of my acquaintance anyway – take a little thing like motherhood right in their stride. Working as long as they feel fit; right up to the baby's birth in some cases; then up and about again a fortnight afterwards. But if you're unwell, of course, there's absolutely no question of expecting you to – well – "

"No. I see. Thank you."

In spite of my gruesome display of badinage and bonhomie, of course I knew perfectly well what was upsetting poor Deb.

It was upsetting me, too. The idea of her having that wastrel's child battening inside her made me feel quite queasy with disgust, so I could well understand what effect it must be having on her. But what could I say to reassure her? That, when the child was born, she would certainly love it, in spite of its paternity?

I didn't dare hope for so much.

I decided the time had come for action, so I let go of her hand. "Look," I said cheerfully, "why don't you let Lucinda help you get up? It's splendid on deck this morning. The sea air – "

"Will do me good. Well, perhaps." Wanly, the poor girl smiled. "Yes," she agreed, "I'll get up."

"Excellent," I said.

I got up myself, and left her.

I had to get away.

The ship made good progress now, and as Fred and I came up on deck one clear October morning, we found the crew scurrying about all over the place, at action stations with a vengeance today.

"Must be land," said Fred, grinning. "Come on."

So we went to look. And, through a telescope belonging to the second officer we did indeed descry land. We saw trees against the skyline, and just rising above the waves was a green, undulating shore.

"Long Island, sir," said the officer. "Tomorrow, you'll be on dry land again."

At eight the following morning a large steamboat came alongside the barque and we were decanted into it, to be taken to the shore. We berthed, and transferred ourselves to a hackney cab. And even as Lucinda gabbled and exclaimed and stared, the negro driver cracked his whip and we were merrily bowling along. We had arrived in New York.

In those days it was a town of painted wooden houses, red and white, yellow and grey, all with bright green shutters. Wide roads and broad pavements made getting about easy enough, but when on foot one had to take care not to stumble over the great fat pigs rooting in the gutters. Apparently New Yorkers turned their hogs out to graze each morning, and each evening the animals returned safely home, ambling along as easily as – well, as hogs going home to their supper.

"Do they never go astray?" I enquired of our landlord one morning, well aware that any unescorted porker parading along High Holborn or the Strand would have been enticed away and turned into bacon within ten minutes of wandering off by himself. "What I mean to say is, might there be a risk of a pig going missing?"

"No sir, there might not," replied the American, firmly. "Do not, sir, confound the citizens of the free United States with those of the corrupt kingdoms of Europe. Do not assume that we in this republic behave as you do in the Old World, where rapine and corruption universally prevail."

"Well, no," I murmured. "No, indeed."

"The citizen of Europe," declared my mentor solemnly, "is a poor, brutalized thing. But the citizen of the New World is a moral being."

"Yes. He must be." Chastened, I nodded and agreed. I was indeed impressed. But as I privately wiped his saliva from my lapels, I wondered if all the citizens of the New World were as prosy as my host.

Hot as an oven, even in October, New York was nevertheless no paradise on earth. Full of giant ants and enormous buzzing mosquitoes, who bit and stung and sucked our corrupt Limey blood with true republican zeal, we swatted and stamped until we were tired, but in the end we admitted defeat and accepted that there was to be no respite from the attentions of these beasts.

"Seen the bedbugs?" grumbled Fred. "Big as bloody cockroaches. Stinking place."

Indeed, Fred seemed resolved to hate America. Lucinda was interested in and delighted by almost everything she saw, but he complained and moaned all the time, finding fault with our accommodation, our food, our reception, the theatre, the people – especially the people – until Lucinda declared that if he didn't shut up she would throw his false teeth into the Hudson River and he would have to mumble his lines through his crabby old gums.

Our first engagement, playing *School for Scandal* in a little green and gold theatre hardly bigger than a hat box, was not a great success. Or so I first thought. "You'll find Americans a touch phlegmatic, sir," one of our ship's officers had told me, and so they were. For our first three nights the theatre was barely half full and the (entirely male) audience was almost completely silent. We then did *The Taming of the Shrew* for an apparently mystified, equally taciturn and half-empty house.

But then things picked up. It was as if the New Yorkers had given us a test, and we had passed. By the following week we had become so famous that tickets were almost unobtainable, for droves of spectators came to the play, to enjoy our version of a splendid eighteenth-century English comedy, and to see the English actors.

"Ladies out front tonight!" hissed Lucinda, peering through the curtains just before the start of our last performance at the end of our second week. "Seven of them, in the two best boxes."

"Let me see." Feeling much better now she was on dry land, Deb squirmed under Lucinda's arm and looked for herself. "There are four more coming in now," she whispered. "One old woman with three very pretty young ones, all in silks and ribbons and bows."

"Excellent." Fred had joined the party and now he too gave the females a once-over. "I'll play to the one in the mauve tonight," he announced, with a leer. "That one on the right, with udders like a cow."

"Ugh." Digging her heel sharply into his foot, Lucinda flounced off. "He's such a *pig*," I heard her tell Deb, as they stood in the wings waiting to go on. "I don't know why I put up with him, truly I don't, so perhaps one day someone will tell me, for indeed *I* don't know."

We were made welcome in New York. In England we were despised as vagabonds and socially on a par with thieves, harlots and beggars, but in the New World we were showered with praise and presents, we were invited to parties at private houses, we attended public balls and we went to civic fêtes, at one of which was the mayor himself.

"Welcome, welcome," he cried, "thrice welcome, noble sir!" and he shook my hand until my arm almost rattled in its socket, before moving on to Fred and attempting to dislocate his shoulder too. Deb and Lucinda got off lightly, merely having their fingers kissed.

But the double honour of being treated as a lady and a celebrity was lost on Lucinda. "Look over there," she hissed to Deb, as she retrieved her hand from the mayor. "See? My dear, that cap!"

"It's not a cap," whispered Deb, "it's a fried egg."

They giggled so much that the American lady whose headgear they were abusing turned round to stare. "Ladies, please," I muttered. "Lucinda, I'll speak to you later."

"I'm sorry, darling." Lucinda pouted. "But you must admit, it's a horrid cap." She shrugged, then grinned. "Oh, Henry, don't be cross with me, not when Deb's smiling! Isn't it delightful to see Deb smile?"

I had to admit that it was.

Back at the theatre, we found our American colleagues generally enthusiastic, friendly and charming; but they were lackadaisical about rehearsing and on the whole incapable of remembering their lines. They made up the play as they went along, which was unnerving for us until we got used to it.

"Bloody imbeciles," was Fred's universal verdict, but this was unfair as they were generous and well mannered, and would have been excellent company if only one could have discounted their disgusting habit of spitting all over the place. At rehearsals (when they deigned to come), on stage, in the dressing-rooms, in the front-of-house itself it was spit, spit, spit, all day long, and yellow gobbets of tobacco-streaked catarrh lay everywhere.

A phlegmatic nation indeed. And this filthy habit was not confined to players. It was universal. Once, in church, I saw the priest turn aside to spit on the altar steps even in the act of elevating the Host.

Lucinda Tolland was surrounded by new admirers. Prints of her, both garishly coloured and perfectly plain, appeared in all the stationers' shops, and gangs of loungers hung round the stage door each evening, eyeing her up and down as she went in and again when she came out. She was in a fair way to being mobbed and would have been, had not Fred glowered so sourly at any man who came within a yard of her that her devotees kept a respectable distance.

"Feller with a glare like that don' need no bowie knife," observed a fan of Lucinda's sourly, in my hearing. But the rumour was nevertheless put about that Fred went heavily armed. I suppose that salved the Americans' smarting manhoods.

Fred had had no particular desire to visit America, and his sole purpose in coming was to relieve the American theatre-going public of its ready cash. After our initial hiccups we were now managing this very well. Actors are two a penny in England but in the New World we were as welcome as the flowers in May. All the same: "They're nothing but a rabble of bloody tobacco chewers," growled Fred, as he inspected the flecks of dried spittle on his new greatcoat, collected as he'd walked the short distance from our lodgings to the theatre. "Don't you think so, Henry?"

"Yes indeedy, he sho' does," said Lucinda, laughing at him. "His o-pinion is, that these Yankees ain't nothin' but a tarnation mob. An' rowdy with it."

"Let me speak for myself, Lucinda," I said, but I couldn't help smiling. In some ways, certainly, she wasn't so very far from the truth.

I suppose we remained a little standoffish, keeping ourselves to ourselves. Each morning the four of us sat down in my dressing-room to take our eleven o'clock coffee, brought in by a black servant boy belonging to the theatre manager. The child's actual name was Nebuchadnezzar Highpole, but he answered readily to "Here, Nebbo!" In fact, he was like a well-trained dog, and although he was clumsy and haphazard in all things, he made up in enthusiasm what he lacked in savoir faire. Deb was determined that one day she would teach him to wash up the dishes and leave them cleaner than when he began, but I had no high hopes she'd succeed.

That morning, like any other, Nebbo set out grubby cups and grimy saucers, then poured out for us. "Here, Nebbo. Go out and get me a meat pie, there's a good lad." Fred gave the boy a ten-cent piece and a wink. "Hang on a minute, though – anyone else want some grub?"

"No," I said.

"No." Lucinda was busy scoffing her way through a box of chocolate caramels sent in by a fan.

"No, thank you." Deb gave the boy a smile and another dime. "Get a pie for yourself though, hmm?"

"Thank *you*, ma'am." Nebbo took the coin and tossed it high in the air. He grinned enormously, his large white teeth splitting his black face almost in two.

"Why did you give him that?" asked Lucinda, as Nebbo's bare feet flapped off down the passage and out of the theatre.

"Because he reminds me of myself," replied Deb simply.

"Oh yes, he would." Fred grinned. "As an English actress, you've a great deal in common with a black American servant boy."

"Yes, I think I have," rejoined Deb. "And I'd like to do something for him one of these days."

"Before you say it, Fred, shut up." Lucinda pushed the script she'd been looking over aside and yawned. "Well," she announced, "Mr and Mrs Lee have invited me to go to the races with them tomorrow." The Lees were our landlord and his wife, a pair of crooks who smiled charmingly while they fleeced us right and left.

"Is that so?" Fred slurped his coffee. "You hardly know the buggers," he muttered. "Not going, are you?"

"Of course I am." Lucinda shoved her last caramel into her mouth and wiped her sticky lips on Fred's dirty pocket handkerchief. "You're invited too."

"Damned if I'll go." Fred glowered. "Wouldn't trust a Yankee bookie with a five-cent piece."

"I'll go by myself, then." Lucinda looked from Deb to me. "Unless either Mr Collis or Mrs Minot would be so gracious as to join the party?"

"I have a great many letters to write," I said. It was true, I had. The amount of paperwork involved in shifting the four of us about North America was staggering.

"I don't think I can. I must do some shopping." Deb put down her coffee cup. "Nebbo's agreed to come with me and help carry things," she said.

"You watch him," warned Fred. "Half your stuff'll end up in his bloody pockets.

"I don't think so." Deb shrugged. "He's a nice lad. Do you know, he was sent here from some estate in Alabama when he was such a little child. He can't even remember his parents. Isn't that sad?"

"Heartbreaking," replied Fred. "A soft touch, girl – that's what you are."

Lucinda went to the races and lost seventeen dollars. Mrs Lee won twenty and Mr Lee broke even. Fred insisted it had been a put-up job, and that even now Mr Lee was gloating over Lucinda's eight dollars fifty, this being his half share in the sting. "All tarred with the same brush, these bloody Yankees," he muttered as we sat at breakfast the following morning, eating Mrs Lee's hot rolls, hash browns and bacon slices, for which I had no doubt we'd be charged as much as if we'd been feasting upon turtle soup and Beluga caviare. "Nothing but a rabble of thieves, swindlers and rogues."

"Sour-faced misery," retorted Lucinda, who had enjoyed herself despite her losses, for she'd been introduced all around the race course as, our charming guest Miss Lucinda Tolland, the famous Shakespearean actress, lately of Covent Garden and Drury Lane. "Well, I have walked *through* Covent Garden and *down* Drury Lane," she'd told me later, unblushing. Now she glared at Fred. "Swindlers and rogues, forsooth," she muttered crossly. "Being a mere strolling vagabond yourself, I'd question *your* right to give yourself airs."

"Go and eat your bonnet," growled Fred. "God, you're a stupid bitch. You really think – "

"Fred. Lucinda. That's enough." I looked sharply at them both, for I'd just noticed that leaning on the sill of our ground-floor breakfast room window, which was half open that morning, were three young men in top hats and fancy waistcoats. Listening fascinated to every word we said, they were chewing tobacco in a ruminative, peaceful fashion and spitting neatly into the flower bed on which they stood, no doubt crushing Mrs Lee's late geraniums into pulp with their great boots.

"G'mornin', Mr Collis," said one, grinning as he caught my eye.

"An' g'mornin' also to Miss Tolland there," added another, tipping his brim to Lucinda, who smirked graciously in reply. "An' to Mis' Minot and Mr Hammer."

They spat in unison. "Lovely mornin' for a stroll 'cross the Park, Miss Tolland," remarked the first one. "If you was thinkin'' of goin' out, that is?"

As the three of them leered at her, Lucinda smirked even more. Fred's face grew purple. He muttered something so obscene that Lucinda slapped his hand hard. "Don't grind your teeth," she hissed at him, urgently. "They'll break!"

Of course I invited the three men in, to share the remains of our breakfast. By now I'd been in the New World long enough to be only slightly surprised when, without ceremony, they pushed the sash window open wide and climbed right into the room.

Taking off their coats but keeping their hats on, as do all American men, even in the theatre and in hotels, they seated themselves down between us and gobbled heartily, calling for more coffee and bacon and sending Silas, the negro servant, scuttling off to the kitchen to fetch more rolls "an' be quick about it."

Lucinda flirted shamelessly. Deb smiled as brightly as her

usual early morning nausea would allow. Fred fondled his side whiskers and looked gloomy and Byronic.

"You're leavin' us next week, we hear." The man in the brightest waistcoat, his mouth full of bacon and yellow tobacco juice, grinned at me. "Goin' on to Phil'delphia, ain' it?"

"That's right," I agreed.

"To repeat your great triumphs here," said his friend, ogling Lucinda.

"To delight Phil'delphians with your O-phelia," added the third, winking familiarly at Deb.

I could have sworn I heard Fred growl. In fact, I might well have done, for now one of the men turned to him. "Well, Mr Hammer," he said, "that Mac-beth you played last night. Say. What a feller, eh?"

"What?" muttered Fred, coldly.

"A real cool customer," explained the American, laughing. "Wouldn' be anxious to meet the likes of him on the trail, no sir. Stick you through soon as look at you, I guess." Our guest cleared his throat noisily, then spat neatly on to the rush matting. "Couldn't control his other half though, could he?" he ruminated. "That Lady Mac-beth. A she-wolf, sir! I tell you, a she-wolf."

This lucid critique of Fred's interpretation of the role made Lucinda and Deb giggle and Fred glare. For once in his life he seemed at a loss for words. But then he turned away in disdain and muttered to Deb that he'd make sure we kept the bloody windows shut in future.

We left New York at the end of November, going on to Philadelphia for six weeks. For Deb, the journey was very arduous, for she was seasick in the calmest waters and the choking fumes of the coal stoves used in both railway carriages and steamboat saloons made her heave.

"How is she?" I asked Lucinda as we sat aboard a steamboat on the Delaware River, nearing the end of a thoroughly tiresome six-hour journey by train, coach and ferry. "Is she still unwell?"

"She's lying down in the ladies' cabin. I've given the stewardess a couple of dollars to keep the other women away." Lucinda looked out over the choppy grey-green wavelets. "Poor Deb, she's no traveller, is she?"

"It would seem not," I agreed. Dejectedly, I shrugged. "Maybe we should have left her in New York."

"Oh, don't worry, Henry. She'll be fine once we land." Lucinda smiled encouragingly at me. "She's happiest with you. With us, I mean."

I wondered. The travelling was proving particularly trying for Deb. Cooped up in overheated, overcrowded steamboat cabins or railway carriages, she often fainted and one of us had to keep an eye on her all the time. Our winter engagements would take us to Philadelphia, then to Baltimore, then Washington, by stagecoach, train and river boat. I felt wicked to be putting the poor girl through such torture.

But she wanted to come with us. "Stay in Philadelphia," I urged her, as we made our arrangements to go south. "Stay here, with Mrs Farrier." For in smart, well-to-do Philadelphia we had hit on excellent lodgings and I knew Deb would be properly cared for there.

"I'd like to go with you. That's what I came here for, to see a foreign land." Weakly, Deb smiled at me. "Or were you thinking of cutting my parts? Maybe having an American play them?"

"I wasn't considering any such thing," I replied testily, for I had in fact been wondering about just that. "Where would we get another Ophelia like yours, another Juliet of your calibre?"

"Then I'll come to Baltimore," she said. "And after that, we'll see."

So she sat green-faced on the decks of river boats, she endured the total lack of privacy on these vessels and she forced herself to eat the disgusting slop on which the passengers were fed.

"Of course I'm going on," she insisted, as she sat in the dressing-room on our first night in Baltimore, as white as her gown.

I watched from the wings. I saw her give the audience their money's worth and more. Her delightful, child-like Juliet touched their hearts, making them smile. And later on in the play the pathos of her situation and the halting terror in her voice as she finally took her own life, moved the spectators to actual groans of pity. Ladies in the front rows were in tears.

"Not bad. Not bad at all. But with a face like a wet week, it's a good job she doesn't fancy herself in comedy any more." Watching from the wings as Deb's American Romeo led his Juliet to the centre of the stage to receive ecstatic applause, Fred clapped too.

"She'll be a great tragedienne one day," said Lucinda sombrely. "People will talk about our little Deb in the same breath as they mention Mrs Siddons. You'll see."

Chapter 18

As I have already remarked, Fred seemed resolved to hate everything about America. As for Lucinda, she was only slightly more impressed by the New World, this land of natural justice and universal liberty, this home of the free.

But whereas for years afterwards Fred habitually referred to the United States as "that bloody place", Lucinda, a little more tolerant, laughed good-naturedly at everything and everyone American. More tactful and less aggressive than her lover, she made friends with almost everybody we met. Her sprightly demeanour and pretty face naturally ensured her popularity with the gentlemen, and her gossipy curiosity ensured that she met American women rather more than halfway. All in all, they took to her mightily.

"To think I always heard tell you English was mean as hound dogs and prouder than real Indian braves," remarked one matron, matriarch of a theatre-mad family who had attended all our performances in Baltimore (a town which, in my opinion anyway, had been modelled faithfully on Manchester, right down to the dirty, dingy warehouses, the redbrick terraced houses and the filthy canals). "And to think I believed all them wicked, wicked lies."

This lady, a pillar of Baltimore society, had come back stage to meet us. She smiled in adoration at Lucinda, who smirked and preened in reply, and who, as the result of one particularly fulsome compliment, promptly invited the matron and all her family to dinner with us the next day. I suspect this was partly because Lucinda rather liked the look of the matron's eldest son, a handsome boy of twenty-five. On the other hand, it may have been wholly to annoy Fred.

No matter. The matron was absolutely delighted. "Why, thank you, Miss Tolland," she exclaimed, adding complacently, "I told that there Mrs Perkins over Woodside Heights as she shouldn't judge folks before she knows what she's at. She reckoned to me that British people were stuck up entirely. But I guess *you* English folks are as sociable as glory be."

She couldn't see Fred, glowering behind her.

In the coach from Baltimore to Washington, Lucinda struck up an acquaintance with the Jefferson Delaneys, a family of Washingtonians who evidently thought she was God's gift. On our arrival in the capital, nothing was too much trouble for these kind people, who escorted us to the best hotel, harangued the manager into giving us the best rooms and impressed on him that we were to be provided with every luxury; "These folks here bein' world-famous English actors, an' used to elegant living. They ain't no poor white trash."

"No, *sir*," agreed the manager. Collaring a servant lad, he motioned to us to be seated on the two great horsehair sofas which adorned the foyer. He walked from behind his reception desk and, folding his hands together, he bowed. "Ladies. Gentlemen. If you'll kindly follow me, I'll show you to your rooms. Simeon will bring your boxes up directly."

"There, sir." As I rose to my feet, Mr Jefferson Delaney touched my sleeve. "You won't have no trouble here, I guess." He leaned closer. "Pardon me for axin'," he murmured, "but Mrs Jefferson Delaney wants most partic'lar to know. Does that fierce-lookin' feller you're with dye his hair?"

"Excuse me?" I asked, wondering if I'd heard him aright, for it was a most singular question, you'll agree. "I'm sorry, Mr Delaney, but I thought you said – "

"That's right. I asked if that Mr Hammer there dyed his hair."

I assured him that Fred's raven curls were untouched by artifice. Turning to his wife, he whispered my report.

"Ah thought not," she said. She sighed. "My, but that Mr Hammer's one mighty fine-looking man."

I don't know how I kept a straight face.

"Mrs Delaney is calling for me this morning," announced Lucinda a day or two later, as she gobbled her breakfast of bacon and hominy grits with her customary relish, and urged the rest of us to gobble up ours. "We're going to see the savages."

"Savages?" demanded Fred. "What savages? Wild beasts, you mean? Lions? Tigers? Wolves?"

"Silly man." Affectionately Lucinda grinned at him. "I meant native Americans, of course," she said. "Red men."

"In war-paint and beads?" demanded Fred.

"I *do* hope so!" Lucinda blushed, and giggled.

"I'm sure you do." Fred sniffed. "Just your sort of caper, gawping at red men in war-paint, beads – and little else beside."

Lucinda giggled again, and blushed pinker.

"I'll come with you," declared Fred. Wiping his mouth on the back of his hand, he stood up. "I'm curious to see these buggers myself."

"Oh, they won't interest you, dear." Now Lucinda frowned. "Look, you stay here and relax. Or go to the theatre. Didn't you want to knock his lines into Mr Beaton?" For Mr Beaton, a New World Duncan to Fred's very British Macbeth, was more than usually inventive even for an American actor, making up his lines as he went along and also improvising so copiously in blank verse that Fred had to kick him to shut him up. "Fred, you know you meant – "

"Is that the Jefferson Delaney bitch coming in now?" interrupted Fred.

"Yes. But, darling, she's brought her own carriage, so there's no need for you to escort us."

"I'll come with you," repeated Fred. "Unless you've any reasonable objection, that is?"

"No, but I just thought – "

"You never think, Luce. That's why I'm coming too. To prevent you – "

"Oh really, Fred!" Now Lucinda became angry. "You make me out to be such a fool!" she cried. "Sometimes I wonder if you honestly – "

"Stop nattering and get your bonnet. Your friend's waiting."

So off they went, bickering.

Deb had stayed in bed late, so halfway through the morning I took a break from my everlasting correspondence and went up to see her. To my delight and surprise I found her sitting up in bed and chatting with our landlady, an affable woman whose efficient black servants left her little to do but gossip all day.

"Good morning, Mr Collis," said Deb brightly. She had a tray on her lap and was spreading a new roll with strawberry jam. Furthermore, she looked as if she meant to enjoy eating it.

"Good morning, Deb." In spite of myself, I beamed foolishly back at her. I sat down on the rocking chair at the foot of the bed. "Well?" I asked, in my unctuous uncle's voice. "And how are we today?"

"We're feeling just *fine*," replied Mrs Hallam, refilling Deb's coffee cup. "Much better'n we did, anyways." Maternally, she smiled at Deb. "Mis' Minot's been telling me all 'bout the past few weeks. Seems she ain't a good traveller?"

"I'm not so bad as I was." Deb munched her roll. "And do you know, the sickness I've been having seems quite gone today. I feel hungry for the first time in months."

"That's excellent." Grinning like a pedlar's performing monkey, I looked from Deb to her chaperone. "Might you ladies feel like taking a walk later today?"

Mrs Hallam leaned back in her chair and yawned. "I'm sorry, Mr Collis," she drawled, "but I'm that tarnation busy, I guess I just shan't be able."

"But *I* shall. Give me an hour." Deb smiled back at me, and I saw that today there were roses in her cheeks. "Where's Lucinda?"

"She's just stepped out for an hour," I replied. "I'm sure she'll be back soon. So, if you get dressed?"

But Deb had to make do with me as a walking companion, for Lucinda and Fred stayed out until midday. They returned from their visit to the savages much subdued, although for rather different reasons.

Along with a dozen other gawpers, the red men, and their keeper, they'd spent the morning cooped up in a small room ten feet by twelve. They had gone to learn and marvel and be entertained, but it turned out they had not enjoyed themselves at all.

Red Eagle, the eldest savage, had been the greatest disappointment. Wearing a European suit of clothes, his hair cut close and his face completely innocent of paint, ornamental scars or marks of any kind, he had sat there silent, chewing tobacco and spitting; for all the world like a true son of the new republic, and no more interesting than any of those.

His son Black Elk had been all huddled up in a tartan blanket, visible only from the chin up. He was evidently in a deep sulk, or at best unwilling to enter into conversation, for he sat as silent as his father, chewing and spitting and chewing again. When his keeper had asked him a question in his native tongue, he had scowled and glared, but made no reply.

As for the third red man: well, he had indeed been tricked out in war-paint and beads and worn nothing but some sort of leather apron. His hair had been long, black and glossy, plaited in braids and ornamented with feathers. His skin was oiled, his face was hook-nosed and handsome, his figure was splendid – all in all, he was the sort of fine young fellow the gawpers had hoped to see. But, "Running Buffalo was literally *sitting* on the stove," complained Lucinda. "Honestly, Henry, the place was so close I could hardly breathe."

"Poor devil." Fred sat down and turned to me. "Poor bloody creatures. Henry, you should have seen them. They were like wild animals in a pen. That Running Buffalo fellow would've stuck a tomahawk in my head soon as look at me, given half a chance."

"He did look rather fierce," agreed Lucinda.

"Yes indeed." Fred glowered at her. "Don't think I couldn't see he was giving you a little *frisson*, in spite of the fact that he stank like a tomcat."

"I'm surprised you noticed anything I was doing," retorted Lucinda. "Especially since you were standing there preening yourself and making sheep's eyes at Mrs Delaney."

"She was ogling *me*. When she wasn't making faces at the naked savage." Fred snorted in derision. "Ugly fat sow she is."

"Oh really, Fred!"

"Don't you 'oh really, Fred' me." Fred pushed back his chair and got up. "Bloody country," he muttered. "Land of the free! Balls to that!" He glared from Lucinda to me, scowling at us as if it were all our fault. "Oh yes," he went on sourly, "it's the land of liberty all right. Provided you're a European and can gob a yard's length towards the nearest spittoon. And miss."

"Deb's very much better this morning," I interrupted firmly, determined to steer Fred away from yet another diatribe on the shortcomings of God's own people. "Just after you'd gone she got up, so I took her out for an hour. She's in the dining-room now, gossiping with Mrs Hallam."

"How's she looking?" asked Lucinda.

"Very well. She has some colour in her cheeks and her eyes are bright."

"Fever," diagnosed Fred lugubriously.

"No. She's quite well." Hearing a step in the passage I went to open the door. "Here she is. See for yourselves."

Lucinda and Fred had to agree that Deb did look much, much brighter. The dismal months of constant nausea and wretched depression of spirit seemed to have been succeeded all of a sudden by a calm sense of well-being, and a new curiosity about everything around her. I felt that in spite of all her difficulties, everything would now be well.

Deb disliked Washington. We all did. It was a town in limbo, half-built, its smart new civic monuments interspersed with untidy brickfields and waste land, on which the town's only too well aware that if Fred took it on, he'd play it as most provincial strollers did, turning this essentially tragic role into a piece of low comedy, and throwing Lucinda's noble, eloquent Portia into fits of giggles. Which, of course, destroyed the whole thing.

We agreed that Deb should continue to play two or three times a week, until a bulging, pregnant Juliet or an *enceinte* Cordelia was no longer feasible. Then she should rest up and prepare for the child.

For the remainder of that winter and into the spring, we alternated between the elegant neoclassical Chestnut Street Theatre in Philadelphia and Park Theatre in New York. Both of these theatres were licensed by fashion and patronised by ladies, but yes, in both of them the male citizens of the free republic behaved like swine, coughing and choking and spitting and smoking and eating their way through the performances, keeping their stove-pipe hats clamped firmly on their heads and hanging their feet over the seats in front, if there were space.

As in all public places in America, men and women were stricly segregated. In the theatres the ladies did not mix with the gentlemen, but sat primly in their own private boxes, getting on with their embroidery and talking among themselves.

We were offered more engagements than we could take, and we did so well that even Fred was pleased. He enjoyed counting his money even more than he enjoyed criticising America, and that winter he had plenty of cash with which to salve his finer feelings, constantly outraged though they were.

In February we left Deb in Philadelphia with a particular friend of Mrs Delaney, the lady who had taken Lucinda to see the savages; and who, it transpired, had written to her Yankee friends to tell them all about Fred. We spent the early spring in New York, and here – thanks, maybe, to Mrs Delaney – we saw Fred become something of a dark, brooding hero among susceptible females. In the character of Macbeth he featured in innumerable coloured prints, sequinned cut-out models and finely executed lithographs, which seemed to be on sale everywhere.

Hanging drooling over the edges of their boxes, ladies fainted when he performed. "Who's getting *frissons* now?" demanded Lucinda enviously, after a particularly ecstatic reception one evening, during which Fred had been almost knocked flat on his back by the enormous bunch of flowers hurled on to the stage from a jam-packed ladies' box. "Who's too big for his bonnets tonight?"

"Can't help it if they dote on me, silly bitches." Smugly, Fred grinned at her. "Face up to it, Luce – some of us 'as that star quality and some of us 'asn't."

"Horse shit," retorted Lucinda eloquently, kicking him hard in the shins and stamping off to sulk in the green room for the rest of the night.

And my Hamlet? Well, I'd been obliged to replace my ideal Ophelia with an American girl, whose Boston snuffle grated horribly but who no doubt sounded as Danish as I did, and I was expecting lukewarm notices at best. So I was surprised and delighted when the New York *Evening Post* hailed Mr Collis and Miss Wyatt (the Boston snuffler) as the great triumph of the spring season.

Chapter 19

What do they *do* with hot water and lengths of string? We – that is, Fred, Lucinda and myself – arrived at Mrs Delaney's friend's house one fine bright Sunday morning in April just as a servant girl went dashing upstairs with a pitcher of hot water, closely followed by another girl with a second pitcher and a pocketful of twine.

The place was in an uproar. Female voices shouted orders and black servants cowered and hid. Lucinda was already taking off her bonnet and shawl and rolling up her sleeves. "Well, it's not as if we weren't expecting it," she said calmly, as footsteps scurried overhead and an agitated female voice shouted orders to what sounded like a regiment of minions thundering about upstairs.

"I think I'll go and walk around the Park," I said, unwilling to remain within earshot of any screams of pain.

"I'll come with you," said Fred, snatching up his hat and jamming it firmly on his head. "Nothing for us to do here, eh?"

"Men. Babies themselves, that's all *men* are." Sweetly, Lucinda smiled at the pair of us. "Well, I'll just pop up and see if I can be of any help," she said.

"You, Luce? What do you know?" asked Fred.

"My mother had thirteen." Lucinda pushed her hair back from her face and began securing it tightly with pins. "I delivered at least four of them myself."

So Deb's baby first saw the light of day in Philadelphia, a Quaker town and the elegant capital of the free state of Pennsylvania. Philadephia's fresh, clean air, green open spaces and pure white marble public buildings, the beauty of which I have never seen surpassed, made it a great favourite with us all (except, of course, with Fred) and I was glad that since Deb's pretty springtime baby had been born a citizen of the United States, she was also a native of what was undoubtedly the fairest city in the Union.

As it happened, I need not have been so squeamish about hearing Deb cry out, as, according to Lucinda, the birth was an easy one, and the following day the young mother was well enough to receive visitors.

"Mr Collis," cried Deb, beaming at me as I went sheepishly into the bedroom, "how kind of you to come!" She was wrapped in a white poplin dressing-gown and she looked so lovely I couldn't help but smile like a half-wit offered a barley sugar twist.

"Good morning, Deb." I wanted to take her in my arms. I wanted to kiss her and hug her until she begged for mercy. But instead I sat down on the bedside chair and, since I had to do something, I looked at the child.

She looked back at me. Channing Minot's light blue eyes stared solemnly into mine, and I felt a distinct stab of unease which wiped the inane grin right off my face.

For the child was so like him. Black-haired, blue-eyed, she had his heart-shaped face, his arched eyebrows, his damn-you expression. No, I thought then, I'm being fanciful here. How can a day-old baby look like anything but a baby? But now Deb seemed to catch my mood, and she too looked anxiously at the child. And *her* face seemed to ask, is my daughter an enemy too?

Enough of that. "What a beautiful little girl," I said heartily. "An absolute charmer." To my relief Deb's face brightened. "Has she a name?" I asked.

"I thought of Caroline. Or maybe Adelaide." Deb took one of the child's small hands in her own. "Look at her little pink nails," she said, wonderingly. "Like tiny sea shells. Perfect, each one. Mr Collis, do you think Adelaide suits her?"

"It's excellent." Seeing the child flail her other hand about, I let her grasp my finger and was surprised at the strength of this newborn's grip. "Well then, shall it be Adelaide?"

settlers are portrayed as evil aggressors and the red men as virtuous savages. The part of the Indian chieftain would be perfect for Fred. Mr Collis, I think you have what Mr Rayner used to call a slayer here."

So it turned out to be. We played *Powahatac's Bride: or, the Red Man Betray'd*, by Zachary B. Lawless, to packed houses. Fred was excellent as the tormented Indian chief, Lucinda had them all crying their eyes out as his unfortunate wife, and I enjoyed myself hugely playing the villainous Yankee fur trapper who betrays the Indians – who have befriended him and saved his life – to the army in exchange for gold. I was hissed and execrated night after night after night.

"Beast! Murderer!" At each entrance, I was reviled and cursed to high heaven. "Hope you die like a dog in a ditch!" I've never had a more gratifying reception, before or since. I never knew I could be so convincingly wicked.

I was amazed by the play's astonishing success, and can only assume that the image of the noble savage, valiant in defeat, touched something deep in the Americans' souls. Of course, on a workaday basis, they continued to enslave and deport and murder and rob the native Americans on the grandest scale.

We had hoped to have Deb back at work by June, but it was not to be. She simply did not have the stamina to go back on the stage night after night, so I was obliged to retain the services of the Boston snuffler until her affected, overacted Ophelia had almost driven me to distraction.

But then, at the very tag end of the season, Deb travelled back to New York and declared she would appear twice a week, if I wished her to, once as Juliet, and once as Cordelia. She would not do Ophelia, she said. She did not wish to tread on the snuffler's toes.

I doubted if Deb was properly fit for work, but she insisted she was better, so I had bills printed. On her first night back I was as impressed as the audience. Her tribulations seemed to have given her a new maturity, a new depth of understanding, and she gave New Yorkers the most moving Juliet the critic of the New York *Evening Post* said he ever hoped to experience.

Ladies usually find the play affecting, but grown men wept openly as this Juliet died. At the end of the evening, the house rose as one man, stamping and shouting and cheering (American audiences do not often clap their hands) until the building shook on its foundations.

The theatres closed for the summer break, but now we had invitation after invitation to do concert parties, recitals and entertainments, so we were busier than ever. September came and I realised we had been away from England a whole year. I thought it was time to go home.

Our passages were booked and our farewells made when Deb remarked it was a pity to have been in America so long and have seen so little of the country. "Being laid up so much," she sighed, "I've done and seen nothing. What a waste."

"Maybe we'll return," I said.

"You'll be fools if you do," growled Fred, predictably enough.

"Take no notice of him," said Lucinda. "I'd like to come back here some day."

"We could stay a little longer, perhaps?" I suggested. "Do a month or so of the new season? The management of the Park would be delighted to have us, so if we wanted to take on a few more engagements, we could."

"God, no." Fred snorted. "Get out while the going's good, that's what I say."

"Lucinda?" I asked. "What do you think?"

"I don't know." Lucinda frowned. "I've come to like America. But on the other hand, I do miss England."

We left that discussion hanging in the air, but then, two days later, the manager of the Park called at my lodgings to ask me if I'd consider making some guest appearances with the regular company there. The financial rewards would be substantial.

I accepted his proposal. I agreed to take part in six performances over the next three weeks. Deb and I postponed our departure for a month.

A few days after my first performance, Deb and I were

walking down Broadway, the Oxford Street of New York, idly killing time. We were looking in shop windows and trying to keep out of the way of homicidal omnibuses, hell bent on running over anyone who stepped in their way. We turned away from a display of fabrics in a shop window and as we did so Deb suddenly clutched my arm. "There's a man watching me," she said.

"Where?" I glanced round. "What man?"

"The one over by the column. I saw his reflection in the shop window." Deb sounded terrified. "Do you see him now? He's a black man, but not an ordinary negro."

I looked, and saw a nondescript black man in servant's clothes lounging against a wall. He appeared to be half-dozing in the sun. "He's probably waiting for his master," I said. "Come now, Deb. He's just a servant wasting time."

"I'm sure he's not," she insisted.

"Well, who is he then?" I was disposed to humour her today.

"I don't know. But I feel he doesn't belong here. And I know he was watching me."

"Well, maybe he was. You're worth looking at, after all. Perhaps he saw you on stage?" For although in this land of liberty negroes were not admitted to the main body of the theatre, servants and coachmen could be stuffed into a segregated gallery to yawn away the play and drop nutshells on their supposed betters below.

"Perhaps." Deb shrugged. "But he's not – "

"An ordinary black man? Of course he's not." I smiled at her. "My dear, in New York we've seen human beings of all the shapes, colours and sizes God ever put on the earth. Black, white, yellow and all the shades and hues in between. An 'ordinary black man' would be very difficult to find. In fact, I doubt if there's any such creature."

"He's looking at me again," was her reply.

So we walked quickly on. Distressed, Deb clung to my arm and stumbled blindly, at one point cannoning into a pair of great fat hogs which were ambling along perfectly peaceably amid the well-dressed human strollers. I looked at her face and saw how pale she was – in the bright sunlight her complexion was almost transparent. "Perhaps he was staring at you," I agreed. "But in this free country, a man is allowed to look at a woman, you know."

"I know." Deb shrugged. "You think I'm very foolish."

"You've been ill," I said. "When you get all your strength back, you won't have these sick fancies any more."

Chapter 20

Artistically, financially, and in every other way too, our tour of North America had been a great success. I'd been afraid that Fred's disgust with the Americans and all their works might finally boil over and lead to a public explosion which would get us all lynched. But he managed to control himself and eventually learned to confine his expressions of disgust to his intimate circle. Much to my relief.

On October the third, Lucinda and Fred were due to sail, or rather steam away, taking their loot with them. Although Lucinda had begged and besought and even offered to give up flirting with other men for as long as she lived, Fred had refused to make a visit to Niagara Falls, insisting that he wasn't going to stay a day longer than he had to in the New World. But as for Deb and I – well, we would see the Falls, and some of New England too.

I had decided she wasn't really fit enough to travel by sea, and that she would benefit from a really good, long holiday. I'd been diffident about suggesting myself as a sole travelling companion, however, so I'd practically gone down on my bended knees and begged Lucinda to reconsider her decision to depart.

"Couldn't you stay a month longer?" I'd pleaded. "Send Fred home, certainly; but go on a later passage yourself?"

"I don't think that's possible. The old bear would fret himself into a decline away from me." Lucinda had laughed. "I'm not sure I could do without him, either."

"No. I suppose you couldn't, really." The depth of Lucinda's affection for Fred never ceased to impress me, and I often wondered if a more devoted woman ever lived.

"Do you think Deb would *want* just my company?" I asked. "Would it suit her to be alone with me, I mean?"

"I think maybe it would." Lucinda took my hands in hers and held them. "Poor Henry," she added, smiling. "Sometimes, you're such a silly man."

"What's that supposed to mean?" I demanded, annoyed.

"Nothing." Lucinda shrugged. "My dear, I'd stay with you, you know I would, but Fred – "

"Yes. And it might be as well to get him away while the going's good."

"Exactly." Lucinda nodded in agreement. "Well then. We'll see you in London, shall we? Next spring?"

"I hope so."

"So do I." Lucinda leaned forward and kissed me on the cheek. "She needs someone like you," she whispered. "So speak up for yourself, won't you? When you get the chance, that is."

And then Fred entered the sitting-room, and she had no opportunity to say any more.

That October I had more ready cash available than I've ever had, before or since. I had money from my own benefits, I had my share of the takings and as manager of the group I'd drawn a salary higher than any I'd ever been able to justify before. I'd bought myself some decent suits of clothes, so I looked more like a gentleman than a vagabond. It was just as well I was so rich. All American inns overcharge Englishmen on principle, and in my fine broadcloth coats and smart top hats I suppose I appeared better off than I was, egging them on to even further extortion.

Since Deb turned out to be very much in favour of a little sightseeing and disposed to accept me as a companion on her travels, we went to Boston for the autumn. We enjoyed the crisp, clear air of New England, and the red and gold scenery both refreshed and exhilarated us. But I had heard that winters this far north were exceptionally severe, and I doubted if the child would prosper cooped up next to a stove until spring, so I looked at the map of the country, marking the extent of railroads, steamboat routes and European settlement.

Virginia. Carolina. Georgia. The very names sounded warm and welcoming. We would go south, I decided, to these warmer states of the union. We'd escape the fierce northern winter, we'd put the roses back into Deb's cheeks and make Adelaide bloom like a little peach.

As we sat near the stove in the sitting-room of our Boston lodgings, I took the child on my lap and told her mother my intentions. "We'll travel slowly, at a pace to suit you," I assured her. "We'll have a private coach – "

"What they call an exclusive extra?" she put in, with a smile.

"Yes." I loved to see her smile. "We'll need to use steamboats sometimes. But now you've had the baby, you'll probably be a much better sailor."

"I doubt it." Ruefully, Deb shook her head. "But I'd like to see the country, so of course we'll do what you suggest."

"You must have some new clothes, then," I told her. "Lighter things – cottons, silk. Listen, you go to one of the stores here and buy the material. Have it made up into whatever you need."

"Yes." She bit her lip then. "I'll have to see what I can afford," she began. "I must try to save."

"I'll pay," I cut in. "I'll buy your clothes, and our travel expenses will be mine."

"I see." She twisted the chain she wore round her neck, the tarnished gilt chain from which hung the green glass ornament that was now an essential part of her costume as Juliet. Sometimes, she wore it with ordinary clothes. The baby liked to suck it and play with it, and I was afraid she might cut her soft mouth on the glass – but I supposed her mother had thought of that. And just now Adelaide began to whimper and fidget. "I think she's hungry," said Deb.

"She must be." I handed the child back to her mother, and got up from my chair.

"You don't have to go." Quickly unbuttoning her gown,

Deb put the baby to her breast before I'd had a chance to leave her.

"I'm sure you'd rather be private," I said, looking away.

"Yes. But I don't mind you being here." Again Deb smiled at me. "Go on with what you were telling me about your plans for us."

So I sat down again and while Deb fed her baby, I sketched out a possible itinerary for us all, using the railroads, river routes and the public stage-coach connections with both. I was well aware that even on fresh water Deb was a bad sailor, but as the country had been opened up and was now largely colonised along the banks of the great rivers, it was almost impossible to get anywhere without using the paddle steamers which plied these wide waterways of the new world.

As I talked, my gaze was drawn again and again to the child, and I watched fascinated as the baby took her milk, as her little hand caressed her mother's breast, as she closed her eyes in bliss. I decided then that there can be no sweeter sight than a mother nursing her infant, and I felt such tenderness for both of them, and such an overpowering need for Deb, that I ached.

But as for Deb, I doubt if it so much as crossed her mind that it might be improper to nurse her child in front of me. I suppose being in the company was to blame for that. After all, most actresses tend to scurry around back stage in varying degrees of undress, and an actor is usually so busy himself that he hardly registers the naked legs, bare breasts and more as they dash by. I had seen Lucinda half-naked scores of times, and felt hardly a passing interest in *her* (very considerable) charms.

I wondered what Deb thought of me. If she thought of me at all. I supposed she saw me as a father figure. As a replacement for Charlie Rayner. Well, in her eyes I was probably nearly as old, and only slightly better looking.

"What's the matter?" she asked, as I let out an involuntary sigh.

"It's raining again," I said. "We can't go out today."

While in New York I had mentioned to a businessman,

whom I had met at a private party, that I should like to see something of the southern states one day. He had responded by issuing an open invitation to look up his family in Georgia, should I ever visit the south.

From Boston I wrote to him, reminding him of our acquaintance, telling him my plans and asking his advice on hotels, routes and sights to be seen. He replied with much good advice – and an offer of hospitality. "I have been in contact with my cousins," wrote Mr Perry, "and I find that the idea of having you and Mrs Minot as house guests is very gratifying to them. I'm enclosing timetables and other information which you'll need to plan your journey. Now, if you yourself would get in touch with Mr James Macgregor – "

So we were to go and stay with the Macgregors, a family of rice planters in southern Georgia. I booked passages. To anyone who asked, I said that Deb was my near relation by marriage, a young widow taking a recuperative holiday to get over her recent loss.

We set out in late October, and in due course we reached Richmond, Virginia, where I had my first experiences of southern hospitality, southern friendliness – and of being constantly among slaves. Since arriving in North America, I'd met dozens of coloured people, both bond and free. Some had seemed cheerful, some wretched; I had come across apparently contented slaves and perfectly miserable freemen; so, while the whole institution of slavery is repugnant to me, I must admit that in these southern states I hoped to see well-ordered plantations on which I'd find smiling black labourers and charming dusky children, all working together under a benevolent southern sun. In Virginia, however, the slaves looked mostly wretched. It didn't bode well for my hopes.

Our journey south was to be made by railroad and river boat. We decided to go more or less directly to the Macgregors' estate, to stay there until we tired of them or they tired of us (we had an open invitation to stay as long as we wished) and then to travel slowly back north, stopping as we pleased on the way.

So that is what we did. We took trains, steamboats and, on those many occasions where the railroad came to an abrupt end and the river-boat connection was still some miles distant, exclusive extras.

These often turned out to be mere covered carts, driven through cypress swamps by emaciated, fever-shaken settlers. Or, worse still, superannuated stage-coaches rattled over primitive stony tracks and corduroy roads – routes through marshland, made up of tree-trunks laid side by side as railroad sleepers are, thus ensuring a hideously gut-churning, spine-dislocating ride – by over-enthusiastic negroes, whose skills with the reins left much to be desired.

But Deb did not complain. In fact, despite the overall discomfort she suffered and the unremitting attentions of the ubiquitous biting insects which I now realised must infest the whole wretched continent, she seemed to be enjoying herself. It was I who had the misgivings and doubts, I who thought it would be a miracle if we reached the Macgregors' plantation sound in body and mind. And Adelaide? Oh, the baby simply slept through everything.

On the river boats Deb was far less sick than she had been while she was pregnant, but she was so troubled by mosquitoes, which raised great red bumps on her arms, face and neck, that she and Addy frequently took to the stifling ladies' cabin and left me to promenade the decks by myself.

I was lonely then, but not alone – one could never be alone on an American river boat. Everything tends to close society, and I could not pause to look into the murky water without a fellow passenger coming up to stand beside me, spit noisily into the water, and demand to know where I was headed.

Thanks to the universal habit of expectoration, the men's cabins and saloons were perfect piggeries which I avoided as much as I could. This was no hardship, for I found neither the company nor the conversation to my taste. Seated in the ubiquitous rocking chairs, my shipmates rocked to and fro, hawking and spitting and chewing tobacco, and judiciously criticising the governments of both the new and the old worlds.

As an ignorant Limey playactor (as opposed to an enlightened American moral being) I found I was not expected to join in the discussions, but to listen and be improved. I learned a great deal. To my horror I discovered that back in London, England, the Queen could summon a subject to Windsor Castle and have his head cut off "any durn time she pleased". Furthermore, when the Queen rode out in her golden coach, with her diamond crown set upon her head, any subject who failed to kneel as she passed by would be taken to a convenient post and publicly flogged.

On retiring, the gentlemen took themselves off to sleeping cabins and stretched themselves out on narrow shelf-like bunks, taking a last good long spit before turning over and going to sleep. I put off going to bed as long as I could, and generally slept late in the mornings.

"The mosquitoes don't bother you, do they?" Deb asked ruefully, as we sat together on the main passenger deck one evening, in the cooler twilight air. One of the lady passengers had lent her a protective muslin shawl, and she kept this close about her. "They don't bite you at all."

"No, they don't." Now I swatted a pair of the beastly buzzing things, bringing their courtship to an abrupt conclusion. "Perhaps you ought to go back inside."

"I'll stay up a little longer. It's so close in the cabin." She smiled at me then, and as usual my heart turned over. Then she touched my sleeve. "Oh, just look over there," she whispered. "A heron! Isn't he beautiful?"

"He's magnificent." But I wasn't interested in herons or anything else while Deb was by my side. And now, as the other passengers started to drift towards their sleeping quarters and the light began to fade into wonderful purples and scarlets and golds, I thought I might speak seriously to her about her future. As Addy's godfather, I had some legitimate interest in the welfare of her child; but more than that, I wanted to know how things stood between the two of us. If, on her return to England, she meant to go back to her husband, or if perhaps –

"Deb," I began, "I've been meaning to ask if you – "

"And look at that!" Something else had caught her eye now, and, glancing across the boat I saw a great river alligator this time, swimming idly in the slip stream with a full complement of parasitical sparrows, or something of the sort, riding sedately on his back. Watching the evil-looking brute, Deb clapped her hands. "Isn't he splendid?" she demanded.

"Yes." I laughed. "Two or three very fine travelling cases there."

"Mr Collis!" Deb frowned in reproach. "How could you think such a thing, when he looks so happy here?" She gazed around her, at the swampy river and the encroaching banks, and she sighed. "Isn't this lovely?" she murmured. "So wild. As the world was meant to be."

The final stage of our journey was by paddle boat down the swampy Altamaha River. From the decks of the boat I watched alligators slither and slime into the murky water, I saw jungle creatures with great fangs slinking away into the forest, and I gazed as brilliantly coloured birds rose up and whirred away into the tangled undergrowth, above which towered dismal swamp cypresses, growing thickly right down to the water's edge.

Every so often there was a clearing, on which was a landing stage and maybe a cabin, already rotting and sliding back into the soupy water.

Eventually we reached Balthazar Island. This was a town built on a sandbank, into which it was slowly sinking. The captain of the steamboat told me that the river floods at least twice yearly and when the waters recede it's found a little more of the land has disappeared, that the houses seem a little lower on their foundations, and that where a man once had an orange grove he now had a paddy field.

It was altogether a wretched place. I had expected bright sunshine but there was only haze, the heat hanging in a sticky, vaporous curtain over everything. I had hoped for health-giving sea breezes, but the air was full of the smell of sweet rottenness. I leaned on the rail of the boat and looked into the green water. Adelaide in her arms, Deb stood by my side. Together we watched the landing stages come into view.

Suddenly Deb caught my arm. "Look," she cried, "over there! It's a dear little church, with a tiny wooden spire. Isn't it pretty?"

Pretty? Even from the boat I could see the little white-washed church was leaning crazily, ready to topple into the swamp upon which it was built. The whole area was decaying, sliding slowly into the great river.

I began to doubt the wisdom of this trip.

We left the steamboat without much regret, and stood like two forlorn ducklings on Balthazar Island quayside, waiting to be met by our hosts.

There was not a soul in sight.

In his letter, Mr Macgregor had told me that each paddle steamer arriving that week would be met. But as the minutes ticked by, as a quarter of an hour became a half, then a full sixty minutes, as the afternoon became warmer and Addy grew ever more fractious, I began to be afraid that this whole journey had been a wild goose chase. That no respectable Southern gentleman would have dreamed of inviting a pair of strolling vagabonds to be guests in his plantation house.

We were victims of an elaborate practical joke.

Leaving Deb sitting in the shade with the baby and the luggage, I walked round one of the rotting sheds which embellished the quay, and eventually I discovered a living being. Lounging against a capstan, spitting vacantly into the scummy water and whittling a piece of wood with a rusty bowie knife, was a dirty, unshaven fellow in a white suit and broad-brimmed hat.

From him I learned that we were indeed within a stone's throw of Mr Macgregor's estate, and that the plantation house itself was a mile or so distant, up a tributary of the Altamaha River.

"Is it possible to hire a boat to take us there?" I asked.

"Well now," replied the whittler, "there's a coupla' free niggers works for Mr Naylor on the quay here. They gotta boat."

"Where are they?" I asked. "Could we hire their services?"

"Hm." The whittler considered, spat, scratched his head and considered again. "You could," he replied. "Ain't nothing exactly to stop you. But I reckon that if Mr Macgregor was expecting you, he'd have sent his own niggers to fetch you."

Of course he would. "Oh," I said glumly. "I see. So what do you think I could –"

"Sounds to me like a boat's coming now." The whittler grinned. "An' there's Mr Macgregor's nigger shouting out. Ain't no mistaking that boy Franco's holler."

Sure enough, I returned to the other side of the quay to find a large rowing boat being tied up. Its crew of three smiling negroes shouted a welcome to Deb and then, all at once, began asking her where she wanted to sit, in the prow or at the stern.

"At the back, I think," she replied, pointing.

They handed her in, and amid much chattering and cautioning – "Take care wi' the baby, missis. Don' you trip now, missis" – she and Adelaide were made comfortable on the cushions at the end of the boat.

The negroes then hurled our luggage into the bows. As he threw a small case to his friend, one of them glanced up and noticed me. "Mas' Collis?" he demanded, grinning hugely.

"Yes, that's right." I held out my hand to him. "And you are?"

"Franco, suh." Still beaming, the man ignored my outstretched hand and barked an order to his fellow crewmen. Courteously they helped me into the boat, and within five minutes of tying up we were away.

Deb and I sat side by side in the stern of the vessel, reclining at our ease. Our dusky boatmen rowed and sang, and shouted exuberant greetings to workers in the steaming paddy fields which bordered the slimy green water. I gazed over acres and acres of flooded paddies, each field divided from its neighbour by dykes, on which we could see people walking to and fro. "Is all this land Mr Macgregor's?" I asked Franco.

"Yessuh! All Mas' Macgregor's." Franco's face split into a gleaming white grin. "Mas' Macgregor, he very rich man."

"Here rice. Down river by the sea, cotton," added another negro. "All Mas' Macgregor's."

"We comin' to the house now, sir," added the third. "On the left bank, you see?"

I don't know what I had expected a plantation house to look like, but when the Macgregors' mansion came into view it took my breath away. Quite beautiful in its simplicity, it was a large, square, timber house, white-painted, with big windows, wide balconies and a regal colonnade running the length of the frontage. Its spreading green lawns were planted all about with magnificent cypress, juniper and what looked like evergreen oak or chestnut trees, which gave dappled shade from the hot Southern sun.

"Finest house on the whole river, yes *suh*!" declared Franco, observing I was impressed. Then, taking up a large shell which was lying in the bows, he put it to his lips and blew.

At this signal, a dozen or more negroes appeared from nowhere, running towards the jetty where we were tying up. Variously howling and shouting and singing and exclaiming, they handed us out and set us on dry land again. Our luggage was out of the boat in seconds, and carried away. And Adelaide and Deb were surrounded by a sea of black faces, their owners all apparently in ecstasies to discover this "lil' alabaster baby" and her equally alabaster mother.

"Oh Massa, see! Come, Massa, Missis, see!" The commotion intensified. The servants parted ranks to let the newcomers through. And we were, at last, introduced to our hosts, Mr and Mrs James Macgregor, of Paradise, Harrison County, Georgia.

I have never, before or since, been so graciously received. Mr Macgregor beamed at us, and pumped my hand until it ached. Mrs Macgregor smiled with real Southern warmth, and took Deb into her embrace like a mother. "You must be so tired," she cried. "You and this poor child here, coming all this way – you must be exhausted. Jasper! William!"

At her bidding, two black men came running up.

"Bring the little trap round," she ordered, "and take Mrs Minot here up to the house."

In vain did Deb protest she could walk the hundred yards or so to the mansion. She was delivered there in style while I strolled up with Mr Macgregor, glad to stretch my legs.

The house had been built by his grandfather, so Mr Macgregor told me, but had been much improved by himself. He was responsible for the modern kitchens, the large airy drawing-rooms on the ground floor, and the laying out of the gardens. As he looked enquiringly at me, obviously wanting my reaction, I smiled my complete approval. I told him with perfect sincerity that he had done an excellent job.

In one of these elegant drawing-rooms we were introduced to his daughters, Miss Flora and Miss Jane. These girls, at eighteen and nineteen more or less of an age with Deb, took their lady visitor and her baby away directly, cooing and fluttering like a pair of great gauzy doves.

"Your daughters are delightful," I told Mr Macgregor, for so they were. As pretty as the dawn, pink-faced, fair-haired, in billowy white gowns sashed with pale blue and lilac, they were quite lovely to look upon, and what is more they seemed amiable with it.

"They take after their mother, sir." Mr Macgregor beamed fondly. "You should have seen Mrs Macgregor at eighteen. Belle of Harrison County. Still is, in my opinion," he added.

I glanced at my hostess, who smiled graciously and smoothed her silk gown. I nodded. There didn't seem any reason to disagree.

"They're so kind, aren't they?" asked Deb. She and I had been taken to inspect our quarters and asked to come down again when we were ready, and it so happened that after washing and sprucing ourselves up we found we were alone on the ground-floor verandah, looking over the gardens behind the house.

Deb smiled at me. "Do you know," she continued, "I have

a quite beautiful sitting-room, and a bedroom, and there's a dear little box bed for Addy, just right for her now she's growing so fast. And when I went to the dressing-table there was a tray laid out with silver brushes, and combs, and there was a great bottle of cologne, which must have cost fifteen dollars at least. And there were hairpins and clips, and bandoline – everything.

"I have a little black maid, called Juley. She's the sweetest thing, so obliging; she's rocking Addy to sleep right now. And Miss Jane said that if I needed anything at all, to send to her directly. Is your room pleasant, Mr Collis?"

"Extremely." It was. I had a large, well-furnished bedroom and dressing-room on the north side of the house, and I'd been introduced to Nathan, an affable negro lad who would be my valet during my stay. I described all this to Deb, who nodded her approval and pleasure on my account.

"Well, I think we'll be very happy here," she said, contentedly. "Don't you think so?"

"I don't see any reason why we shouldn't be," I replied. Indeed, the place seemed like the very perfection of Paradise to me. "Perhaps," I added, "while we're here, you might address me as Uncle, or Cousin? We are supposed to be related, after all."

"So we are." Deb smiled. "Very well then, Cousin, isn't it charming here?"

"It certainly is," I replied.

Meeting our hosts in the drawing-room ten minutes later, I assured them that our accommodation was all we could desire, and more, and I thanked them sincerely for their kindness.

"Well, it's a great honour to have your company, sir." Mr Macgregor grinned. "Was hearing from Cousin Perry in New York the other week, an' he sent me some snippings from the newspapers. Seems you're quite a celebrity up north, sir."

"Not really," I replied. "Mrs Minot was the great sensation of the last season."

"Ah yes. 'The most affecting Juliet of the modern age.'

That was in the *Post*, if I remember rightly." Dreamily, Mrs Macgregor sighed. "The theatre's a great love of mine," she confessed. "When I was younger I lived up in Baltimore for a year or two, an' I must have gone to the play 'most every week. Twice or three times a week, even."

She glanced shyly at Deb. "Perhaps, Mrs Minot, you and Mr Collis here might consider giving us a recitation or two? One evening, that is? Or could we maybe get up a little concert party? Have the folks here and round about over for an afternoon?"

"Martha, don't be so forward." Mr Macgregor shrugged apologies for his wife. "She doesn't mean it," he said.

"But we'd be delighted to entertain you and your friends." I smiled at Mrs Macgregor, who was blushing furiously. "We could discuss it tomorrow, perhaps? And put a programme together?"

"You'll have them picking cotton next," said Mr Macgregor, but he grinned amiably at his wife and seemed more than obliged to us.

So, over the next few days, Deb and I worked up some pieces. A couple of our more genteel comedy sketches, a short one-act play, some recitations, and a few of the latest popular songs made up a respectable afternoon's entertainment.

We discovered that Miss Flora and Miss Jane both played the piano and sang, so we invited them to join in with us. Deb taught them some new songs and the three of them arranged a few duets and trios and glees, which sounded very pretty and were sure to go down well.

Perhaps you will say it was scandalous that we were expected to sing for our supper, as it were? Maybe you'd be right. But I was perfectly happy to oblige such charming hosts. As a player and a vagabond I have been treated as a criminal in my own country, so I have no false pride about my place in society. And I'm well aware that people want to see actors act.

We embarked on a life of pleasure. Waited upon hand and foot, dining like kings on the freshest fish, finest mutton and the most delicious game imaginable, encouraged to please ourselves in every respect, we could not help but be content.

After we'd settled in I had Nathan call me early in the morning, and on each new day, before the rest of the family was up, I went for long walks along the dykes. There, as the dawn broke in pink and purple glory, I watched flocks of brightly coloured birds rise from the water's edge, beating their wings in excitement as I approached. I observed great fat alligators slithering into the green water at sight of me, and laughed at the hundreds of jack rabbits bouncing off across the fields, panicked by a single stranger who did not even carry a gun.

Heaven, I thought, must be just like this.

Chapter 21

My early morning rambles were marred for me only by the occasional sight of a gang of field hands going off to work. These people not did not jostle and shove and chatter in groups like a gaggle of English peasants, but marched in single file, silent, some of them in shackles even, in the custody of a slave driver on a mule.

The drivers, I observed, were black men, slaves like their charges. But the driver was set in authority over the gang, and he had a whip, which he was empowered to use.

There'd been a flogging on the day we arrived, as it happened. Miss Flora told us about it later, when she was incidentally complaining about her own maid, whose brother chanced to be the man who'd been whipped.

"I told that Constance," said Miss Flora, as we took a break from our morning music practice, "I told her good and all, if you don't mend your lazy ways and get my gowns ironed up nice and smooth like they should be, I'll see you're given a dose like your brother had."

"What dose was that?" asked Deb idly, turning over some sheet music.

"My Pappy had him properly whipped." Now, leaning over Deb, Miss Flora pencilled in an extra line of notation which I suppose, in her opinion anyway, improved Handel's original air no end. "He was uppity with the overseer, you see – said his back pained him and he couldn't work no more that day, so the driver was told to give him fifty lashes. Then they staked him out in the sun for the afternoon." Miss Flora tweaked a wayward curl back into place. "Seems he has better manners since."

The calm, matter-of-fact way in which this slip of a girl imparted this unsavoury information made me wince. "Is it usual to beat slaves like that?" I asked casually. "I mean, fifty lashes merely for making a complaint – it does seem a little excessive, wouldn't you say?"

"It's the usual thing, surely." Unabashed, Miss Flora smiled at me. "Now, Mis' Minot, this here air, shall we take it verse and verse about?"

I continued my morning walks, but nowadays I was fast becoming more and more depressed by what I saw. Flocks of brightly plumed birds no longer delighted my eyes, the sight of a dusky blue heron rising gracefully from the marsh gave me no pleasure, for if I turned the other way I could see slaves at their back-breaking labour, I could observe emaciated women, some of them with stomachs bulging in the last stages of pregnancy, toiling in those swampy fields under a pitiless sun.

But, "strong as an ox, your nigger woman," affirmed the white overseer, whom I met one morning and who took it upon himself to accompany me for a little of my stroll. He pointed to a vastly pregnant adolescent, who was labouring in the rice field. Bent double, her bulge must have obscured her vision and the stance was obviously most uncomfortable for her. "Now that Delilah there," he said, "take her. Comes out to the fields each day, does her work, good as gold. When her time comes she'll go lie down on a dyke and just drop it, get up again and go on home."

He grinned at me. "I know a man's been to Africa, seen nigger women there drop their pups and just get up again, go on working. Here, they get three weeks' holiday to recover."

"What happens if a pregnant woman can't work?" I asked, carefully keeping my voice neutral.

"Yes, well, there's your lazy bitches, up and pretend they can't go to the fields when they're in whelp." The overseer grinned again. "I jes' give them a taste of Teaser here."

"Teaser?"

"That's right." He shook his whip, then cracked it. "Just a little taste, you understand. So's not to harm the babby."

"I see." The very idea of a man lashing a pregnant – or indeed any – woman, revolted me, and I hurried on, saying I was late for breakfast.

On the way back I got lost and, following a winding path which looked as if it must lead somewhere, I finally came across a cluster of broken-down wooden sheds. There was a strong smell of dunghill, and other rubbish – cabbage stalks, meat bones, corn husks and the like – was strewn about everywhere. The stench from this rotting waste was vile. Chickens were scratching outside one of the sheds so I thought, ah, hen coops.

Then, out of one of these coops, crawled a skinny, scrofulous child. An elderly woman with a heavily bandaged foot followed it. Startled, she looked at me. "G' morning, Massa," she began, nervously.

"Good morning to you." I smiled at her. "Are you collecting eggs?"

"No, Massa." She looked puzzled. "Mas' Lucan, he tell me to stay home today. An' this child, she sick."

I recollected that Mr Lucan was the overseer. "So this is your *home*?" I asked, incredulous.

"Yes, Massa." The woman shrugged. "You want something, Massa?"

"No. Nothing." So these were slave cabins. This was where the labourers lived. "Well," I said, changing my mind, "perhaps you could tell me the way back to the plantation house?"

"Yes, Massa. Want me to take you?"

"No." The very smell of the old woman was making me feel ill, and I didn't want her company at all. "Just tell me the way, would you?" I asked.

When she'd finished giving me garbled directions, I fished in my pocket and found a five-cent piece. She took it without comment and I could tell she was relieved to see me walk away.

Although the field hands were uniformly wretched, the

house servants, at least, appeared to be well cared for and relatively happy. Deb's maid Juley, a well-developed mulatto with plenty of meat on her bones, grinned constantly and sang as she did her work. Another housemaid, Tonette, was a woman of great personal beauty, who went about her day's labour with a regal dignity which put every other female creature in the house to shame. Her voice had a soft, deep, musical quality which made me long to get her up on a stage, for someone so like my idea of the real Cleopatra I never heard or saw, before or since.

About a fortnight after we'd arrived a couple of new guests came, distant cousins of the Macgregors, but entirely lacking our hosts' charm of manner or desire to please.

"Actors, eh?" demanded Mr French, on being introduced to us. "Never go to the theatre myself," he observed, in the kind of tone which he might have used to inform us that he never frequented abattoirs, low-class brothels or lazar houses either.

His wife was a stringy, yellow thing with a catarrhal cough and a suspicious frown. She addressed her husband as "Mr French" and did not call Deb or me anything, since she resolutely ignored us.

"Did you sleep well last night, Mrs French?" asked Deb on the morning of their third day, evidently determined to hold a conversation with her breakfast neighbour.

"I did not." Mrs French's tight little mouth pursed crossly. "No, young woman, I did not sleep at all."

"Oh?" Deb looked solicitous. "Why was that?"

"Well." I braced myself for half an hour's chat about flutters in the chest, indigestion and nervous palpitations. But it was not to be. "Well," said Mrs French severely, "it was those house niggers mostly. Those that have their quarters down by the stables."

"Oh?"

"Yes." Mrs French sniffed. "If I was Mr Macgregor, I'd discipline them. But he don't discipline them at all, you see, and this is the result."

"I'm sorry," said Deb, "I must be very stupid, but I don't understand you."

"All night they were at it," Mrs French grumbled. "Ululating – that's the word, I think. *Is* that the word, Mr French?"

"It is, Belinda Josephine," he replied.

"They were ululating, then. One in particular was yelling her mouth off and the others were encouraging her, they kept crying out, 'Sing it, Simone!' So of course the wretched woman kept on and on." Mrs French shuddered, making her leathery jowls wobble like dried-up jellies. "And when you consider that those partic'lar nigger quarters are at least a hundred yards from the house – well!"

"I'm truly sorry, ma'am." Mr Macgregor had listened to his guest's complaints with real concern. "I'll have someone speak to Simone," he promised. "It won't happen again."

"Thank you, James." Mrs French simpered. "You jes' see that it don't."

Deb and I had assumed – if we assumed anything – that the slave whose singing had so offended old mother French would merely be ticked off and told not to yowl through the midnight hours again. So you can imagine the horror we felt when later that day we heard that Simone was to be flogged.

"That can't be right," I told Deb, whose maid Juley had brought her this intelligence, and who was now bitterly reproaching herself for letting the poor slave in for a beating. "It's not your fault," I added, "you weren't to know that the old bitch didn't sleep last night. And Mr Macgregor said he'd have someone speak to her, for God's sake. Not have her whipped!"

"But Juley said so," cried Deb, distraught, "Juley insisted – "

"Juley is not blessed with the world's greatest intellect," I said. "Look, Miss Jane's downstairs in the morning-room, I'll go and ask her."

I returned to Deb's little sitting-room with bad news. It seemed Simone was indeed to be beaten. And that we were bidden to watch justice being done.

If I hadn't gone to speak to Miss Macgregor, perhaps we

shouldn't have been thought of as spectators. But now we were cordially invited to the stable yard where the whipping was to take place.

Even as I spoke to Deb, Miss Jane came rapping on Deb's door, urging her to make haste. "And bring a parasol," she advised. "Sun's high over the yard just now."

So, we assembled at the appointed place. Eventually, supported by two other black women and followed by a villainous-looking mulatto driver in a red wool cap, the miscreant was brought out.

Simone was a woman of about thirty, a dignified, tidy, nice-looking person, neatly dressed in a blue cotton gown. Her head was bound up in a purple spotted handkerchief, her ears sported large brass rings, and in any other circumstances it would have been a pleasure to look at her. At this point I was informed by Mr Macgregor that since there were ladies present, the beating was to be carried out by the overseer, a white man, and not by the half-caste driver – an honour I doubt poor Simone appreciated at all.

I had expected the woman to be beaten on the hands, perhaps, or maybe given a few light strokes across the backs of the thighs. But now, to my horror and disgust, she was stripped to the waist. The driver jerked her arms above her head and tied her wrists to a branch of an overhanging magnolia tree, while her ankles were made fast to a ring set in the flagstones. Now she'd be unable to flinch away from the lash.

Looking at her face I saw there were tears on her cheeks.

They let her dangle for a full five minutes – to think on her sins, I suppose. Then the overseer came out, wiping his mouth on the back of his hand. Cracking a leather whip, he sauntered over to his victim. "You'll sing out even prettier now, nigger," he remarked. He cracked his whip again, then leaned back to strike the first blow.

As he drew back his arm Simone screamed in anticipation, and she kept on screaming all the time he was striking her.

I hear her screams still.

Mrs Macgregor was not present at the flogging, for she'd

gone on a shopping trip to Balthazar Island, but her daughters supplied her place admirably. Pretty as pictures in their white gowns, they looked on with satisfaction, twirling their parasols this way and that as the slave took her ten lashes.

And what of Deb? Deb had been by my side when the first blow was struck, but when the poor creature was taken down and helped away by her friends, I looked round to find her gone.

I discovered her later in her own sitting-room, being sick. Tears flowed unheeded down her cheeks. Her hair had come loose, and strands of it were floating in the bowl into which she was heaving up her heart.

"I hate this place!" she cried, as she saw me. "I hate it, Mr Collis, I hate it! I shall leave today!"

"Oh. Er, well, my dear," I began, "I don't think we can just disappear. Not like that."

"I said, *I* shall leave." She glared at me, a distraught Medusa. "You do as you wish. But I shan't stay another day in this filthy hole!"

"Deb, don't shout," I said. Reaching for a cloth, I leaned across her to wipe her face. "My dear child, you're very upset. Hysterical, even."

"Of course I'm upset!" Dashing away my hand, she shouted even louder. "Of course I'm hysterical! And so should you be! So should anyone who calls himself a human being! Or did you enjoy the spectacle? Were you edified by the sight?"

"It was horrible," I said. "But Deb, dear Deb, you're making yourself ill now, you're – "

"These people are monsters." Narrowing her eyes and hissing through gritted teeth, Deb glowered at me. "These Macgregors are not humans, they are devils. It's not just what's happened today," she added. "This is just the last straw."

"What do you mean?" I asked.

"Well, have you seen how their slaves live? *Have* you?"

"I came across some cabins a day or two ago, and I will agree that they weren't exactly luxurious. But I did not actually see inside them."

"*I* have seen." Deb sat down and began to weep afresh. "I have seen inside the wretched little hovels these poor people call their homes.

"Mr Collis, yesterday Tonette took me to visit her mother. I'd heard from Juley that her mother was ill, so I decided to take the woman some nourishing food; a pint of broth, maybe, or a piece of ham.

"Of course I didn't know the way, so I arranged to meet Tonette and go with her to her mother's cabin. I must admit I was curious – I wanted to find out if the mother was as beautiful as the daughter, you see. Tonette is extremely beautiful, don't you think?"

"Yes, she is."

"Mm." Deb sighed. "Well, we saw her mother. She's ill because she's worn out. She has had fifteen children and ten of them are dead. She has been allowed to stay at home this week because she has an ulcer on her leg. It will not heal, and even the overseer agreed that she must rest up.

"Oh, and thanks to the life she has led, she doesn't look like Tonette. She's ugly, toothless and old."

"Deb, my dear – "

"On the way home, we passed the slaves' hospital. Hospital's the wrong word, it was a dirty hut with an earthen floor. There were no beds, no nurses, no blankets – nothing, except two women in labour, an old man in the corner dying, and rats. There were plenty of rats. One of the women kept shrieking, so Tonette said she would go and fetch the midwife – one of the old slaves, I suppose. I just stood there. I didn't know what to do."

Deb was weeping freely now, tears coursing down her cheeks. "I am leaving now," she said. "Addy and I will not accept the Macgregors' hospitality for another hour more."

"You can't go now." I took her hand and rubbed it, trying to comfort her. "Look, we'll go on Thursday. We can't leave before, there isn't a boat."

"I'll walk. I know how. I'll walk across the dykes to Balthazar Island and hire a boat, I'll – "

"Deb, please be sensible. It's Monday now. I'll speak to

Mr Macgregor before dinner, make our excuses and arrange to go."

"You don't have to leave," she muttered.

"I want to," I said. "I hate what goes on here too."

"Oh." Deb pushed her hair out of her eyes. "I shall talk to Mrs Macgregor," she said. "She can't be aware of what goes on. She wouldn't allow it."

I had my doubts on the subject of Mrs Macgregor's ignorance, but I kept them to myself. "I shan't be rude to her," added Deb then, seeing the expression on my face. "I shall tell her I wish to know more about the plantation, that's all."

She stood up. "If I were a negro slave," she muttered viciously, "if I were Simone's husband or father, I'd get an axe and murder the Macgregors. And the Frenches, and all their other horrible friends, including the two of us. We deserve to die. We do nothing to stop the outrages here."

Deb returned from her interview with Mrs Macgregor stony-faced and grim. "I didn't offend her," she said quickly. "I just asked for instruction. And I received it."

"What did you talk about?" I asked.

"We discussed the plantation for a while. She told me how Mr Macgregor's grandfather had reclaimed all this land from Indians and swamp, and turned it into the place we see today. She told me all about her own family; her parents, her cousins in Baltimore, and her grandparents from Louisiana, who have a sugar plantation there. That got us on to the subject of slavery."

"And what did you learn about that?"

"I learned that the Bible says it's right to turn subject peoples into slaves. The Jews did it, so the Christians may do so too. I learned that just as women are inferior to men, black people are naturally inferior to white. That on the plantations here the negroes benefit from moral and spiritual instruction that they'd otherwise never receive."

"I see."

"I let her think I was accepting all that nonsense. And then

I asked her if she thought flogging was the only way to enforce discipline among slaves. I asked if she had her own daughters beaten for every little fault.

"She laughed. She took my hand and said, 'Lord, Mrs Minot, don't confound us white folks with black cattle!' Then she said, 'Look – if you had a dog wouldn' obey you, would you say, "Please, Fido, sitty down here peaceable and listen to me. You'll just have to quit bitin' all those folks, 'cos I won' have it." Eh? Course you wouldn't. You'd whip old Fido good an' all, I guess, so's he wouldn' bite no more.'

"So I said to her, well, Simone wasn't biting anybody, she'd just been singing. And *she* had powers of reasoning and understanding; so wouldn't it have been sufficient just to ask her to leave off her singing while the house was abed?

"And Mrs Macgregor said, 'If Simone had been a white gal, yes. Simone being black, no. Let a nigger woman have an inch of loose and she'd take a mile; she'd be insolent and unmanageable in no time at all.' And she patted my hand and said if I'd lived in the South all my life, as she had, I'd understand that the only way to control slaves was by force. It was all they understood. They expected to be flogged now and then, and they didn't really mind it."

Deb looked at me. "I didn't take her to task on the rights and wrongs of slavery," she said. "But she was anxious that I shouldn't score any points, and she remarked that slavery had been the rule in the Caribbean islands until about ten years ago. That she didn't think English folks on the whole could have much tender feeling for the black races.

"Then she went on to ask, wasn't it true that the English beat their convicts? That English women were flogged in public and that the English regularly had their sailors and soldiers whipped? And didn't I think it disgraceful that *white* folks should be used in such a fashion?

"And she looked at me so triumphantly then – I don't think I've ever seen such a superior smile."

"But soldiers and sailors are beaten only for serious offences," I said. "As for convicts in prison, they are criminals anyway."

"No, Mr Collis, she had a good point." Deb's sweet face became even more troubled now. "When I was a child, there was a crippled old man living in our court. He'd been a soldier in all the French campaigns, so the neighbours said. One day, while the army was on the march, he told an officer that a young private soldier was wounded too badly to continue on foot. He asked if the man could be carried on horseback.

"The officer said no. The soldier insisted that the man would die otherwise. So the officer had the soldier charged with insubordination. He received two hundred lashes and was very ill because of it. He was turned out of the army without a pension.

"Mr Collis, that man's health and spirit were broken because he tried to help a friend. I think that perhaps the Americans have learned their cruel ways from us."

"Maybe." I couldn't see the point of arguing. "I've arranged our passages on the *George Washington* for next Thursday," I said.

"What did Mr Macgregor say?"

"That he'd be sorry to see us go, that he wished us a pleasant journey, and he hoped we would visit here again."

"Oh." Deb grimaced. "We'll soon be back in the frozen north," she said.

"I'm afraid we will," I agreed.

"I'm glad." Deb smiled at me then. "I know what it's cost you to do this," she said. "I know you think I'm uncouth and ungrateful."

"I don't."

"You do. And I'm obliged to you for humouring me."

"My dear, I would prefer that you didn't call it humouring."

"I'm going to speak out," Deb said. "I'm aware that some Englishmen are treated worse than slaves. But I know now that to have the power of life and death over another human being is wrong, and should end. I'm going to write a pamphlet saying so."

"As you think best," I said.

But, I thought, suppose the slaves were freed? What then? Where would they go? How would their former owners find money to pay them wages? Surely the whole economy of the country would collapse? I imagined a South full of freed slaves, destitute, illiterate, for whom their former owners felt no responsibility; hordes of people who had no understanding of trade, or commerce, no ability to look after themselves.

Whatever happened, I saw trouble ahead. On one hand there was a real possibility of bloody revolt against the whites – on the other, the equally real threat of total economic disaster. Mulling it all over I gave myself a headache and got nowhere.

By Thursday our trunks were packed and we were ready to leave. I can still see the scene in the front porch, our hosts thanking us again and again for the pleasure of our company; and I can still see Deb's face set hard and unsmiling as the Miss Macgregors cooed and fussed over Adelaide.

Then, suddenly, I felt faint. My head spun and my vision blurred. Before I could even stagger to one of the basket chairs in the lobby, I collapsed, hitting my head so hard on the flagstones, Deb told me later, that I knocked myself out.

Chapter 22

I was so ill that they didn't dare keep me in the plantation house itself. Instead, a couple of slaves carried me to a sort of Chinese pagoda in the grounds of the mansion, in which there was a day bed and two rocking chairs. It was comfortable enough; in fact it was positively luxurious when compared with a slave's cabin.

A doctor – if he was that – a red-eyed Irishman in a ginger wig who'd been summoned especially from nearby Jonas Creek, came in to look me over. "Your husband, ma'am?" he asked Deb.

"No. A near relation," she replied.

"Ah." The doctor gave her a knowing wink and drew her away from my bedside. "Well," he said, "it's a type of ague common round here. Poisonous thing it is. There's cramps, and vomits, and purges, and sweats – all that. Body forgets itself entirely. Goes to pieces."

"I see," said Deb, no doubt remembering her own fever, contracted just after she'd had Adelaide.

"Calomel, that's the stuff this fellow needs. Four grains a day. And bleeding." The doctor opened a dirty canvas bag and took out a box of knives, curettes and cups. "Don't mind the sight of blood, do you, ma'am?"

"No," replied Deb. "No, I don't mind it at all. But are you sure that bleeding *is* the best treatment?"

"Sure as I'm alive," the doctor assured her, hiccuping. "All the same, though," he added, "this sort of fever's often mortal. So you, being a mother an' all, you'll not want to nurse this poor soul through his last agonies." Pushing up my shirt-sleeve, he prepared to bleed me. "I'll send in one of Macgregor's slaves," he muttered. "There's an old nigger woman works in the kitchens, she knows exactly what to do."

"Send her, since she's familiar with the illness," said Deb. "But I shall stay too."

"Mrs Minot, that's altogether not very wise."

"I shall stay," repeated Deb. She came over to my bedside and looked down at me. "Sleep," she said softly. "Sleep's the best thing for this."

The black nurse arrived later that evening. I had seen her several times before, for she was a house slave. Lisa-Delight they called her, or sometimes Aunt Lisa, for she was more than old enough for this honorific to be bestowed.

Blue-black as pitch, bony as a skeleton, her huge, flat, bare feet (no slave on the Macgregor plantation ever had shoes, even in winter time) slapped like flippers on the stone-flagged floors. "This the massa who sick?" she enquired as she stood in the doorway of the summer house, beaming at Deb.

"Yes." Deb stood up. "Come in and sit down, Lisa-Delight."

Lisa-Delight did as she was bidden. She looked all round the temporary sick room and clicked her tongue, grinning even more broadly. "Well, Mis' Minot," she exclaimed at last, "you *are* comfortable in here!"

She glanced towards me. "Now, for the massa here, this what we must do."

Lisa-Delight took over the management of the sick room entirely, and with Deb as her lieutenant she began the long drawn out business of dragging me back to health. Dr Hogan came in to bleed me and give orders, but Deb and Lisa-Delight nursed me, washed me, fed me, shaved me, watched me through tediously humid days and sticky Southern nights, and performed the meanest, most degrading offices for me.

The sickness exhausted me. I became as weak as a newborn baby, and just as helpless. I could observe, I could hear – but I could hardly lift a finger to help myself, and the idea of even trying to speak was more than I could bear.

During the hours of daylight I dozed between sleep and waking, seeing faces from the past, faces from the present, and ludicrously mixed up combinations of the two; all of them swimming in and out of focus so maddeningly, that I know I cried out in exasperation. I was jerked into complete consciousness only by the slave's exhortations to "Sit up, Mas' Collis, do," and to "Drink this down, Mas' Collis, this'll see you well again."

The slave had been astonished that a white woman would willingly dirty her hands in the sick room. I was often dimly aware of her cries of, "What for you wash him, Mis' Minot? Let Lisa do that!" And then again, "Don' you take 'way them dirty sheets, Mis' Minot! You'll mess you clean white hands!"

But Deb did wash me. She did change my soiled bed linen. And she coaxed liquid down my dry, aching throat and she combed my damp hair back from my sweating forehead. Tending to my most intimate needs, she messed her clean white hands a dozen times a day, and she performed these disagreeable tasks so neatly, quickly and kindly that I had not the slightest discomfort nor suffered any embarrassment. Although now that seems odd to recall.

"Where's Adelaide?" I managed to ask her one morning, as she helped me out of my sweat-stained shirt and into a clean, fresh one.

"With Miss Flora and Miss Jane." Deb touched my hand, to see if I was still as fevered, I imagine. She smiled kindly. "Henry, don't worry about Adelaide. Just think about getting well."

She'd used my Christian name, for the first time ever. I thought, I *must* be dying.

I was aware of two or three more days and nights passing – but then I began to feel a little better. I took my first supper of solid food, and kept it down. The next morning Hogan came in, drunk as usual, and congratulated me on my progress; but the worthy doctor stumped off in a huff when I declined to be bled yet again.

I was awake for the rest of that day. I sat propped up

in bed and watched the shadows dancing on the walls of the room, I monitored the progress of the sun through the heavens. "I want to go back to New York," I told Deb, as she settled things for the night, rolling down the greased paper blinds which would keep at least some of the biting, sucking, chewing insects away.

"What did you say?" she asked, for she'd been turned away from me, busy with the blinds.

"I want to leave!" I repeated querulously. "I want to go tomorrow!"

"You're not strong enough to travel yet," she said. She lit one of the spirit lamps and carried it over to the bedside. "When Dr Hogan says you can be moved, we shall go. I promise."

"*Doctor* Hogan!" I snorted. "That man received his diplomas from the University of Hard Liquor. What does he know?" In spite of being bled almost white by that half-wit Hibernian, I'd managed to sit up all by myself that evening, and I could feel some strength returning to my legs. "Look, Deb," I said, "I'm obviously not going to die, so there's no reason why we should stay here. We'll make our excuses and leave."

"You couldn't walk as far as the landing stage, and you know it." Deb sat down at the foot of the bed. "Patience, Henry," she said. "Patience, yes?"

"Yes, I suppose so." I lay back on my pillows and looked at her, this lovely girl who had nursed me through a distressing and dangerous illness, risking her life to preserve mine; and I felt weak again, but with love.

"You saved my life," I said, unable to take my eyes off her. "I'll never be able to repay you. Never."

"Lisa-Delight saved your life," said Deb. She smiled at the woman who was standing by my bedside, holding a glass of my evening cordial. "It's Aunt Lisa here you have to repay. Not me."

"I'll buy her freedom." I reached out to take the slave's hand. "Lisa-Delight, I'll buy your whole family's freedom!"

"My family?" Lisa-Delight cackled like an old hen. "Got no

family," she laughed. "All dead. Babies dead, brothers and sisters dead, everybody dead 'cept Lisa." As she told us this, Lisa-Delight's grin did not falter. "Don't want no freedom," she added, and passed me my drink.

"Why not?" I asked, sipping.

"Wouldn' know what to do with it." Lisa-Delight beamed. "Lord, no."

"But, Lisa, wouldn't you like to end your days as a free person?" I asked. "To live in your own little house, and be able to come and go as you please? Not to have to work except for wages?"

"No. Them things is only for white folks." And Lisa-Delight shook her head and laughed, poor woman, she actually laughed out loud. "Mas' Macgregor good man," she continued. "He kind massa. Never sells chillen 'way from parents. Never sells wife 'way from her man. Not want to go 'way from him."

"She likes it here," said Deb, when we were alone together, for although she was nursing me, Lisa-Delight still had to go and scrub pots in the kitchen. "She actually likes being a slave."

"Does she?"

"Yes." Deb plumped up my pillows. "She was telling me a day or two ago, all the slaves here think the world of Mr Macgregor. As far as they're concerned, he's a kind master. He doesn't split up families, you see. He lets the slaves keep pigs and chickens, and the old people and pregnant women are never flogged."

"Well, I should hope not."

"That's not the general rule, you know. Lisa said that on the plantation where she grew up, children were often sold away from their parents. A woman could be flogged until she miscarried, then flogged again for losing her baby – her master's property, you see.

"Once a slave was taken out and burned alive for stealing a leg of pork."

"Oh God." I shuddered. "Poor Lisa. I suppose she can't imagine being anything but a slave."

"No, I don't suppose she can."

"This is a wicked place." I sighed bitterly. "A wicked, wicked place."

"It seems to compare favourably with others like it. And it's true, the Macgregors are kind."

Deb was humouring me. I knew she hated it here even more than I did. I looked round the wooden cabin. "You could go back to the house tonight, if you like," I said. "I expect you would like to get some sleep."

"I sleep here." Deb sat down on one of the rocking chairs and put her feet up on the edge of my bed. "I don't leave you unless Lisa's here."

"You haven't been to bed since I became ill?" I demanded, incredulous.

"I sleep very comfortably where I am now." Deb yawned. "I shall sleep very well tonight."

Later she got up and came over to settle me down to sleep. "I'll make arrangements to leave," she promised. "Henry, in a day or two, when you're stronger and able to walk by yourself, I'll see Mr Macgregor and ask him to book passages for us."

She leaned over me to smooth my pillows. And then she kissed my cheek, as a mother would kiss a sick child.

It was the first of many such kisses. I'm sure that each one burned its impression into my flesh, never to be erased.

I kept begging her to get us away from the plantation, and at last she agreed that I was fit enough to be moved. Now she argued with that incompetent sot Hogan and was diplomatic with the Macgregors. She brought Mrs Macgregor to see me and clamped her lips tightly together when that lady sniffed around the summer house and said tartly, "Well, you can surely smell there's been a nigger as good as living in here."

She said she hoped Deb and I hadn't been too bothered by Lisa-Delight's bodily odours, for Aunt Lisa, like the rest of them, wasn't too particular about her personal cleanliness. "But she's a very old woman," went on Mrs Macgregor, forgivingly, "and, oh glory, you can't be going on at them all the time, they don't understand anyways." Patiently, she sighed. "But the Lord knows these old women can be a trial and a tribulation and no mistake."

Yes indeed, I thought, yes indeed.

In due course we boarded the SS *Georgia Belle* at Balthazar Island quay, and set off for the north. After a horrible journey which I'd prefer to forget, the three of us arrived back in New York just in time for the Christmas holiday.

We kept this very quietly, but I can honestly say that there in New York I passed the best Christmas of my life, those few days spent in the company of the two people I loved best in the world. We had warm, comfortable lodgings in the house of Mr and Mrs Shawcross, an Englishman and his American wife. Here we stayed for ten weeks while I tried to get my health back. I sat most of the day in a rocking chair, near the stove. I nursed my god-daughter, I read, I dozed – I led the life of an old, old man, and even this exhausted me.

Deb, on the other hand, was very busy with the Abolitionists, of whom our landlady was one. During the day she was out at meetings or readings, and in the evenings she worked on her pamphlet, detailing her experiences on the Macgregors' Harrison County plantation.

As she sat scribbling furiously, covering sheet after sheet of foolscap, I lounged in the chair by the stove. "You don't mention the Macgregors by name, do you?" I asked her one evening, as I watched her reading over her previous hour's work.

"No." She shrugged. "I don't see there's any need to name names. After all, it's the whole plantation system which must be destroyed." She looked at me. "And we owe some gratitude to the Macgregors themselves, after all."

"But you don't feel it's ungrateful or disloyal to write condemning the way of life of people who were so kind to us?" I asked. Devil's advocate, as ever.

"Henry, I feel no animosity towards the Macgregors." Deb laid down her quill. "As slave owners go, I now understand that they are kindly, tolerant, humane – by their lights, anyway. But as I've said before, it's the whole rotten edifice of slavery which must be pulled down and trampled upon."

"Charmingly expressed," I murmured. "Did you make that up yourself?"

"No." Deb blushed, and fiddled with the green glass pendant she wore about her neck today, her Juliet pendant as I thought of it myself. "I think I read it somewhere," she said. Then she rose from the table and came over to me. "I know I'm an ignorant, half-literate simpleton," she said quietly. "But I know good from evil, and I recognise oppression when I see it. Having seen what I did, I could not rest if I played no part in the struggle to free the slaves. The Abolitionists' cause is a just one. Don't try to divert me from my work."

"I wouldn't dream of it." I rubbed my eyes and lay back in my chair. "You go on with your pamphlet," I added. "I'll give Addy her bread and milk tonight."

"Tabitha could do that," said Deb, taking up her pen again. "You stay by the fire."

Tabitha was our landlord's maid of all work. Needless to say, she was black. "Don't you think Tabitha has enough to do?" I asked gently.

"I particularly asked Mrs Shawcross about Tabitha's duties," replied Deb, not looking up. "She told me that all the household laundry is sent out. There is an Irishwoman employed in the kitchen – she does all the cooking and most of the other scullery work. All Tabby has to do is wait at table and keep a small house clean and tidy. She has a comfortable room and you can see for yourself that she's clean, cheerful and well-fed."

Deb glanced up then and smiled wryly at me. "I have been a housemaid myself, and I can tell you that if I'd had a mistress like Mrs Shawcross, I would probably be a housemaid still."

"All the same, I'll give Addy her supper," I said. But I felt that Deb had scored a point.

So, many an evening I sat watching Deb write, until my eyelids grew heavy. I noticed she'd become very thin, and I felt guilty, sure I must be responsible for that. But then, lulled by the heat from the stove, I would doze, and dream.

In my imagination Deb would come and sit by me and, smiling in that beguiling way of hers, she'd take my hands. She'd lean across and kiss me, not on the cheek as she often had in reality, but full on the lips. She'd take me in her arms and embrace me with all the passion I felt for her; and then we'd be lying naked on the warm rug before the stove, and I –

And then a coal would fall against the grille and I would wake with a start to find her indeed next to me but fully clothed, pulling a shawl closer about my shoulders or asking if I wanted tea – acting out her role as a loving sister or daughter to me.

"Are you in pain, Henry?" she asked me one evening, rousing me from a doze. "Does your head ache again?"

I opened my eyes and stared at her stupidly. "No," I replied. "No, why?"

"You groaned in your sleep. You seemed to be talking to yourself."

She looked so solicitous that I almost laughed. Or cried, I'm not sure which. In my dream I'd been with her in my bed, I had been just on the point of possessing her completely, and the fulfilment I'd desired for years now had nearly been mine. And she had taken away even my dream.

We sailed for England in early spring, me a weakened yellow creature looking twice my actual age, Deb grown more robust and bright, cheerful and happy, and Addy a sturdy, smiling, apple-cheeked one-year-old. The steam crossing was uneventful. No storms rent the sails or tore the rigging, in fact the ocean was a great, silent millpond, and Deb was not seasick at all.

Arriving at Liverpool, Deb managed everything, talking down the Customs men, arranging our transfer to a good hotel, and ordering the removal of our luggage there.

From being flush with ready cash, I was now hard up indeed. Those three months in New York had made a great hole in my capital and I foresaw that in a few weeks' time I should be literally penniless. This was nothing new to me, of course, but it was going to be some time before I was fit enough to work. I would have to ask Fred Hammer for a loan.

"I'll write to him today," said Deb. "Henry, don't worry about money. We have six trunks full of clothes – we can sell those if we need to." She smiled at me so charmingly, so confidently; but, alas, there was never the merest suspicion of flirtation on her sweet face.

I saw I had indeed replaced Charlie Rayner. I was her lost father and she was the daughter I'd never had. With that I'd have to be content.

5

Esther Harris

1845

Chapter 23

Of course, I recognised the pendant as soon as I saw it. It was old Haskell's, taken in lieu of payment for the keep of her charity child. I must say it looked better around Deb Tanner's smooth white neck than it had ever done bumping against Ma Haskell's bony chest. Not that Haskell wore it often. She didn't want to lose it, you see.

Deb Tanner, that pasty-faced doll whose very existence had blighted my miserable childhood, had grown up into a remarkably pretty woman. Thick, soft, russet brown hair, dark eyes and a pale, clear complexion were natural assets for which I myself would have killed; and now added to these were a good figure, decent carriage and a pleasant speaking voice learned, I suppose, from those beggarly strolling players. Her accent had been as Brummagem as a cheap tin button when we were children.

"She's too skinny," said Rameses, when I was sitting with him one evening and complaining of the unfairness of it all. "Too gawky by half. Her bones stick out all over."

"Do they, Ram?" Comforted a little by this solacing fiction, I patted his smooth brown hand. "I could wish her finger bones stuck through her finger ends."

"They will," he murmured. "Sooner or later, they must."

"The sooner the better." I looked at my own hands, at my cracked nails and flaking skin. "The day that rids the world of Deb Tanner can't come too quickly for me."

"Well, she looks like a death's head already." Ram grinned. "A mask on a pole, that's all she is. A hard winter will be all it takes, believe you me."

But, whatever Ram said, Deb Tanner wasn't a hay rake,

not yet. True, she had arrived back in England very slim, but now that she had lost all the puppy fat of childhood, the fine bone structure of her face and the elegance of her figure could be properly appreciated.

Rameses likes his women meaty. Fat, even. That's why he likes me.

Who was Rameses? Oh, I'll come to him in a moment.

Ugly caterpillars may turn into beautiful butterflies, but I have to admit that my own looks had not improved with time. My hair had become so thin that these days I was obliged to wear a wig. My eyes had sagged at the corners, my nose was bulbous and spongy at the tip, my teeth were all but gone. My skin was crepey and mottled and in places crusty with eruptions, which no ointments or lotions could even alleviate, let alone cure.

"You look like a toad," Deb Tanner had told me once, when we were seven or eight years old. I suppose I must have said or done something to upset her, but I can't for the life of me remember what. "You're an ugly, scabby, dirty toad!" she'd cried, dancing around me, laughing and making faces all the while. She was kicking up such a racket and making such an exhibition of herself that the whole court came out to watch her. "Esther Harris is a slimy, crawling, bulgy *toad*!"

I'd cried into my pillow that night. But she was right, I did look like a toad, and now I was more toad-like than ever.

You think it's unreasonable that I should hate her so much? You believe that thoughtless insults should be forgotten, that life's too short to bear grudges?

Then all I can say is, you've obviously never been cut to the quick yourself. You've never had your self-esteem so cruelly wounded that it's been dying by inches ever since. You're lucky, aren't you?

But life has its occasional compensations, the guilty are sometimes punished, and I have seldom been more gratified than I was that afternoon when Deb came barging into her bedroom to find me and Channing in her bed. The sight of her handsome husband in congress with such a creature as me had sickened her. Made her physically ill with disgust.

Good. Why shouldn't she suffer now and then? What right has Deb Tanner to a charmed life?

When Channing Minot first eyed me in that speculative way in which some other men – a good few men, in fact, and not all of them half-blind, either – have eyed me in the past, I felt a surge of elation which must have made me glow. There we'd sat, in my little office, sizing each other up, and suddenly he'd grinned at me. "You don't spend all your time on business affairs, do you, Miss Harris?" he'd asked.

What a silly grin he had. "No," I replied carefully. "Why?"

"I just wondered." More grinning. "What are your leisure pursuits?"

"I go walking," I replied. I returned his grin. "I am extremely fond of walking."

"Street walking?" He winked at me. Cocky little devil. "You like to walk our London streets?"

"Sometimes."

"Of an evening?"

"Of an evening, yes."

"And you have friends, whom you meet?"

"I have friends, whom I meet." I was getting almost too excited now. My hands were sweating and I was itching like fury. "My friends and I meet for mutual pleasures," I said. "As friends do."

He looked at me, I looked at him, and we understood one another. "Perhaps," he said, "when you next chance to go walking, you might meet me."

"I think that's very likely," I replied.

We went on from there.

You may think – I'm sure you *do* think – that there's no good reason for a man married to a woman like Deb to go walking, and more, with a woman like me. But Channing had desires and needs which that whey-faced fool had no ability nor, I would have guessed, inclination, to satisfy.

I'd seen her face that day. It wasn't just the fact of her husband's adultery which upset her. He was drunk, he was drugged, and he was doing something to me for which he could have been hanged. And while I was in Paradise, his wife had been so shocked and horrified that she'd been sick.

My most persistent memories of Channing Minot are not, however, of bliss. They are of Channing drunk, being sick as a dog who's eaten a mouldy meat pie. Of Channing constipated from the effects of too much opium, straining on the close stool, yelling for a cup of strong coffee to encourage his unwilling gut to contract. And then there are the recollections, far too many of these, of Channing lying to me, stealing my money and insulting my servants.

"No, I never saw it," he would declare, looking me straight in the eyes with the selfsame banker's draft actually sticking out of his waistcoat pocket. "Where's that filthy nigger of yours? I shouted for my boots half an hour ago."

But none of this really disgusted me as it would certainly have revolted his lily-white bride. And anyway, I suppose a man who's done away with both his parents, who has brought himself to snuff out the two lives who gave him his own being, must be capable of anything.

He murdered his parents?

Oh, yes indeed.

How did he carry out this terrible crime?

Oh, in a typically mean and furtive fashion. He drugged them with laudanum and very soon they fell into comas from which it proved impossible to rouse them. Old Minot's manservant, Tripman I believe his name was – yes, that's it, Abel Tripman – found his master unconscious in a mess of his own vomit, with his wife in the same state beside him. Poisoned, apparently, by bad oysters.

Channing told me all this – in strictest confidence, of course – when he was drunk.

I wonder why he was never suspected of murder. I wonder why the police so readily accepted the story he cooked up, that both his parents were inordinately fond of fat Colchesters and liked to eat upwards of three dozen at a sitting, washed down with new ale.

I wonder why Tripman, who seems to have suspected the

truth from the first, did not inform the police of his suspicions; although I must admit it has been more lucrative for him to blackmail the son and heir.

Not that Channing actually inherited all that much. Old man Minot had debts, large debts, which not even the selling of his bookshops could clear. The son, bred to a life of idleness and fit for no profession, had no means of attaining solvency.

He was desperate when he met me. The Hebrews are eminently sensible gentlemen, and they wouldn't lend him another farthing. They recommended him to a few gentile money lenders who quickly sent him packing, and in the course of his luckless wanderings he met my servant Rameses. Who brought him to me.

I liked the look of him immediately, and lent him what he wanted. Lent? Well, yes, I suppose I had no very lively hope of repayment. I gave him what he asked for. I got something in return.

"Why do you not capitalise on your own assets?" I asked him one day, when he was bewailing his fate and lack of fortune. I was well aware that he was so stupid, he would not understand what I meant.

"My assets?" he demanded sourly. He had no money at all that day, and was in dire need of a drachm of opium; which I was withholding, just for the fun of it. "What assets do *I* possess?" he asked.

"Your looks, of course. Your handsome face and splendid figure – they're assets, aren't they?" I stroked one of his finely boned wrists, which were so unlike the coarse, knuckly joints of most men. "Find a rich old woman to support you. It wouldn't be difficult."

"I wouldn't want to be kept by a *woman*," declared the idiot, sticking out his jaw and trying to look like a man's man. I wondered what he thought he was doing now, if not being kept by me?

I have often debated with myself whether it is better to have brains or beauty. Well, both, of course – with beauty, *I* could have conquered the world. But it's a tragedy to be possessed of beauty alone. Without a sharp intellect, it's useless. Worse than useless.

Poor Channing. With something like sympathy, I looked at him. Lacking his usual comforter, that morning he was fidgeting and shaking badly. I opened the door. "Rameses," I called, "bring Mr Minot his cordial."

Channing's face brightened. He was like a child offered a toy, a dog about to be taken for a walk.

What a very boring little person he was.

While he slept off the effects of the cordial, dreaming, I don't doubt, of money and power, Rameses and I got out the books and did our monthly reckonings. The accounts looked very healthy that month. I wasn't rich, certainly, but I felt I had done very well for a tinker's child.

As I went through the records, Ram's black-backed fingers moved lightly, sorting bills of exchange, arranging banknotes in order of denomination, making little piles of copper, silver and gold. Weighing a coin in his pinky-brown palm he sniffed. "Alloy," he muttered, biting hard on the edge. It was hard, too hard to be gold. He dropped it into a mug of acid kept for the purpose, and the coin blackened. "I know who paid with this," he said, rapidly sorting out nine others like it.

"No undue violence, Ram," I cautioned. I knew the defaulter well, an old gentleman too fond of cards who had probably been duped himself. "No broken bones this time. Just a few bruises, eh?"

When Rameses went out to deal with various defaulters and collect some revenue, I sat by the fire and dozed. My life flickered before me in the flames. I looked back over the past couple of years, and sighed. I hadn't done so badly, really.

After I'd filched and disposed of as much stuff as I dared, I left the Taylors' employ, sneaking away from Orchard House one midnight with most of the family silver in Mr Taylor's own travelling valise.

I went back to Ma Haskell, whose anger with me was slightly appeased by the sight of some decent plate, but who grumbled that with a distinctive pattern like this one we could never sell it. We would have to have it melted down and sold as scrap, getting only half its present value. She wasn't much mollifed when I produced another thirty-odd pieces of assorted gold and silver, including Mrs Taylor's pretty silver needle case with the tiny red glass laudanum bottle secreted in the lid.

If I learned ingratitude from anyone, it was from old bitch Haskell. I stayed with Ma Haskell for a month or two, but then I became restive, and anxious to branch out on my own account. Through some of old Haskell's contacts I began to receive items generally considered a little too hot for the respectable fences to handle, and on the proceeds I started to lend money, but in a very small way.

I was clever. I was never caught, nor even came under suspicion. But all the same, Birmingham is a small town and there were too many fences operating over too small an area, and it was becoming a little warm for us all.

I had a contact in Shoreditch who suggested setting myself up in London. This appealed to me, so, without poaching on an established patch – which was not easy, I assure you, for I had to buy my little area of business from a set of *very* evil and grasping persons – I set up in the City at my old trade of receiving, and I lent a little money on the side.

There's a delightful anonymity about London, which makes it possible for one to be one's own woman, and keep company with nobody very much – it's far safer that way. But now I couldn't do without Rameses, who appeared out of the blue one day and asked for work. He had heard of me, he said, through my Shoreditch friend.

Lascar, Egyptian, whatever he was, misbegotten bastard anyway, Ram is sharp and intelligent. We took to each other right away. These days we're very good friends.

He had kept Deb Tanner (I'll never call her Deborah Minot, never) in sight all over America, he'd reported regularly by letter – yes, he's a paragon, he can even read and write – so I knew exactly where she was and what she was up to.

I needed to keep tabs on her, you see. For now the seeds were sprouting. Soon the flowers of fulfilled ambition would blossom. I already had her husband. Eventually, I'd have her child. Anything and everything she held dear would be mine.

Oh yes, I intended to have that child.

Or something of equal value.

Chapter 24

Having Channing Minot at my beck and call was doubly delightful. He was Deb's husband, and it was fun to make Rameses just a little jealous. Dear Rameses. With his unnatural desires and perverted fancies, he was a perfect match for a misshapen creature like me.

Of course, Ram loathed Channing Minot. Hated him like poison. "He's no good," he would insist balefully – as if I had declared Channing to be all perfection. "No good at all. He takes your money. He sleeps in your bed. And for what?"

"You shall sleep in my bed tonight, Ram," I told him one morning, more to shut him up while I worked out some particularly complicated accounts, than because I especially wanted him there.

But when Rameses and I met together for mutual gratification, I had to admit that as a sexual partner I much preferred dear Ram to Channing Minot. Channing was lazy, while Ram was energetic. Channing needed endless stimulation and encouragement while Rameses was as anxious to *do* as to be done by. Channing was drawn to one or two very obvious perversions, while Ram was endlessly inventive.

One evening when Channing was out, gambling away my money most probably, Ram informed me that in Islam it is a sin to have hair on the body. He then produced some evil-smelling stuff with which he proposed to anoint me, in order to rid me of mine.

"Why is it a sin?" I enquired, curious to know.

"It is displeasing to Allah," he replied, as if that settled the matter.

"But why?"

"Infidel, you ask so many foolish questions." Rameses grinned at me. "Come upstairs," he said. "I shall make you very beautiful tonight."

"I doubt that," I said. But I complied.

"I didn't know you were a Muslim, Ram," I remarked, as he splashed the stuff on.

"Didn't you? Hold your arms above your head." He pushed his hand into a stone jar and then began to slap great dollops of viscous slime into my armpits. "This stuff is used in the harem of the great Sultan himself," he said.

"Then where did you get it?" I demanded.

"I have my methods," he replied.

"Oh yes, I dare say you have."

He continued to scoop and slap until I was covered from head to foot in the stuff, which now began to burn and make me itch. "Wait," said Ram, as I reached for a cloth to wipe it away. "Wait a few minutes more."

I waited, fidgeting. But when I saw the pernicious lotion was now raising great weals and blisters on my skin, I jumped from the bed. I ran naked to the kitchen for water, and threw bucketfuls on my burning flesh.

Wet and slippery, on fire from the caustics but now totally hairless, I turned to see Ram leering at me in anticipation. "You look wonderful," he croaked. "Like a houri sent from Paradise. Come here."

Flattery is the greatest aphrodisiac of all. We embraced on the flooded kitchen floor.

When we were exhausted and replete, we lay comfortably entangled for a few minutes more, but then Rameses got up. He made coffee, and, while it was standing, went across the road to a chop house. He returned with a hot rabbit pie, which we devoured very companionably at the kitchen table.

Yes, I thought as I munched, if Channing Minot should ever become difficult, I can safely leave it to Rameses to explain to him how things stand. When all is said and done, Ram is my best friend.

All the same, I still wanted to have my fun with Channing. Of course, the attraction there was my power over him. I did like his looks, I admit – what woman wouldn't have? – but everything else about him was insipid and dull. As for *his* talents in bed – well, I could have given myself more pleasure with a carrot and a pot of grease.

After she left Channing, Deb lived in some unsavoury ménage with a common stroller, name of Hammer, and his actress whore. I forget what she was called. A black-haired bitch she was, blowsy-looking, ugly as sin – altogether a very disagreeable person. Lucinda Tolland. That's it.

But then, when she returned from her travels, Deb took lodgings with another actor, Henry Collis. This was the decayed-looking fellow who'd been with her in America and was now her keeper, I supposed.

"Does she look happy?" I asked Rameses, who had tailed her round London for a few weeks now, watching her comings and goings and noticing whom she met.

"She's busy, and preoccupied," replied Ram. "I wouldn't say she looked happy, but she doesn't seem sad either. She takes the child with her everywhere."

"Ah. And the child is sickly, weazen?"

"No. She's a fine big infant, very bonny."

"That's a pity." I considered what to do. Deb had been on a loose lead for far too long now. Eventually I decided to arrange a meeting between husband and wife.

First of all I primed Channing, rehearsing with him what he should say. He promised to be circumspect. Well, we'd see. Then I sent Ram to deliver a message from Channing, and after some toing and froing of notes a rendezvous was arranged, at my house in the City.

I wondered if Deb would come.

She did.

As soon as she entered my little office I saw that Deb Tanner was still very pretty. Pale, and these days slim almost, but not quite, to the point of gawkiness. Oh, I'll be honest. She was more than pretty. She was beautiful.

When her eyes met mine, she flinched. "Good morning,

Deb," I said, smiling in welcome. "How pleasant to see you again. How well you look."

She ignored me! She turned her back on me and looked at her husband, who was sprawled in an easy chair before the fire. "Good morning, Channing," she said.

When he had heard Rameses letting the visitor in, Channing had started to squirm with excitement, and he was grinning like a monkey now. "Good morning, dear wife," he said. He got up and walked towards her. "It's like a dream come true," he went on, still grinning. "My own precious Deb, come to see me at last." He stretched out his arms in welcome.

"Don't touch me!" Deb started back from him as if he'd been a poisonous snake. "Channing, if you come one step nearer, I'll, I'll – "

"You'll what?" But now Channing dropped his arms to his sides and stood where he was. "I heard you had a child," he said. "My child?"

"Of course she's your child!" Stung into righteous outrage now, Deb kindly handed me my trump card. If she'd told Channing that the child was somebody's bastard, he'd have lost interest in it, and how much better that would have been for both mother and babe! "What do you take me for?" she demanded, looking Channing straight in the eye.

"My wife," he replied soberly. "I take you for my wife. And as for the baby – "

"Adelaide. Her name's Adelaide."

"And I take Adelaide for my daughter." Now Channing looked so concerned, so solicitous, so contrite, he would have deceived a bishop. "Deb, may I see my child?"

"No, you may not." Deb pulled her shawl tight across her bony shoulders. "Why did you ask me to come here?" she demanded.

"I wished to see you, of course." Channing shrugged, the picture of injured innocence. "You're my wife, I love you. And you ask why I want to see you. Oh Deb, Deb . . ."

"Oh, be quiet." Deb glared at us both. "I have decided I no longer wish to be married to this man," she said. "I want a separation, a legally binding separation. You can send for a lawyer now." She gave me a baleful stare. "That woman there can witness what I say."

"Why do you want a separation?" asked Channing.

"Why?" Deb's eyes flashed. "You go with common prostitutes. You lie. You steal."

"I lie and steal? Oh, come now, Deb, what evidence have you of that?"

"Well – you whore, anyway." She turned to look at me. "You've committed adultery with that woman," she spat. "You've dirtied my bed with that thing, that creature – I called it a woman, but it's scarcely even human!"

She was so foolish. I held my peace but I thought, oh Deb, you're such a simpleton, do you think I'll ever forgive you for that?

"You have no proof of adultery," said Channing. "You have no witnesses, no material evidence whatsoever."

"I have the evidence of my own eyes."

"Not worth a ha'penny." Channing laughed. "So you accuse me of adultery with Esther," he said. "Look at her. She is not rich, she is not desirable, she is not handsome. Who would believe you?"

Thank you, Channing, I thought. You will pay for that.

"The world knows about you and Henry Collis," he went on. "Everyone can see you living openly with that vagabond, sharing his table and, I don't doubt, his bed." Channing grinned. "So I'm an adulterer. Many men are, and in most circles going after whores is an acceptable weakness in a man. But what are you, Deb? A runaway wife. An actress – almost by definition a harlot. Whereas I am a – "

"You're a scoundrel!" Deb cried. "A beggarly, cowardly, unprincipled villain, a filthy beast who – "

"Whereas I am a gentleman born and bred, who courted a penniless girl and married her for love. I may have some little defects of character, but I do not deserve to be insulted and browbeaten by a woman who has taken my child from me, to be brought up among vagabonds by a man who rogers her mother!"

Channing pushed his hands into his pockets and looked reflective. "I think I shall have the child brought here," he said. "There's room for a child and a nurse here."

"No!" Deb was ashen now. "No," she repeated, "you can't have her!"

"Can't?" Channing smiled. "My dear Deb, if I want my daughter here I'll have her here. She's my child – you admitted as much before a witness. Therefore I shall do with her as I think fit."

"You can't have her," Deb repeated. But she looked worried now, for she knew Channing was right.

We let her dangle there for a few moments, but then at a nod from me Channing went on. "We could perhaps make a bargain," he said.

"What sort of bargain?"

"There's a certain pendant you sometimes wear. We want it."

Oh God. Channing was so clumsy!

"A green glass pendant," he went on, a bull at a gate. "Give me that and I shan't trouble you any more. I'll give up all claim to Adelaide, I'll never even see the child."

"You want my pendant?" Deb was clearly astonished. "A bit of glass, you want that, you'd exchange your living child for that?"

"Yes, that's right."

"Oh." Deb's eyes were round. "Why do you want it?" she asked

"Aha." Channing tapped his nose.

"It's just a fancy of his," I said, glaring at the fool who had now ruined everything. "Merely a whim." I smiled at Deb and spread my hands. "Deb, you know Channing and his whims. After all, you were a whim yourself, weren't you?"

"Was I?" Deb glared at me so fiercely that you'd have thought we'd offered her a rat sandwich rather than a fair bargain. "And what interest have you in this, Esther?"

"I'm fond of Channing," I lied. "His pleasure is mine, that's all."

"*His* pleasure." Scornfully, Deb regarded us both. "His

filthy, depraved, disgusting pleasure, his horrible fancy, his revolting, villainous – "

I stopped listening. I let her rant on a few seconds more but then I interrupted her. "Think about it, Deb," I said curtly. "A piece of green glass. That's all Channing wants. Give him that and you need never hear of or see Channing or me again."

"I'll think about it," she replied. "I'll think about it and let you know next week."

"You'll let us know by Friday." I smiled kindly at her. "You'll make a sensible decision, I'm sure."

"Before I can decide anything I'll need to breathe some fresh air." Deb tied the strings of her bonnet. Then she opened the door and went out, almost running across the hallway, not even waiting for Rameses to open the front door for her.

"Well," said Channing, "I think we frightened her rather nicely. Esther, we're a good team."

"Mm." I toyed with a heavy brass paperweight, trying to decide whether to throw it at his stupid head or ram it down his throat.

"I need something to relax me." Channing yawned, stretched and grinned at me. "Send Ram out to the apothecary, would you? I'd like a cordial, of Mr Sherratt's own mixing."

"Ram can make one up for you himself. He knows what you like." If Channing had not been in the room I might have told Rameses to up the dose of laudanum to a fatal one, I was so angry.

When Channing had drunk off his cordial he closed his eyes for five minutes but then, just as I thought he'd dozed off, he opened them again. He stirred, got to his feet and came over to me, leering. "Let's go upstairs," he said.

"I'm busy," I replied.

"Let's go upstairs!" he repeated pettishly, a child who wants his own way.

I thought about it. It might be a good idea, for he'd sleep very soundly afterwards. But this would definitely be the last time, for I'd had enough of entertaining the greatest sexual bore in Christendom. "Very well," I replied.

Let him find another playmate, I thought, as I gave him relief. Let her be obliged to exercise her imagination as I have done, and let her receive as little gratitude as her reward.

Afterwards I left him sleeping and went downstairs. I wrote a letter, which I sealed up and gave to Ram to keep in the pocket of the waistcoat he wore always. In the event of my disappearance or coming to harm, I told him, he should present the letter at the nearest police station.

"He's no good for you," said Rameses casually, pocketing the letter. "He's a wastrel and a fool, and he can't even fornicate like a man."

"Watching, were you?" I shrugged. "You're quite right," I agreed. "Perhaps one day we'll have a game with him, shall we? Make him squeal."

"Yes." Ram's dark eyes glittered. "Now that is a *good* idea."

"Mm." I was sore, for I had a bad patch of eczema on my left arm and Channing had grabbed me roughly there, tearing the skin and making it bleed. "Rameses, you must keep the Tanner woman in view. Do you hear me?"

"Yes," he replied.

"Good. Now, what about some coffee?"

"Later." Rameses looked shifty. "Is he asleep?"

"I imagine so. Coffee!"

"I could do it now." Rameses grinned. "I'd leave no marks."

"I dare say not." I patted his arm. "But no."

"Why?" Ram glared at me. "Why not?"

"We still need him. Not for much longer, I assure you – but we cannot do without him yet."

"Oh." My servant was crestfallen. "Oh. I see."

"Patience, Ram, patience." I smiled at him. "You'll have your chance one day."

"You promise me?"

"I promise you."

"Good." Ram knew I would not lie to him, and was satisfied.

Rameses loathed Channing, as he loathed all parasites. He would have killed him with as little compunction as he'd have killed a flea, squeezing it between his finger and thumb nails until the creature's shell broke. As for Channing, he abused dear Rameses to his face, referring to him – in my hearing, the half-wit – as "that idiot nigger". Now that was as foolish as it was unkind and untrue.

Ram had not heard that conversation between Deb and Channing and me, he'd been out on an errand while that was going on. But my servant was acute. He was right about Deb's stupid husband.

As I drank my coffee I understood that very soon Channing Minot would become as useless to me as a worn-out slipper, and be fit only for the soil cart.

6

Deborah Minot

1846–1851

Chapter 25

When we returned to London, the town was dead. The theatres were closed for the summer, and the cholera was cutting a swathe through the population with no respect for age, class or sex. Our best friends, Fred and Lucinda, were in France, doing a series of concert parties. Apparently they were performing in French. I had not known they were so versatile.

In spite of the cholera bringing prices down a little, we could not afford to stay in the town; lodgings there were far too expensive. Through an acquaintance, however, Henry Collis found a room for me and the baby in a house kept by the widow of an actor who had once worked with him. This house, in a pleasant Middlesex village, was at least half an hour by coach from Covent Garden; but the railway was already built and when the station opened this leafy backwater would, I was sure, soon become a mere suburb of the great city. Henry took a room for himself in a lodging house a few minutes' walk down the village street.

In spite of being still weak and run down, he went into town daily, to meet his friends in the profession, to sit in the coffee houses with them and talk, to try to arrange engagements. Few offers were forthcoming, and those which *were* made were for ridiculous things like a fortnight's walk-on work in Aberdeen or a stint as a scene painter at the Lane.

"I've no objection to manual work," he said, as the three of us walked out in the mild summer air one July evening, "but I've no skill whatever in the painting line and could not draw a column or a nymph to save my life. I'd be out on my ear after the first day."

He took Adelaide from me and swung her on to his shoulders, something she loved. She giggled and pulled his hair. "Perhaps I'd better stay here and look after Addy," he said ruefully, "while you go out and see what *you* can find. I could start a nursery school. What do you think of that?"

"I'm going into town first thing tomorrow," I replied. "I'm determined to find something, even if it's only walking on in a burlesque."

I couldn't find anything at all.

We were so hard up that our prosperity of a few months ago seemed like a dream. After our rent was paid we had scarcely anything left over to buy food, and by the last week of July we were absolutely without money.

I wondered where Adelaide's next bowl of bread and milk was to come from; but then, one balmy evening, just as I was screwing up my courage to ask my landlady for a loan, Henry walked in. He was looking so pleased with himself that his haggard features were transformed.

"What's the matter?" he asked, seeing my frown.

I told him.

"Ah." He picked up Adelaide and kissed her. "Well, this young lady shall have beef broth tonight. I've found a job."

"Have you? Doing what?"

"Teaching singing to brats." Henry pulled a face. "Yes, well – I'm aware I have no qualifications. But I sing a little, I can play the piano, I know a few songs." He grinned at me. "I taught you to breathe out and in."

"Yes, you did," I agreed. "But whatever shall I do without you?"

"Without me?"

"Yes. You'll need to live in town, won't you?"

"I'd assumed you would come with me." He frowned now. "The cholera's passed, the bills of mortality are right down now, so I think Addy would be safe."

I looked at him, he looked at me, and we both reddened.

"You mean you would need a housekeeper?" I asked, to save face.

"Yes, I'd need a housekeeper," he replied.

We paid off our lodgings in Middlesex and moved to Sydenham Road, Clerkenwell, a shabby, seedy area as full of thieves and prostitutes as honest working men. Here, cheap chandlers' shops stayed open until all hours, and second-hand clothes merchants and pawnbrokers plied lucrative trades.

There was no refuse collection in this part of the city, so consequently household rubbish lay about everywhere, rotting in festering heaps all over the roads. As it was high summer, the place stank.

"We could certainly do with a few of those Yankee porkers around here," remarked Henry, skirting a pile of reeking offal as he walked with me past a cheap butcher's shop one day. "Do you know, when we first went to New York, I thought using those hogs as scavengers was a revolting idea. But now – "

"Now you think it's an excellent scheme. So do I." I sighed. "I'm missing New York."

"I miss Philadelphia." Henry was carrying Addy, and now he tickled her under the chin. "That's where you were born," he told her. "It's the most beautiful city in the Union. A paradise of wide green open spaces and pure white marble halls. No rubbish in the streets there."

Adelaide was unimpressed. She merely burbled in reply, and pulled Henry's hair.

Every day I went out to look for work, but I found nothing. Nothing at all. I began to think I'd be obliged to hire myself out as a servant, a maid of all work, for in addition to keeping myself and my baby, I knew I should be keeping my promises to my American friends and sending money to the Abolitionists – whose cause, now I was away from America, seemed just as pressing.

More so. In my shabby but comfortable lodgings I thought of the slaves in their squalid cabins, and knew I was indeed blessed. As I curled up in my warm bed, I remembered that sick and dying slaves lay on bare earthen floors. As I watched my daughter learning to stand upright, heard her burble and chatter and try to talk, I saw poor Simone's terrified face and heard her dreadful cries.

Henry took a room adjacent to mine, for which he paid the rent. He also gave me money to buy food for all three of us. "Very well, it's a loan," he said irritably, when I hesitated about taking his cash. "In our profession, we help each other out. If you were in work and your friends were not, would you stand by and watch me or Lucinda starve?"

"No, of course not." I took the money. But I knew I had to find, or earn, some cash of my own!

I looked at my pendant, my green glass pendant which Esther and Channing had wanted so badly that my husband had been astonishingly eloquent in his attempts to persuade me to give it up. Of course, I had no intention of gratifying any whim that repulsive pair might have, but I did wonder why they wanted my necklace so badly. Perhaps I could sell it? If it were valuable enough for Esther Harris to hanker after it, perhaps someone else would part with a few pounds for the privilege of owning the thing. Or maybe I could pawn it. I decided that when Henry came in from teaching the tone-deaf children of ambitious mammas to wobble up and down the major scales, I would ask his opinion.

I put Addy down for a sleep and went downstairs. We could not afford coals for fires in our rooms, so, on the dirt-encrusted range in the lodging-house kitchen, I cooked supper for the three of us. Tonight, it was large platefuls of boiled potatoes, liberally doused with the savoury gravy from the smallest possible bit of pot-roasted beef.

We ate it sitting together on my bed. Afterwards I took my pendant from my pocket – for these days I always carried it with me – and held it up to catch the evening light.

"I wonder why Esther wants it so much?" I asked Henry, frowning.

"I thought it was your husband who wanted it?"

"No," I replied. "It's Esther who wants it. She just made Channing ask for it."

"Perhaps it's an emerald after all." Mopping up the last of his gravy with a bit of stale bread left over from breakfast,

Henry grinned at me. "It's the crown jewel of an Indian prince."

"I don't think so." Peering closely at my supposed crown jewel, I could see that over the years the facets had been chipped and damaged beyond repair. Here and there the stone had been rubbed to a smooth opacity, and now it looked just like a piece of one of those green glass bottles used for keeping liniment in.

"No," I said, "it's not an emerald. It can't be. Can it?"

"Take it to a jeweller," suggested Henry. "Ask the value."

"And be laughed at? Or handed over to the constables?" I closed my hand protectively over the stone.

"Take it to Mr Lockett, then." Henry got up and collected the dishes together. "Ask Bob Lockett's advice."

"You mean the pawnbroker down the road?"

"Yes." Henry dropped the tin dishes into a bucket and put it outside the door for the slavey to collect. "I'll come with you," he said.

"What if he asks how I came by it?"

"We'll say it was a present from an admirer. An anonymous gift." Henry laughed at my frown. "Don't worry. Bob Lockett's an old acquaintance. He's not in with the police, and he wouldn't inform on a client."

"All the same, Henry, don't you think – "

"Look, when you went to see that woman who's keeping your useless husband – who must, by the way, be quite insane to be attracted to *him* – "

"Thank you, Henry. Thank you very much."

"I'm sorry. Who must be temporarily infatuated in the way the best of us may be once or twice in our lives, you said she seemed very anxious to own this bit of rubbish. More than anxious."

"So she was."

"Then get it valued." Henry pulled me to my feet. "Find out what the wretched thing's worth. Then you can sell it to the silly woman for a fair price."

"Well, maybe."

"Trust me." Henry plonked my bonnet on my head and

picked up my daughter, who snuggled happily into his embrace. "Come and see Mr Lockett," he said.

So we did.

Mr Lockett turned out to be an old, shrivelled gentleman dressed in garments so various and decaying that it was said, so Henry later told me, that he acquired them from corpses in the public mortuary. He smelled like a dead rat left behind a wainscot.

"From an admirer, Mrs Minot?" he asked, screwing his jeweller's glass into his rheumy eye. He squinted at the pendant. "Ah," he said.

"What?"

"Gold," he murmured.

"Oh?"

"Plated, that is." He grinned at me. "Most of the plate's rubbed off. It's cheap alloy underneath."

"I see."

He transferred his lens to his other eye and peered at the stone. He tapped it with a short ivory wand. He touched it with the tip of his tongue. "Glass," he said, shaking his head. "I thought it might be beryl, but it's just glass. Worthless. The stuff they make bottles with."

"I thought it might be."

"Then you're not disappointed. Good." The old man removed his eyeglass. He grinned at me again. "It's a pretty trinket," he said kindly. "I could lend you – ah, let me see – half a crown. Would that help to tide you over?"

I needed just such a sum to send some letters off to America. "Thank you, that would be a great help," I replied.

I accepted the florin and sixpenny bit. I watched as the old man wrote out the pawn ticket. "I hope to redeem it soon," I said.

"It'll be here waiting for you." Mr Lockett still smiled at me, and his watery eyes were still kind. His ill-fitting false teeth slipped over his grey gums, and he jerked them back into place. "I'll put it in my box, just here," he said. "I'll keep it for you."

The summer passed. The ambitious mammas took their children away from their singing lessons and put them back to reading and writing, so Henry found his services as a maestro were no longer required. I had had no success in finding work, so now both Henry and I were unemployed. Soon the Clerkenwell rent was in arrears.

"We'll try the Northern Circuit," said Henry as autumn arrived and our lodgings became even more cold and cheerless than they'd been in summer.

"Playing to Irish tinkers in Liverpool?" I asked.

"Playing to whoever will pay good money to watch us." Henry shrugged. "We must go where our living is, after all. Paupers can't be proud, can they?"

"Can't they?"

"No. Or if they are, their pride mustn't show. So courage eh, Deb? Be brave."

A tall order. "I'll try," I agreed.

"Good girl."

As I looked at him, he smiled, and I wondered how I could ever have been afraid of this man, ever thought him cold and unkind.

In America he'd been kindness itself. When I was ill and fit for nothing he'd encouraged me and cheered me up; it was he who'd helped me to get well. And he'd been a father to Adelaide, as good and kind a father as any child ever had.

I shuddered as I recalled that horrible fortnight when he'd been sick with fever. I'd been ill with fear myself, and I'd been on my knees daily, praying to God to preserve my friend, my dearest friend, who was wasting and dying before my frightened eyes.

"What's wrong?" he asked now.

"Nothing. Why?"

"You looked far away." He smiled at me. "Don't worry. We'll get there, in the end."

Henry wrote to an actor manager in Carlisle, who controlled a great area of the north-west. He drew attention to our successes in America and offered the services of us both. To our great relief the manager chose to be impressed and we were offered a short season on one of the northern circuits, playing mainly in the Liverpool–Manchester area and doing everything from walk-on burlesque to Shakespeare.

If we were going to Manchester, I decided, I wanted to put my affairs in London in order. Well, of course I could do nothing much about my husband, but I did not wish to leave anything of myself in that dirty city, so I packed up everything I owned and sent it by rail to Manchester, to be called for.

It was only when we were about to leave that I remembered my pendant. I had to have that back, I had to have that in my hand, if only because Esther Harris wanted it. I borrowed three shillings from our landlord, promising to repay him with my first Saturday's wages. I redeemed my property. I was unreasonably glad to get it back.

As I walked out of Mr Lockett's frowsty little shop I brushed against a woman standing on the pavement, counting coppers from one hand to the other with a fixed stare of concentration. She looked up as my skirts swished by hers – and knew me at once. "Mrs Minot," she said, without surprise or emotion. "It's Mrs Minot."

"Kitty." I was both glad and embarrassed to see her. "Kitty, how are you?"

"Badly, Mrs Minot, very badly." Kitty looked at me with dull eyes. She sighed, and I could smell spirits on her breath. "I left that house," she said. "I had words with Mr Minot, you see. He said things I never thought to hear from the son of such a dear, good woman as his mother was."

Kitty dabbed at her eyes. "I left the day after you did," she continued. "I live with my married sister now, in Seven Dials. I don't get on with her husband, but where else can I go?"

"What brings you to Clerkenwell?" I asked.

"The same errand as brought you." She glanced back towards Mr Lockett's shop. "I can't live on air, Mrs Minot."

"Have you seen Channing since you left Holborn?" I asked.

"No." She sniffed. "Nor do I want to. The house is sold," she added. "He's living with some woman now. I say woman. She looks like a frog."

Poor Kitty, I thought. Once so lively, energetic and busy, she sounded like a prisoner in the condemned cell today. "I met Abel Tripman a month or so back," she went on. "There are things you ought to know."

"What things, Kitty?"

"Just – things. I can't talk here in the street."

"Oh, Kitty!" Her glazed, hopeless demeanour brought tears to my eyes. So active, sharp and spry before, living in Seven Dials had changed her. I expect, though, that existing on a brother-in-law's cold charity in one of those foetid alleys, in a mouldering slum far worse than any in Birmingham's squalid courts, might have changed me.

"Look, Kitty," I said, briskly now, "I am leaving London tomorrow, and I expect to be away for a month or so. But if you give me your address, I could see you when I return."

"Could you, Mrs Minot?" In gratitude, Kitty pressed one of my hands. "I'd heard you had a child," she said, looking at Addy who was asleep in my arms.

"She was born in America." I drew the shawl back from the baby's face. "She has Channing's eyes," I added, in case Kitty wondered if my daughter was somebody's bastard.

"You're well away from Mr Minot now you have a child." Again Kitty wiped her own eyes. "Mrs Minot, I never had any of my own and I've no right to instruct my betters, but if I were you I'd keep that baby away from Mr Minot."

"Why, Kitty?" This was strange advice. For all his faults, I'd never have thought of Channing as a danger to a baby. "Kitty, what are you trying to tell me?"

"Old Mr Minot was a harsh father." Kitty pressed my hand again. "Oh, I know a child must be corrected and disciplined, of course I do. But old Mr Minot whipped that little boy from the time he could crawl. There'd be seven nights in a row when his mother and I would have to go to him and try to comfort him – his mother gave him Gregory's by the bottleful so he'd cry quietly and escape more beatings still."

I felt cold. "What did Channing do to be beaten?" I asked. "Was he a bad, wicked child?"

"No, not really. He took biscuits from the kitchen. He

broke a piece of china now and then. He was naughty sometimes, answered back once or twice – but don't all children do that? Mrs Minot, whatever his faults, he didn't deserve all those beatings. And I used to think to myself, that boy will grow up to think it's natural to whip children half to death, and he'll treat his own babies as his father treated him. I'd keep your little girl safe with you, if you can."

"Channing and I are separated," I said. "I've no intention of living with him again, so you need not fear for my daughter."

"Good." Kitty shrugged. "I must go," she said, and hurried off without even bidding me goodbye.

Slowly, I walked home. Poor Channing, I thought. I recalled now that when those men had attacked us in the Covent Garden alleyway, he had been almost out of his mind with fear. He'd been so terrified of being hit that he was prepared to see his own wife violated before *he* suffered a beating. Again I could hear him whimpering and pleading.

Just like a little, frightened child.

Chapter 26

We arrived in Manchester on a dark, rainy night, strangers in a strange, dirty industrial town even sootier and filthier than Birmingham. Henry had the address of the theatre in his pocket, but now it was ten minutes past midnight, everywhere was shut up, and we had nowhere to go.

So the wheel had come full circle. After all our successes in America, back in our own country we were mere strolling players again. People outside the pale of decent society, the fit companions of thieves and whores, and of no account whatsoever.

"*Courage, mon amie.*" Taking Adelaide, Henry fastened her inside his greatcoat and smiled encouragingly at me. "First," he announced, "we get something to eat. Then we find a place to stay."

All we could get at that time of night were stale sandwiches and bottled beer. The only lodgings we could find were two stinking rooms above a butcher's shop, for which the landlord demanded three weeks' rent in advance. Henry offered him fifteen shillings on account, which he eventually accepted, but not without a great deal of grumbling beside.

I looked round the room allotted to me. It was dark and dirty, with scratched, stained walls and woodwork, and the floor had not been swept since Adam was a boy. The sheets on the beds were ragged and damp. The cockroaches rattled and scurried behind the flaking plaster. The water supply was a rusty pump in the back yard.

But Henry was cheerful and optimistic, and he raised my flagging spirits. He rocked Addy to sleep, then made us both some hot rum and water. He sat beside me on my sagging bed and hugged me close. "To the success of us both," he said, raising a grubby glass. "God knows, we deserve it."

"We do indeed," I agreed, and drank my cordial down.

We played in about a dozen theatres all over the northwest, and it was good to work again, to dizzy my head with that exotic smell of the theatre which I'd first sniffed with Charlie Rayner such a long time ago. On the negative side, however, the promised dramatic roles did not materialise, and we spent our time feeding lines to low comedians, walking on in burlesques, singing patriotic songs and prancing about in absurd versions of the Highland Fling (very popular just then, on account of the Queen's current obsession with all things Scots).

The audiences in these little circuit theatres were hardly genteel. As the performances went on they ate, drank, smoke, talked among themselves, spat nutshells, belched and farted. The opposite of reticent, they liked to make their views known. "Will you be after showin' a bit more leg, now," yelled the Irish tinkers in the pit, trying to look up the dancers' skirts. And then again, "Look at the size of her, why don't ye, now there's a big girl for you an' all."

This latter observation was directed at a great fat soprano in Salford, who had a face like a frog but sang like a lark ascending. She was wasted in Salford. She should have been at the Italian Opera House, Covent Garden, and I told her so. "I don't think so, my dear," she said sadly. "I'm far too old and plain to think of that."

Perhaps she was. But it was a pity. She was an excellent example of the wasted talent and blighted hopes which pervade our wretched profession, in which an actress is valued only if she is young and pretty. I saw myself at forty, too old to be of use to anyone but a skinflint manager on the northern circuit, who would pay me ten shillings a week, if I was lucky. And the idea depressed me extremely.

"Go on, do your best," whispered Henry one evening in Wigan, as I stood in the wings preparing to go on and face the usual sort of rabble. Dressed as a village maiden, my face was painted like a Dutch doll's, my skirt was up to my knees and my bodice was splitting all down the back. I had to dance a tarantella, and was sure my costume would never survive the evening. The heel was coming off one of my shoes already.

I turned to Henry. I wanted to hide my face on his shoulder and weep. "I feel such a fool," I said miserably. "Just look at me."

"Look at *me*." Ruefully, he grinned. He was got up as a comic doctor, in checked pantaloons and a bright red wig that Dr Dermot Hogan of Jonas Creek would have killed for. I laughed in spite of myself. "That's my girl." Henry grinned. "Rise above it," he whispered. "Off you go. You're on."

So on I skipped, to a chorus of catcalls and whistles and requests that I show the audience my arse. I smirked and flounced and wriggled and despised them all.

While I worked, I'd been obliged to leave Addy with a succession of unsatisfactory minders who had doped her with Atkinson's or Gregory's and otherwise ignored her completely. But although she'd been drugged into insensibility, my poor baby would not starve, for we returned to London from Liverpool with our pockets lined, if not exactly with gold, then with enough ready cash to see us through the next few months without worry.

I had sent our Clerkenwell landlord the rent owing and also the three shillings I'd borrowed, and he met me at his front door with a crooked grin and the comment that he'd never expected to see his money or me again. "Come in," he said, "come in. Now which will you have, the parlour or the first floor back?"

I took my old room again, which had been occupied in my absence by a very dirty fellow who drank, smoked and spat, and it took me and the slavey three days to get it decent again. Henry went into town to see what he could fix up in the way of work for us. He couldn't find anything, and then on the evening of that third day's cleaning up he came in with a very long face indeed.

"What's wrong?" I demanded, assuming he had disagreed with a manager or failed an audition.

"Mr Lockett's shop has been burned down." Sombrely, he

looked at me. "Mr Lockett's body was discovered in the ruins today."

"Mr Lockett?" I was horrified. "Henry, when?"

"Last night. We smelled smoke, remember? We knew there must be fire engines; we heard their bells."

"Yes, so we did." Upset and shaking, I sat down. "So, how did Mr Lockett – "

"The body was badly charred, but the story I've heard is that the police think he was dead before he was burned."

"Murder?" I whispered.

"It would seem likely." Henry sat down beside me. "He was a good man," he said. "Helped me out many and many a time." Heavily, he sighed.

I did not sigh. Once I had recovered from my initial shock, all I felt was anger. Damn Esther! For I was sure Esther Harris must somehow be behind this. Of course I had no proof of her guilt, I could not march into a police station and demand they arrest her immediately, but I knew, in my heart, that Esther was involved in this. I considered what to do. I wondered if perhaps I ought to talk to Kitty.

But I had lost Kitty's new address. Search though I might among the papers at the bottom of my trunk, in that mess of playscripts, notes, bills, receipts and all the other clutter with which I seem to encumber myself everywhere I go, I could not find it.

I decided that I did not like the idea of venturing into Seven Dials on a wild goose chase. Kitty might no longer be there, and I was certain to emerge from that filthy labyrinth with my pockets slit, or worse.

I brooded about Mr Lockett's death for a week or more, becoming more and more convinced that that she-devil must be involved somehow. Finally I could contain myself no longer. Leaving Adelaide in the care of the slavey, I went to Esther's lodging.

It was mid-morning when I arrived. I was admitted to the house by a thin-faced messenger boy, who announced my arrival then scuttled off, presumably on Esther's business.

I found Esther about to take coffee. She and Channing

sat at a table, on which there was a huge mass of papers in Esther's untidy handwriting, and on top of this pile of litter was a tray. A black servant, whose face seemed familiar from somewhere other than here, poured fragrant liquid into fine china cups. He served Esther's perfectly; but Channing's he carelessly slopped into the saucer, without even a murmur of apology.

Channing seemed neither to notice, nor care. "Good morning, Deb," said Esther coolly. "I've been expecting you a month or more since."

I was not invited to sit, so I stood. I was not offered refreshment, so I went without. I could see Channing was ill at ease and fidgety, so I decided it was worth a try. Also, I needed money. I was in funds at the moment, but I did so want the security of a little bit saved, and unless I found work soon I would need to spend my precious tiny capital. Once again my child might be crying for food and my shoes be in holes.

"What do you want, Deb?" asked Channing, condescending to notice me at last.

"Last time I was here," I said, addressing Esther, "you told me you wanted a certain piece of jewellery of mine. I've decided I'll sell it to you. For fifty pounds."

Esther was in the act of raising her coffee cup to her lips, and I was interested to see that as I told her my intention her jowls wobbled and her coffee spilled. She coughed. She cleared her throat. "You still have it, then?" she asked, or rather croaked. Channing, I was fascinated to observe, had gone as grey-white as his rather dirty shirt.

"Yes, I still have it," I said. "Did you think I had lost it, then?"

"No." Recovering now, Esther shrugged. "No, I hadn't thought about it recently at all. So what did you say you wanted for it?"

"Fifty pounds."

"Indeed." Esther laughed. "My dear Deb, it's worth less than a sovereign. But since Channing has a yearning to possess it, I'll humour you both. I'll give you ten pounds."

"Fifty," I said firmly. "Otherwise it stays mine."

"Does it, now?" sneered Esther. "Such brave words. Deb, we could have it for nothing, if we chose. We could take it by force."

"I doubt if you will, though." I went over to where Channing sat slumped, looking worried. "Channing," I said softly, "I know what you and Esther did. If you don't make it worth my while to keep silent, I'll go to the police and inform on you. Then you'll both be dangling from the highest gallows in the land."

Bluff. Sheer bluff. But I thought it was worth a try.

It seemed to work. Channing's face lost what vestige of colour it had had. "What do you mean?" he demanded, ashen, but forcing a smile.

"I mean there's been an untimely death," I said. "I mean a poor old man was killed and his house set ablaze. I mean that certain people in this room might know something about all that."

"I don't know what you're talking about." Channing's smile was sickly now, and sweat stood in beads on his forehead. However could I have thought him charming, handsome, loveable, kind? He was a reptile. No, that comparison degrades reptiles.

"You *do* understand what I'm saying," I murmured. "Channing, if you refuse to co-operate now, I'll certainly pay you back for all you've done to me. I'll teach you a lesson you'll never forget."

"I don't think so," he said softly, but he was still sweating. He glanced at Esther, whose face was stony. I had a feeling he was afraid of Esther – but then he was afraid of most people.

She glared at him, then at me. "What a pair of fools," she said scornfully. "What a pair of useless, ignorant fools."

I took that to mean there was to be no deal. I let myself out of the house.

On the way home, I wondered what I should do next. If Channing really wanted some bit of worthless rubbish, and would leave Addy and me alone if he got it, it might be worth my while to let him have it. For fifty pounds, of course. I'd have to get him on his own, and browbeat him into agreement. He'd never do anything if Esther was there.

I yawned. I was very tired. Addy was teething, cutting some of her back molars, and that week I was getting very little sleep. I decided to let Channing sweat a bit more, then go and see him again.

The last place I expected to see Channing's name was on the third page of Henry's daily newspaper, a fortnight later. I would probably never have seen it at all, had not Henry brought it to my attention. "I'm sorry, my dear," he said, as he handed me the page, "but I suppose you would want to know."

To my absolute amazement, I read that Channing Minot had been arrested for murder. Not for the murder of Mr Lockett, as I'd have expected – but for that of his own parents, more than five years ago.

I sat down and stared at the page in front of me. His parents had been dead for a long time, their bodies had long since mouldered into dust. So when, and how, had the matter come to light at all?

The evidence, it appeared, was in the form of an anonymous letter to the police. This epistle included a confession of guilt purporting to be the murderer's own, taken down verbatim by the honest citizen who had also written the letter. And when Channing Minot was visited and questioned, it became clear that the letter wasn't a hoax. The interviewee admitted everything. The police appeared to have a case.

I was astonished that Channing had confessed to a crime to which there had been no witnesses.

But confess he had, and, it seemed, at length.

Incredible.

But then I remembered his extreme cowardice, and while I hesitate to suggest that the police had beaten a confession out of him, I was sure that a very little physical pressure would have made him talk, regardless of the consequences. "Take her, then," he'd told the thug who'd threatened me. To save himself a thrashing, he'd have watched his own wife being raped in a public street.

"When will he be tried?" I asked Henry, still stunned.

"At the next quarter sessions, I assume." Henry eyed me narrowly. "Did you suspect it?" he demanded. "When you married him, did you ever imagine anything like this?"

"No! Never!" I stared at him. "He said his parents were dead. What of that? People *do* die!"

"Indeed they do," said Henry drily.

"I can't believe it's possible," I said. "I *know* Channing!"

But then, even as I said it, I knew that wasn't true. I didn't know Channing at all. Everything he did took me by surprise – his gambling, his affair with Esther Harris, and now this – all of these things had come to hit me out of the blue, and they'd shocked me to the core of my being.

"I'm being blackmailed," he'd said, when he was explaining why certain of his debts could never be paid. He hadn't told me why, and I hadn't asked. How naïve I was then. How childish, how stupid, how impossibly ignorant!

"Would you like some brandy?" asked Henry gently, seeing I was staring into nothing.

"No." I blinked rapidly, and turned to him. "No," I repeated firmly. "Well – what happened to you today?"

"I received an offer." Henry shrugged. "I have an engagement for two months, at the Princesses. I was coming back to tell you but then I met a friend who asked me to go and have coffee with him. As we waited I glanced through my paper – and discovered all that about Channing Minot. So I felt I should come home, and – "

"Henry, Henry, stop a moment. You did say the Princesses?"

"Yes."

The Princesses! This was a great leap from the ridiculous to the sublime, for the Princesses was one of the best theatres in London. I was astonished again, but delighted this time. "You'll play with Mr Macready?" I demanded.

"Yes. I'm to have Laertes, Macduff and Cassio."

"Heavens." I clapped my hands to my mouth. "He'll mangle you," I declared. For in addition to being the greatest classical actor of the age, William Charles Macready was well known to be a man of limited self-control, fierce temper, strong passions and great physical strength, who had a wide and apparently well-deserved reputation for undue violence towards his fellow players. And Henry Collis was nowhere near fit enough to be thrown across the stage of the Princesses three or four times a night. "Henry," I said solemnly, "he'll kill you."

"I'm rather afraid of that." Wryly, Henry smiled. "I only have the parts because Mr Traynor, who was playing them until yesterday, is at home with a broken collarbone. He says he's had enough of being Macready's prime victim and some other fool can take his place. *I* must try to keep out of the old fellow's way."

"That'll be difficult."

"Well." Henry grinned. "I may be mangled, as you say. But anyway, it's work."

"I must try to find something myself. Henry, I owe you hundreds of pounds."

"Don't fret about that." He smiled at me kindly. "Keep me company," he said. "Bind up my wounds. Care for Addy. That's enough for you to do just now."

Bind up his wounds, he said. This turned out to be a prophecy, not a joke. Every night from then on, I met him at the door of our lodgings with liniment and bandages, ready to deal with all the cuts, bruises, scrapes and strains he collected over the next few weeks. "He nearly had your eye out tonight," I told him one evening. I dabbed at a very nasty cut just below Henry's left eyebrow. "Was that during the sword fight?" I asked.

"Yes."

"I thought so." I wondered about sending out for a doctor, as I thought the cut might need to be sutured. "Look, Henry – don't you think perhaps you've suffered enough now?"

"You mean I should give up?" he demanded.

"I think you're being given more punishment than is good for you. You're not a prizefighter, you know."

"I sometimes feel like one." Henry winced. "But I can't

give up. These few weeks are probably the high point of my life. 'See this scar? I was given it by the great Mr Macready himself.' What a tale to tell my grandchildren!"

"You haven't any grandchildren."

"Perhaps I shall have, one day." Henry rubbed his face. "My teeth on this side rattle," he grumbled. "If he's not careful, I'll start to hit him back."

But as he'd said, it was work. He was paid handsomely for being Mr Macready's punchbag, and even began to save something towards our next season of rainy days.

The old actor wasn't deliberately vindictive, either. He just got carried away. The day after he slammed Henry against a flat, breaking his wrist and almost dislocating his jaw, he sent round a handsome apology and a case of best champagne.

"Do you wish to visit him?" asked Henry one day, a month or so after we'd first seen the report about my husband.

"Visit Channing?" I shrugged. "I don't think so," I replied. "It would look as if I were gloating."

"He might want to talk to you. To make his peace before he – well, before he – "

"Dies. No, I don't want to see him."

"But he is your husband." Reproachfully, Henry looked at me. "I think you ought to go. Just once."

"No!" I jumped up and glared at him. "No, I'll never visit him! Let that woman see him, if she wishes. Let her comfort him!"

"My dear Deb, the man's in prison. Soon he'll be on trial for his life. This is no time to be jealous of his affection for someone else." Henry touched my hand. "I really feel you ought to go."

"You don't understand." I snatched my hand away – but then I shook my head. "We mustn't quarrel," I said. "Please, Henry, let's not quarrel. Not over Channing Minot."

"Don't you want to see him ever again?"

"I'll see him on the scaffold," I replied.

But I did not have to decide whether to attend the trial, let alone the execution. In the event, Channing fell ill in prison, and died of a putrid fever before the court could try him, before the hangman could break his neck.

I was glad he'd died in prison. What he'd done was horrible, and I'm sure many people would have agreed he deserved a disgraceful death, with the hangman pulling on his legs to choke him and the crowd jeering as he expired. But I could not find it in my heart to regret his escape from that.

The newspapers said the prison chaplain had been with my husband when he died. That he had repented at length and prepared his soul to meet his creator. I wished I could believe he'd repented of his wickedness; but I doubted it. I imagined he'd lied and fudged and shifted until the last.

And I wondered what part, if any, Esther Harris had played in this. If I'd seen that anonymous letter, would I have known the hand?

Some weeks later, a great boxful of books and papers was delivered to my Clerkenwell lodging. Inside I discovered a mass of family documents all relating to the Minots. The box contained no covering letter, however, so I could only assume that my husband had taken all this stuff with him to prison, and had asked for it to be delivered to me when he was dead.

Most of the books were in French, so I could not read them. I sold them to a dealer, by weight. I sorted the papers into piles, a tiresome business. I turned up only one item of interest, a newspaper cutting about the marriage of Channing's grandparents, Pierre Minot of London and Anne Parker of Newbury, Berkshire.

There was also a family Bible, printed in French. This recorded the births of Thomas Minot, Channing's father, and of a sister Elisabeth, whom I supposed had died young. For Thomas there were additional details of his marriage to Jane Gibbs and a record of the birth of his son Channing – but for his sister Elisabeth, there was nothing more.

Then there were letters, dozens of them, old yellowing things. Among these was a note from Alexander Channing's widow, asking Thomas Minot for a loan. I assumed that this

Alexander Channing was the man after whom my husband was named.

In the end, I couldn't be bothered to sift through all this stuff. So much waste paper, I thought. So much useless rubbish. I threw it all away.

But I kept the Bible. To the Minot family record I added the date of Adelaide's birth. What a heritage, I thought. What a bloodline, poor child. I was almost glad I did not know who my own forebears were.

I looked down at my hands. I twisted my wedding ring round and round, and sighed. So now I was a widow. I was free again, at liberty to choose another partner if I pleased.

Another partner. As I sat in the deepening twilight, it came to me, it hit me like a thunderbolt. I knew, and I had known for years now, who I wanted my partner to be.

Chapter 27

"It's the only way," said Henry. He was still nursing two broken fingers and a badly bruised jaw, but his engagement opposite Mr Macready had otherwise been a success, and led to his hearing about another opening in East Anglia, of all places – in Ipswich, I believe.

"My dear Deborah," he went on, seeing my long face, "what else can I do? I owe Fred six hundred and fifty pounds. I've saved two hundred of which I'll let him have half, and I'll use the other hundred on this venture. Look, I'll be away five weeks. Six, maybe. Seven at the most."

"Oh," I said. I could not conceal my dejection. I did not even try.

"Cheer up." In his usual fatherly fashion, Henry patted my arm. "Two of the people in this company are friends from years back," he continued. "The fellow managing them is getting old, he's not really fit enough for touring. I might take his place; set myself up again."

"But couldn't you do that in London?" I demanded. "Look, if Mr Macready likes you, perhaps he could help?"

"Macready doesn't own theatres. He doesn't manage circuits." Henry shrugged. "I'm afraid that going to America was, in retrospect, a very bad move. But if I can now get half a dozen people together, if I can take over an established company, our troubles should be over. There'll be a place in the group for you, of course," he concluded. "If you want it, that is."

I turned my head away. "Oh," I said, "you have no obligations to me."

"On the contrary, I have obligations of the most particular

kind. Those born of gratitude, affection, esteem – "

He took my two hands in his and, raising them to his lips, he kissed them. "I'll always feel obliged to you, my dear," he said. "You'll always have my most sincere friendship, and my absolute trust."

But not his love. He did not say, his love.

There was no question of trying to prevent his going, of course. What could I have said, or done, to make him stay? That I was ill, and needed him? It wouldn't have been true.

But I was not *well*. I had had so much worry and anxiety that these days my health was poor, to say the least. My eyes were shadowed, my complexion dull, and, never robust, I had now declined dramatically and become very thin. So thin, in fact, that when I was walking down High Holborn one day, carrying Addy in my arms, a gentleman had stopped me and pressed a couple of shillings into my hand. He'd advised me to get myself to a pie shop, without delay.

Henry gave me a banker's draft for thirty pounds, with which I should keep myself and Addy while he was away. "By the way, Lucinda and Fred are back," he told me. "I met a mutual friend in the Strand today, and he gave me their new address."

The following day Henry went off on the tour of East Anglia, which he hoped would set him up again. He intended to put together a company for that coming season, and take it round the country. In fact, we'd be right back where we were when I first met him, he would be the manager of a group of strollers and I would be a wandering vagabond too.

If I chose.

But did I really want that? Did I honestly wish to trail all around England tied to a man who kept me with him out of *obligation*?

I could work on my own account, I thought. I could even put together my own small company, I could become a manager myself.

An impossible dream? Maybe. I was a woman, and although women did manage theatree troups, they were a rarity in what was still almost entirely a man's world. I did not have Henry's contacts, nor his enormous circle of acquaintances. But I knew what to do, and how to do it.

Perhaps, I thought. Perhaps.

I hugged the idea to myself, like a lover. And like a lover, it warmed me.

I resolved that I would not fret. I saw Henry off, then I dressed myself and Addy in our best clothes and went to see Lucinda and Fred.

They were living in the grandest style. Giving my name, we were admitted to smart new lodgings in one of London's most fashionable squares. I was taken upstairs by a powdered flunkey, then shown into a flower-filled vestibule by a French maidservant, whose gown was considerably newer than my own. The maid took my name again. One minute later, we were taken into milady's *salon*.

"Darling!" The toast of Paris and now dressed in the height of French fashion, Lucinda swept Addy and me into her embrace, almost suffocating us with her perfume. "Darling Deb," she cried, "darling, darling Deb, where have you *been*? Have you been working? Someone told me you were in Liverpool, was it true?"

"Yes, I'm afraid it was."

"How horrid for you! But never mind, you're here now. Oh, my darling girl and darling baby, I've thought about you constantly and now here you are and it's all too much for me."

She blinked back tears. "How is darling Henry?" she demanded. "And why isn't he with you?"

"Henry's gone to Ipswich. Didn't you know?"

"No." Lucinda's eyes grew round. "Fred, do you hear? Henry's gone off and left her. The wicked, wicked man! Very well then – let's talk about him. Let's call him all the most horrible things we can!"

I didn't mind what Lucinda called him. In spite of all my strong-minded resolutions, it eased my heart just to hear his name.

I brought Fred and Lucinda up to date. "So he's off on another wild goose chase, that's what it boils down to," said Lucinda crossly, when I'd finished. "But then, that's Henry all over."

"What do you mean?" I asked.

"Oh, you know perfectly well." Irritably, Lucinda tapped her patent leather shoe on the polished floor. "He's so wrong-headed. So wilful. I've never known a man so deliberately blind to his own interest as Henry Collis is!"

"But, Lucinda!"

"But nothing." Lucinda took my hands in hers. "My dear Deborah," she said earnestly, "all men are fools. But some are so extraordinarily foolish that they verge on the imbecile. Now, Henry Collis – "

"Henry Collis what?" enquired Fred, frowning to hear his friend so traduced.

"Be quiet." Lucinda grimaced. "Deb, I think you already know this, but it'll do no harm to say it again. Henry needs to be pushed, and pushed hard. He needs to be taken to the water, told he needs to drink – *and* shown how to do it! If ever there was a perfect fool to himself, then Henry Collis is his name. And so – "

And now Lucinda abused Henry at length, talked of her beaux in Paris, then came round to abusing Henry again.

"Do you think Henry will ever marry?" I asked idly, as she paused for breath.

"*I* don't know. Plenty of women would have him, if that's what you mean." Lucinda sighed. "I've always thought him attractive. Extremely attractive, in fact. Far more so than this blue-jawed oaf," she added, smirking archly at Fred.

"Go and boil your bonnet, Luce," said Fred composedly, from behind his newspaper. "And stop tormenting poor Deborah here."

"I'm doing nothing of the kind." Lucinda turned back to me. "I'll never understand why he was so fond of Pen Gaynes," she went on reflectively. "Temperamental, bossy, dictatorial, *fat* – why do men like fat women?"

"Something to get hold of in bed," muttered Fred. "All that blubber – something to grab at." He laid down his paper. "Can't see the attraction of steam barges myself. Never could."

"There's no accounting for taste." Primly, Lucinda folded her hands. "I wonder if he will marry?" she murmured. "Sometimes I see him as – "

"A typical single man," interrupted Fred.

"No!"

"Yes." Sarcastically Fred grinned. "A social butterfly, flitting from flower to flower. Sipping the nectar and fluttering on, with ne'er a backward glance at all the broken hearts he's left behind him."

"But I *can* see him as a family man," insisted Lucinda. "At his own fireside, with a babe on each knee."

"And one day, goats will fly," laughed Fred.

If I had hoped to be comforted by hearing Lucinda speaking Henry's name, I was disappointed. I came away from her lodgings feeling more miserable than when I'd set out.

Fred was right. Henry was a typical single man. He did like women built like steam barges. I put the fact that there were no steam barges in evidence these days down to his late illness, but I did not doubt that in the new company there'd be blubber enough to take his fancy. As for me – I was slim to the point of emaciation these days.

Then something happened which, in the course of twenty-four hours, caused the little flesh I did have on my bones to melt away.

Adelaide went missing.

It happened two days after I'd seen Fred and Lucinda. The woman I'd paid to mind her while I went to see the manager at a theatre in Edgware had "slipped out for a moment" and come home to find her gone.

I arrived back in Clerkenwell to find the nurse absolutely frantic with anxiety. She was a good woman, a mother of six who took in washing and mending and generally worked her fingers to the bone for her family, and I'd left Addy with her before. I'd trusted her completely. I'd never have imagined she would let me down.

Now here she was at my lodgings telling me she'd lost my baby.

I leaned towards her and sniffed. No gin. "Calm yourself,

Mrs Hawkins," I said, far from calm myself. "Tell me again, how long were you away?"

"Ten minutes, Mrs Minot. I went across the way to the chandler's shop. She was fast asleep after her dinner, you see, so I thought there'd be no harm in it if I just slipped out. Oh, Mrs Minot, what can have become of her?" And the poor woman wept.

As she sobbed, I heard the front door slam. And then the slavey brought me a folded piece of paper. "Black man give it me," she said, shaking. "Black man wiv big white teeth. Said to hand it to you directly."

I was acquainted with only one black man in London.

My heart sank.

I unfolded the paper, and read.

"If you mean to keep that pretty face of yours and if you want to see Adelaide again," ran the note, "do just as you are bidden. Come to meet me at seven this evening. Bring the pendant with you.

"*Tell no one.*"

These last three words were heavily underlined.

The note gave an address in Bermondsey. South of the river. Unknown territory to me. I assumed this was one of Esther's bolt holes in times of trouble.

For who could be writing notes like this except Esther Harris?

If she had not taken Adelaide, I would have ripped her ridiculous letter to pieces and trodden it into the mire. If she had not stolen my child, I would have gone to see her that minute and sorted things out between us once and for all, for I was sick and tired of her meddling in my affairs.

But any mother will know how I felt about Adelaide. And I was dealing here with a person who, I was almost certain, had been implicated in at least two untimely deaths; and who would not, I believed, have any compunction about getting involved in a third.

"Tell no one," she'd written. But, aware of how ruthless Esther could be, I felt I had no choice but to involve the City Police.

In terror for my child, my anxiety growing by the minute so that my stomach became knotted and my throat dried, I wrapped myself in my shawl. Glancing nervously to the left and right, looking for Esther's shadowy servant, I slipped down the street, not stopping until I reached Chancery Lane police station. I went timidly inside.

A young sergeant with great black shadows under his eyes yawned as he took down my story. "What will you do?" I asked, for he seemed very bored and disinclined to believe a word I said.

"I'll ask one of our non-uniformed officers to step round to your lodgings." He yawned again, hugely. "So you just hop back home and wait for him to come."

So I sat at home, worrying lest I had been spotted going into the police station. I had no real hope of being visited by any detective. I looked at the clock, wondering when I should set out for Mill Street. I saw that I had hours yet.

My imagination ran riot. I decided that Esther was quite capable of killing a baby. Tearfully I hoped that at least I would be given the body of my child. I hoped that at least I would be able to visit a grave.

To kill time, I hunted out some sheets of writing paper and pens and wrote to Henry, asking him return, begging him to return, for Adelaide had been stolen and I did not know how I could bear it alone. I was just sanding the letter when the slavey rapped on my door and opened it, showing two young men into my room.

"B-beg your pardon, Mis' Minot," she began, "but these gennelmen 'ere wouldn' 'ardly let me bring 'em upstairs, let alone step up an' announce 'em. I told 'em, I said you was busy."

"That'll be all, thank you, Dolly," said one of the men, taking the slavey by her skinny shoulders and firmly turning her out.

He closed the door behind him. "Detective Police, ma'am," he added laconically, eyeing both me and my room. "Sergeant Gower said it was a matter of urgency, so I hope it is."

I assured them that Sergeant Gower had been quite correct,

and both men grinned. "Very well then, Mrs Minot," said the man who had not yet spoken, "let's get to the point. This woman you described down at the police station, the one whom you reckon's taken your child – we know her as Mrs Jarvis, Mrs Weatherall, Mother Cobb, the Opium Queen – "

"And many, many more," said his colleague, gently rubbing a great wart on his chin. "The child's still missing, I assume?"

"Yes."

"Right. So we'll pay Miss H a call. Would you have the goodness to come with us?"

"Yes, of course." I glanced at the clock. "She said to come at seven."

"Quite so. Now, here's what we'll do."

So I set off with my companions, who in fact looked exactly like a pair of strolling actors down on their luck and who, if I met any acquaintances, could easily be passed off as such. One, a lanky, down-at-heel fellow in a blue coat and very dirty fawn trousers, had a sharp, rakish, swaggering air which marked him out instantly as a comedy lead; while the other, the one with the wart, was rather more lugubrious, a seedy provincial Malvolio if ever I saw one.

They took me by cab to London Bridge, where we all alighted, then they gave me precise directions to Mill Street, on the south side of the river.

"Off you go then," said Wart, as I agreed I'd understood their instructions. "We'll be close behind you."

"Don't lose your way," added Blue Coat, grinning.

The policemen were so casual that I was convinced they thought of this as a game. I was trailed along the dirty highway and, glancing back occasionally, I would see Blue Coat idly inspecting a vegetable barrow, Wart pushing a crowd of dirty, ragged children aside, Blue Coat biting into an apple while Wart kicked a stone across the road.

I had never been south of the river before, and it seemed like a different world. Although Clerkenwell was seedy, it was positively genteel compared with this district. Here, old clothes shops lined the pavements, spilling malodorous rags from rickety trestles, offering goods which already looked like so much waste shoddy to me. Barrowmen offered rotten fruit and vegetables for sale, and scrawny women haggled over the price of a bagful of blackened potatoes or yellowing cabbage leaves. Thin, dirty children sailed paper boats down gutters full of visible sewage.

From the doorways of collapsing, crumbling buildings came unappetising smells of cooking, reminiscent of dirty laundry. Parker's Court had been a light, airy, desirable place of residence compared with Mill Street's repulsive slums.

I looked back over my shoulder to see Wart still shambling along. Now he had a dirty felt hat pulled down over his face, while Blue Coat was got up like a poor tradesman, a carpenter perhaps, with a ruler sticking out of his jacket pocket.

I thought, I must be nearing the place. I stopped a dirty urchin, and asked directions. "End of the parf," he said, jerking his thumb behind him. "Can't miss it. Last 'ouse before the rivvah."

The policemen contrived to reach the house just as I did. Well, I call it a house, but that suggests a home. This was a crazy, rotting building at the end of a muddy lane, so near the river that I supposed it must be flooded during the spring tides. Certainly its walls were green and mildewed, suggesting that the place was permanently damp. It smelled of dead animals. A door, once painted blue, hung off its hinges. Peering inside, I could see nobody. In front of me were some dangerous-looking stairs. "Go on," whispered Wart, coming up behind me. "We'll be here. Get her talking, if you can."

So, alone, I began to make my way up the staircase, clinging to a wobbling banister. The policemen melted into the shadows.

When I was halfway up, the door at the top of the stairs opened and I saw her. "Come on, Deb," she coaxed, mocking. "Nearly there."

She went back into the room and I followed her. As I entered this apartment Esther locked the door behind us and pocketed the key.

The baby lay upon a narrow iron bedstead, and looked so peaceful that I knew at once she was dead. "I gave her a little Gregory's," said Esther offhandedly. "She was fractious, you see."

"Damn you!" Tears filled my eyes and flowed down my cheeks. "Damn you, damn you! May you rot in hell for ever!"

I snatched up the baby and held her. To my unspeakable relief she was just breathing. But she was limp and pale. In my arms, her head lolled and her eyelids rolled back, making her eyeballs clearly visible. I stared into those sightless eyes, I repeated her name over and over, but I got no response.

She was in a deep, drugged slumber. But at least she was alive.

"She's come to no harm," remarked Esther carelessly, obviously enjoying my distress. "She's asleep, that's all."

"When did you dose her?"

"Hours ago." Esther shrugged. "I only gave her a couple of teaspoonsful."

"It looks as if you gave her a whole bottleful!" I glared at Esther so angrily that even she flinched a little. "You idiot, don't you know that stuff can kill?"

A silly question. Of course she knew.

"Did you bring the pendant?" asked Esther.

"Yes." I handed it over without demur.

Esther examined it closely and grunted, satisfied. She looped it over her wrist. "Very well," she muttered. "You may take your brat, and go."

I stood where I was. Get her talking, the policeman had said. "Before I leave," I said, looking pointedly at the pendant, "tell me why you want that."

"What?"

"Tell me why you want my necklace. Just out of interest." Now I had Adelaide safe, I could relax, and I smiled at her. "Tell me, Essie," I wheedled, using the childhood name by which I'd called her when we were friends. Well, sort of friends. "Tell me, what is it to you?"

"It's just – no. Why should I tell you?" Esther's beady

eyes became nearly invisible. "Why should I tell you anything?"

"It wouldn't do any harm, would it?" I rocked Addy, and she whimpered. Soon, she'd begin to recover. All she needed was time. "I offered to sell it to you," I reminded her. "But you wouldn't buy it."

"For fifty pounds?" She laughed. "Deb, I'm not a charitable institution. Never was."

"So why – "

"Oh, stop whining. I'll tell you." I realised now that Esther Harris was rather drunk. Her hands were shaking, and I could smell spirits on her breath.

"I never told Channing," she muttered. "He thought it was just a valuable jewel." Gummily, she grinned. "It's the key to a fortune, that's what it is."

"I don't understand," I said. Where were those wretched policemen? Why didn't they burst in and arrest this creature, why? "You'll have to explain."

Esther sat down on the bed. "When you were left with old Haskell," she began, "you were just a baby. Your mother was a common whore and your father – well, I suppose he was some idle vagrant passing through. He turned up in Birmingham now and then.

"Some said he was an actor, but Haskell thought that was all nonsense. He was usually too drunk to walk, let alone get up on a stage; so I expect he was just a beggar, or a rogue.

"Anyway. The whore was a conscientious mother, she paid Haskell every week, regular as you like. But then she became ill and couldn't go out looking for customers.

"Old Haskell cut up rough." Esther grinned. "God knows, the old bag had screwed enough out of the poor harlot, she'd always been paid on time; but she wanted this week's cash, she said, or you'd be out on the street.

"So, since the woman hadn't got any money, she gave Haskell the pendant. I suppose some client gave it her. Or she pinched it. I dare say old Haskell meant to pawn it, but then she changed her mind. She wore it now and then but later she sewed it up in the hem of her cloak."

"The one you stole," I put in.

"I borrowed it." Esther glared at me. "It was you who stole it."

"Unwittingly. I thought it was mine." Bitterness welled up inside me then. "You branded me as a thief!" I cried. "You had me hunted as a criminal, you blackened my name!"

"Oh, that's old history." With a wave of her pudgy hand, Esther dismissed my complaint. "You were such a fool, Deb," she said, grinning. "So easy to frame. Well, after you ran off things got a bit warm at the Taylors', so I left Orchard House and went back to Parker's Court. When old Haskell heard you'd scarpered and taken her pendant with you, she threw a fit. Hit me. Said she'd had it assayed, been told it was an emerald. Always was a liar, old Haskell. Anyway, what she didn't know was – "

"What?"

"This." Esther took out a pocket-book and riffled through a great wad of bills of exchange and other documents. "Here it is," she said and handed me a yellow, faded, crumbling piece of newspaper. On this was an advertisement for information, and a drawing of a pendant.

My pendant.

Unmistakeable.

There was the stone, and curling round it the metal snake. The drawing was meticulously done, the detail exact. Beneath this, unnecessarily, was a description of the object in question and a request that anyone having information of its whereabouts should write to Mr Charles Heeling, attorney at law, in Bolton Court, Fleet Street.

"How did you know about this?" I asked, handing the cutting back to her. "And why is that thing the key to a fortune?"

"I came across the advertisement by chance. Then I made investigations of my own. I have my contacts, you see." Esther shrugged. "England's such a small country," she said. "Sooner or later – and if you're in my line of business it's usually sooner – you're bound to meet someone who knows someone."

"I dare say." I yawned. The room was fuggy, I was suddenly very tired, and I had had enough of this nonsense. I just wanted to go home.

I had given up all hope of those policemen arriving. By now, I thought, they'd probably sloped off to a tavern, or been distracted by the prostitutes who infested this district.

"So I saw the lawyer myself," said Esther, "and I told him I might know where this thing was to be found."

"Whose was it?" I asked.

"That he wouldn't tell me. But I did come up with some information."

"What?"

"The person who placed this advertisement is rich. Very rich. Owns a large property in Berkshire and another in Kent."

"So what are you hoping to get out of this?" I asked. As if I didn't know.

"None of your business. It's time for you to leave." Esther's face was hard now. "Go on. You know the way."

"You'll have to unlock the door," I said.

"Oh yes." With an effort, Esther got to her feet. "That husband of yours," she muttered, as she searched for the key, "he was rather interesting once. But he became very tiresome, in the end."

"In the end?" I looked at her. "So it *was* you who wrote that letter?"

"Of course it was." Esther shrugged. "Did you think I would – "

But by now the policemen listening outside the door had wearied of this, and even as Esther at last took the door key from her pocket, the sound of splintering wood filled the room.

"Don't move," cried Blue Coat. "You, Harris – hand over that pendant."

But Esther wasn't going to be told what to do by a scruffy little plain clothes detective. As the policeman walked towards her she stepped back and threw my pendant from the window, into the muddy steet below.

When Wart and I went to look for it, of course it wasn't there.

Chapter 28

Henry wrote to tell me that everything was going well for him. As usual, his letter began with "My dear Deborah," and concluded with "Yours most affectionately, H. R. Collis."

The meat in this sandwich was made up of facts. There were no protestations of affection, no telling me he missed me, nothing which could have tickled Lucinda's fancy at all. It was a letter from a father to a grown-up daughter. From a guardian to a ward.

He was acting again, he told me, and had come to an arrangement with the retiring manager of the Ipswich company. So now he was getting together a group of his own, to put on the plays he wanted to perform.

"I have got hold of a couple of very good men who can turn their hands and talents to most things," he said, "and now I'm looking out for another lady or two." Preferably blubbery ones I reflected, sourly.

I turned the page to read the last paragraph and had a surprise. Henry had, he concluded, mentioned me to a Mr Franklin, a circuit manager he'd met passing through Colchester. This man had taken a London theatre for a short season, and was anxious to find a young actress capable of playing comedy and tragedy, for his current leading lady had let him down.

Run off with an earl, I supposed.

Mr Franklin remembered seeing me in Liverpool, and thought he might consider me for London work. When he arrived in town, he would be in touch.

I put the letter in my box and walked over to the window. So the manager would be in touch, would he? He'd consider me for London work? If only he would! I was so anxious to find something that, in return for a firm engagement and a weekly salary, I would have agreed to walk on in burlesques, turn cartwheels, dance on a high wire – anything. I wished Mr Franklin would contact me.

But if wishes were horses, beggars would ride. Wishes wouldn't feed Addy or keep me in stockings. Two weeks went by, my small stock of ready cash dwindled even further, and I heard nothing.

And then, to my astonishment, Mr Franklin called me for audition at the New Globe in Southampton Row.

"You could begin directly, Mrs Minot?" he asked, when he'd ascertained that I could act, sing, dance and be heard at the back of the gallery.

"Certainly." It does not do to seem too eager, I suppose, but I *was* eager that day. I was desperate. "Yes," I said, "I could begin tomorrow."

"Excellent." Mr Franklin slapped his knee and grinned. "We start rehearsals tomorrow. I'll see the printers today."

It was a miracle. Out of work and near destitute that morning, by afternoon I was signed up to play Juliet, Viola and Rosalind and several good parts in some brand new plays, at one of the best theatres in London.

So it was that, a week later, I saw bills going up to proclaim my first appearance on any London stage. Nervously I wondered how much capital Mr Franklin had tied up in this.

But perhaps Mr Franklin was more astute than I'd imagined. Plenty of people came not to watch *Twelfth Night* or *As You Like It*, but to gawp at me. To have a good stare at the widow of Channing Minot, the man who had cold-bloodedly murdered both his parents. Whose mistress, a common criminal, was now languishing in prison on a charge of kidnapping my infant daughter (and an assortment of other crimes).

"When do you expect Henry back in town?" asked Lucinda, who of course came to see me on my first night, bringing with her a great gaggle of friends and hangers on, all gentlemen.

"Within a week or two." I was removing my paint and now

I scrubbed at my face so hard that Lucinda would not notice my blush. "Has he written to Fred?"

"Oh, Fred's had a bankbill and a short note. Came last Friday, I believe." Lucinda grinned. "It's been eight weeks or more now. I'd have thought he'd have written some nice long letters to you?"

But I didn't want to discuss Henry with Lucinda. Instead I went over to reclaim Addy from the scene-shifter who had been minding her while I worked.

"I don't think you ought to leave this little precious back there," announced Lucinda, as we drove home. "Why don't I look after her?"

"Would you want to?" I asked.

"I'd love it." Lucinda took Addy in her arms, and cooed like a nesting dove. "Will she come to stay with Aunt Luce then, darling?" she burbled.

Addy burbled in reply, and pulled Aunt Luce's hair.

So it was settled. Adelaide went to stay with Lucinda, who was resting after her triumphs in Paris and being kept in the lap of luxury by Fred. *He* was in great demand as a villain in pantomimes, a hero in Shakespeare, a comic lead in farces – his star, it seemed, would burn ever brighter, for these days his kind of ranting, howling and roaring appeared to be the very thing to bring in the London crowds.

"He *is* an old fraud," agreed Lucinda affectionately, when I said I thought Fred's growling, prowling portrayal of the baron in an otherwise terrible melodrama was the only good thing about it. "Yes, my dear, I'd say he was a *great* fraud."

"I didn't quite mean that," I said quickly, terrified that Lucinda would go straight home and announce, Deborah thinks you're a fraud. "I meant he was so energetic. So enthusiastic, as well."

"Yes, he's an energetic, enthusiastic fraud." Lucinda laughed and patted my hand. "Don't worry, he knows he's all wind and flurry. And he's well aware that compared with dear Henry, he's a blustering, bombastic amateur who couldn't *act* his way out of a brown paper parcel. How is poor Henry, by the way? I can't help wondering."

"He wrote to me earlier this week," I replied. "He hopes to be back in town on Wednesday."

"And it had quite slipped your mind," said Lucinda drily. "Oh well. Have you seen yesterday's papers?"

"No. Why?"

"Such goings on." Lucinda giggled. "Look!"

I looked at the page she offered me and I saw that Esther had escaped from prison.

She was being transferred from a gaol in London to one in another part of the country, and had been locked up for the night in a police station en route. When, the following morning, a policeman had gone to take in her breakfast, he had found a patient figure waiting for him. Bonneted, head bowed, she was a bulky person clad in regulation prison garb – who had looked up at him so suddenly that the bright dark eyes, black face and sharp white teeth had frightened the officer out of his wits.

He'd dropped the bowl of food with a crash and fallen gibbering against the wall, crossing himself and muttering that he'd seen the devil. The black man walked out of the cell, up the stairs and out of the police station entirely.

Advertisements for information leading to his arrest were soon up all over town, but these posters showed a caricature negro. A grinning black face, its great mouthful of tombstone teeth took up half the visage; it was a face no human being ever possessed.

"It would make the most capital burlesque," said Lucinda thoughtfully. "Take it very fast, put in a bit of banter, some of the usual business."

"Mm," I agreed. "Fred could put something like that in his next pantomime."

"Yes!" Lucinda clapped her hands and laughed. "He could play the negro himself," she said. "I've always wanted to see him in blackface. But blacked up *and* in a gown, bonnet and ringlets – my dear, I shall die!" She threw back her head and guffawed.

Other people also saw the theatrical potential of the exploit, and for the next few weeks all the London theatres were featuring sketches about a white woman who could turn at will into a black man, who walked through walls and opened locked doors as easily as if they were garden gates.

How had Esther escaped, and how had her black servant substituted himself for her? This was never established. And although I knew her escape would annoy Blue Coat and Wart no end, and that Esther richly deserved to be in prison, in spite of myself I smiled.

So we never knew what became of Esther, or the pendant. I myself did not much care, for the absence of one more than compensated for the loss of the other.

And Henry finally came back to London. As I was putting Addy to bed one Sunday evening, someone came into the lobby downstairs. I heard a man's voice say something to the slavey, there was a chinking of coins, and the girl giggled. Poor thing, Henry was the only man who ever took any notice of her.

I went on to the landing. "Henry?" I called, peering into the gloom.

"Deborah!" Seeing me at the top of the stairs he bounded up, and in seconds he was with me. I was in his embrace and we were laughing, talking and laughing again, all at once. He hugged me for a full five minutes. And then he drew back and took my hands.

"Oh, my dear," he cried, "I have missed you! You received my last letter?"

"Yes." I was sniffing now.

"Mr Fearis has a room for me?"

"Yes. Your usual one. Downstairs."

"What's the matter?" Henry touched my face and brushed away some tears. "Deb, what's wrong?"

"Oh, nothing." Blinking, I swallowed hard. "It's just that it's been so horrible here and you've been away so long – and I'm *so* glad you're back!"

"So am I." He hugged me again. "Where's Addy?" he asked. "I've missed her, too."

* * *

I had intended to forget about the pendant, but for some reason it was always there, lurking like a shadow at the back of my mind. I could see the advertisement asking for information about it; but to my great annoyance I could not remember the name of the attorney who had placed the wretched notice.

However, I had plenty of other things to do. I was appearing five nights a week at the New Globe and I was rehearsing the female leads in four new plays which Henry had bought for his recently formed company. Any time left over found me occupied like any other stroller, stitching costumes and head-dresses in readiness for my new parts, and mending tears in those used for my old.

For, of course, I had agreed to join the company – but, I am happy to add, on my own terms. Remembering what Lucinda had said about Henry needing to be pushed, and pushed hard, I decided to try forcing his hand a little. "This new company," I began, watching his face. "It is to be *our* company? Yours and mine, that is?"

"Yes, of course," he agreed.

"With *our* names on the bills?"

"Well, yes." Looking up from the newspaper he was scanning, he knitted his brows. "'Under the management of Mr Collis and Mrs Minot', or something of the kind. Unless you feel your name should be first? Personally, I think it trips off the tongue better with mine in first place; but if you have any strong preference for the other way about?"

"No, none." He was right, it did sound better that way. "That sounds fine."

"Good." He looked at me. "What's the matter?"

"What do you mean?"

"You're frowning at me."

"I'm not." I put down my sewing. "Oh, I suppose I expected you to argue. That's all."

"Argue? About what?"

"I thought – I wondered – well, this new company of yours – "

"Of *ours*." He clasped his hands together and smiled at me. "I could not even think of undertaking this venture without your participation," he said. "You'll take all the female leads. And I was hoping you'd deal with the salaries and general day-to-day accounts, too."

"Well, if you wish." Certainly I could do that. These past couple of years had made me as sharp and careful an accountant as any in the Bank of England itself. "Well, then?"

"It's all settled." Henry grinned. "You still look surprised."

"And you're the one who's surprised me," I said. "Would you make me some coffee? Very strong, with a little brandy?"

"Of course, madam," he replied.

Henry planned to take our new company on a tour of the Home Counties, and then he hoped to rent a season in a London theatre. While in London, we remained in our Clerkenwell lodgings, of which we'd grown rather fond.

Having more ready cash than I'd had for a long time, I smartened up my bedroom and took a separate sitting-room next door to it, in which Addy could also sleep.

She was beginning to talk now, and every morning she woke me by shrieking "Mama! Dink! MAMA!" at the top of her voice. Then she would lob her rag doll at my head, and she was a remarkably good shot. She would not be quiet until I took her into my bed.

If I had come home late from the theatre, I found all this rather wearing at five in the morning.

I employed a girl to shop and cook for me. One day, as she was unloading her shopping basket, unwrapping her purchases while I added up what I owed the chandler, I saw it. Grabbing the sheet of old newspaper from my astonished little cook-housekeeper's hands, I stared at it and saw that, yes, it was the same, it was an advertisement asking for information, and there was the picture of my pendant, my green glass pendant, the stone encircled by the gilt snake.

"What's the matter?" asked Henry, who walked in just then and retrieved a piece of cheese from the dusty floor. He saw I was pale and his concern was obvious.

"It's nothing," I said, trying to smile. "Nothing at all. I

thought I saw a notice about Fred, I wanted to read it – but it wasn't about him at all."

My little servant could not read. Henry looked at me shrewdly, but asked nothing more. He sat down at the table. He was looking very smart that day, handsome even, in a charcoal-grey coat, black trousers and a very dark blue waistcoat. His fair hair was newly cut, he was neatly shaven and his sallow face even had a bit of red colour in it. In fact, he looked in better health and spirits than he'd been for a long time.

"What are you staring at, Deb?" he demanded. "Has a pigeon left its calling card on my shouders?"

"No, no." I sat down too. "You look – it's just that you look – "

"Like an undertaker's man. Yes, I know. I've been to see Mr Macready," he explained. "These are my humble suitor's robes."

"Why did you visit him?"

"Ah well, I thought to myself, if one doesn't ask one doesn't receive, so I went to his house in town and asked if he'd consider leading two or three performances for me next season."

"You've secured the New Globe, then?" I demanded.

"Yes. Franklin's taking over the Victoria. I saw the lessees today."

"Why didn't you tell *me*?" Angrily, I glared at him. "I'm supposed to be your partner. Yet you go off without saying a word, you sign a contract behind my back! Why?"

"Deborah, listen." Henry ran his fingers through his hair. "Why have both our names on the documents? Why have both of us declared bankrupt next spring?"

"What do you mean?"

"I mean that, if this fails, I shall be in the debtor's prison this time next year. And I don't want you and Addy there with me."

"It won't fail. We'll have a brilliant success." My pendant forgotten, I beamed at him. "My dear Henry, we're bound to succeed. But I must say this now."

"I know. Don't go behind your back again."

"Exactly."

"It's agreed." Henry stood up. "You're not working today, are you? Shall we go out to dinner tonight?"

"We could eat here," I replied. "Judy will cook, and serve."

I wanted him all to myself.

Chapter 29

The season at the New Globe was a wonderful success, I suspect for all the wrong reasons. My notoriety as the widow of Channing Minot still guaranteed good audiences whenever I appeared, and now it was rumoured that, while my wretched husband languished in prison, I had become Henry Collis's mistress. It was said I had even borne him a child, though where this spectral infant was to be found, no one knew.

But fortunately Mr Macready appeared to believe none of that, and his guest performances gave us wide popular appeal. "Asking Macready to perform with us was the smartest thing I ever did," said Henry smugly, as the bills went up and the takings poured in.

"Was it, indeed?" I asked, teasing, pleased for him. "Smarter even than engaging my services, all those years ago?"

"Well. Certainly *as* smart. And he says he'll do another three performances for us." Henry grinned. "I can't think why the old bear's being so affable. I think he must have fallen in love with you."

"Perhaps," I replied. Personally, I thought the great man still felt guilty about knocking Henry about so much, and this was his way of making amends. Although it was true that, in spite of being the most faithful and uxorious of men, Mr Macready was notorious for his sentimental attachments to personable young women, especially actresses.

And what did I think of him? Well, although he was nearing retirement he was still extremely fierce and violent in both speech and manner, and he frightened me half to death. Both off stage and on.

He was terrifying in *Macbeth*, showing up Fred Hammer's interpretation as the burlesque it really was. Fred played Macbeth as a pantomime ogre, a noisy brute who crashed about the stage creating utter chaos; in short, playing the sort of rather uncouth person you would not want in your drawing-room, in case he broke the furniture.

Mr Macready played him as a fiend. He roamed and foamed and growled and prowled about the stage, making retainers flinch and spear-carriers tremble. He spoke his lines so forcefully, so compellingly, that whenever he paused – for effect, of course, not because he'd forgotten his words, as our unfortunate new prompter one night assumed, hissing them audibly across a mesmerised void – the audience hardly dared breathe into the silence.

His dramatic presence was so overpowering that whenever he came anywhere near the front of the stage, the people in the pit shrank back in fear. I've even seen women cross themselves. The pretty ones fainted. Overcome with emotion, I asssume – or to draw attention to themselves. Did they hope the great man would leap from the stage and come over to revive them, to kiss their hands in tenderness and assure them he was only playacting?

Perhaps I'm being unfair. As Macbeth, Macready was the very personification of evil.

It had been agreed between him and Henry that I should try Lady Macbeth. But, playing the monster's equally wicked lady, it was obvious to all that I was as afraid of him as everyone else, and I'm sorry to say that this threw the play off balance completely. And Mr Macready very bluntly told me so.

"But you're v-e-e-e-ry young," he drawled graciously, as he finished demolishing my performance so conclusively that he had me blinking back tears and half resolving never to get up on a stage again for as long as I lived. "You'll c-e-e-e-rtainly improve. Eh, Collis?"

"Er – yes. Certainly." Poor Henry looked from me to Mr Macready and back again. I think he was as scared of the man as I was, although he'd have died rather than admit it.

For his last performance with us, Mr Macready played Othello, with Henry as Iago. Henry was bruised and thumped around the stage all evening, and as for Desdemona – well, I was horrified to see how she was mauled, tossed and worried, I thought at the end he'd killed her in earnest.

I need not tell you how relieved I was that for Desdemona Mr Macready had insisted on using Miss Beatrice Harley, his own leading lady from The Princesses. Leaving Emilia (a much safer part) for me.

"Did he hurt you?" I asked Miss Harley, as at the end of the evening we removed our paint in the large dressing-room we shared.

"Hurt me?" Miss Harley held out her arms, on which half a dozen red welts were now evident and some fine purple bruises developing nicely. "What do you think?"

"Why do you let him?" I asked.

"He doesn't mean it. When he's on stage, he's possessed." She shrugged, then smiled. "At heart," she said, "he's the kindest of men. When my mother was ill, he sent her his own physician. And a new shawl, and some bottles of port wine, and he paid for a nurse for a month, too."

"Ah." I smiled myself. "When he mauled Henry, he sent him champagne."

"There you are, you see." Miss Harley stood up. "If you're ever in any sort of trouble," she added, "be sure to apply to Mr Macready for assistance. If he can, he'll help you."

I thought to myself, I would have to be in some truly tremendous trouble to apply to Mr Macready for help. The very idea of confronting that fierce unblinking stare, of being questioned or rebuked in that languid drawl, gave me the shudders.

I was worried that after Mr Macready had given his last performance with us, our shooting star of success would fade; but after finishing at the New Globe, our company secured a season at the Theatre Royal, in the Haymarket.

"Modern drama. That's the thing," declared Henry, looking doubtfully at the sheaf of new plays he'd already been sent by dozens of hopeful new playwrights. "Well, Deb? Shall we make a start on these? You find us another *Powahatac*, eh?"

I didn't find a *Powahatac*, but I did find two excellent melodramas with perfect parts for both Henry and myself. We read them over to the company, and found the other actors equally enthusiastic. With these two new plays and a production of *The Tempest* (recently revived by Mr Macready and all the rage just now) we began our new season, and very well we did, too.

As well as acting on stage, Henry and I found we were in great demand for private entertainments and public festivals, and our programme of readings, recitations and sketches by Mr Collis and Mrs Minot attracted large and appreciative audiences wherever we went.

We even turned work away. "I don't particularly want to go all the way to Newcastle," remarked Henry one morning, glancing over a gold-bordered invitation to grace a civic event, in return for a handsome consideration. "It's too far, and the railway is so slow."

"And I'd have to leave Addy," I said. "No. Tell them we're already engaged."

"They're offering us seventy guineas for the evening. And suites at the Station Hotel."

"Still no." I shrugged. "I'd rather have an evening at home, I think."

"So be it." Henry opened another letter. "Ah. Now, how do you feel about three days in Exeter, hotel bills and all other expenses paid?"

"I'll seriously consider that one," I replied.

To think that there was a time when I'd have gladly travelled to Carlisle in a tinker's cart, to walk on in a pantomime for ten shillings a week.

As the invitations poured in, we realised we were becoming quite famous, happily as much for our talent as for my incidental notoriety. I don't suppose it mattered much – indeed, I expect it helped – that we were the constant target of speculation, that we were said to be secretly married, that Henry was whispered to be Addy's true father. Although no respectable woman would have invited me into her drawing-room as a guest, only as an entertainer.

But, in spite of all this bustle, I could not put the pendant out of my mind. Eventually I told Henry about the advertisement. "What do you think I should do now?" I asked, over a glass of hot rum and water in my room one evening, just before we went to bed. "If you were me, Henry, what would you do?"

"Nothing." Henry added more sugar and lemon to his drink, and stirred it with a stick of cinnamon. "Don't think about it any more," he said. "Lose the piece of paper and forget the lawyer's name."

"Why?" I asked.

"Raking up the past is often unwise," he said. "You have everything you need – a sufficient income, a child, a growing reputation. What would you have to gain?"

"What would I have to lose?" I replied.

"Oh, I don't know. Why ask me anyway, why do you want my advice? So that you can do the reverse of what I suggest?" He got up from my table and yawned. "I'm tired," he said. "I think I shall turn in."

It wasn't like him to be so sharp. "Henry," I began. "Henry, just before you go – "

"Yes?"

"You're angry with me. Why?"

"I'm not angry." He shrugged. "I told you, I'm tired. Just tired."

He left me sitting in the gloom. It was on the tip of my tongue to call him back, to say, "Don't go, don't leave me. You hear what people whisper about us, so why don't we behave as they think we do? Sleep together by night, as well as act as a pair by day?"

So what stopped me?

Propriety? Decency? A fear that if I suggested such a thing, he would despise me for a whore? That I'd lose his friendship, that he'd abandon me and Addy to our fates?

No, not really. Not at all, in fact. We were partners in business after all.

What was it, then?

Well, just recently I'd been noticing the way he looked at other women. For instance, Miss Harley. As she'd acted Desdemona to Mr Macready's Othello, I'd watched Henry watching her, and I'd seen his eyes follow her round the stage, seen him stare fascinated as Macready throttled her to death.

Miss Harley was plump and pretty, a little older than me, and fair-haired. By any standards, she was a beautiful woman. Desirable, certainly. And, as far as I knew, unattached.

Did Henry want her?

Possibly.

Then there was Dorothea Jackson, a girl we'd just enticed away from a Sussex circuit. She was chubby and rosy-cheeked, and I was certain Henry liked her. More than liked her. Engaging her had been all his idea, and it was fast becoming plain that she could neither sing nor dance with any proficiency, so why did he want her?

She was his sort of woman, that was why. She was blonde, blue-eyed and just made for hugging and kissing. He wanted her in his bed. Henry had been celibate for too long. He was over his illness now. He was looking for a new mistress, and I knew who she was going to be.

Chapter 30

The end of the season was approaching fast. Audiences were still good enough, but were certainly falling off now. Deciding that the company could spare us for a few days, Henry and I took Addy to the seaside for a long weekend.

Walking along the strand, I had time to think – and to worry. I was still anxious about Henry, sure I was closing my eyes to an affair he must have started by now and was probably carrying on right under my nose. But worse than that, I could not put that wretched pendant out of my mind.

When we arrived back in London, I sought out the offices of Mr Heeling, the lawyer. These were in a tall, narrow, crumbling building in a dirty court off Fleet Street, a foetid hole full of rubbish and the previous autumn's dead leaves, which eddied and swept about rustling and whispering among themselves.

Little ghosts, I thought. Souls of those who fought lawsuits in Chancery and died of despair before judgement was given.

A warning to other fools.

I turned my back on the place and walked away. But, against my will, I was drawn back there again. I wanted to *know*.

I thought about it for a few days more, and then, in spite of my own and Henry's reservations, I went to see the attorney. I would trust his confidentiality, I decided, but I'd also be very careful about what I might say. At the back of my mind was the thought that this might be a trap, though who had set it and who the intended captive might be, I had no idea.

At eleven o'clock one morning, then, while Henry was

at the theatre supervising some rehearsals for our summer concerts, I was in Bolton Court. Entering Mr Heeling's grimy outer office I was received by a clerk, an old, old man in threadbare greenish black who would have made a perfect apparition, except that ghosts are not supposed to smell of foul linen, stale tobacco and gin. "May I be of service, madam?" he enquired, wheezing like a pair of rusty bellows.

"I wish to see Mr Heeling," I replied. "I don't have an appointment."

"Ah." The clerk smiled gummily and wheezed more. "He's a very busy man, you know."

"I'm sure he is." I smiled in return. "But all the same, perhaps you could ask him to spare me five minutes? Two minutes?" I laid two half-crowns on the old clerk's desk. "One minute, even?"

"I'll see what I can do, madam. If you'll please be seated?"

I sat in that grubby, frowsty outer office for half an hour. I counted motes in the dusty spring sunbeams, I read the spines of a hundred ancient law books, I stared at antique copies of the *Newgate Calendar*.

This lawyer was never going to speak to me.

But just then, as I was about to admit defeat and go home, I was summoned to the inner sanctum. Introductions were made, tea was offered and declined, and finally the lawyer and I sat down, facing one another.

Mr Heeling was ancient. If his clerk was old and decayed, this man was actually moribund. His hands were gnarled and spotted brown, twisted with rheumatism. His head wobbled precariously on a thin stalk of a neck and his false teeth slipped and clicked.

As I'd entered the room I'd thought I heard him mutter to himself, and now he was doing it again. Mumble, mumble, mutter, mutter, like an old man talking in his sleep. "I'm sorry?" I said gently, as if I had not heard a question. "Mr Heeling, what did you say?"

"Nothing, Mrs Minot. Nothing at all."

As if roused from a pleasant dream, the old man nodded

graciously at me. For the first time he looked me full in the face. He stared for a moment, and I supposed this was for the usual reason. He had seen me on the stage and was curious to know if I was as fair as I was painted, or if without rouge and powder and other aids to beauty I was a sallow, withered crone.

But perhaps it wasn't that at all, for now he shook his head. "It's extraordinary," he said, talking to himself again. "Quite uncanny."

"What is?" I asked.

"Strange," he murmured. "Very strange." But then he recollected himself. "I'm so sorry, Mrs Minot," he said. "You gave me rather a surprise, you see. A shock, even."

"Did I?" He surprised me too, for here he was babbling and gabbling away about shocks and surprises and I had not even stated my business yet. "I'm sorry to hear that."

"No matter, dear madam. No matter at all. Excuse me." He opened the drawer of his desk and took out a package, which he unwrapped. It was a small painting in an oval gilt frame. "I was looking at this only last week," he said, and handed me the picture. It was a miniature of a lady.

"Now, Mrs Minot," he said, "I am a lawyer, I do not break the confidences of my clients. But I look at this portrait and then I look at you. I see the same face in life and in paint. What am I to make of that?"

What indeed. I looked at the picture and I saw that the resemblance was indeed very strong. Coincidence? Possibly. But, being an actress, I have studied my own face closely over the years, I know where its strengths and weaknesses are; I know how to make my eyes look larger, how to make my mouth seem smaller, how to disguise the slight bump on the bridge of my nose.

And as I looked at the portrait I could see that this lady's eyes were the same colour, size and set as mine, that her nose (except for the bump, which a tactful artist had of course not painted in) was the same shape as my nose, that her generous mouth was the image of my own. "Where did you get this?" I asked.

"Ah, I'm allowed to say nothing." Mr Heeling sighed. "In my younger days," he murmured, "I was close. Very close. Secretive as an oyster, secure as Newgate Gaol. No one got anything out of me. Now, I talk too much. Well, my dear madam – what may I do for you?"

I told him I'd seen his advertisement and that since I had once been in possession of the pendant in question, curiosity had moved me to visit him, so that I might learn more of its history.

"You do not have the item in your possession now, Mrs Minot?" he asked.

"No, I'm afraid I don't," I replied. "Mr Heeling, *do* you know its history?"

"Yes indeed. It's a copy of a French piece. Referred to in various documents as *le bijou de serpent* – in English, the snake stone, I suppose. I believe the original is in the possession of a family in La Rochelle, name of Minot."

The lawyer's head wobbled and he smiled a wavering smile. "Now, there's a coincidence, wouldn't you say?"

I gaped at him. "You did say Minot?" I whispered.

"Yes." His old head wobbled more. "A coincidence, yes?"

"Yes indeed." It was my turn to be shocked and surprised. "So, Mr Heeling, was my pendant – the snake stone, I mean – "

"The person who owned the copy of the snake stone has long since disappeared."

"Ah." I felt hot, then cold, then hot again. "And is this person you speak of the lady in the picture?"

"Why do you ask that?"

"*Is it*?" I almost shouted.

"Yes." Mr Heeling shrugged. "Yes, it is."

"You must tell me everything," I said, excitedly. "Everything you know."

"Must I?"

"Yes!"

"And why is that?"

I tried to be calm. I told myself that there was no point in upsetting or frightening this frail old man. "I think I have a right to be told," I said. "I believe, and you must agree, that I have some connection with the person in this painting. You tell me that my pendant is a copy of one owned by a family which bears the same name as mine. If you were me, would you not be anxious to know more? And would you not hope that anyone who *did* know anything might tell you what he knew?"

Mr Heeling sucked his false teeth. "I could tell you something about the lady in the portrait," he said. "But my dear Mrs Minot, believe me when I say that most of this affair is a mystery even to me."

"Tell me," I said gently. "Please tell me what little you know."

"Well then." The lawyer rubbed his lank cheek. "Well then, the lady in the portrait was born into a comfortable, even a wealthy home, but soon after she reached her majority she became estranged from her family."

"Why?"

"She conceived a passion for a young man. An actor. But an alliance with a gentleman in the acting profession was not acceptable to her parents, and they forbade her to have anything to do with him."

"And then?"

"I believe the lady ran away. I say I believe – in truth I do not know whether she ran away, or was turned out. In any case, I do know that the alliance – "

"With the actor?"

"Yes, with the actor. The alliance produced a child."

"A boy or a girl?" My heart was thumping now and my head spun.

"A girl." Mr Heeling shook his old head at me. "Mrs Minot, I must ask you not to interrupt me again. I lose my thread so easily these days."

"I'm sorry. Please go on."

"Where was I? Oh yes. The person who paid for that newspaper advertisement was the unfortunate lady's own mother. She had lived in seclusion for many years, she had completely shunned her family and been shunned by them, but in her last illness she became anxious to be reunited with her daughter.

"Aware that this daughter had once been in possession of that curious jewel, she decided that an advertisement mentioning it, rather than the actual person she sought, might produce more acceptable results. In short, it might serve better to keep impostors away.

"Nothing much came of these enquiries. Various persons came to my office, claiming knowledge of the pendant, but no one could produce it and I dismissed them all as frauds or rogues. And then, last month, I heard that the person was dead."

"The person who had placed the advertisement?"

"Quite so." Mr Heeling spread his hands. "So you see, Mrs Minot – "

"And what about her daughter?" I asked, forgetting that I had been asked not to interrupt him.

"I was coming to her." Mr Heeling sighed. "The daughter was never a married lady," he said. "As I told you, she had a child; but she never married the father."

"Why was that?"

"Oh, the usual reason, I suppose. He was probably married to someone else.

"But now, here's the strange part. A week or two ago I happened to hear about an unproved will – my colleague here and I do some probate work, you see – leaving some little property, about two or three hundred pounds in value, to a Miss Deborah Tanner, the only child of a Mr George Francis Tanner, an actor.

"My colleague made some enquiries, and it turns out that Miss Tanner had a very odd history indeed. Her mother was not married to Mr Tanner, whose work necessarily took him to all parts of the country, and indeed abroad. The mother of the child was frequently ill, and it seems the infant was brought up by a woman in Birmingham, for it was there she was born and there the mother settled for a while after the birth. I suppose the actor had been playing in the town, for there seems to be no other connection with the place."

For the moment, I could not speak. My head ached and I felt faint. Trying to make sense of all this, I closed my eyes and tried to collect my thoughts. "Was Mr Tanner's mistress the lady in the portrait?" I asked.

"I don't know," Mr Heeling replied. "But this is the strange thing. Mr Tanner's will refers to his mistress. Her name was Elisabeth Minot."

"And is she alive?"

"She is dead." Mr Heeling looked at me. "She died of consumption when her daughter was six or seven years old."

"I see. Mr Heeling, my maiden name was Tanner."

"Was it, indeed? Could you prove that?"

"I could produce witnesses who would agree that before my marriage I always went by that name."

"Ah." The lawyer nodded. "I see."

And now, painfully, I dragged all these facts together. "And of course," I said, "the lady's mother, the person who placed the advertisment – her name was also Minot?"

"Her maiden name was Parker. After her daughter left home, she was separated from her husband and returned briefly to her own family. I believe she soon quarrelled with them. She resumed her unmarried surname and was known as Miss Parker from then on."

"Ah." I looked hard at Mr Heeling. "Was Miss Parker – Mrs Minot, I mean – the mother of a son as well as a daughter?"

"Why do you ask?"

"*Was* she?"

"I don't know. It's possible, I suppose." Mr Heeling narrowed his eyes at me. "What are you thinking?"

"My late husband's grandmother was Anne Parker. I found her name in a bundle of documents which I came by after my husband's death."

"I see." Mr Heeling shrugged. "Parker's a common enough name," he said. "There are probably a hundred Anne Parkers in this city alone. And if this lady was your husband's grandmother, as well as possibly – and I do stress, possibly – your own, why was she never in contact with her son or grandson? Why have you never heard of her before?"

"Because she was a recluse – you said so yourself. Because

she shunned her family and was shunned by them – you said that too." I looked at the old man sitting in front of me. "Mr Heeling, Channing never spoke of his parents or grandparents to me. Not to put too fine a point on it, my late husband was hardly a man of family feeling."

"You're drawing conclusions now," said the lawyer. "Mrs Minot, it's never wise to draw conclusions until you have all the facts."

"I think I have all the facts," I said. "I think we know everything now, don't we? Anne Parker married Pierre Minot. She had two children, Thomas and Elisabeth. Thomas had a son, Channing. Elisabeth gave birth to a daughter. Mr Heeling, Channing Minot and I were cousins."

"It's possible." Mr Heeling sighed. "Yes, I have to admit it's possible. Mrs Minot, perhaps at this stage you should know that there is no money involved here. Mrs Minot senior made several very unwise investments in recent years. She died a pauper. My own bills remain unpaid."

"Ah." I hadn't expected to learn I was an heiress. And if Mr Heeling was thinking of trying to touch me for my putative grandmother's legal fees, he could think again.

"You look pale, Mrs Minot." The lawyer's voice broke into my thoughts. "Let me send Harold out for tea. I have some brandy in my cupboard, perhaps you'd like – "

"No." I rose to my feet. "Thank you for your time, Mr Heeling," I said. I held out my hand. "I do not imagine we will meet again."

The lawyer shook my hand. "Mrs Minot," he said, "after consideration, I do feel we might substantiate your claim to Mr Tanner's bequest. So, if you would like to take this matter further?"

"Let it go to charity," I said. "Let them give it to the poor." I took my hand away. "If there's anything left after the lawyers have taken their fees."

Chapter 31

I walked home through the dirty London steets, thinking, thinking, thinking. When I eventually arrived back at my lodgings my mind was still in turmoil.

I was not working that evening, so I told Addy's nurse she could have the rest of that day to herself. I gave my daughter her supper and then put her to bed. I went into my own bedroom and tried to settle to some sewing, but I couldn't. Irritably I walked about, glancing through the grimy window, picking at my cuffs, fiddling with my hair, twisting buttons round and round. Sometimes I found myself singing, but then I was silent, then almost tearful – but then I was singing again.

I wondered what Henry would say about all this. Might he frown and be annoyed that I'd visited the lawyer, that I'd disregarded his advice? Would he refuse to listen to anything? Or would he be interested and want to know all about it? Looking through the window for the hundredth time, I willed him to come home.

When he finally did come and I told him what I'd discovered about myself, his reaction was neither one of bored irritation nor of fascinated surprise. Instead, he listened patiently, not saying a word. When I'd finished, he bit his lip and sighed. And I found it was I, not he, who was asking questions and demanding answers.

"What's the *matter*, Henry?" I repeated. "Why are you looking at me like that?"

He continued to look at me, long and hard. "I knew I'd seen your face before," he said, at last. "I thought you must resemble someone I'd seen only briefly – a woman in an audience, perhaps, whose face had stuck in my mind. That happens sometimes. But now I can't imagine how I could have been so stupid. You see, I knew your parents."

If he'd hit me across the face, I couldn't have been more astonished. "My parents?" I stared like a mad thing. "You knew my parents?"

"I believe so."

"Well." I was amazed. "How did you meet them?" I demanded. "*Where* did you meet them?"

"In Manchester, I think it was," he replied. "The first company I ever played with was there for the autumn season, and the manager took on an itinerant and his wife. Well, we assumed she was his wife, we didn't actually ask them, we didn't – "

"And they were my mother and father?" I interrupted.

"They must have been," he agreed. "They called themselves George and Elizabeth Weston. He was a player born and bred, had been on the road since he was a little child. She didn't act, but the company needed someone to sew and help the ladies dress – she made herself useful.

"She was always ailing, though. She coughed all the time, she spat blood. As for him – well, perhaps I shouldn't say it, there's no need."

"Tell me, Henry," I demanded. "You must tell me."

"He was always drunk. So he wasn't often in a fit state to go on." Henry looked at me. "But when he did, he was magnificent. He was a splendid Othello. I never expect to see a better Macbeth. But the trouble was, three days a week at least, he was useless. Eventually the manager had to let him go."

"But Henry, Charlie Rayner was always drunk, and he never missed a single performance."

"They were different sorts of men, my dear. Charlie's body was pickled in the stuff, but it had no effect on his brain. Whereas with George Weston – "

"It was the other way about." I shrugged. "Did they ever mention a child?"

"No, never."

"So she didn't regret giving me up." I chewed my lip. "She didn't miss me at all."

"I didn't say that." Henry reached for my hand. Sitting on my bed, he pulled me down beside him. "I've shocked you," he said. "Poor Deb, you're pale as death. Shall I fetch you a cordial?"

"No. I shall be quite well in a minute or two." I sniffed. "Tell me about my mother."

"She was ill," he said gently. "She was thin and pale, she had no stamina at all – and a theatrical company is no place for anyone weak in body or mind. Well, you know that yourself. But it seemed to me that her trouble wasn't just bodily. She was pining for something."

"You're just saying that to make me feel better."

"No, it's true." Touching my chin, Henry turned my face towards the light. "Poor creature," he said sadly. "Poor woman, she was the picture of you."

And yet she left me, I thought bitterly. She left me with that woman in Birmingham, to be worked like a little slave, to be worked to death for all she knew, or cared. "Did you like them?" I asked, coolly. "Henry, were they pleasant people?"

"Yes, they were. Well, she was, anyway." Wryly, Henry smiled. "Your mother was so gentle," he said. "Always sad, always quiet, but kind. I think I fell in love with her a little. But then I was a boy. Boys are always falling in love."

"Whereas men seldom do," I muttered, turning away.

"You think not?" Henry's hand still held mine, and now he pulled me round to face him again. "The truth is, a young fool merely becomes an old one."

I looked at him. Unable to read his expression, I shrugged and shook my head. I thought I might start to cry. He must have thought so too, for now his arms went round my waist. Pulling me close into his familiar, fatherly bear hug, he held me. He kissed my forehead.

I lifted my face to his, but as I was about to speak his lips found mine – and he kissed them. Henry Collis kissed me on the mouth, and with such passion, such hungry, desperate desire, that I almost fainted. He held me so tightly that I gasped for air.

I had dreamed of this moment, rehearsed it a thousand times, but the reality was almost too much to bear. Now it was as if a dam had burst, as if waters were swallowing the land. My head spun, and I was drowning. And all the while he was calling me his love, his darling, his angel. And the kisses went on, and on.

I kissed him back. I could not help it. Months of longing would not be denied, and they let loose their spring tides of desire, washing over and engulfing me again and again. I found I was aching with need. I wanted him to know it. I took his hand, to guide it to my breasts.

Then suddenly, from the next room, there was a cry. The wailing, snorting moan of a little child.

It was Henry who heard it first. He drew away from me and listened again. "That's Addy," he whispered. "Deb, had you better go to her?"

"She's fast asleep." As her mother, I well knew the difference between Addy's waking cry of distress and a snuffle deep in sleep. But Henry seemed concerned, so I released him. "Go and look at her, if you wish," I said.

"If you say she's asleep," he replied, "she must be."

But Addy's cry had broken the spell. Now Henry sat silent. He still held me in his arms, but he would not look at me. "What is it?" I asked, threading my fingers through his buttonholes, rubbing my face against his shirt front, sniffing fresh linen and the warm, human smell of the man himself. "Henry, what's wrong?"

"Nothing," he said.

"Nothing?" I glanced up at him. "Don't look so solemn, then."

He shrugged, and let me go. In fact, he almost pushed me away. "I'm sorry," he said.

"Sorry? For what?"

"Don't tease." He looked at me. "I love you," he said. "I've loved you for years. And I know you don't want me."

"You think *that*?" Needing to touch him again, I reached